Very early the next morning, Constantine Quiche was traveling with his hostess Regina Marqab by the sea shore when they saw it.

"What is there?" Constantine asked. "There, south of Monaco, and going into the distance forever? A fog bank? But it is too thick for a fog. And it looks as if it were a bright green. And what are those high bridges coming out of the Principality itself? What sort of channeled waters are they crossing?"

"Why, it's a great mirage," Regina said. "It is like a cloud bank. You can see the dawn under it."

"Listen," Constantine said. "Ship whistles—they are too near the shore. And there is no way there should be so many ship whistles. It sounds as if all the flotillas in the world are assembling here. Regina, something strange is happening. This is nothing like Monaco."

It was like nothing that had ever been seen before. This was a green land extending south eternally, a color-drenched land with pastel-colored cities.

"Oh how could this be?" Regina cried in rapture. "It is the paradise on Earth, and how have we forgotten it?"

APOCALYPSES
R.A. Lafferty

PINNACLE BOOKS   LOS ANGELES

APOCALYPSES

Copyright © 1977 by R. A. Lafferty

An original Pinnacle Books edition, published for the first time anywhere.

ISBN: 0-523-40148-5

First printing, October 1977

Cover illustration by Ron Walotsky

Printed in the United States of America

PINNACLE BOOKS, INC.
One Century Plaza
2029 Century Park East
Los Angeles, California 90067

Table of Contents

APOCALYPSES

Where Have You Been, Sandaliotis?

CHAPTER ONE

Highways are often a detraction from a landscape. They are scars upon it. They are cuts, sometimes bleeding cuts, in it. They are an unnaturalness intruded into a countryside.

There aren't a hundred highways in the world of which this isn't the case. There aren't more than a dozen that actually add a new and striking beauty to a beautiful countryside. The Grande Corniche is one of the few that, running through really beautiful country, adds a new and extraordinary touch to that beauty.

Constantine Quiche drove a new Sassari Twelve, tooling along just east of Nice. He was on an assignment, and he might stop with friends if it seemed likely that it could further the carrying out of the assignment, or he might veer away if that visit seemed to call out "Danger!"

He had fair directions and a permanent invitation to a villa that the Marqabs had rented some months before. With a gala sundown at his back, Quiche believed that he could locate the Marqabs by dark. He could find anything that it was necessary for him to find. He was the best detective in the world.

He had a very recent memory of an encounter so violent and colorful that he had not yet assimilated it. There were unreal elements about it as of something that had happened underwater. And he was in a glorious purple daze from it. He had driven out of that unreality onto the Grande Corniche that was at least half real. Now he drove off into scenery so splendid that it almost had to be contrived. He began to find that central element of scenery that is often ignored by the eyeless. He knew that he was very near to the Marqabs and their sort. This was exquisite. The central element of scenery, the one feature of that whole region that can hardly be duplicated elsewhere, is "People as Scenery." Here that central element was outstanding.

The French people at large have an angularity and awkwardness to go with their sincerity of body and their originality of movement. But the very best of them do not have this angularity and awkwardness. The Italians in ordinary have a sloppiness that is the "beyond" of carelessness and that almost gets in the way of their beauty, and they have a shoutingness that is the "beyond" of lyricism. All except the most excellent of them have these things. The Corsicans have the provincialism of all islanders, and the rocky faces of all peoples who come from rocky coasts. All except the most superb of the Corsicans have these things. But here, along the Grande Corniche and the sundown lanes that led off from it, here were the best, the most excellent, the most superb of all these peoples. They were on the blue coast, on the beaches, all through the beautiful hills, around the villas and cabanas. These were the beautiful people so necessary to a grand scenery.

There were other sorts of people there also, Britons and Americans and Norwegians, Germans and Poles and Turks, and the people of the parts of Libya around Cyrene. All these people were extraordinarily scenic.

Constantine Quiche, with the eye of the best detective in the world, picked out the two most scenic persons of all. They were his friends, Salaadin and Regina Marqab. They were standing by their own villa in the evening. It is true that there was something that called out "Danger!," but it called in an ambivalent voice. Constantine did not veer away. He stopped. He was there.

This was delight, but the rituals were observed on the meeting.

"An evening full of linnets' wings," Constantine spoke and bowed.

"Oh lost sheep of the house of Marqab, alight!" Salaadin added his ritual.

"Bless by your visit our poor house," Regina Marqab completed the ritual. They all hugged and kissed and were happy. (And yet something bothered Constantine a little. "Wherever did I learn this ritual that comes so naturally?" he asked himself. "And wherever did I know these Marqabs who are my best friends? The hound has eaten a piece of my memory.")

"Where did you get it, Constantine?" Salaadin asked, referring to the second guest, the splendid automobile. "And where was it made?"

"The car? I got it in Marseilles today. There was no way I could refuse it. It is a Sassari Twelve, the first one I have ever seen. There was an old monitory voice that shrilled at me, Salaadin, "It is bait: it has a hook in it: do not take it or you are hooked." But I took it, so I suppose that I am hooked. Yes, I am hooked on it as I am hooked on the two of you. Oh, it was made in Sassari."

"Sassari, Sardinia?" Salaadin asked.

"That's a funny thing about it," Constantine said. "All the papers on it say that it was made in Sassari, Sandaliotis. Sandaliotis? I will have to look that up. I believe that it is a very old name for something either in legend or in geography. Are Sardinia and Sandaliotis the same place? Have they revived an ancient name for the island, and why? I hadn't heard about such."

The Marqabs brought Constantine in for a fine supper then. A place had already been set for him, or for some extra person. There were other guests, three of them. Julien Moravia was there, Amelia Lilac from England, and John Seferino from Istanbul. Oh, they were like three bolts of evening lightning named "Danger" and "Love" and "Death." It was both a pleasure and shock to come on them there, an especial shock in one case since Constantine knew that one of these three persons was dead.

These were three more of the exceptionally scenic people who inhabited that region like gorgeous ghosts that night. Constantine knew who all of them were, though he could remember meeting or knowing only one of them. Towards Amelia Lilac, Constantine had the memories of the twin passions of love and death, one old, one new.

Julien Moravia had the air of a totally cultured and urbane person; and it was out of that air and impression that he often spoke crudely and cruelly. Amelia had the name of being very beautiful. That she was so almost had to be accepted: really, there was no way to get a good look at her. She seemed always to be wrapped in a lavender cloud or shadow. But she did give the impression of almost total beauty.

John Seferino was somehow different from other people, and it always took a while to decide in what that difference consisted. He was very much larger than other people, that was it: but why did one have to seek for that explanation?

Constantine joined them all at table. Mushroom quiche was the opener, already there.

"It is for you, Constantine Quiche," Regina said, "after your name and flavor. Someday I will devise the excellent dish, the Constantine quiche, full of cucumbers and cheeses and sour fruits and pomegranate cider. But for now it is the mushroom quiche in your honor."

"But you did not know that I was coming," Constantine said, "and one does not make mushroom quiche in a moment."

"But of course we knew that you were coming," Regina Marqab said. "Would God send us such a special guest and not tell us that He was sending him?"

"Ah yes, I am sure that God told you that I was coming, told you through some strange instrument," Constantine murmured, casting his eye over the other three guests. "And yet no one could have known, for I had not decided to come here for certain until I saw you two Marqabs standing against the green and gold sky. And the invitation to me was an open one given some months ago. But my place was set here, and this dish has a tie-in with my name. Which stange instrument might it have been?

"For here are Julien Moravia and Amelia Lilac and John Seferino, three famous "agents," though nobody knows whom they are agents for. I know them by their fame and by their little pictures on their dossier clips. But I have met only one of you three before, *and that one of you is not here now.*"

"But, Constantine, our friend and our companion and our ghost, is it not a clever counterfeit of that person who *is* here?" Amelia Lilac spoke as if out of a lavender shadow. That girl carried mystery around with her.

"The surrogate, I believe, surpasses the original," Julien Moravia spoke as if in admiration of someone present. "Then let us exalt the surrogate and demote the original."

"Have you not heard, Constantine Quiche, the account of the person who went out dressed like a shoddy impersonation of himself?" John Seferino asked. "He easily convinced all the curious persons that he was a counterfeit and someone other than himself."

"I have heard it, I have done it," Constantine said, "but this here-present person is not a shoddy impersonation. Really, the impersonation is almost too perfect, almost too splendid.

"Three "agents" here. You are the three people in the world I would least want to run into in a nervous situation, though I admire you all and perhaps love one of you. All of you are here in the home of my very dear friends, and what are the odds against any of you three even knowing my very dear friends? They are very long odds for even one of you three. They are prohibitive odds for all of you together. And yet I am certain that there are sincere accounts of the connections to be had. Are there not, bright dove Regina?"

"Oh, I knew Amelia in England many years ago," Regina said.

"You are not even many years old, Regina," Constantine told her. "And who knows Julien Moravia?"

"Why, both Salaadin and myself have known him for a very long time," Regina said. "Why are you mistrustful tonight, Constantine? Do you not recall the story of the man with his neck in the noose and his feet on the trap who still reassured himself 'These are my good friends. They have *got* to be kidding.' "

"I recall the story, Regina. I am the one who told it to

you once. You and Salaadin have known Julien for a very long time, you say?"

"They have known me for a very, *very* long time," Julien Moravia gave it the escalating echo.

"And John Seferino?" Constantine asked as if he were a dog worrying an old rag.

"Oh, Constantine, Seferino and I have business together," Salaadin said. "We have business in Levantine Lands and Waters. We are both members of a very secret and very rich-to-be corporation right now."

"We could get you into it, Quiche, for some rather startling profits," John Seferino said, "but discretion is required. Constantine Quiche, you, the best detective in the world, do you believe that you have enough discretion to enter into corporation with us?"

"No," Constantine said. "Sometimes I haven't any discretion at all. There are five of you here. Two of you, my hosts, are very dear to me, my very best friends. The other three of you are living legends. Ah, pardon there. Two of you three are living legends. The third one of you is a legend who has died very recently. But how, among the five of you, are there no tears? Have you no grief at all for someone who has been very close to you and now is dead? In five such sensitive and superior persons, there should be at least a trace of tears."

"Why should we shed tears in your happy presence, Constantine our love?" Regina asked.

"Oh, for the one of you who has died today," Constantine said. "I find it quite sad."

"One of *us* has died today, my friend?" Salaadin asked.

"Yes. One of you five here present. Died about two hours ago, I guess it was."

"Sad, yes," Julien Moravia said. "Very sad. Where did it happen?"

"Marseilles."

"How did he or she die, best detective in the world Constantine?" Amelia Lilac asked with easy merriment out of her self-contained shadow.

"I killed him or her," Constantine said. "Really, I had to."

"And you are not startled when you come here and see

8

that person to be alive, yet or again?" John Seferino asked.

"Only half-startled," Constantine said. "I half expected it."

There was the beauty of old but bright art about this company at table. That painted beauty was here, and there was an unearthly thrill when such painted beauty moved and spoke. It gave one the feeling that the old legend was true, that there had once been a singular and extraordinary race of beautiful people whose homeland had been destroyed and who had scattered into small enclaves in many nations. The legend said that these people still maintained a small but tight nation even in their scattered exile, and that the people of that nation would always recognize each other.

Five of the six people at this supper table could well belong to that mysterious nation of the beautiful people. One of them, Constantine Quiche, could not. To some other nation, to many other nations he might belong, but not to the nation of the beautiful people.

"Is it not possible, Constantine, that not just one of us, but all three of us whom you call 'agents' have been killed?" Julien Moravia asked. It seems either comic or tainted to speak of beauty in a man, but how else could one speak of Julien? "Is it not possible, astute detective, that there are three rather than one interloper here with you at this table? Would it not balance it out right to have three dead persons and three live persons here? You said that you had met only one of us three agents before, the one who isn't here. Yet I recall that we have all been in company together before. What if all of us here are false agents?"

"I don't know," Constantine said.

"And what if none of us is false?" John Seferino asked. "And what if you killed no one at Marseilles? What if you have only thrown that rock into the pond to see what sort of eddies it can stir up?" (If there had been a separate nation of *elegant* people, John Seferino would have belonged to it also.)

"For that small part, I know what I know," Constantine said. "And you do not."

9

Bec rouge onion soup had followed the mushroom quiche on the table.

"Ah, but what if you did not kill, but instead were killed, at Marseilles?" Amelia Lilac proposed. "And what if another person were substituted for *you*? Should we not be very alert against you then?"

"In that case, I would not be here at table with you," Constantine said. "It would be another person here. But it isn't. It is myself. I happen to be sure of this."

(But he wasn't quite sure. He lied a bit there. He had the unreal feeling on him and had had it for several hours.)

By and by, they had salmon in aspic. They all ate with a vigor that belonged to them by right. Superficial people are at their worst when eating. But these beautiful people ate beautifully. And boar was being roasted outside. Boar is the test.

"What case can the best detective in the world be working on now?" Amelia Lilac asked out of those pleasant shadows that always surrounded her. (It was as though the light that was bright on everyone else was dimmed on Amelia, and she was picked out instead by a muted, lavender spotlight.) "Not only is the best detective in the world here, but the three most mysterious agents in the world are here also, seemingly to thwart him. Is it High State Doings that you are on, Constantine?"

"Possibly, possibly," said Constantine, "or it may be very low doings by very monstrous states or corporations."

"Is it International Intrigue, worthy opponent?" Julien Moravia asked.

"Possibly, possibly, international or interworld," Constantine Quiche told them.

"Is it genocide, or war or murder? Or is it perhaps a securities or a real estate manipulation?" the elegant John Seferino asked. "Oh, it must be a grand case!"

"The only thing grand is in the name," Constantine said, "for I believe that it is more on the order of a grand larceny."

"The best detective in the world on a case of larceny? It must be grand indeed," Amelia remarked. "It must be

10

a very special case of larceny to have such a cast of characters starring in it, you and ourselves."

"And will you catch the thieves, Constantine?" Julien asked.

"Catch them easily. And prevent them, I hope."

"And what is it that the thieves are trying to steal?" Seferino asked.

But Constantine Quiche seemed a little embarrassed by that question.

"It is an awkward thing," he said, "and I am not at all certain that it will even be attempted. I work on a tip here, and the tip may be in code, to bring me to the area. I would rather not say what it is that the tip indicates may be stolen."

"Oh come along, prediletto," Regina said. "Salaadin and myself are among your best friends. You can distrust us or you can trust us, but we will still remain the best of friends. And these three that you believe to be agents, if indeed they are here to thwart you, they already know what is to be stolen. And if they are not here to thwart you, then they are as innocent as ourselves. What do you believe that someone will attempt to steal, my Constantine?"

"Monaco."

"What? Do you believe that the casinos will be robbed? But that is done quite often, Constantine. And, just as often, the thieves are apprehended. This happens even without the services of the best detective in the world."

"I mean that there may be an attempt to steal the principality of Monaco."

"What? All of it?" Salaadin asked laughing.

"All of it, yes," Constantine said glumly. He didn't like this scatter shot.

"What, Constantine, will they line up every person in the little realm and rob them?" Julien asked.

"No. My information is that they may attempt to steal the entire principality. They may attempt to steal the two square kilometers of it, and the 50,000 inhabitants of it, and the 50,000 visitors also. They may attempt to steal the two cities of Monaco and Monte Carlo, and all the buildings and all the land, and all the water, too, I suppose. And, on another hand, nobody may attempt anything remotely like this."

"What would they haul it *off* in?" Amelia Lilac asked.

"I don't know," Constantine said. "They have some pretty big equipment. They couldn't take it all in one bite, but they could take it all in a dozen bites. Or maybe they won't take Monaco or anything else away. Maybe they will bring something instead and leave it."

Constantine Quiche felt rather out of it for the remainder of the evening. He couldn't shine at all in this bright company. The best detective in the world had never been much of a shiner.

They all went out of doors to eat roast boar on wooden tables and benches. The really beautiful people do not use silver or plate to eat roast boar, and they do not eat it inside. The boar was unjointed by a servitor with a bone saw. It was hacked apart by a second servitor with a hacker. And it was cut up by a third servitor with a two-tined fork and a set of long knives. The weathered-wood tables had first been drenched with lime juice and then with sour yellow wine. They had been salted and peppered. And then the joints and cuts of boar had been flung directly onto them.

The boar was eaten bare handed and bare faced. You had to belong to the beautiful people to eat it this way. Nobody else could get away with it.

"I wonder how long it has been since boar was last eaten in this manner?" Constantine asked, feeling himself an outsider now.

"Oh, on Sandaliotis, they have never ceased to eat it this way," John Seferino said. Seferino pronounced it 'San-dal-EE-o-tis.' Seferino was a completely elegant person, so his pronunciation had to be the correct one.

"This is the second time today that I have encountered the name Sandaliotis," Constantine said.

There were crocks of quince vinegar there. When eating boar, one dipped the hands into this vinegar sometimes to cut the grease. There were pandanus leaves there on which one wiped the fingers if one wished, but one felt that they were an imperfect substitute for something.

"No cubs, wonderful hostess?" Amelia Lilac asked Regina.

12

"No cubs," Regina said. "That is a disadvantage of living in the world. There are so many things that one assumes will be available, and at the last moment they aren't."

"What are the cubs?" Constantine asked.

"Oh, on Sandaliotis, bear cubs are always there to lick the diners' hands when they eat boar," Seferino explained it. "This is the old custom. I could never abide the vulgarism of having hounds instead of cubs to do it. No, the pandanus leaves are better than the hounds. Any thing is better than the hounds."

Constantine ate it awkwardly. It was as if he were of a lineage that did not even extend back before utensils and plates.

"Who is going to steal Monaco, Constantine?" Amelia Lilac asked out of her own aura of lilac shadow.

"I don't know," he said weakly. "I suppose I will have
All the beautiful people ate the boar beautifully. Only
to find out if I am going to stop them."

"I hear that there is a general breakdown in the art of gathering intelligence," that elegant Seferino was saying. "And I hear that World Interpol is about to fall on its face again in one of these deals. And the bleakest and most lost department even of World Interpol, they say, is the Sortilège Department. It is pathetic the inept things that are going on in that organization. Quasi-law is simply not what it used to be, and larger things than Monaco are likely to be stolen unless competence is brought to it.

"Whom are you working for now, Constantine Quiche, best detective in the world?"

(How could this man Seferino remain so elegant when he was up to his big elbows and ears in roast boar?)

"For the Sortilège Department of World Interpol," Constantine said, "as you know very well."

"Oh, for World Interpol?" said Julien. "Have they *real* people working for World Interpol now? I had heard that it was otherwise."

Of course none of them at the boar tables laughed. And certainly they did not titter. But there *was* a titter there. It was something like the sound of night insects, of cicadas or crickets. Who was the bug master or cricket

13

master there? Constantine had the feeling that somebody at the table was bugging him with bugs.

"What wine is this?" Constantine asked. They had been drinking cup after cup of warm, sweet wine; not very good wine either.

"Falernum," Regina Marqab said. "It's very strong, but you can let yourself go on it; you're with friends. It's the only ancient wine that burns freely."

"But Falernum hasn't been made for sixteen hundred years," Constantine objected.

"On Sandaliotis, they have never ceased to make it," John Seferino said, just as if there were such a country as Sandaliotis, just as if this really was old Falernum.

The "agents" had begun, as agents often do, playfully to pretend that they were drunker than they were. But Constantine was much drunker than he pretended. Why were the others not so? There was a treachery about this false Falernum. It has been laced for Constantine, and not for the "agents," and not for the Marqabs.

Constantine, by careful effort, began to unconfuse himself, but that forced him to recognize just how confused he had been. The confusion had begun back at Marseilles where someone had been killed. It was very unprofessional for the best detective in the world to be going around in such a confused state. But any other than the best detective in the world would not be going around confused: he would be dead.

Constantine had to admit now that he did not know where it was that he had known his two best friends the Marqabs. How odd that he could not recollect where he had been acquainted with his two best friends in the world, nor how it had become so securely set into his mind that they *were* his two best friends.

He did not recall where he had known the violet-clouded Amelia Lilac, though he was sure that he had once had some very spirited and ambivalent dealings with her. He did not know at all where he had met the other two agents, Julien Moravia and John Seferino, though he had recognized them both on coming to them, and one of them had said that they had all been in each others' company before.

And he did not remember who had assigned him to this

14

most important case in this area; he did not remember who his superior at World Interpol was; he did not remember anyone else at World Interpol; and he hadn't any idea at all how that ridiculous story about thieves stealing the principality of Monaco had come into his mind and onto his tongue.

Constantine suddenly left the party when the Falernum was burning the brightest. But he did not go to his room in the house of his two best friends in the world, and he did not go to his car ("It's death-trapped, it's death-trapped," he had sense enough to whisper to himself), which was in front of that house.

Instead, he scanned back over the winding landscape that he had come through on his arrival, and he remembered every detail of it. He recalled, from a second long flashback one of the false lanes that he had followed for a while on picking his way there, a rock heap in a crackling thicket. It was a rock heap that would be hidden from almost every view.

Constantine moved there very quickly, and not by roads. He had an animal way of moving; not a way of one of the beautiful animals, a way of one of the scurry animals. There was swearing after him in beautiful-people voices. There were rapid footsteps after him, and he gave the slip to those footsteps. The darting and scrambling people can sometimes move with more cunning and stealth than can the beautiful people themselves. And one does not get to be the best detective in the world without having certain talents of movement and escape.

Constantine slept in that concealed rock pile that night. There is something very safe about rock piles in the midst of crackling thickets when they are chosen on the impulse of the moment. The best detective in the world had slept on rocks often and he did now.

Through the night, he was interrupted only once, not into wakefulness, but into a dream. The rock pile seemed to have become an under-ocean rock pile, a grotto, a cave, a booming tidal cavern. A female dolphin visited him there with her springy fish-flesh and her cool ways. She smooched him in that slurpy way that female dolphins have, and there was an underwater echo to it. Then he felt the needle stabs that are so often a part of those strange-species kisses.

"They have needled me with more confusion before I was out of my old mix-up," he said. "Well, I will have them yet, I will have all of them. They leave a trail whenever they meddle with me, and I can follow any trail."

The rest of the night, until an hour or so before dawn, he slept as easily and restfully as anyone can sleep on a rock pile. And yet he recalled in that sleep a few of the words that the female dolphin had whispered to him before she gave him the needle:

"We live in caves under the ocean and we have a dog that lives in the sky. Sometimes we come up. We whistle to our dog and we both gambol.

"If you hear anything else of us, do not believe it. This is all that we do.

"Will you not come and see me in my cave sometime, after this little ritualistic action that we are engaged in now is finished with?"

But the best detective in the world is always receiving various sorts of communications.

CHAPTER TWO

But very early the next morning, Constantine Quiche was traveling with his hostess, Regina Marqab, by the sea shore.

"See, you have foiled them," she said. "Monaco hasn't been stolen. It is still there."

"But what else is there?" Constantine asked. "What is that south of it, and going into the distance forever? A fog bank? But it is almost too thick for fog. And it looks as if it is bright green. When the morning sun hits it it will change, I suppose. But it seems to come right up to the principality. And what are the high bridges coming out of the heights of the principality itself? What sort of channeled waters are they crossing?"

"Why, it's the great mirage," Regina said. "It even has a name, I believe. It is not seen once in five years. But it is more like a cloud bank. It doesn't come clear down to the ocean. You can see the dawn under it. It would be too spooky otherwise. I don't know how the effect of the high bridges is obtained. Sometimes they do look like bridges, and sometimes they are only shimmers."

"The ship whistles, the ship whistles, there are too many of them," Constantine said. "They are too near off shore, but then there are more distant ones too, farther to the south. There is no way there should be so many ship whistles. It sounds as if all the flotillas in the world were assembling here."

"There is only one sort of ship whistles like those," Regina said. "They have been advertising the ships everywhere for three weeks, in every paper in the world I believe. It sounds as if there were thousands and thousands of them, like gulls barking before a storm."

"Excursion-boat whistles!" Constantine said. "You are right. There are no other ship whistles like them. But where can they all be going? There aren't any ports there to accommodate them."

"I'll bet that there are now," Regina said.

Constantine had been up quite early this morning. Sleeping on rocks in a scenic wilderness is pleasant and it is stimulating, but it is also conducive to early rising. He had checked his new car, his Sassari Twelve. Why, it would hardly have been a death trap for him, even in his befuddled condition of the night before. The wiring and the bombs were absolutely amateurish. It gave him a small feeling to be treated to such an inept and small-time operation. Why, that had been no more than a bit of banter, such a childish placing of the explosives! They had been having fun with him, and only long-shotting on killing him if they had intended that at all. No, the explosives hadn't been intended to kill the best detective in the world, not even if he had really been so bombed on the wine the night before. Such death threats could have been no more than good-natured warnings.

"What was in my wine last night, Regina?" Constantine asked as they rolled along in the Sassari, that purring luxury cat of a car.

"Galveston Gimlet," she said. "It's just one of the older and more basic knockout drops from the States. I didn't do it, of course, but it was fun to be in on it. Oh you do go goofy in the face when you find out that you're being taken! They play rough in the set lately. They have deals going on for a while. And then the rough play is partly from being so jaded and surfeited and all. We were betting when and where you would fall, but you gave us the

18

slip (and you *couldn't* have, to turn one of your own phrases). Where *did* you fall?"

"In a rock pile, in a preselected rock pile. And there I was visited by an intoxicating creature, as if I needed any more intoxication. It was not you was it, Regina? Are you of dolphinish flesh?"

"It was not I, Constantine. I must have a rival in your affections. Who do you know who is a dolphin? And you didn't have any trouble with your car this morning? I worried about that a little bit. But they all said that, if it killed you, it would prove that you weren't the best detective in the world after all."

"No trouble with it, Regina. But, in a way, it proves that they are not the best 'agents' in the world. Agents should not be jaded or surfeited. They should be avid and hungry.

"Is it not almost lustful the way this car rolls along, Regina? That little arrangement at the car, it was only to amuse me, I am sure; but I haven't the same humor as they have in the 'set.' I am not too sure that Monaco is still safe, though she is still there. There seem to be strange flags flying over her this morning. Can she have been 'stolen' by a coup? And physically there are too many lines and attachments to her. And that mirage, that cloud, I just don't trust it at all. There are really two of them. There is a low cloud on the surface of the sea that is green, and there's a high cloud bulking downward in the air and it's a sort of lavender color; it's much thinner than the green cloud. It's moving down entirely too low now. It will touch the surface cloud."

"Can we drive under it, Constantine? Let's try it. I never rode under a mirage before. If you would just veer a little bit more to the right, Constantine, we could do it. We're not on the old road anyhow. You've jumped it. We're just on the rocky shore, but they're using a lot smoother rocks this morning."

"Regina, for the last half mile we've been riding over land that was always ocean before."

"You are sure?"

"I'm sure. But is it not a well-paved road that we come onto now? It is so light and springy, as if it were built out of air. Springy? But it does not have the look of extreme newness. It has the look of being under water for a long time and until very recently. Yeah, until as recently as about an hour ago. What kind of road is this? Light and springy? Built out of air? Not new at all? Been under water so recently?

"And look at those bridges above us. They are bridges, inasmuch as they are anything. Whoever saw such light and airy engineering? Airy again. What is this all? They can't hold up anything if they are as light as all that, but they are holding up something. There are cars moving over them now, rather airish-looking cars too. We may as well resign ourselves to the whole world being light and airy today and not built out of very much of anything. Shimmering bridges, dawn-beam bridges, but they must be a little bit more substantial than shimmers. Look at the cars. Most of them look like Sassaris, as mine is, and I never heard of the make till yesterday. And no two of them are very much alike. They must make an incredible number of models.

"And look, Regina, your mirage is a little more detailed as the day gets brighter. Now there are rocks, cliffs, headlands, promontories, bays, capes, timber, towns, harbors, and ports, ships (well, what is wrong with ships, though I never before saw the flags that some of them are flying under), excursion boats (Regina, they must be hauling a million people here! Yes, and there is this *here* that wasn't here before), canal boats, tug boats. I don't remember either canal boats or tug boats off the coast of Monaco before. We won't be able to drive under the mirage, Regina."

"No. Let's drive over it then. We're on a road that was always ocean before, but we are shoreward (to the Monaco shore I mean, there's another one now) from the canal."

"A canal has no more business here than has a caravan of camels," Constantine said.

"This road looks as if it continues along the shore just a little bit back from the docks and slips and basins," Regina said, "and we'll go under the high bridges. Or we can take a turn off on one of these ramps and go. . . ."

"Yes, we can go around and up and around again, and go *over* one of those high bridges, and drive out onto the

20

mirage itself. It looks much more substantial than it did, and the lavender cloud is coming down lower and lower on it; they will merge. I do believe that the high bridges and high roads are elastic and that they are contracting to take up the slack when everything comes into place. Do you know, Regina, that a single string of molecules is unbreakable if properly shaped and linked? I read that in the 'Science and Stuff' column this week. Some of those bridge cables look almost as thin as a single string of molecules. But they are holding it all up.

"Do you see what the bottom hundred meters of the violet mirage really are, Regina? It's underwater sorts of rocks and shelvings, and whatever is it doing up in the air and in that transparent form? It's as though it were the ghost of certain underwater strata. It is the roots of a land hanging in the sky, and now those roots have touched down to the blue water and the new green land. Easy, easy does it. Does it not come down gently? It's almost like a blessing. There will be some turmoil, but, at its present rate of descent, in 10 minutes' time, the water line of that purple fog will be down to the real water line. So that is the way that the demiurges and titans build land, is it? Oh yes, let us drive upon it."

"Constantine, where did you get the weird idea that Monaco might be stolen? Not that there aren't other weird things going on, but how did you ever get the idea that Monaco might be stolen?"

"Oh, that's what an 'agent,' of a sort, said under his death torture. We play rough in our set too. He had broken before his death, of course, and his words were not rational. But some of our experts can put things together out of images dredged out of torture deaths, and what they put together was a great change in the neighborhood of Monaco. And there was the idea of something being stolen from the world. I was sent here then, as the best detective in the world, to find out the meanings behind those things. I believe that Monaco *has* been stolen, but not taken away: she has been adjoined to something that has arrived. There has been some special meaning all along to Monaco holding onto a technical independence. She was part of, she was a token of, something that had gone away for a while and left her as titular head of it."

21

"Would World Interpol be that worried if someone *did* steal Monaco? What are they really worried about? Monaco doesn't even subscribe to the services of World Interpol, as I understand, and whenever did World Interpol have any concern for a nonclient?"

"What we are really worrying about, Regina, is a bomb, a big one, more than 300 miles long, that is coming towards earth and is to be intruded inside our defenses. A ticking bomb that big is dangerous. It may be a world bomb, and it may be intended to destroy the world, so at least is some of the coded advice."

"Did World Interpol get that coded advice about the possible world bomb from another 'agent' under his death torture?"

"Yes, I believe so, Regina. But how did you know that?"

They missed one turn-up ramp but they took the next one. They went up on a spiraled trestle. Spiders spun more substantial-looking things than that trestle was. Whoever had ever seen such light and clean engineering? This was like 'exchanges and bridges' in free flight.

There was a toll booth where they straightened out on the high road coming onto the bridge, and a good-natured man in it was jingling coins and singing a little tune.

> *"Un franc, un florn,*
> *Un lir, un corn,*
> *Un cal-ke-vil*
> *Por pont d'Eghil."*

So Constantine paid the good-natured man a franc and they drove over Eagle Bridge.

"They must go alphabetically," Regina said. "This is E, Eagle Bridge, but why is it Eghil instead of Aghil? And it is the fifth bridge from the west."

Constantine almost forgot to wonder how he had understood the man, but it would have been impossible not to understand his little jingle:

> *A franc, a florin,*
> *A lira, a crown,*

A what-you-will
For Eagle Bridge.

"It's like one of those little languages that people invent out of romance roots to be International Tongues," Constantine said.

"Constantine, all that fish dip you were telling me, about the 300-mile-long bomb and all, maybe it's just what you'd like me to tell the 'agents' you're working on. Maybe it's not really what you're working on at all."

"Maybe not," Constantine said. "Maybe it's just what my superiors are telling me I'm supposed to be working on," Constantine said. "What I am really working on at the moment is dolphin flesh. I'm not even sure that I *am* Constantine Quiche. Maybe Constantine Quiche is just a code way of referring to me and I'm a different sort of person altogether."

It was beautiful to wheel along on the high road above the canal, for a canal is what it was below them, a boat-filled and ship-filled canal that cut through two isthmuses of land that connected a huge new peninsula to the underside of a continent. One could see for endless golden and blue miles from the high-flying Eagle Bridge, and the best detective in the world allowed himself to be overwhelmed by the wonder of it.

"Oh pull off here!" Regina cried. "We cannot go on till we have seen all of this."

They pulled off into a little green observatory park. To the north was the principality of Monaco as they had known it, well mostly as they had known it. Monaco seemed to have a case of morning nervousness over the great thing dangling off south of it for so many miles into the sea. Two isthmuses, each about two miles wide and 10 or 12 miles long, and perhaps 15 miles apart, connected the huge appendage to the main land. The isthmuses were deep cut by the canal, as was the intervening water and the shallows outside them: and the whole of the isthmuses and the water between them was high spanned by the shimmering bridges.

But this new land was nothing like Monaco. It was like nothing that had ever been seen before. This was a great land extending south eternally, a color-drenched land with

23

rocky shores and green-and-blue valleys inside, and with white- and pastel-colored cities. And Constantine and Regina were, in the parkwayed order of the interchanges, right at the entrance throat of a fine city.

"What country *is* this?" Regina asked a handsome lady with mahogany-colored hair.

"Sicoro, L'es *Sandaliotis*," the lady said. "No conostu?"

"Where have you *been*, Sandaliotis?" Regina cried in rapture. "Oh how could this be? It is the paradise on earth, and how have we forgotten it?"

"Have a small care for the snakes, Regina," Constantine said, "that you do not tread on them or they on you. Snakes are always a danger in paradise. And have a small care also that you do not overplay it. You know much more about things than you pretend."

"It is the story of my life," she said. "It has got me where I am today, on a piece of land that wasn't here yesterday with a fellow whose tag says that he's the best in the world."

Oh the scenery of town and country and coast that could be seen from there, or waterways and beaches and cliffs, and commerce! And oh the scenic people who were going by! Constantine had come through the drenchingly beautiful scenery of the Grand Corniche the day before and this morning, and he had never seen such scenery as this.

There was a public phone there on a little kiosk. Constantine shoved francs into it and found that it accepted them. Possibly, like the toll booth, it would accept any sort of money. Was it possible that phones in this country that hadn't been here before were connected in to the phones of the world? Constantine punched a number, and pretty soon he had someone on the line.

"Quiche," he said. "Monaco is physically all right, though possibly in morning shock. Monaco has not gone, but something else has arrived or is happening. There is a complete new country here now. It is a peninsula and it attaches to Europe at Monaco. It extends south as far as the eye can see."

"About a thousand miles in the air is it, would you say?" the voice asked. Constantine was a little bit relieved

24

at hearing the voice, for it was familiar and it brought pieces of memory flooding back into Constantine. But he was also furiously exasperated by the foolishness of it.

"No, no, Grishwell," he said. "It sure is not a thousand miles up in the air. It is right here in the Mediterranean Sea and I am right here on it. I know it is hard to believe, but there is a whole new country here that wasn't here before."

"Instrumentation shows that there is an object about 300 miles long that is hovering about a thousand miles high," the man on the phone said. "Likely there is something wrong about your data or about you. How high did you say that it was?"

"I am on the high point of it, for the region close around here. I am about a hundred meters high. There are some spiraled highways going up here and some spanning bridges. The roots of the thing are deep under the sea now. It is integrated now, though earlier this morning it seemed to be made out of a green fog down on the sea and a lavender fog up in the air. They combined. It is big and it is not hovering up in the air. It is a peninsula in the middle of the sea. It is here."

"Oh my God!" came the voice on the phone. "We are too late then. How have they done it? Has it landed for sure?"

"Landed and rooted, yes. But we don't seem to be talking about the same thing. This is a peninsula with people living on it. And thousands of people arriving to it by— get this, Grishwell—by excursion boats. There are a thousand excursion boats coming into dozens of ports. I never saw a peninsula with so many ports."

"Is it—oh my God, Quiche, what can we do?—is it armed?"

"I suppose that it is, Grishwell," Constantine said. "If it is intended to be armed, then it is. This looks like a complete country with roads and cities. The only armed person I see is a policeman of sorts. He has a happy look about him, but I wouldn't want to tangle with him. He is armed with a service revolver and a snapdragon."

"A snapdragon? I never heard of that."

"Nor I either, Grishwell. The name of it just popped into my mind, but I'm sure that it's the correct name. It's

25

a neat little contrivance. Why didn't I think of that? With a snapdragon in one hand, you could, well you could easily snap a man's neck and kill him."

"Where are you calling from, Quiche?"

"From one of their own public phones. The name of the town on whose edge I am is Civita do Nord or North Town. The name of the country is Sandaliotis. Both, as far as I can find out, were born new this morning after a gestation period that seems to have been no more than three to six weeks and was mostly talk."

"They have phones there, on a country that wasn't there yesterday, by which you were able to dial my secret number here?"

"Yes, I tried it, Grishwell, and it worked."

"Have they clocks there, Quiche?"

"I suppose so. This is a complete city, apparently, and it would have everything. Yes, I see a clock in the tower of an insurance company building."

"Call me every 30 minutes then, Quiche."

"Should the best detective in the world be tied to the end of a telephone? I'll call you from time to time if I think it necessary."

"Is it ticking, Quiche, is it ticking?"

"Is what ticking, Grishwell?"

"The thing you are on, the bomb which the instruments say is a thousand miles in the sky and you say is on the surface of the Mediterranean Sea, the bomb which seems to be camouflaged to resemble a country. Is it ticking?"

"I will let you know if I find out."

"There's only two explanations. Our altimeters are a thousand miles off or—Quiche, when you move about on whatever it is that you're on—"

"Yes?"

"Wear a parachute."

Constantine Quiche hung up the phone. He needed a moment to adjust to his different sorts of data. It was as if he were seeing one world with one eye, and Grishwell were describing a completely different world to his other eye, and he had a split head from trying to focus the two together. The parting suggestion seemed to make no sense, but what could it hurt?

Constantine went into a mod parachute shop that happened to be the nearest building. He went in and bought a parachute. He fitted it about his waist and turned himself into a little pudgy man. A parachute! What nonsense! If it hadn't been for the possible saving of his life he wouldn't have bought it at all.

But was there ever a discovery like this one? Columbus had never come onto anything as new-made as this, and John Chancel had not. Here was a brilliant new world planted down into the middle of the oldest and most storied sea, and it wasn't apparent yet how much the sea was perturbed over the thing. It was the morning of the third day and the Creator had just said "Let the dry land appear," and so it was. It was the morning of the third day in an African cosmology also when the turtle had just swallowed all the seas and made the dry land appear and had decided that it was too much land. And he had spit part of the water over his shoulder then to cover a part of the land and to create again some of the sea. But who since that morning turtle had seen such new land?

Here was a brilliant new world planted down in the middle of a variety of different old worlds and lands. It had its alien elements, but they were not too confoundedly alien. One could understand the talk of the people pretty well. One could read the newspapers, even if you didn't know what language they were written in. It was a little bit like the languages that rich and multilingual children at school in Switzerland put together for fun. It was a little bit like the languages that philologists put together seriously to serve as common tongues. It was gibberish, but it could be understood and read.

But this new-discovery world was an unprecedented situation. At the Sortilège Department of World Interpol, they believed that this was a 300-mile-long world-bomb that had been set down through Earth's defenses during the night, and that it might be ticking off the moments until "Moment Destruction." And who was to say that it wasn't such a world-bomb?

Who knows what a highly sophisticated, highly camouflaged, 300-mile-long bomb might look like when it was trying to put on its most deceptive appearance? But how to find out whether it was such a mechanism—what else could it be, if such a thing was known to have been hovering over the Earth?—how to find out whether it was really that dread, ticking bomb?

No, no, they hadn't gone to any extraordinary trouble over it, not if they were already going to the trouble of blowing up Earth. A few hundred or a few thousand technicians along its 300-mile length could as well play the roles of an innocent populace of a newly appeared country as any other roles. But what was the delay now? Did it have to activate itself? Could it have gotten through Earth's defenses and sensors if it had already been activated then?

"Is it ticking, Regina?" Constantine asked Regina, his hostess of the evening before as he found her again after he had phoned to his superior.

"Sandaliotis, you mean?" she asked. "You'd better believe that it's ticking. This is one ticking country! I talk to the people who go by, and they sure do have things moving here. They have a common law here that is so old and full of holes that you can do almost everything with it. I can get a Unilateral Divorce from Salaadin in one minute. Then, after a three-minute interval for 'seemliness,' I can marry you. And they're having a honeymoon special at the hotel across the street. They're doing a raging business with the real estate people: there are more than a million of them arriving on the excursion boats and they are all looking for a change. This *is* the other side of the fence, the advertisements say. The grass *is* greener here. This is really bargain day.

"Then I can have both the divorce and the marriage set up on a one-hour or two-hour or three-hour rotation, or whatever basis I want, so they will revert and put me back into the *status quid quo*, as they say it here. Salaadin certainly couldn't object to that, especially if he doesn't know about it, and if I'm married back to him automatically before he knows I was divorced from him. Well, come on."

"Regina, just where and when was it that you and Salaadin became my best friends in the world?"

"I'm puzzled about that too. I know it's true, of course, but I don't remember about it, not how it happened at all. Well come on!"

"Aw, Regina, I'd like to, but there are responsibilities

28

that go with being the best detective in the world. I'm in the middle of a case, you see, a big one, and—"

"All right, all right, all right, you best detective in the world you! I'm not sure you're as sharp as you're supposed to be. I say maybe that's why the robbers beat the cops 19 rubbers out of 20. I'll just go across the street and say yes to that young man there who asked me. He's waiting for an answer."

But Constantine, after spending ten minutes over a local newspaper to perfect himself in the language, went into the big library. It was five minutes till seven in the morning. The sun was up. It lighted everything and dispelled all possible unreality. As he went in, there were patriots in the street, high on morning wine, singing with ringing melody and with tears:

> "*Oh nine times risen from the Sea,*
>   *With Meadows green,*
> *Oh SandalEEotis our land,*
>   *Where have you been?*

> "*Oh land where every day is Yule!*
>   *Thou Saint Sardine!*
> *Oh gracious land, Oh beautiful!*
>   *Where have you been?*"

"I have never seen such patriotism anywhere in the world," a real estate man off one of the excursion boats said to Constantine. "Are you a native?"

"No, this is my first visit here," Constantine said.

"I have never seen such burning patriotism in my life," the real estate man said.

"Nor I," Constantine agreed. He went on into the library and he knew what to do there. One does not become the best detective in the world by not knowing how to operate in a data center. The indexing system was not quite the same as in other libraries of the world. It was slightly different and slightly better. And the service was fast. Constantine ordered six different histories of Sandaliotis at random, and he was ear-deep in them when a young lady came and tied a napkin around his neck.

"What is this?" he asked.

"A napkin," she said. "Do they not use them in your country? One is not allowed to eat breakfast in the library without one. One gets butter and marmalade on the books. You know how it is. Will you order in particular, or would you rather receive the breakfast of the day?"

"The breakfast of the day will be fine, young lady," Constantine said.

"All right, I dial it in," she said. "Is that not easy? Shall I rub your neck while your breakfast is coming? Many gentlemen like their necks to be rubbed in the mornings. They find it relaxing. Do you not? You are not a native of Sandaliotis? You are one of the outer barbarians then? I understand that many of the outer barbarians are greatly puzzled this morning by the very fact that there *is* a Sandaliotis, but all of them are wanting to buy land here. Their eyes had been darkened before and they had not been able to see our country."

"Do the people of Sandaliotis have dolphin flesh?" Constantine asked.

"Oh, what a way to put it! Dolphin flesh! Many of the people of Sandaliotis are of the dolphin clan, but I'm not. I'm a sardine. As you may not know, Sardinia was an ancient name for one of the provinces of Sandaliotis. There are quite a few different clans in our country."

"And what a country!" Constantine cried. "If this is fakery, then some faker has gone to a lot of trouble."

"A lot of trouble, yes, but not quite as much as it might seem at first eye. This is North Town. We make it look good here. And then there is Ichnusa, the capital. They really faked it there. But most of the rest of it is still blank. Nothing looks so blank though when you color it green.

"But on the larger scale there is no faking. Only an outer barbarian would speak of God as a faker. How gross of you! But I overlook it because you are ignorant and I am magnanimous. You are something big, you believe, like a real estate man maybe, so you cannot see with common eyes. But the common people of the barbarians, the fishermen, the mule-drivers, the octopus-trappers, the grape-treaders, the bee-herders, olive-pickers, slate-miners, fig-breeders, cheese-makers, card sharks, sponge-divers, they have always known about Sandaliotis. They have visited us here freely, and they have worked here as itinerant workers. There have been no problems with people on the common level.

"And there have been no problems with the exquisite people (for many of you outer barbarians *are* exquisite). They have always known about Sandaliotis. I mean the kinetic philosophers and the goat-hair prophets, the attenuated artists and the music makers, the high comedians and the soul people, the best of the detectives and of the corporation chairmen, they have always understood about us. It is the great middle class of the outer barbarians who never could see us, for reasons not easy to explain. Today they can see us and our land, and it will confuse them for a little while. We must unconfuse them as much as we can. I will unconfuse you, and then you can unconfuse some of your countrymen."

"Is Sandaliotis nine times risen from the sea, young lady?"

"Yes, but these times are not in sequence. It is as though one should say 'nine times strong' or 'nine times glorious.' Sandaliotis is always nine times risen, but she does not rise and sink again. It is more like the eyes of dim persons blinking open and shut and open again, so they do not see her all the time."

"Young lady, is all that rigamarole you are giving me true?" Constantine asked.

"Well no, not all of it. But some of it may be true in a special sense. And there are several clearly true items imbedded in the matrix of parable. It is really just a little entertainment that I devise to tell you while your breakfast is coming. And here it is."

One does not get to be the best detective in the world by doing just one thing at a time. Constantine Quiche ate his excellent library breakfast, matched chatter with chatter with the gracious young lady employee of the library, squeezed the juice out of six different histories of Sandaliotis, dialed for other books, and spun contingent theories in his neat and foxy set of brains.

The six different histories of Sandaliotis gave a consistent (though, to the great middle class of the outer barbarians, seemingly impossible) account of the peninsula of

Sandaliotis. It had always been there, right where it was now, in the middle of the eastern Mediterranean Sea. The reason that it had not always been seen was that a sea-mist (the *velo*, called anciently the *peplos*, the veil) often surrounded the land and made it invisible. Sandaliotis had always been the great and beautiful peninsula between Italy and Spain, somewhat kindred (though several degrees superior) to them in culture and inclination. It had been visited by all the same early visitors, by the people of Phoenicia, of Tyre and Tharsis, of Crete and Egypt and Greece and Asiatic Greece. It had always been peopled by the same Mediterranean stock (always beautiful people, but most beautiful in the case of Sandaliotis). It had been an inner ally and affiliate of the Roman Republic and Empire, though not an intrinsic part of Rome. It had known, it had seduced, it had civilized all the same conquering barbarians. It had been redeemed by the same Christ and churched by the same Church (that patriarchate of Ichnusa of Sandaliotis was the most ancient of them all except that of Antioch, and one history said that it was more anciently established even than Antioch, by one year). Sandaliotis had been sickened by the same heresies, and its reigning heresy was "elitism." It had stood slightly outside of the Industrial Revolution, or perhaps it had had its own slightly superior industrial revolution. The industrialization of Sandaliotis was based on the mining of white coal or leukophanoko, that superior fuel that is mined nowhere else in the world.

Why then had so much of the rest of the world been in ignorance of the very existence of Sandaliotis? It must have been a sort of eye-disease suffered by the rest of the world, the histories said, something even beyond the obscuring effect of the veil or sea-mist.

The ancient references in these histories gave one a sort of lilt of impossible recognition, for they referred, by number and description, to certain lost books of Pliny and Strabo and Tacitus and so many others. These books, lost to the rest of the world, were not lost to the people of Sandaliotis.

When Constantine had finished his breakfast, the lady attendant washed his face and hands and kissed him. Then she went off to attend to other clients. But she showed him how to dial for her, or for another assistant, if he needed aid in anything.

Constantine had recalled that Sandaliotis was the ancient name for Sardinia. In fact, his remembered data now told him that the Greeks had given the name of Sandaliotis to the Island of Sardinia because it was shaped like a sandal. Yes, that was a good enough explanation, except that Sardinia *wasn't* shaped like a sandal.

The Sandaliotis histories that he was perusing said that the Greeks had given the name of Sandaliotis to their peninsula because it was shaped like a peninsula. Yes, that was well enough. The maps in the histories revealed that Sandaliotis *was* shaped like a sandal, much more so than Italy was shaped like a boot. But it was only full Sandaliotis that was so shaped, and not Sardinia. The maps of Sandaliotis were fascinating.

The ends of the drawstrings of the sandal were the two narrow isthmuses that attached Sandaliotis to the continent of Europe at Monaco. The full shape of the peninsula, which included Corsica and Sardinia swallowed in it, was a sandal exact. It was not the low sandal with the strap passing between the toes. It was the real *sandalion*, the *solea*, the *crepida*, the high sandal, the *coturnus* with its red straps or strings. Constantine knew that the two straps or strings, the two isthmuses that connected the peninsula to the mainland, would appear as red strings from the air, for he had already seen their incredible red flowers and their russet countrysides and the red-tiled roofs of the isthmus towns. This was the classical sandal, and if one wanted to know what it looked like, it was the sandal that the people of Sandaliotis still wore.

Constantine dipped into the accounts of the literature of Sandaliotis, of the drama, the art, the music, and the politics-as-art of the Sandaliotistics. There were many of the named names that had a familiar ring. There was the painter Theotocopuli who had gone to Spain to live with the people there. He had been in trouble before he had left home, and he did not tell the people of Spain for sure where he had come from. And neither did he correct them when they guessed wrong on him. Besides, El Greco makes a better nickname than El Sandaliotistico.

There was a little corporal from northern Sandaliotis

who had become a big man among the French. But that raised again the question in the mind of the best detective in the world. Where did Corsica and Sardinia fit into the conception of Sandaliotis? Both of them were included in the outline of the peninsula as shown on the maps. And the names of Corsican and Sardinian mountains were found in their right latitudes and longitudes as mountains of Sandaliotis. Someone was playing free and loose with these things.

Constantine dialed for an aide girl, and one of them came. It was not the girl who had given him his breakfast, but another one. It would not matter greatly. There was not that much difference between the girls. All of them were beautiful and all of them were charming. And if it did not matter which one of them was which, that also fit in with a theory that Constantine was about to devise about Sandaliotis. It *should* make a difference which girl was which, in any other place and condition.

Constantine explained his difficulty to the girl, that there seemed to be a contradiction here; that there seemed to be, in these particular cases, two sorts of lands occupying one and the same area.

"How can there be a Sandaliotis, and at the same time be a Corsica and a Sardinia in parts of the same places?" he asked fairly enough. But the girl nearly became exasperated, except that such a thing would not be possible to one of the pleasant inhabitants of Sandaliotis.

"Have you no black cattle in your own country?" she asked defensively. "Have you no sheep in the closets of your own houses? Have you no unburied bones in your own attics, and no striped snakes in your own cellars? Oh, these are not things that we are ashamed of, but they are things that we would wish were better. There are ways of seeing parts of us, but there are better and more accurate ways of seeing those same parts. So we are double dealers sometimes? Will we never live that down? There are the beasts inside of us, but there are more pleasant and higher creatures inside of us also. The Corsica and Sardinia are sometimes seen by the outer barbarians (and it is an embarrassment that such people should be able to look into our most dismal nightmares), and the waters that are seen about those 'islands' even when those waters are not

34

physically there, these are concretions of our psychotic unconsciousnesses and they are not meant to be seen by daylight. They are our shaggy manifestations; they are our wooly anxieties and our unsettling agitations. It is good to be able to send them off to high and waste places. But they are not the real essence of those places, no more than the morning dew is the real essence of a meadow that it covers briefly. When there is dew on the meadow, it is technically under water. When there is a peculiar dew on parts of Sandaliotis, they are technically under water, and the other parts, the parts not affected by the dew, seem to be islands. But if people would look at things our way and not their own way, they would know that Sandaliotis has always been here, complete and unchanged."

"You must have very deep dew here," Constantine said.

"Oh yes we do," she agreed happily. "In certain areas, we have the deepest dew in the world."

"Is this map of Civita do Nord, of North Town, accurate?" Constantine asked, and he showed her the map he was studying in one of the histories. "I have been studying this map and I now have it engraved on my eyeballs."

"I have an uncle who engraves maps on walnuts," the girl said, "but how do you engrave them on your eyeballs? Yes, the map is correct in every detail, but the city itself might not be correct all the time. They had workers making those streets and alleys all night until daylight this morning, but they got only about a third of them finished. Then they had to stop. They weren't supposed to be making any of the things after the real estate people and other visitors got here."

"Is all this that you have been telling me really not a long jabberoo that says hardly anything, young lady?" Constantine asked.

"Yes it is," she said. "I will have to shorten it and sharpen it up. But some things are not so easy to explain. They instruct us 'Make up something to tell them if they question you on that aspect.' Or they instruct us 'Tell them something without telling them anything if they question you in that area.' A person would have to be a barbarian to know what sort of questions you barbarians

35

were going to ask and to have answers ready. It isn't easy to make up things for every occasion."

"What about the waters around and between these islands," Constantine asked, "the waters which this map here says do not exist. Isn't there a place where very deep fog becomes tolerably deep ocean? Ships and boats have sailed for ages in these waters where this map shows land, where in fact I would probably find land if I went out looking on this unnatural morning. Fish have swum for ages in these waters where this map and yourself say that there are no waters, where you say that there is never more than deep dew."

"That is false," the girl said. "How have ships and boats sailed right through the place where Sandaliotis is? How have fish swum through here? Give me the name of one ship, of one boat, of one fish that has done this. Go ahead. Give me the name of the leastest fish that has done it. I do not ask for the name of any big thing. Only of a fish no longer than your finger. You cannot document what you say. If it had happened, it would not be so hard for you to come up with the name of just one little fish."

"Ah, young girl, I will inquire the names of the ships and boats and fish later," Constantine said. "Now I am going to visit a hotel that I used to know in the mountains of Sardinia. The mountains still have the same name on the map of Sandaliotis that they used to have in Sardinia. That one hotel in the mountains, I will not forget it. I will see if it is still there."

"With all burning hope for your success," the young library girl said, and she kissed Constantine affectionately. There has always been a legend of a very affectionate people in a Mediterranean land, but is it possible that the Sandaliotists are the people of that legend?

Constantine, on his way to the airport and a plane to take him to a certain mountain, stopped at a phone and punched a number.

"The library here is better than those in many places," Constantine said to himself. "I will give it a citation for excellence if it ever falls in my way to do so."

And then the person came onto the line.

"Quiche here," Constantine said. "Grishwell, I have known bombs and I have known realms, but I am not sure that I have ever known a real combination of the two. But from where I stand, on the surface of our item of discussion, I believe that this is a realm, impure and not simple. I do not believe that it is a world-bomb."

"Quiche," Grishwell said, "there is something wrong. Instrumentation (which of course can be fooled when the stakes are as high as they are now: our survival or extinction) shows that the world-bomb is still in hover a thousand miles above Earth. We cannot get a visual on it; it's too sophisticated for that. We cannot get a radar or a magnetic on it; it is certainly too sophisticated for that. But we do know that it is there, or that there is a meteorological disturbance in the shape of a 300-mile-long bomb still hovering there. It could, of course, have left the disturbance in a high hover and itself come down through our defenses. We cannot say."

"Are you sure that there *is* a world-bomb?"

"Of course not, but we must act on the possibility."

"If there isn't, then what am I on?"

"I don't know, Quiche, but stay on it. And keep it there."

"How does one keep a 300-mile-long peninsula here if it decides to move?"

CHAPTER THREE

It was just eight o'clock in the morning. Lesser detectives might just be getting up then, but the best detective in the world had been up and doing for hours. Out of the library and into the streets of Civita do Nord (North Town, this was the name of that northernmost City of Sandaliotis) Constantine Quiche began to run into people he knew in too high a proportion. This, he discovered, would always be a characteristic of Sandaliotis, just as it was the characteristic of dreams and of intensity states, to encounter an inordinate number of persons with whom one was already acquainted.

First there was Regina Marqab, his host of the night before and his companion of that early morning. She introduced Constantine to a new husband.

"But this is not the same young man that you joined earlier," Constantine said.

"Oh him. No. That didn't work out at all," Regina said. "But I'm on an hourly rotation now. Maybe I will settle down a little bit later in the morning. They will set it up for you that way here, and their rates are very reasonable. This is Conrad Squarehauser. He is in real estate and is authorized to buy land on Sandaliotis for more

38

than eight thousand persons. There is a great hunger for land, he says, and all the land on Sandaliotis is so green and new looking! There are a million and a half real estate people who have landed on Sandaliotis already this morning, he says, and there are more coming yet this morning. They are landing at more than a hundred ports.

"I have phoned Salaadin to join me here and have told him how much fun it is. I believe we should buy land here and settle. Both of us are of Sandaliotis ancestry. He is furious though, about my divorcing him mostly. But he'll come around to my style of life when he sees how much fun it is. And we can always marry again any hour we wish to. By the way, I have an eleven o'clock open if you're interested. I was always very fond of you, as you know. I am one of your best friends in the world."

There were many tourist-strangers about who clearly did not come from Sandaliotis, but who just as clearly liked it. They had pleasant but odd appearances. They were either Scandinavian or off-world. These were in addition to the thousands of real estate people. They spoke of having old ties with the place. "Your grandmother came from here," a lady was telling her little girl. "Is it not lovely here?"

"No, Regina, I'm not sure where I will be at eleven o'clock," Constantine said. "Right now I am going to travel quite a distance south to a place where I have visited before. There I will try to find the answer to one aspect of the situation. Do you have any answer to the Sandaliotis phenomenon?"

"What is to answer? It is the life-style. You like it or you do not. I like it."

"Regina, you weren't like this before, were you?" Constantine asked. "Or were you? Though you and Salaadin are my two best friends in the world, I just don't remember you before."

"No I wasn't, except sometimes on perverse streaks. Sandaliotis does this to some people, they say, if they already have leanings to openness. I'm not sure that this is entirely good for me. When I was talking to Salaadin on the phone, I reminded him of the old proverb 'When in Sandaliotis, do as the Sandaliotistics do'. He says that there is no such proverb, and he says that he doesn't believe that most of the Sandaliotistics are like that at all. What I have run into here, he says, is a bit of border-town morality. He says that I'm acting like a typical border-town girl. I suppose that I am."

Regina went away with her latest husband, Conrad Squarehauser.

The streets were now completely overflowing with real estate people wanting to buy the bright buildings and the bright building lots of the city ("Yes, we can have the building by noon," a Sandaliotis huckster was heard to say; "we are the fastest and best builders in the world, and you can see that there is beauty and utility in every line of every one of our buildings"), and green acres in the countryside. There were hundreds of guides and Department of Federal Real Estate Transactions people (with their lavender armbands) herding the many thousands of real estate people and speaking to them from observation platforms and from Living Master-Map areas. One of the DFRET persons was the first young lady who had assisted Constantine Quiche in the library.

"This show has a chance to make it," Constantine told himself. "Everybody is willing to double in brass." But he didn't at all understand the intense activity. It was as if all the shimmering green land of Sandaliotis had to be sold that very day.

Then Constantine saw Julien Moravia, one of the "agents" who had been in the Marqab's house the night before, Julien the beautiful man. Julien was dressed in magistrate's robes now and he was followed by a retinue of bravos.

He saw Constantine, and his face brightened in the most ambivalent look ever, sheer delight at seeing him and sheer evil for some opportunity here, the impulsive waywardness of the rich and mighty, and the glittering cruelty that is to be found near the surface of all beautiful men.

"Arrest that man there!" Julien ordered and he pointed at Constantine. "It will be necessary to take him into custody and possibly to hold him for a very long time. Or it may be that he will break under the torture very quickly. So many of them do nowadays. He is an enemy of the realm and an obstruction to our civil policies."

40

"Julien, this is me myself," Constantine Quiche called out. "You know me. We have shared the same hospitality. Oh, this is a grand joke!"

"Arrest that man at once," Julien cried again. Though he was choking with laughter, he seemed to mean it, and the bravos moved to arrest Constantine. "He is wanted for murder on the mainland," Julien was saying, "and we have to throw a few bones to the mainlanders as evidence of our good faith. They will have so many evidences of our bad faith this morning that we must do something to counteract. He is a murderer and he is a conspirator."

No, no, they were not about to arrest the best detective in the world so easily as that! In the library, Constantine had memorized the map of Civita do Nord and held it firmly in his mind, every street and alley of it, every jurisdiction marker and boundary. The girl in the library had said that the map was accurate but that the city might not be because, for some reason, it had not been finished in all details.

But Constantine knew where the airport was, and he had noticed that it was in a different district from Civita do Nord; it was under the police of the Air Ministry. It would require authority from a different set of magistrates to effect an arrest there. Constantine knew just about what streets and alleys would lead to the airport while seeming to lead away from it. It was a complex of streets and byways which by their very shape had to be designated as "quaint."

Constantine broke into a run, bowling over two bully boys as he made his break for it. With the parachute turning him into a pudgy little man with a bulge around the waist, he could not run as well as he had counted on. Maybe that didn't matter. But he was still the best detective in the world, and he was in the best shape of the world.

For, oh, oh, oh, this was a patterned chase that quickly developed. Constantine could win this. There wasn't even a cut-off man sent out. There wasn't any flanking or herding. The pursuers let Constantine set the directions and conditions of the chase. The strong and chesty and bronzed Sandaliotis runners simply ran after Constantine, and they didn't run quite as hard as they might. It really seemed as if they had compassion on him, and in a perverse corner of his mind he complained about it, that they weren't making a good enough show. And Julien Moravia was left far behind, and Julien had the look of a conditioned and fleetfooted man. He was left behind, all except his voice. His voice belled grandly as if he were coursing and urging hounds on a country chase.

Oh, this had excess of pattern! It was the jumbly-alley run, over-the-fence, down-a-dark-passage, through-an-abandoned-warehouse, over-another-fence, and down-another-alley pattern. There were all those alleys and no streets. There were all those backs of houses and buildings and no fronts. There were all those meetings of three or five alleys, but no straight crossings. Yes, this was a quaint part of town. On his cutbacks, Constantine never had to bowl over more than two pursuers on one foray, and the pursuers were eminently bowl-overable. These chesty bravos were not patsies. Well then, they were secretly on his side. Why were they? Or were they really?

This had a nightmarish quality, and that broke through especially in the belling voice of Julien Moravia who was always in the background. This was like being chased by automatons, by puppets on strings, and being oneself a stringed puppet. This was all thimble theatre stuff, and that will shrink a free person more than anything in the world, to be abridged into such a setting as that.

Constantine reached the airport. He was out of the old jurisdiction, and no new jurisdiction had been alerted to pick him up. There had been no time for that. The pursuers now stood and gnashed their teeth at him, in real or in simulated frustration. What sort of pursuit had it all been? Julien Moravia cried out his theatrical frustration, in a rich belling voice, at his prey having escaped him.

And the timing was perfect. It was all perfect. There was a plane just leaving, and it was going very near to Constantine's destination.

Not until he was in the air did Constantine question himself:

"Have I been made a hopping fool of by the 'agents' and knaves? Has the best detective in the world been had? Are they showing me that Sandaliotis does not follow behavioral laws any more than it follows physical laws? And who was it who put it into my mind to go to a mountain inn in the boondocks of Sardinia? Why was I allowed to escape from such an easy trap in North Town? There were several jaws of that trap that opened of themselves and let me out, as I see it now. Why in law-abiding Sandaliotis should a magistrate have the authority to arrest an innocent man? And what gave me the idea that Julien Moravia in a clown suit *was* a magistrate? How has this indecision and easy acceptance been put into me?

"Oh what dark things will be done in Civita do Nord while I am tricked away into the lonesome mountains of the south? Oh, probably none."

This was a fine green countryside that they were flying over, iridescent green, twinkling green, light-suffused green, enchanting green. But what was that green made out of? A crop-duster was one of the things that Constantine Quiche had been on his way to becoming the best detective in the world, and he knew what crops looked like from the air.

"Young lady, what is that growing down there?" he asked of a stewardess. "It is beautiful, and it misses by a very little bit a tiresome uniformity. Yet it is all apparently of one thing, and I do not know what. It is too fine grained for trees or brush. It is not grapes or olives or almonds or dates or chestnuts. It is not lemons or grapefruit or apples or quince or medlars. It is none of the cereal grains, nor wheat or buckwheat, or rye or barley or oats, nor yet rice. I know what all of them look like whether green or brown. It is no sedge or cane nor reed nor lichen nor clover nor grass that I have ever seen. It looks like wonderful cropland, and I have never seen rolling land so beautifully green; but what crop is it?"

"Oh you poor man," the stewardess said. "That land is not for cropping; it is for selling."

But a Sandaliotis man with an official look to him corrected this.

"She is joking," that man said. "Of course it is for cropping. That is the new magic plant, candle-grass. It is the perfect food for man and beast both."

They came down at Lanusei which now had its name shortened to Lanos. They were in sight of the mountain which Constantine intended to take as a verification point

43

of reality. And the mountain looked the same as it used to. It looked real.

"Where can I get a conveyance to take me to Monti del Genargentu, or nearly there?" Constantine asked a tall and bearded young man who was on the fringe of the airport. He was reassured by the appearance of this young man. He looked like a genuine piece of old Sardinia, not of new Sandaliotis. The man turned his back and refused to answer. Yes, he was a piece of old Sardinia, that was sure. Yet this irritated Constantine, as he believed that he knew this man slightly. Peasants and mountain wranglers do not turn their backs on the best detective in the world without a scathing. Constantine caught the big oaf by the arm and spun him around.

"I asked where I could get a conveyance to take me to Monti del Genargentu, or nearly there," he repeated firmly. Say, that was a big and muscular man that he was swinging around that way!

"Why do you want to go *nearly* there?" the man asked sullenly. "You are nearly there now." The man spoke the old Sardinian dialect instead of the new and more simple stuff of Sandaliotis that sounded like a hedge-child of Esperanto. "And faggots now call it Mont Genorg."

"I'm no faggot. I don't call it that," Constantine said, speaking Sardinian now. "How do I get there?"

The man seemed to mellow a little bit on hearing the old dialect used, but he still had plenty of bristles. He was one of those mountain hedgehogs.

"You can walk," he said. "Or you can go by mule. You can see the mules on the slopes there. Go catch one, mount it, and be gone."

"I want a mule caught and bridled and ready for me!" Constantine swore.

"That one man should catch a mule for another would be as craven as that one man should chew the food for another," the tall and rough man said, "and neither of them could any longer pass for men if it were done."

They were independent, these Sardinians. The Sandaliotis superimposition hadn't changed them much.

"What is this 'nearly there' to the mountain that you want to go to?" the man asked.

"The Inn that Old Grimaldi runs," Constantine said.

44

"Why should you go to old Grimaldi's Inn if you can't even remember Young Grimaldi?"

"Be you the last man!" Constantine cried suddenly, recognizing the man finally and challenging him to the race. He raced up the slope towards the wild mules. He got there first too, before the tall and rough young man. But he had some slight trouble catching and mounting the mule that he selected. Constantine was a good man and he had wrangled mules before, but he was quickly mule bit and mule kicked and mule rolled upon, and he even got a little fast-blooded enjoyment out of it. But when he was finally astride the hooting demon, he saw that Young Grimaldi had long been mounted and was laughing at him.

It was about twelve miles to the Grimaldi-Inn-half-way-up-the-mountain. It was just 10 o'clock in the morning when they came there.

Then, in a very little while, after Constantine had been given a chance to rope up a bucket of water from the well and to wash his hands and face in a stone basin outside of the Inn door, he was with several of them in the big wine-and-dine room of the Inn, drinking black wine and eating hard cheese and hard bread. And also they were giving each other hard looks. Even the closest of friends do not have easy looks for each other in that place.

"This is the test, this is the test," Constantine said to himself, "and it passes the test here. Where there is even one immutable, the world has not gone completely awry. And mountain Sardinia remains that one immutable."

And then he spoke out loud. "There is a puzzle here," he said and he pointed out of the glassless window. "I can see out of the window there all the marks where the old coast used to be, and there was crashing water beyond it. Now I look at the same old coast marks, but there is green land beyond them."

"I hope it won't be this way always," Old Grimaldi said. "I don't like it this way for all the time. I wish the water were back, just for a while now and then."

"It makes a trouble, yes," Young Grimaldi said. "We used to drive the wild boars against the ocean down below. We'd have them off the narrow rock shore then. We'd follow them into the surf with our old hunting pikes

45

and we'd kill them there. Boars cannot swim nearly as well as they imagine themselves able to. But how they can run! They can run up to their own best ideas of themselves and beyond. And now, whenever there are those miles of new meadowland beyond the old shore, there is no killing or catching them at all. They can run forever.

"If there weren't so much money and promise of fortune in this new way, I wouldn't like it at all."

"Was anything like this change of old water into new land ever heard of before?" Constantine asked with exasperation.

"Yes. We begin to remember that it often happened," Old Grimaldi said. "In fact we are instructed to remember it that way. We have always had such days when the big land intrudes on the oceans. We always used to have it that way, one or two days a month. But we didn't like them then and we will not like them now if they are to be permanent; not unless the money to be had out of the new ways changes our mind we won't like them. There is talk that the new land will be made permanent. And there is shakier talk that the new land is going to go mighty fast when it goes, all at once."

"I have been on Sardinia, on and off, six or seven months in all," Constantine said, "and I have never seen this arrangement of the big land before. If it always happened one or two days a month, why have I never seen it until this morning?"

"We used to trick our guests," Old Grimaldi said. "Whenever we felt a day of the big land coming on, we would pray for rain. Then we would keep to our houses and our guests would do it also, and the rainfall would not allow us to see the illicit land. Anyone who runs an Inn in this country knows tricks to cover up almost every disadvantage.

"In the far north, on the mainland, they have had the same trouble. There they also pray for rain when they feel a big land coming on. But their prayers are not answered as regularly as ours, for they are not nearly as holy a people on the continent as we are down here on our island. So they invent stories. They say that it is a big cloud bank. They say that it is a big mirage. And they pray for fog and get it. One needn't be nearly as holy to pray for

46

fog as to pray for rain. But mostly the people on the main land do not look out to sea at all. There could be elephants leaping like dolphins in the sea and they would not notice it."

"I did not mind the big land once or twice a month," Young Grimaldi said. "I would take my wagon and go down to the new land and steal sheep and goats that the promoters had turned on the land to show that it was full of profit. I would fill my wagon with such flesh. Or I would fill it with olives or grapes or cork. They have a little trick, the promoters, where they raise a land in all its fertility and with its plants and animals already thriving on it. That is, some of the promoters have this trick, but it is wearing out. I have become a promoter myself now, but I can't find that trick at all. And I will not like the land here all the time, not even if it is full of profit.

"I will vote against it, but they will not even put it to the vote. They simply impose it. There will be blood flow if we can't drive a better bargain than to have the big land here all the time. And there will also be blood flow if the land is taken away so catastrophically as to kill or cheat numbers of people.

"You are from the north today? Do they have any idea in the north about how these things happen? We have never understood it at all and we live here. About the appearances of this particular day, there is something wrong with them. Someone is being looted and I don't like it. But I suspect that I've joined the looters' league without knowing it."

"I heard from one person that the peninsula and commonwealth of Sandaliotis are to be permanent things now," Constantine said. "I heard in fact that they had always been permanent things, and that everything else about it is nonsense. But I'm not convinced of this. And I have heard that the Islands of Corsica and Sardinia, when they rise above the surrounding land and make themselves out to be separate units, are like black dew that is only an appearance for a while and not a right essence at all. They say that your islands, in their separated aspects, are nightmare things. They say that they are madnesses or bad dreams cropping out. They say that they are mind-sicknesses and person-sicknesses."

47

"Oh, they are a good ways correct there," Old Grimaldi said. "Throw that rock and hit almost anyone. We do have a lot of degrading appearances on us and we must live with them. We must be strong enough to shine through them. Someone must provide the dark strength and suffering of the world. Somewhere there must be a place where they can dump the ash. Somewhere they must bury the bones. Somewhere the Gadarene swine must run, those who did not drown, and it was only a small sounder of them that did drown. Somewhere the noisome miasmas must have their harbors in the hills. This is a torturous thing to talk about.

"We've been fertilized by that dumped ash and cemeterial substance for a long time. There are old ghosts plowed into our mountain gardens and they give some splendid and stenchy blooms to the plants. The whole Sandaliotis business, for the fact of that, is such a splendid and stenchy bloom. It used to appear, as they said, only in the time of the lavender moon. Now they are trying to stretch out that time.

"And then we, in our hills, have always been the refuge for things too horny to be allowed anywhere else on Earth. The old things reigned in the cult circuits a long time ago; and then, after they were clear discredited, they came to our islands to end it all. But they do not die. Or, if they do, they still make appearances after they are dead. Our hills are full of bleak spirits and monsters. Some of them have never been in honest flesh at all. They're phantoms. Why, a person a thousand miles away may be sick or corrupt of soul! And then, for his cure, he may be able to cast something out of himself. He never sees it, or he would be horrified to his own death; and it is not seen by anyone else in his place either. But, when it is cast out there, it will come here to our hills and it will be seen here, as a mad dog, as a mad ape, as a devil.

"We are mightily plagued by creatures out of the centuries before the Redemption. And we are mightily plagued by creatures out of what the Austrians in our own century call the Unconscious. This is a new name for an old and shabby country. These incarnate creatures are not so much from the unconsciousness of people around here, no: our own interior ghosts sometimes break out in

48

violence, but they do not break out in such wandering and bodily manifestations. And then you must consider that we are mostly sweet-minded and do not have so many interior ghosts as people in other places. These incarnate creatures come from the unconsciousnesses or the underminds of people in the Germanies and the Russias, from all the frostbitten and stuffy lands, from the crabbed countries of the Balkans and from all the coal-chimney towns of the central countries that have no suns or oceans to bring them health. They are cast out, those pernicious spirits from the dark places, and they go howling away. But they are canny, and they think while they howl, 'Oh, how can we make a good thing out of this?' And then they see the opportunity. 'Oh Lord, cast us out upon green hills,' they beg. And the Lord, in His mercy, casts them out on the greenest hills that are, our own.

"There is another thing that tends to give us a bad name here," Old Grimaldi continued, "though it does not spring from any evil of us, but rather from our compassion and noble-heartedness. A strong man from among us, one able to bear every torture and unpleasantness, will have compassion on those in the smoky place itself. He will look over the brink (we do have a place in our country where one may look over the brink and down into the everlasting pit itself), and he will point out the most miserable and the most suffering person that he sees there. 'I have an unemployed day today,' the big-hearted man will say (or maybe it is only half a day that he has free), 'Let me take the place of that one there. He's a mean-looking one and undeserving and no one else would give him spell. But he has really had it and he needs a rest.' 'All right,' the person on duty will say. 'We are always open for trades.' So the noble-hearted person will go down to hell to suffer for the other one for half a day, and that other one will come up here to lie on our green hills and rest; and our hills will get a bad name from him.

"It will be forgotten what a noble people we are— (what other people will trade places with damned souls even if for only half a day?)—and it is remembered only that our hills are filled with horrors and frightful spirits. They sprawl on our mountains, and they look up at our blue sky and are refreshed; and all this is on the side of

49

charity and compassion. But you get a few hundred of those fields of hell lying around on a nice day, and you get a bad name. And most of them were not even raised around here. They are foreigners.

"It is a good thing that our island is never submerged, either when the big land is here or when it is not. The noisome ash and rot in our hills would contaminate the sea if it swept over it, and it would kill the fish."

This was more than Old Grimaldi usually talked. He was silent then.

"We didn't even pray for rain today," Young Grimaldi said, "even though we knew that the Big Land would come. There is rich profit to be had in showing and selling the new land today. Do you know that chickens have more wits than people have as to knowing what the weather will do? If there is a downpour that is to be for only a short duration, they will take cover from it and will not come out again till it is over with. But if the downpour is to be for a longer time, they will know it immediately, and they will not withdraw from it. They will be out in it and going about their daily business of eating. That is our case now, and we have a little bit of this chicken wisdom in the business about the big land coming. If it comes for only one day, we will withdraw from it for that one day. But if it comes for a much longer time, we will know it at once, and we will not withdraw from it. We will live with it as well as we can, but we will not like it. It has come for that longer time now."

"And yet Sandaliotis, the Big Land as you call it, seems an altogether pleasant place," Constantine Quiche ventured to remark.

"So does Hell seem an altogether pleasant place, when it comes with its both hands full of enticements," Young Grimaldi said. "Ah, I may have a hell of a time with this Sandaliotis business the way I am entangled in it more than I intended." Oh those bristling hedgehog-men of the Sardinian mountains!

They were silent for a while, looking out of the glassless window at the tumbling green beauty of the hills drenched in sunlight.

"Has either of you heard the story of the world-bomb

that is three hundred miles long?" Constantine asked them after a pause.

"That is a dog-bomb," Young Grimaldi said. "It is all fizz and spark and no explosion. It is a dead-flash, a dud. It is the dog that is all howl and no fang. I say to put the dog killer on it. It is a sheep-killing dog, but it will not harm any person who is not a sheep."

"What that three-hundred-mile-long bomb is is one of the sandals of the devil named Haziel," said Old Grimaldi. "It is the famous sandal with the red strings or straps on it."

"He must be a very big-footed devil to have a sandal that is three hundred miles long," Constantine remarked.

"Oh, size isn't a particular characteristic of those fellows," Old Grimaldi said. "One of them can be quite large one day and much smaller another, and so can be the things that they wear. But the day that Haziel lost his sandal, that sandal was three hundred miles long."

"He is wanting it back," Young Grimaldi said. "That's what's making a lot of the trouble in the area right now."

"You are too wise to believe in tales like that, Young Grimaldi," Constantine said.

"Me wise? When was I ever? A tale like that is like a wild mule. I can catch one of them quicker than you can, I can mount him faster, and I can ride him faster. A man who is mule-bit and mule-kicked and mule-rolled-upon should be a little careful about what other fast-footed thing he tries. This tale, as you call it, is faster-footed than you'd imagine."

"How is the sandal a bomb, Young Grimaldi? Or how is the object, whatever it is, either a sandal or a bomb?"

"Oh the bomb, the sandal, the dog-island in the sky, it is what the chaired doctors now call antimatter and what the unchaired people have always called evil. The Earth and its furniture are all made out of real matter which we call good. Oh, you can pretend that it is something else, and you can degrade our Earth with your mouth, but it is still essentially good, that is to say that it is positive matter. If the sandal, or anything else composed of evil matter or antimatter, should come into contact with Earth, then there would be a great explosion, a mutual destruction. Haziel would not care. He has gotten another sandal

51

in the meanwhile. Even of the people of the Earth, there are many of them who are antimatter in their allegiance, and they would not care. But I would care. I will do what I can and I will warn everyone that I can. I will warn you since you seem to be interested: no good thing ever came from Haziel."

"Is there a connection, do you think, Young Grimaldi, between the bomb sandal of Haziel, and the sandal-shaped peninsula which you call the big land?"

"Oh, there are some compromising stories told that connect the two of them. It is said that a dolphin whistles under the sea, and a dog answers her from the sky. I don't know how much there is to these stories. You must be on a curious case, best detective in the world."

"I am, Young Grimaldi. How can I best get to Salerno in Italy? I am full of hunches and intuitions today and I think I should go talk to a man in Salerno. And do not tell me to go by mule. There isn't any mule road that goes all the way."

"With all the big land that is out there today, how can you be sure, detective? But I have a plane here. I'll take you quickly enough."

"You, young Grimaldi, a bristly hedgehog of the Sardinian Mountains, you have a plane and you will take me there just that easily? And how do you happen to have a plane?"

"Oh, I'm in the real-estate business, for this one long day anyhow, though my heart has gone out of it already. But I have the plane for that, to show areas to the people, for some of the plots are vast. Yes, I will take you to Salerno just that easily, best detective. Why should we make it hard? Is it the Master Forger you will see there? No, do not tell me there is no way I could even have known that there was a Master Forger. You have worn out the variations of the 'there-is-no-way-you-could-have' line. Go phone whoever it is that you will phone, and the plane will be ready."

Constantine Quiche made a phone call from the one phone in Grimaldi Inn, and he quickly had his man on the line.

"Quiche," he said. "Grishwell, does the sanda—ah, the

three-hundred-mile-long bomb come from a world named Haziel?"

"We think so, yes," came the answer. "The world doesn't go by that name in the catalogs though. There is no way you could have known that there was such a world."

"You have worn out the variations of that line, Grishwell," Constantine said. "Is the bomb an antimatter device?"

"We suspect so, yes. What have you found out? Where are you?"

"I'm in the Sardinian mountains. People used to tell me things here. Now they just talk as they used to do, but they don't tell me as much."

"Don't let the peninsula of Sandaliotis leave, Quiche. Keep it there. We don't know what it's doing there, but it may be in the berth of the bomb and blocking it out. That would be to our advantage. Don't let it leave."

"I am to prevent a peninsula the size of Italy or Iberia from picking up and leaving? All right, Grishwell, I won't let it leave."

CHAPTER FOUR

It was a Sandaliotis-made plane, an Ichnusa, that Young
Grimaldi had. As with much Sandaliotis equipment and
vehicles that Constantine had seen, it made up for any
other deficiencies it might have by its striking style. It was
a plane to be proud of.

And young Grimaldi was proud of it, and Constantine
got the idea that the tall man had had it only a short time.
Young Grimaldi had a lot of style in driving it also, but it
was no worse than riding one of the wild mules of
Sardinia.

They went up high, and the beautiful geography of
Sandaliotis was unfolded more strikingly than any map
could show it. There had never been such colors as that
land showed, greens, blues, reds, yellows, browns,
purples, blacks, and back to greens always. There had
never been any such water as was around the new land,
green and blue and white water with an exquisite
sharpness of color. The haze, where it bulked above the
sea, was a lilac color. This was all like a pendant jewel set
down into the Mediterranean, and every part of that jewel
Sandaliotis was illuminated with a new light.

The master Angelo DiCyan (by coincidence he was the

man that Constantine was now coming to see) had once given pen to the idea that the Mediterranean would have been of a color as dull as that of some other seas if it were not for the lands of Iberia and Italy and Greece going into those waters like brands of light ('and one other, the invisible peninsula, which has visible effect'); he believed that these four baffles or reflectives were what caused that sea to be filled with such a suffusing light.

Young Grimaldi brought Constantine Quiche down at a little port between Avelina and Salerno, and then he seemed to wish to explain something else. But he could not quite bring himself to that.

"I notice that you have the parachute, best detective in the world, so you must understand a little bit of it. I cannot tell the things that I only half guess, and besides I am working and taking money from the other side of the street. But keep that parachute on, best detective in the world!"

Constantine noticed that there was, in the port terminal, a booth marked "Travelers' Aid, Sandaliotis Division," and it did not seem to be new. There were so many connections and top offs of events that nobody had noticed until that day! Constantine took a taxi into Salerno, and he came to the home of the master Forger Angelo DiCyan. It was 11:45 in the morning.

"The Master will *not* receive you, Mr. Quiche," said a workman with a huge mallet in his hand. "The Master does not rise before noon ever, and he has an utter contempt for those who do. Please do not make the obvious remarks about us workmen being at work earlier, Mr. Quiche. The clock that I am working by, you will notice, says 12:45. That is the present time in the town where I was born. That keeps things to an honest basis with me. The Hindu there who is faking Hindu statuary has a clock that is set even later. No, I am sure that it will not do any good to tell the Master that you are here. In addition to his contempt for all people who arise before noon, he has an even deeper contempt for all persons of the policeman class."

"I will have that fancy little puppy by the ears in a moment," Constantine said. "I have given him several lessons in the past about what persons of my class can do to those of his. I had thought that I had taught him to temper his contempt in my case."

There were three pianos playing there. One of them was doing an old Scott Joplin rag; one of them was playing a Clarence Sweet Rock-Bottom; one of them was playing a sequence of Profile Jazz by Schrade. Young persons of unknown sex were playing these things on the pianos, and other young persons were recording them and scoring them. There were already playbacks going on all three, blending in with the new play, to form syntheses that would have forgotten their beginnings. These were the first steps of those efforts that the Master would work up into some of the best forgeries in the world.

"Tell him that I'm here anyhow," Constantine insisted. "*I* have a contempt for people who keep me waiting. I assure you that the effect of it is lost on me. And, after all, it is only twelve minutes to the hour."

"Certainly not," the workman said. "The Master has these very high standards. He probably will not see you even at 12:00. He gets up at 12:00, or sometimes much after, but his routine varies thereafter."

"Tell him that the best detective in the world is here," Constantine kept after it, "and that the best detective in the world doesn't like to be kept waiting. Tell him that the best detective in the world has ways of doing things about things like this."

"Oh, he will simply tell me that he is the best forger in the world; that there are far fewer top forgers than there are top detectives; and that he delights in keeping the best detective in the world waiting."

Constantine Quiche caught the workman roughly by the throat, and the workman banged Constantine roughly over the head with his mallet. They both stepped back then, hurt in feelings and body.

"Why not tell him that I'm here?" Constantine wouldn't give up yet, and he was feeling his head that had a new knot on it.

"Because he isn't here," the workman said, "and because I'm never supposed to say that he isn't here."

"Oh, what a way to run a false house! That Scott Joplin piece they are forging, is it the Sycamore Leaf Rag?" Constantine asked.

56

"Oh no, it's the Box-Elder Leaf Rag," the workman said. "It's very new."

"So new that the Master still hasn't put the finishing touches on it?" Constantine asked. "He will still have to come up with the sheets of old music paper, but I am sure that he has that for every period. He will still have to note it and score it in Joplin's intense hand, but he has often forged Joplin before, I believe. Oh, there is no forger like him! And, yes, he has a wonderful bunch of workmen working here. You are his guarantee of excellence."

"Thank you," the workman said. There were a dozen or so young persons there roughing in masterpieces of forgery. They knew their period materials, their canvases and pigments, their marbles and bronzes. And there were some glassmen there mouth blowing forged-glass masterpieces as people used to do it a long time ago.

There were essence blenders making vintage wine, and bottle founders making vintage bottles. And there was a lady typing at Edsel Schrock's own genuine Fret-Jet typewriter for which DiCyan had outbid everybody at a famous auction. There was even one of Schrock's battered trunks there that DiCyan had had for a song, other persons not foreseeing the power of the honestly sworn-to "from-the-bottom-of-the-trunk" attestation. Yes, there had been quite a few really superior works come out of the bottom of that old trunk in recent years, no matter that they had rested in the bottom of the trunk for only ritual seconds after they had been completed. (If a forger neglects the rituals, he is lost.) In honesty it must be said that these latter-day discoveries were better than anything that Schrock himself ever wrote.

"Oh what this Master Genius and Organizer could have done if only he had gone straight!" Constantine glowed out the words in admiration.

"Spare us," one of the workman said, and he rolled his eyes. "The best detective in the world would be much better if he stayed off of stale remarks. Besides, the 'straight way' is greatly overrated; and, if you knock off the post-humous accruals, it pays hardly anything at all. Most of us here tried it, as did the Master himself. This pays so much better, and it offers so many more opportunities for creativity. In fact, the Master always refers to the work that we do here as 'Traditional Context Creativity.' There is nothing so beautifully ordered as forgery. And much better than the straight road is that beautifully sweeping curved road (we never call it the crooked road) where the really superior scenery is to be found."

The Master Forger Angelo DiCyan came in the front door. It was exactly twelve o'clock noon. Angelo was winy and briny from a long night of it, and he almost looked wilted. But he took a scissors and snipped a very little bit off each side of his moustache, the amount the ends had grown in the last twenty-four hours. He discarded the red night rose that he was wearing and put on a yellow day rose. Then he was fresh again for a new day.

"I understood that you did not rise before noon," Constantine said.

"I do not," the Master said. "I rise now. The other that you see, that is a disreputable person who sometimes inhabits my body during the night hours. Quiche, I consider your coming here to be in the nature of an intrusion and aggression. Our free and easy air here is not meant to be breathed by detectives or other infidels, not even by the best detective in the world. Lay off me, Constantine! I have no time for your petty harassments. I have been working on something that is so big that it is completely beyond your reach."

This Angelo DiCyan did have reputation and status. He had so much of them that he had sold incredible, newly discovered masterpieces as his own forgeries, because there had grown up so strong a market for his avowed forgeries. Among the forgers, that is status. But Constantine Quiche had his own status to maintain.

"No, man, no," he told Angelo. "I do not harass you. We will not reach any accord this way. I want your good will. I want your cooperation. I want your help. I want your advice. I want your judgment. I want your fine appraisal. And my group will pay well for all services. And, if I cannot have these things from you in genuine form, then I will accept your forgeries of them. They may serve even better."

The Master Forger Angelo smiled a bit then. He appreciated the praise that Constantine heaped upon him. He

58

led Constantine into other rooms secluded from the workshop.

"All right," the Master said, "so long as you understand that it is a forgery of my good will and not my good will itself, then we can consult. But it will have to be very confidential. I cannot have it known that I am working with the right side of the law. Let us go into my inner rooms which are even more secure."

"We *are* in your inner rooms. We have just come into them. How big, Angelo? That is my first question. How big a forgery could there be?"

"Oh, as big as the biggest figure that could be written on the biggest tab that the customer could lift. There is no other limit. I could forge this very world that we are on, and I could forge it convincingly enough for your most astute planet-buyer. All I would need is money enough for the project and a place to set my fulcrum."

"Yes, all right," Constantine said. "I didn't know it could be done quite that big, and this isn't a question of it. As big as a country or a realm, yes, but not as big as a world. Then there is the other part of the inquiry. How about a forgery—how shall I say this?—a forgery of which there is no original."

"Oh, certainly, certainly, there are instances of that, Constantine. That is almost too easy sometimes. To do it best, one has to reject the 'too-easy' and 'too-cheap' solutions. Then you have really quality forgeries of which there are no material originals. This thing is difficult only because it places the forger on his honor, or at least on that forgery that he may delegate to serve as his honor. It is so hard to check it when there is nothing to check it by, and the commissioning of such a thing might be subject to abuse.

"And there is another detail which not-quite-master forgers sometimes overlook in doing forgeries-without-originals. There is one small thing that *must* be done. One *must* make a slight change in the world first: a silent, slight, adaptive change in the world itself so as to produce such a world as would accommodate this missing masterpiece. But we all of us change the world continually.

"Nor let us be misled by such a term as 'missing original.' That is not the same thing as 'no original.' I have in mind one of my own nearly perfect forgeries, the 'Weeping Hermes of Praxiteles.' I made this forgery of an unavailable original. I made it very much as Praxiteles would have made it. And I made it as good as Praxiteles could have made it. The original had been the Landmark Greek Sculpture of the fourth century B.C., and I made it to be so. But I had already rambled through the mind of Praxiteles by means of many of his other sculptures, which is what made my forgery-without-an-original such a superior one. But it wasn't as if there *had never been* an original. There had been. I could study that missing masterpiece in its effect on all later works. I could study the written descriptions of it that have come down to us. Really, I already had the impression, as it were, from the mud in which it had lain. I had only to pour the mud mold full of molten marble.

"Incidentally, I *have* found the missing Praxiteles, the 'Weeping Hermes' itself, and I am ruddy foxed if I know what to do with it. It isn't as good as my version which is now accepted as the original. Even as one of my 'authentic' forgeries, it would lower my reputation a bit. But I will keep it a while, and then I will find a way to turn it to best advantage.

"But you are talking about the forgery of something that never was, and yet *could* have been?"

"Yes I am, Angelo," Constantine said. "And perhaps that could-have-been context would have to be, maybe has already had to be, forged also."

"Oh well, many things are able to grow their own contexts about them. Sometimes a thing will seem right for a while, and then it will seem just a bit wrong. Like yourself."

"Like *myself*, Angelo?"

"Yes. Weren't you absolutely secure and sure of yourself as the best detective in the world for a while? And, in the last eighteen hours or so, haven't you come to feel that there was something just a little bit wrong with you in that role, with you in any role?"

"Yes, that's so, Angelo. What of it?"

"Maybe you here present are only a forgery of Constantine Quiche. Maybe *I* forged you."

"An interesting idea. At least I would be a masterly forgery then."

"You were speaking first, Constantine, about a very large forgery. And now you are speaking about a forgery without a corresponding original. I suppose that they belong to the same case?"

"Yes."

"This costs money even to talk about, Constantine. Who is paying me to talk about it?"

"World Interpol."

"Well, working for them would not necessarily put me on the side of law and order. I could salve myself by saying that it would put me on the side of the law and disorder, but I do not like disorder in any company, surely not in the company of the law. I really am for order all the way, and let the law go hang. Every real artist lives within the lines of order, and a forger must live within them still more strictly than any other. He is not *allowed* to slip. What is it that is to be forged, Constantine?"

"A country. That is what is to be forged, or is being forged, or perhaps was forged a long time ago. Or perhaps it falls into another case altogether and I am mistaken about it. It may be that there is no forgery. That is what I must find out."

"A *country*, you say, Constantine?"

"Yes, a country, a realm, a commonwealth, a consensus monarchy headed up by an appointive tyrant in the present case. It is a commonwealth coexistent with a peninsula in our own Mediterranean, peninsula a little bit bigger than your Italy."

"A *country*, you said, Constantine. A *nation*?"

"Yes, Angelo. A master forger has surely heard of out-of-the-way set-ups before. I want to know whether this country is a valid original (which does not seem possible to me), or whether it is an outright forgery (and I believe it is), or whether it is something else that I have trouble even positing. I want to know how good a forgery it is, and how well it will stand up. I want to know where it has been and where it is going, either as forgery or original. I want to know who did it, and why."

"Oh this is unfair, Constantine!" the Master Angelo wailed and he held his head in both his hands. "You

61

present me with a staggering conception that would be absolutely paradise to any master forger, and in the same presentation you tell me that it may already have been done. I do not want it to be already done! I want to do it myself! To forge an entire country, what would I not give for that? Constantine, what is this all about?"

Was it possible that Angelo was protesting too much? With a forger, how do you tell?

"If you did not 'sleep' till noon, you would know, Angelo," Constantine said. "It has been the wonder of the world this whole morning, I'm sure of that."

Angelo the master went to a door leading into the workshops.

"Bring the journals," he called to one of the men there. "Instantly, instantly, bring them." And the noon journals, just out, were brought almost at once.

"Ah, ah, ah," Angelo cried, reading and comprehending swiftly. "This is something out of the usual, Constantine. Let us go to my inner rooms and examine this situation more fully."

"These *are* your inner rooms," Constantine said.

"Oh, I suppose so, but in my mind I always picture myself as even richer than I really am, and as having suite after suite of rooms, each much more inner than the others."

Angelo was through the journals then in a fury of activity.

"Ah, they treat of it with a sort of hysterical humor," he said then after only about three minutes of cramming. "They are afraid yet to treat it any other way. The world, for six or seven hours now, has been in a state of suspended disbelief. There are no real facts here. There are no details. But the overall shape and color of it is here. Oh, is it not done boldly with a brave hand! I am eaten up with envy. Could even I, with every facility possible at hand, have done it so bravely? Or do I have a master and superior somewhere whom I have not even dreamed of?"

"Angelo," Constantine said, "I believe that you are sufficiently acquainted with all aspects of the Mediterranean civilization and culture to give a balanced judgment here. You are the best man for it that I could think of. If it is not too big for even you to give a balanced judgment on—"

"Constantine, you committed a redundancy when you spoke of Mediterranean civilization and culture. To me, at least, there is no other of either. I am a member of the body of the Mediterranean achievement and I know its flavor. No, I do not believe that it is too big to give a judgment on. It would be only (or perhaps it was) a medium-sized province of the Roman Empire. We will not be intimidated by size. Give me unlimited funds. And give me (just to have an interval to refer to) about four years to make the preliminary survey. Then, perhaps, we can go more deeply into it."

"Perhaps we are inextricably deep into it already," Constantine said. "I would like to have the survey and appraisal made today, as early today as possible. I am not sure that even today will be allowed to run its full course."

" 'There shall be new lands and rumors of new lands, but the end is not yet,' " Angelo quoted. "Let us not be intimidated by the *speed* of events. The peaceful, perhaps overly peaceful arrival of the new land does not seem to constitute an attack. Sandaliotis has claimed Monaco as an intrinsic part of its country, but there hasn't been any blood shed there yet, in spite of several flags being run up and pulled down again. In fact, such a peaceful surprise appearance seems to break all the teeth out of a surprise *attack*. The surprise is all gone now. If it is a danger, then it is no longer a quick danger. Anything that could have set down a three-hundred-mile-long peninsula in the middle of the Mediterranean could have done almost any damage that it wished. I am a forger and I like to consider forgery in everything. But first let us consider whether this may be genuine, and not a forgery at all.

"There is the real possibility that the place has been there all the time. There have been elites all the time. There have been hidden-knowledge people all the time, illuminati and cognoscenti and intelligentsia. And there has been real substance to some of these people in spite of the puppet types with which they have surrounded themselves for purposes of camouflage. And there has al-

63

ways been a sort of national resemblance among the high esoterics.

"Why should they not have had their own homeland? And, as to the fund of hidden knowledge itself, well one of the earliest pieces of hidden knowledge to be encountered, in whatever context, is always the knowledge of invisibility and the manipulation of it on a selective basis. Oh yes, the land could have been there all the time, invisible except to the initiated and the intelligent. But, in that case, why was it invisible to me, for I have always been both?"

"Ah, there is also the mystery of the ships and the boats and the fishes," Constantine said.

"Oh, that may not have been too much of a mystery. Ships stay to their own routes, and boats ply their own territories. There is a close-mouthedness about Mediterranean fishermen. There have always been wide areas where they would not go. 'No fish there,' they always say, but some of us on the peripheries of the areas can see the sea leaping with fish. On another hand, there are areas in the Mediterranean, areas strangely corresponding to Sandaliotis on one of those hasty maps there, where *there aren't any fish.* Constantine, I have a strong suspicion that there isn't any water there either, though there appears to be. You know that the other side of invisibility is always *seeing something that isn't there.* If you don't see something, then you must see something else in place of it, even if it is colorless background. As to the fish themselves, the Mediterranean has great quantities of blind and confused fish that are like fish that have been swimming in huge underground pools and are strangers to the light.

"(By the way, I have forged fish, Constantine. I have forged nine ponds full of fish for certain country lords in my own Italy here. They are alive, and they swim. They are organic, and they look like fish. And they are forged. Remind me to tell you about it sometime.)

"As to the selective invisibility, I have learned a little bit of that myself. As one who often operates outside the law, this has been quite necessary to me. When you yourself once had my establishment searched, I made many incriminating objects invisible, objects that were involved

64

in my forgeries. And there are objects in this room right now that you cannot see because I will not let you see them. Well, even the strongest and most adept mind couldn't make an entire country invisible, or make a functionally invisible country visible either, but a few million minds brought into close concert might do it."

"How about context, Angelo? You said that many things are able to grow their own contexts about them. Does it seem to you that Sandaliotis has done this?"

"Yes, very much so. It is growing or projecting its own context, or it is making apparent the 'has-always-been' context into which it fits. There is a rush of connectives and coincidences into my mind as though a flood dam had broken. Yes, already I am *remembering* Sandaliotis, and I am remembering its relationships with other parts of the Mediterranean world, from archaic to modern times. I am, all at once, understanding and interpreting hundreds of cryptic references to it, from Strabo to Chesterton. I can already think, for instance, of the names of ninety famous mirages and weather hallucinations in the region whose names are plays on the name 'Sandaliotis', and I can see a common source to even more distant names and a common source to widely scattered phenomena.

"(By the way, I forged a mirage once. It wasn't too difficult. All it took was a directed temperature inversion and an optical counterflux.)

"I now find Sandaliotis as a recurring idea in nursery rimes, and in old collections of riddles. A nonsense line of Rabelais suddenly makes punning sense about Sandaliotis. I find it as a recurring fugue in music, and as a recurring landscape-syndrome in pictorial art. I believe that every great public building in Sandaliotis had been painted in our own art and has heretofore remained unidentified there. These are six pictures of great Sandaliotis buildings in the noon journals here, and I recognize every one of them as appearing in Italian art. This thing is almost explosive the way it touches off connectives. It has been there a long time in one form or another."

"Well, shall we go look at it, Angelo? I do value your opinion as to its authenticity. And if it is a forgery on a giant scale, who would recognize that part of it so quickly as yourself?"

"It doesn't matter, Constantine, whether we go now or later. For a while yet, I can see it as well internally here as I could see it if we went to it. But it would seem more as if I were working for my money if we went. If you want to go there, we will go."

"Yes, I very much want to go there," Constantine said. "There are so many pieces to this that we just have to be there to make out their pattern."

They went to the port. They bought tickets for the next flight to Ichnusa, the Capital of Sandaliotis. There was a ready way to check on one aspect of this slippery reality right now. Angelo DiCyan questioned and found that this was a regularly scheduled flight and not a new flight at all. There were records still at the ticket desk that showed that the flight had been made the day before, and the day before that, and the day before that also, the flights made on days before anyone had ever heard of the city. But nobody there had a *positive* memory of those flights being made, in spite of the fact that they were in the record.

"I will hit their literature of the various arts," Angelo said while they were in flight. (Constantine had told him about the amazing library in North Town, and they speculated that the one in Ichnusa, the capital, would be even better.) "I know that you have done some of this, but there are parts of it that you wouldn't even know where to look for. I will read their accounts of the various *forgeries* in those arts. In the accounts of the forgers, I would look in particular for one name, my own. In France or in Spain or in Italy or in England or in the Netherlands or in the States, my name does appear as that of the great art forger. If Sandaliotis has truly been a part of the community of nations, they will know my name there also."

And Angelo whistled the second chorus of 'Oh mention my name in Sandaliotis.' It seemed to be the new song of the day, for people in the plane, and for the real-estate agents and other visitors going there.

"Do not concentrate so entirely on the arts," Constantine said. "Our clues and our keys will most likely be found outside the field of the arts."

"My dear man, *nothing* is outside the field of the arts," Angelo DiCyan argued. " 'The Arts' is just a way of look-

66

ing at things, the right way of it. Of no substance whatever can you say 'This is in the field of the arts' or 'This is not in the field of the arts.' And as to the Commonwealth of Sandaliotis, whether it is a forgery or whether it is a contingency or whether it is a fact, it is still sheer art in every function and process of it. Being of the Mediterranean world, it cannot be bad art, even if it is faked art.

"The clouds, the clouds, I never saw them acting so perversely. What are they hiding?" Angelo said then.

"What? Which?" Constantine asked.

"The whole array of them from north sky to south sky, that length of cloud, and that length, and that one again, and the thunderheads in the several places of them. They are like children grouping in groups to hide something among them. I have these fancies sometimes, Constantine. It really seems as if the clouds are hiding something."

(Sometimes this man Angelo seemed like a man skimming clay pigeons up in the air to see what fire they would draw. He seemed so now. Constantine suspected what it was that the clouds were conspiring to conceal. Did Angelo?)

They saw from the air why the Mediterranean was an especially bright and shimmering sea, in contrast to many others. The quickened lands combine with the sun to be light sources of the seas, and this Sandaliotis was ideal for it. There was never a land so suffused with light and so reflecting of light. There seemed to be light *within* the green transparency of its meadows.

They came down at Ichnusa, the capital of Sandaliotis, and they came down into an urban dazzle. We think of ancient Mediterranean cities as things of white or ivory or gray stones, magnificent yes, but not quite overflowing with life and color. We forget that in their own times, those great buildings were brightly painted, just as the great statue-stones were. But the cities of Sandaliotis were still in their own time, and the stones of Ichnusa actually shouted and bled with the bright colors of them.

Constantine and Angelo took a swift carriage to the Arts Palace where Angelo believed he might best begin his investigations. "What genius! What genius!" Angelo glowed at the city as they rode through it. "I am on fire with envy. Why was I not directing this great thing? And

67

yet, how could I improve it? Oh, here and there I could. But that, that, I would never even have thought of it."

There were signs of youth and even of childishness around. Grown persons, for instance, were blowing soap bubbles, huge and gaudy, as they walked along.

"Are you capable of such forgery as that, if it is forgery?" Constantine asked.

"I am," said Angelo, "and I myself am a secret soap-bubble blower. I always carry a pipe and a jar of bubble mix in my pocket, but I blow the bubbles only when unobserved. I will blow them openly from hence on."

Angelo popped a pill and offered one to Constantine.

"Take one," he said. "There is nothing like them in nervous situations where you may be subject to various sorts of invasions. They will counteract all mind-numbing devices, and all infusions that unhinge the limbs and will. Hold it under your tongue and forget about it. It will last for many hours. It will give you twelve hour protection against ordinary invasions."

"I always prefer to trust to my own wits," Constantine said.

"I wouldn't, not with yours," Angelo told him. "I'm scarce willing to trust to my own sometimes."

"What is the pill? Who made it?" Constantine asked.

"I made it," Angelo said. "It is my original forgery of Doctor Korkolon's controversial Guardsman Pill. Mine works. His doesn't."

Constantine took one of the pills and put it under his tongue and forgot about it. It was just one o'clock in the afternoon. Constantine did not go into the Arts Palace. It was too beautiful outside.

There was the great sweep of the Italian Stairs down the eastern slope from the Arts Palace, a flight of steps that was a hundred meters wide and three hundred steps down, made out of dazzling hundred-color painted and natural stone. The flight of steps had every sort of pop shop on it. It also had ten thousand bench loungers and step loungers who all belonged to the beautiful people. People as scenery, the concept surpassed itself with the loungers here.

Or north was the great basilica. At the bottom of the great flight of steps were the Ninety-Nine Fountains of

Nekros and their reflecting pools. And still east of the fountains was the Roman Circus where thirteen different streets fed into the great circle. In the green pedestrian island inside the great circle was the Tarshish Tower with its great thirteen-faced clock. If one should stand at the foot of the Tarshish Tower, so local belief had it, sooner or later he would see every person in the world pass by. And if he should close his eyes and count to thirteen while he was standing at the foot of that tower, he would, at the count of thirteen (how childlike and naïve are the Sandaliotistics in some things!), be kissed by a fair one of the opposite sex.

CHAPTER FIVE

The best detective in the world closed his eyes and counted to thirteen. After all, if the best forger in the world could be a soap-bubble blower, could not the best detective in the world play kissing games like a kid?

He was kissed. Oh, by what sort of creature though. He felt the needle punctures, but they were more common than not with kisses nowadays. He opened his eyes. It was Amelia Lilac, the agent of sorts, from England. She was, as always, wrapped in her own shadow or mist. On her, it went well.

"Oh my heart, oh my air, oh my day!" Amelia said.

"Needles are unfriendly, Amelia," Constantine said. "The quick needling like that destroys trust."

"Oh no, it was only a love potion," she said, "to bind you to me. Sandaliotis is more medieval and more Italian even than Italy, and should it not have love potions a dozen times a day?"

"I should have kept Angelo with me a bit longer," Constantine said. "He might have been able to tell me whether you were a forgery. Are you, Amelia? Are you genuine, or are you a fake?"

"Oh, Angelo!" she said. "He is the fake. But whatever

I am, I am still a work of art. Who else can do such things with her own shadow? You will notice now, Constantine, that you are very slightly paralyzed in limbs and volition, and your motions will be just a little bit slow and blurred. So will your brains be. You will be amenable. But, as a compensation, you will be suffused by an euphoria. Is it not pleasant, Constantine? Oh, the love potion was in the needle also, but we must never forget our baser business as well. And now you will come with me. Quickly, quickly, Constantine. You will take the place of someone else, and that someone else will be yourself, the storied best detective in the world. You look so like him. You will call him your 'nephew' if you ever happen to meet his mortal remains, but now you are himself. In this we do things for others, and we do things for ourselves. We will now insert you into a production. Try to handle it, dear. It is a very nice dramatic role. Then we will lift changed elements of you out of that production again for other use. Are we not devious? Come along."

Was Constantine Quiche compelled to go along with Amelia Lilac in her lavender cloud, or did he go along with her willingly in the thought that she was as good a current clue as was at hand? Oh, there was some compulsion to it. Constantine often felt himself compelled to go that first crooked mile with a beautiful woman. As to being slightly paralyzed in limbs and volition, it may well be that Constantine was always so. He was never as free as he wished to be. He was always inhibited. But he could outleap and outrun the next hundred men he would see, in spite of that slight paralysis of limbs and body. And he could outthink and outwill many persons half his age or twice his age, in spite of the slight paralysis of his volition. He wasn't as paralyzed as most people are. And he had always seemed to be amenable, and he had never been quite so, nor was he now.

Did the forgery by Angelo of the Doctor Korkolon controversial Guardsman Pill help at all? Yes it did. It helped immeasurably. It contained the needle assault pretty handily, and it might yet prove the factor to keep Constantine all in one piece.

"I am worried about my new and splendid car that I

71

left in Civita do Nord this morning," Constantine told Amelia. "I am in love with that splendid car."

"And I was jealous that you loved that car more than me. But there is not enough of it left to worry about now, and there are only small nostalgic remnants surviving of it for you to be in love with," Amelia said in her lilac-colored voice. "We did not know for sure where you had gone, you see (you have been 'belled' by this latest injection, but apparently an earlier one had failed), nor when you would be back, if at all. But, if you did come back to your car, we wanted to have a welcome for you. So we gooney-trapped it. And we had to do it again and again every hour. Children would come around and caress the car and get in it, and of course they would be killed by the explosion. We used 'Baited Breath' on it so that we could hardly stay away from it ourselves when we had finished trapping it. And I doubt if you would be able to stay away from it either if you caught even one whiff of it. If you had come back to North Town, you would have been killed at the car just as the children were. We would set the traps again, and the young people would come by once more to ogle it and to play with it. And they in turn would be killed, just as the earlier bunches had been. If I mistake me not, it has just blown up once more (this makes six times in all) and killed only a single person this time. I tell you though, if you'd come back to your car, we'd have had you, Constantine. Not that we don't have you now."

"If you can kill me any time you wish, and in so many different ways, then why am I still alive?"

"Differences of opinion on how best to use you, and changes of mind. We are setting you down as a nothing person, and then we have to change from that. Be a nothing person, Constantine, if you want to stay alive. We go into this building here. It is called the Dungeons of Tertullian. Did you know that Tertullian was a Sandaliotite?"

"He gives them a bad name then," Constantine said. "*I* do not go in here. I am following another inclination to another place."

"A test of strength, is it, Constantine?" Amelia asked. "You fail it then." She went into the building named the Dungeons of Tertullian and she did not look back. Constantine followed her in. He did not absolutely have to follow her, but he was inclined to it. He wished to set the impression that he was more amenable than he really was. And he hadn't any other particular goal. Besides he was intrigued by some of the signs there. "We create realities." "We are making the world you will live in, right now." "Illusive Illusions for every Need." "How deep is your need for Punishment? Come see us in the Tertullian Dungeons." "The Word can be made Flesh, Yours." He could not resist those things. Besides, Amelia might lead him to the place where the bodies were buried.

There was always something a little bit graveyardish about that violet cloud that enveloped her. Amelia had the air of being a very beautiful woman, but it was a thick air that one could hardly see through. Constantine wanted to go where the clues and the answers grew in the thickest clusters, and that might well be in this building named the Dungeons of Tertullian. There was a waiting period when he went in though.

Constantine was putting things together easily and naturally in his mind now. He recollected several of the Sandaliotis maps that he had engraved on his memory and his eyeballs that day. There had been minor details on those maps that now assumed major importance. There were six major east-west canals on some of the maps. And there were the notations of the negative elevations.

Canals, canals, the great traverse canals. There were those six major canals in the three-hundred-mile length of the peninsula. Really, the ships could set routes that would coincide with these canals, and they would be inconvenienced hardly at all. What does determine routes anyhow? The easiest way. They will stay clear of rocks or spits of land or shallows, they will stay clear of shoals or trick currents or of the nests of storms. Ships can be herded into certain narrow paths by little tricks of rocks and shallows; these things will be like dogs snapping at their hulls and keeping them on the narrow course. A little section of shallows can be as effective as a great section of a lowering peninsula in this; and what if they coincide?

With the canals, or with the consensus routes which might be on the same course, ships could still go freely

73

from any part of Spain or any part of France to any part of Italy or Greece or Africa, and they would not really have to go out of their way. And they need not even know that the Big Land was there, no, not if the captain and the navigator and the pilot and all the lookouts and crewmen were all blind at the same time: or if the Big Land itself happened to be sulky or invisible.

And those negative elevations as given in those small red letters and numbers on those maps were tricky. They were not, in fact, simply called "negative elevations." It seemed more as if they had been called "normally apparent negative elevations" of so many feet or fathoms. But what would their elevations really be?

Oh, to the observation of some persons, they would be so many feet under sea level, safe and out of the way, deep-sunken lands. But then there were the small black letters and numbers that gave the real elevations (real to whom?), and these were positive figures (above sea level, so many feet or fathoms). There should have been something illegal about this duality.

Suddenly, inside the building called the Dungeons of Tertullian, Constantine Quiche was seized by a pair of powerful men so forcefully that his arms were nearly unsocketed by the assault. (The waiting period had ended.) He was dragged, carried, hauled into a room that was more dismal than most of them, and he was set down before a forged Inquisitor. (There was a buzzing noise that he could not account for.)

Before a forged Inquisitor? Yes. A true Inquisitor may be known by his towering look of justice untempered by anything, even by mercy. But a false Inquisitor will have a crumbling-tower look, and he will show tempered stone all through the structure. It will not be tempered by justice, but it will be tempered by every sort of inconsistency, and there will be no predicting such a person. Run away from him if you can.

But Constantine could not. This was no amenability that kept him there, no paralysis of the limbs or volition. It was the constraint of strong men. And this forged Inquisitor was far below the level of the other persons that Constantine had seen on Sandaliotis, and well below the level of the strong men and the others who were there.

74

The forged Inquisitor was blindfolded. Oh yes, that gave a little similarity to the image of "Justice." From the lobules of the Inquisitor's ears there dangled little pendants. On each of these was the small hammer, anvil, and stirrup, all broken. And here also were replicas of the three semi-circular canals, all blocked by miniature rock slides. These pendants indicated that not only was the Inquisitor deaf, but that he also had his sense of balance destroyed, for these were all effigies of things in the inner ear.

The forged Inquisitor was talking harshly and inanely, and Constantine did not understand him perfectly. He had an unctuous and false use of the simple tongue. When one loses the sense of balance and becomes a stumbler, the tongue also stumbles or stammers. And one who has been blinded will also sometimes talk blind. The Inquisitor had a mechanical way of talking, and in fact he was reading his words, with his fingers, from a small panel in front of him where the words were projected in raised form, a paragraph at a time. There was something all too vicarious and coldly evil about it.

"Your mother should be condemned for uttering a forgery!" Constantine said angrily. That, at least, should get under the skin of the forged Inquisitor. And that false man did flush, deaf though he was, but he plowed on through his talk. That insult would hurt Constantine here, but he had no patience with forged people or situations.

"Do not think that, because there is no good nor evil, that there is no guilt or punishment," the Inquisitor said. "The latter two things we must have forever. 'In the Beginning was the Guilt' is the scripture that we follow, 'and the World was created to be a Dungeon for the punishment of that Guilt.' If we did not believe that, we would not believe anything. You are guilty, that is the premise. And you must be punished, that is the conclusion."

The buzzing noise that Constantine had been hearing was a camera, but why were such inanities being transcribed and filmed?

"What am I guilty of?" Constantine asked the blinded and deafed and unbalanced man.

"We will put you into the dread clock room of the Tertullian Dungeons," the Inquisitor was saying, not answering Constantine whom he had not heard), "and we will strap you to the dank wall there, almost, but not quite out of the reach of the rats. There will be a noose around your neck, and your own guilt will be in your heart. We will torture you from time to time. And, if your sentenced hanging does not come first, in two days or three you will die from the torture. There is only one alternative for you: that you make a full confession."

"Oh all right then," Constantine said. "I'll make a full confession."

The deaf-man Inquisitor could not hear the little bell that rang on his prompter's panel, but he could feel the vibration of it with his fingers. He waited for the engraved words to appear under his hands.

"Really?" the Inquisitor asked then, reading the words with his fingers. "This is almost unprecedented. All the other prisoners, brave and heroic even in their error, sternly refused to confess and went to their deaths still refusing."

"Better to live one hour as a red-corbelled gross hawk than to die for a thousand years as a lesser speckled monk hatch!" Constantine spoke as bravely as had any other who had ever been before the Inquisitor, and he banged his palm on the table so vehemently that the strong men tightened their grips on him to the point of acute pain. But both the blind-and-deaf Inquisitor and his prompter's panel felt and understood the blow.

"Well said," the Inquisitor acknowledged, reading with his fingers, and yet there was something uneasy about that man. "Yes, yes, I suppose that what you have just said is true," he continued to finger read, "although we are not able to place that proverb in its context right at the moment. Well, proceed with your full confession, though I doubt that it will be accepted. We already know, as the saying goes, more about you than you know about yourselves."

"I will fully confess that I don't have any idea what is going on here at all," Constantine said. "I will confess that I was never so confused and without a lead in my life. I will confess my ignorance of all the prime facts of this case, and I will confess my inability to construct any

76

theory at all to account for it. Does that constitute a full enough confession for you?"

The Inquisitor drummed for a moment with his fingers, waiting for the words to come, and they came.

"No," the Inquisitor read them with his fingers then. "Ignorant of the facts or not, you have got yourself right into the middle of the facts. You have got yourself into this situation, and there were countless ways that you could have avoided it. It is yourself who has put your own neck into the noose, which noose you will encounter in almost a matter of seconds. Every man who gets into such a positively outrageous situation is responsible for it, since it isn't done that easily. Why are you on Sandaliotis? Why do you interfere?"

"I am here because it is part of my assignment to be here," Constantine said. "I am here, I suppose, to find out why Sandaliotis is here."

And the engraved words were coming up under the fingers of the blind-deaf-man Inquisitor a little bit more rapidly now.

"Then why were you near Sandaliotis last night when our land, to the vulgar apperception, was not here yet? Why were you trying to find out why Sandaliotis was here when it wasn't? If you were not guilty of malfeasance, you could not have known that it *would be* here. Man, you are digging your own grave with your own mouth, and do you think that you can undig it with a toy confession? Why were you near the northern canals last night?"

"I don't know, forgie, I just don't know," Constantine said. "By my own instructions, I was there to keep the Principality of Monaco from being stolen. But I had no instructions to keep your land from appearing. Quite the contrary, my latest instructions are to keep you here. By the way, would you tell me just how it is managed that—?"

"I will tell you nothing," the forged Inquisitor read the words that had come up under his fingers so instantly as to startle him. "It is not I who offered to make a full confession," he read. "Can you give us a good reason why you should not be put to the torture in the clock room?"

"Yes. A very good reason. I wouldn't like it," Constantine said.

"*You* wouldn't like it?" the forged Inquisitor intoned

77

after a very short while. He really did read quite well, from the engraved panel, in a theatrical sort of way. "But *we* would like it. *I* would like it. Such things are the very blood and bones to us. I would like it, and I win over you there. Men, to the clock room with him! Put him to the torture!"

Oh, they dragged him down dank passages and broken stairways, where the walls were dripping with saltpeter and moist death, down and around, and perhaps through some of the same passages more than once. Cameras were grinding and clicking. Records and films were being made of this. Why were they? Who was keeping count of all this insane injustice and farce?

They seemed to come into the clock room or torture room of the Tertullian Dungeons through the roof of it, by a dangling ladder let down there, a ladder that went through, or quite beside the giant eye that was the roof of it. It was pretty dark within, but the outlines could be made out by pale ghostly lights, and by the aid of the other senses. There was an awful tearing and crunching sound from the floor, and there were the fear stenches of the other men in the room. Their locations, nailed or strapped to the walls, were clearly given by their stenches and by their moanings.

The clock room was in the shape of a perfect triskaidek-ahedron, a thirteen-sided figure. On each of the thirteen sides there was a large clock, high up, with illuminated numbers. The numbers and hands of those great clocks gave almost all the light there was in that room. This room seemed to be a mockery of the Tarshish Tower, with the thirteen clock faces here turned inward.

Each victim, pierced and transfixed to the wall (Constantine, taking the place of another person who had been removed from the wall and dropped to the crunching floor, had become the thirteenth victim) was held there a prisoner on the oozing and saltpeterish surface, strapped by straps and chained by chains, and it was so arranged that he could not see his own clock above his head, that he could not see his own snake, that he could not see his own light. But the other twelve clocks he could see, the other twelve snakes, and the other twelve lights.

Constantine was strapped in a dangling position with

78

ankle straps, crotch straps, chest straps, and wrist straps. And a noose was put around his neck. The bitter end of the noose rope was tied (so at least it seemed by looking at the other ropes and clocks for Constantine could not see his own), was tied to the minute hand of the clock above him. When this minute hand ascended to the next hour, the pull of the rope would strangle the victim to death. Or, it seemed in some cases, that there were other levers and reductions and gears about the clocks where a man could be strangled in an hour, or possibly in a day, or even several days. Such cases as Constantine could observe, however, indicated that most of the fellow victims would die with him at about the stroke of the next hour.

Oh that panoramic eye in the ceiling of the room, that eye that was the ceiling of the room, was it necessary that it should hum and chatter like that? Are giant panoramic eyes always so noisy?

At this particular moment, a few minutes after one o'clock in the afternoon, the noises did not put any great strain on the victims. Constantine scanned his twelve fellow victims, a mixed crew that was mostly on the disreputable side, and he was shocked at the tension and pathos in the faces. Pain and the fear of death commonly wipes nobility off of faces and leaves a brokenness in place of it. It is not easy to retain the noble look when there are no viewers except that humming eye. Were there many and sympathetic viewers, it would be much easier to die nobly.

But the victim with the most agonized face of them all was talking in a calm and easy, though raspy, voice. Constantine, as an amateur psychologist, knew that this was a sure sign of psychosis, the horribly tense features disassociated from the easy and careless voice.

"The death hour, the ghostly hour, the witching hour, it is not at midnight," old agony-face was discoursing with his unnerving calmness; and the rats were crunching down on the floor below. No need to ask what they were crunching on. It was the body, not quite dead yet, of the man that Constantine had replaced in the straps of the thirteenth niche. The man clearly had his neck broken, but he still moaned and complained. Rats were doing away with his lips and his jaw muscles, and they would soon be to his tongue and through his throat; and then he would moan and complain no more.

"That hour does not come at calm midnight," the agony-faced man was saying. "Where is there any weirdness at peaceful and sleepful midnight? All climaxes come at the very opposite hour to midnight, at high noon. But that is not the death hour either. It is at high noon, yes, that the devil is unleashed ('The noonday devil in the noonday heat,' as the poetess wrote), but he goes roaring about the world for more than two hours after that. This runs it into the dangerous and evil part of the day."

This agony-faced, calm-voiced man was on Constantine's left, and Constantine, alive to the clock analogy, had dubbed him The One O'clock Man.

"There are more murders committed at two o'clock in the afternoon than at any other time," Agony-Face was continuing in his easy raspy voice. (He sounded as though he had cheered too much at the games somewhere yesterday.) "There are more suicides at two o'clock in the afternoon. There are more people who enter hell at that hour, for which reason those auxiliary side doors are opened then that at other times are kept closed. There is a maximum of sin at two o'clock in the afternoon. That is the hour of betrayals and cheatings, of embezzlements and frauds, of dishonesties and infidelities. It is the hour when people, seized with the passion of evil, turn and choose damnation by free choice. It is the hour at which twelve of us hanging here will die today. Why not all thirteen of us? I confess I do not know that.

"In well-run countries it is the hour at which felons are hanged. In this ill-run country it is the hour when innocent men are hanged. I am an innocent man, and I will cry to heaven against my fate from now till that hour comes. The Inquisitor has said that there is a special insulation in the ceiling of this thirteen-sided room that prevents cries raised towards Heaven from escaping from here, from ascending beyond that ceiling. If this is true, then all is lost. I know about the death hour though. Is it for this knowing that they are going to kill me?"

Constantine himself looked up at the ceiling in the dark and he heard the sound and sensed the big panoramic eye. Well, not much could ascend beyond that big eye. It would block out anything going up. It was a baleful eye, and not the eye of Heaven.

Was the agony-faced man, the One O'clock Man, mad, Constantine wondered. The contorting of the face with the calmness and monotony of his voice indicated that he might be. But then Constantine noticed something that he had not noticed of any of them before. The agony-faced man had been reading his words in his calm voice. There was the hushed glow of a prompter's box, of thirteen of them.

In that darkened, thirteen-sided room, the numbers of the big clocks were illuminated, and their sweeping hands also. The only other lights in the room, besides very small signal lights above the head of each victim, came from the radium-glow eyes of the rats down on the earthen floor. But these eerie illuminations were sufficient to give a rough idea of the appearance of the fellow victims there, very rough, very rugged, and with most of the finer pieces left out of them.

The rats on the floor, while still completely covering the slowly diminishing body of the last victim like a seething blanket, did also (some of them) leap at the thirteen victims strapped in their places on the wall. They got them with slashing assault in the feet often, and the victims would roar out in anger and pain. The shoes of the other twelve victims were already slashed to pieces. And those of Constantine, the last and the thirteenth of the men to be strapped there, were half in ruins, and their ruin would soon be total.

But Constantine, that best detective in the world, had been noticing things that others might miss. He had been considering that something was possibly just a little bit wrong with those rats, that their behavior was not quite that of excited rats at all, that it was the behavior of excited machines. But, stumbling onto this thing as he did, he had a shock of them in their new aspect; they were worse than savage and slashing rats. They were more unnatural. Some of the leaping rats, at least, were mechanical.

The Two O'Clock Man, the second man to the left of Constantine, was talking about the rats now.

"On this cursed world," he croaked out, "every leading person has a rat who is the slashing extension of his soul.

81

It is for this reason that the leading persons are able to appear so noble: their baser parts go out of them and into the rats whenever they most wish to appear grand. Do they hunger for the unclean food that they might not eat openly? Then they roil and stir here in their rat persons and feed on the bodiès of their dying victims, for our flesh becomes uncleansed by our suffering and death. Do the leaders lust for those perversions and infidelities that they may not show in public? They will show them here then, in their rat forms, for there is nothing so perverted and faithless as a rat."

The Two O'clock Man roared and howled then, in sudden pain and rage.

"Ah, I burned your ears, did I, rat? And I have your vile slashing in answer to my truth?" he cried, and he kicked it and some shredded portions of his own toes loose from his foot. "Why, it is the evil rat of the Tyrant of Sandaliotis himself! It is the rat of our beloved and appointed Tyrant. And here are the rats of the Security Chief, and of the Master of Elevations, and of the Advocate Judge, and the Arbiter of Culture, and the Madame Dowager First Minister of the Realm, and of the Supervisor of the Traverse Canals. Here is the rat of the Ildephonse of Ideologies and of the Polycrates of Planning. Oh, writhe, you rats. I know about rats. Is it for this that they kill me?"

What was there in the heart of Constantine Quiche that called out "Forgery! Forgery!" at this whole business? What was it that insisted that this was the wrong side of reality? Oh, Angelo DiCyan The Master Forger should be with them here now to brand this whole thing as a superior forgery, or an inferior; to commend it or to dispraise it. It was that baleful panoramic eye in the ceiling of the thirteen-sided room that gave the whole thing the fetid air of reality-gone-wrong.

"There are only two answers, two alternatives," the Seven O'clock Man was bawling out as if he were a huckster calling apples on a corner. "There is the Adoration of the Sky-Bomb and the payment of tribute to the Minions of the Bomb. Or there is Annihilation. There is nothing else for the peoples of Earth. In either case, this will be, happily, the end of the Earth as we have known it. Once the shadow of the Sky-Bomb has fallen on Earth, then Earth has become the Slave. It may be either the living slave or the dead slave, however. This is the choice that we have. Let us choose to be living slaves.

"Oh, Sky-Bomb, remember me who gave testimony in your favor, when you come into your own! Remember me, if that is possible, very very soon, within the hour if that may be!"

The suffering victims were reading the words off of little prompter's panels that were somehow set before their eyes. This made the circumstances and the messages more and not less sinister, just as the mechanical rats had seemed more sinister there, in a sudden flash, than real rats were. These were last cries of agony, and they had to come off of prompter's cards because the speaking souls of the victims were shut up and mute.

"I am the Annihilation and the Dark!" the Nine O'Clock Man suddenly howled out from his place on the wall. It was not even his time to give testimony. The panoramic eye had to groan and wheeze a little bit to concentrate on the Nine O'Clock Man. There were thirteen men, crucified as it were, spread and strapped to the walls, thirteen men to die on this grove of thirteen hanging trees in this room. Thirteen men to be hanged there: but which one of them would it be who would hang himself and then fall down from his hanging, and then burst himself asunder in the middle?

"I am the Annihilation and the Dark!" the Nine O'Clock Man cried again. "It is for this that they kill me." This seemed to be the only message that the Nine O'Clock Man was going to give, and it wasn't the message that was intended for him. His little prompters' panel rattled in front of his eyes with the correct message, but he was blind-eyed and turned within.

As Constantine's eyes became more accustomed to the devouring darkness of the room, they could pick out the faintly luminescent snakes, writhing and nailed to the rotten stone walls above the heads of the victims, each one showing, in the flickering lettering that ran along his flakey skin, the superscription of each of the victims who were to be hanged. Each man would be able to read the superscriptions of all the others (in a minute he would be

83

able to, in a minute yet, when his eyes like screw worms had augured their way further into the darkness): but he would never be able to read his own superscription or to know the name under which he was to be hanged.

"Forgery! Forgery!" called the interior warning to Constantine again, but where was the forgery? There was no scrimping, there was no short-changing here. There must have been thirty thousand fierce rats there, mechanical and real, filling the large room to the depth of a meter with a horrifying and murderous mass. But a mere thirty rats would have done almost as well for quick effect.

There was an excessive verisimilitude about the nooses that now began to tighten about the necks of the victims as 1:30 was past on the clock faces and the minute hands began to ascend towards two o'clock and death. That was not cheap-effect forgery. That was very strong-effect forgery, if it was forgery at all. And, yes, above the snake and below the clock, on the moisture-rotted wall above each victim, there was a small red light like the single red eye of the illyx-dragon. While each victim lived, his light would burn with its very small and very intense bloodglow. And when that blood light went out, it would be a sign that its victim was dead.

Forgery, perhaps. But strong and evocatively dramatic forgery is what it was.

The Three O'Clock Man was speaking with a hollow and croaking voice. He was reading his words from his prompters' box and reading them well.

"I am a patriot," he said with his croaking voice full of pride. "I am sworn to love and defend my land forever and to give testimony to the trueness of it. My oath and my support are absolutely constant. It is the inconstancy of my land before the world that worries me. The old justifications and promises that were once given for my land are no longer given, and belief in them has dwindled. It is said that they are myths. They are attacked by the persons who attack the first promises of scripture, and they are attacked by the same weapons, the gentle incredulity, the superiority of attitude, that appear to a secular authority and consensus which is really as empty as it is imposing, all those base things that are known as the higher criticism. And the false guardians of my land have put me

84

into this prison because they say that I am disruptive, because I say that the great promises are true and not myths.

"It was when Our Lord Himself faced the array of nations and appointed them all that they should do, at the time of His going, that my nation was given its place of 'Incandescent Waiting.' 'Lord, about that Nation there,' said the longest-nosed of all the nations, and it was none other than Italy, our neighbor across the eastern gulf, 'What is it appointed to that nation to do?' And Italy pointed the nose and finger at Holy Sandaliotis herself. 'If I will have her remain until I come, what is that to thee?' the Lord asked.

"It was not said that nothing should be appointed to Sandaliotis: very many things have been appointed to her. But, most of all, it was intended that Sandaliotis should be a Land-in-Reserve, that it should be a guardian against the famine, that it should be a guardian against the future, that it should be a preservation-fire at which torches might be rekindled when all other torches had gone out. 'But if the fire itself lose its spark, how shall it be rekindled?'

"But it does not work that way entirely," the Three O'Clock Man went on. (His prompters' panel had chattered a little bit sometimes, indicating that he was departing from his written lines here and there.) "What is reserved in my land now is a very sharp evil as well as a sharp good. There are germs and viruses of all the old plagues and contagions and heresies still viable here, still on reserve here. There are shattering ideas still in seed form, and if they ever reach soil and water the world may be ill lost over them. These shattering thoughts must not be allowed to be thought at all. I have things in me that are very critical and momentus to say at this time, and there is an impediment in me that will not allow me to say them. 'You will notice now that you are very slightly paralyzed in limb and tongue and will,' a betrayer told me. 'You will be amenable,' I was told, 'but, as a compensation, you will be suffused with an euphoria. Is that not pleasant?' No, it is *not* pleasant, because I will not let it be. The paralysis of limbs and tongue and volition was induced in me by a needled kiss. That is the same kiss that

85

was given to Our Lord on His last night, and He also was slightly paralyzed in limbs and tongue and volition until His death. He also became amenable. You have wondered how it came about that He, who was nowhere else amenable to an evil, now became amenable unto death? It was the cursed kiss that did it, the kiss with the built-in needle or snake's tooth. But the one who gave the kiss will fail even at being hanged, and will fall down a distance and will then burst asunder in the middle."

Constantine had a sudden high, comic vision of Amelia Lilac failing at hanging herself, and falling down in a sharp and slanting place, and bursting asunder. Oh, that was a pleasant and illuminating little vision! Amelia was a creature of puzzling beauty, but what thing more apt and beautifully just than this could happen to her?

"But He rejected the euphoria!" the patriot, the Three O'Clock Man said. "He was not amenable unto that pleasure and accommodation. Nor am I. The agony of my death is necessary for the resurrection of my country. If there is no sharp-enough agony in the world, then mine will help to sharpen it to the critical point. I am the patriot forever, and it is for this that they will kill me."

A snicker of mechanism, a creaking of ropes. Constantine Quiche was suddenly filled with a stifling fear. And so, he supposed, were the other victims. The Three O'Clock Man, in fact, had finished his exhortation with a curdling scream, as if taken by more than ordinary pain and apprehension.

The nooses were all tightened by a quantum as the minute hands of the big clocks swung upwards. Now was the time of the palpitations and the shortened breath, and for the phantoms that always accompany a strangling. Now was the time of the vile sweat and of the fear trembling that releases its own stench.

"Is there any pain like my pain!" the Six O'Clock Man burst out with a really shaking sharpness of voice which the noose prevented from becoming of sufficient power for other than compromised effect. "It is as if the 'brothers' had asked the Lord 'Appoint it that our pain may be more heroic than the pains of any of the others. Appoint it that we may sit on the two thrones of pain on Thy right hand and on Thy left.' But it does not work out like that.

There is nothing heroic about really excessive pain. It is the sick clown who comes out of the great pain, and his motley is a deformity. Others have received the plaudits for their noble pain and have gone away in the nimbus of regard and applause.

"And then, when the show is over and the lights have been dimmed, the real pain begins for those who were never much in the bright light and bright regard, the deforming and grinding and degrading pain that is bad show and bad death, and it becomes in its extreme bad intent and bad effect.

"Is there any pain like my pain? I would hope that nobody else falls so low into so base an expression and reception. It disgraces all the nobility of pain that came to the noble persons before. They must be got off-show before the horror pain begins."

All of them knew that this Six O'Clock Man was right, and their own strangling pain was deforming and grinding and degrading and destroying any grace or reason.

"Do you know that one of us thirteen is to be killed by an 'accident'?" the Eleven O'Clock Man cried out in new alarm as if he had just received that new information. And he had. But his prompters' box was clicking like an insect, as these were not words that it had given him. "By that 'accident,' this will become an outstanding scene, perhaps outstanding enough to win the grand prize.

"But this is wrong and it should not be so. The proportion is all wrong, and the thing itself is wrong. The 'accident' has been cleared in advance with an element of the local law. And then persons will explain away the 'accident', the death. It was only a theatrical device, they will say, and no more than that. And the percentage of deaths of this sort in spectacles has been very low. It is as if they should say that they were entitled to have this one particular death, since the statistics owe them more than one death already. But the one who dies for it will be truly dead. It is wrong for a real person to have to die to give effect to a scene. It is the least known of us who will be killed by the 'accident.' But I am very little known. It may be that it is for this that they will kill me."

One of them to be killed by a contrived accident? Or all of them to be killed on purpose? Or how many of them to be killed by legal sentencing? And how many of them would be killed by sentencing that was a little bit less than legal?

Now they were all a bunch of wolves nailed up to a fence as an example to other wolves. They expired there, and they gave out with their howlings as they expired.

"*I* am no patriot!" the Four O'Clock Man howled like one of those frothy wolves. "I know the secret that carries me through all of this. You can put a stick of wood in my dying mouth to bite on, and that stick will turn black and will smoke when I bite it. That is for hate. My secret is that there is more passion in hating than in love, and that it is more sustaining. And, moreover, hate comes into the mode more often, and it is in now. So I will hate. This is the power and the machinery that every hater has to use: that it is the antilove that can bring the mutual destruction when the opposites meet; and that hate does not care whether it is destroyed and dies the death, so long as its opposite is also destroyed. So it is that hate is always triumphant. Mine is the antireason and the antiaction and the antithought and the antilove. It is our tactic that we take over every good name and use it, and no one else can use it after we have finished with it. We are respected, and we are the inventors of respect. And we are the destroyers who always work outside the lines and bring the lines and the order into disrepute. We make strong intonational attacks on 'stale legalisms,' and on 'institutionalisms' and 'establishments,' and we are the most absolute establishment of them all. We are mad, and we brag that we are mad, that we are not of the orthodoxy, not of the reaction, not of the stale accountability.

"And yet we are an accountability, for we keep count. The mutual annihilation of the primaries and of the 'antis' (ourselves) is what we work for. But there must be something of us left over after the destruction, or at least there must be nothing left over of them. The moment we reach the assurance that there will be nothing left over of them, that is the moment when we precipitate the mutual annihilation, antimatter against matter, antipeople against people, antireason against reason, perfidy against faith, destruction against conserving. We have sworn our allegiance to annihilation, so how can we lose? When we are

88

on the side of total loss, then there is no losing for us in any contest. I am an antipatriot forever, an antiworldite, an antiuniversite. And it is for those things that I believe that they will *not* kill me. Do they kill their own? Perhaps they will kill one person here by 'accident.' Perhaps they will sham the death of another one, and not effect it, and that one will be myself. But, if I have to go, I believe that I will be able to take one or more of the others with me. We have that agreement."

Oh God save us all from the strangling death! The nooses were tightened by another quantum, and life shrank accordingly. There was the small pin-lighted prompter's box that dangled down before Constantine's eyes sometimes. It was for his eyes only. It could not even be seen by the big panoramic eye that was set into the ceiling of the thirteen-sided room.

Constantine knew that he was supposed to read the words of the prompter's box, to speak them out with a tortured eloquence. And he would not do it. He knew that his refusing to say the illumined words created an embarrassment and an awkwardness, and he was sorry for that. But he remained silent.

The Five O'Clock Man spoke in his stead.

"I am an 'agent,' " the Five O'Clock Man said from his crucified prominence. "You may have seen Zucconi's great painting 'The Deserted Agent.' He had caught the unutterable abandonment well. It is the essence of an 'agent' that he be mysterious. He cannot even go across the street for cigarettes without making a great production out of it. He will call for Turkish cigarettes that are not in common stock, and he will be abusive. And, of course, there will be secret messages on the papers of almost every cigarette in that package when he finally gets it. The 'agent' will go in a trench coat and a pulled-down hat on the warmest days, and he will carry an electric flash at bright noon. He is so mysterious that he does not understand himself or his own purpose. But he must rotate about a primary somewhere or he has no reason for being at all. There has to be this unquestioned service to some distant luminary or all his life is in vain.

"Oh, but when the word comes that the primary has disappeared or been destroyed, then the 'agent' is desolate. He can still put the fang on others and say 'You are now slightly paralyzed in limbs and tongue and volition; and you will be amenable.' But what of himself when he loses his primary, or when (Oh, this cannot be, and yet it is the present case), when he forgets what his primary is, when he suffers the amnesia of person and purpose? It is because I have become the 'Deserted Agent' that they will kill me now."

The glow lights (between the snakes and the clocks) had gone out above the heads of several of the victims, which indicated that those persons were dead. Some of the victims made a big fuss about dying, and some of them did it in the most amenable fashion. There was a sort of rend and crack and snap concurrent with the light going out on the Seven O'Clock Man. His straps had broken, or perhaps they had already been cut, and he fell from his supports, and the noose broke his neck. This was the death by 'accident.' But others were being extinguished on purpose. A man could not see his own indicator light, but (as Constantine discovered at the very last moment) he could see the reflection of that glow on something, perhaps from the snake's eyes. At the very last minute he discovered this. Then that reflection went out. He knew that his own light had gone out and that he was dead.

CHAPTER SIX

And after death, the judgment.

The judgment was held in a rather cool recovery room.

"Your imposing silence was rather good, Frenchman," the Director was saying, "just as your earlier 'full confession' to the Inquisitor was a new twist. You are too good to be an actor without a card, too good to be a walk-on. We will make out a yellow card for you. A yellow card is better than no card at all with actors' union. And, if you will give us no details on yourself, we will not push you overmuch. We will find out what we want to know about you, but we will not find it out from you." The voice of this Director was all sounding brass and tinkling cymbals.

"You killed one of the 'victims' by 'accident,'" Constantine charged.

"One of the actors died by unfortunate accident, yes, but I did not kill him. Those were very strenuous roles, as you must know. I believe that he killed himself by putting himself so vehemently into the scene. It did give a masterly turn to the scene, however; perhaps masterly enough to win the grand prize for scenes this year. I should have won it last year but I was done out of it by block voting.

91

"But you yourself created a special role by your silence under torture, Frenchman. You created the role of the mysterious Thirteen O'Clock Man. And, really, the words that were written for you were not the best of the lot. Well, I'll not waste them. I'll use them in something or other, perhaps in a sequel. But could there be a true sequel, do you think, to such a strong movie as this one 'The Thirteen-Sided Room'? We have been working on this very well, and I believe that the death scenes were the best of all. We will see, we will see. Your expressions were wonderful. We caught you in up-shadow and down-shadow and in darkness.

"And your face, yes, I had told you that you had to do something about that shallow face of yours. There wasn't enough landscape to it to pick up the dim lights in the dungeon torture sequences. But you did do something about your face. I'll never know how you did it unless you tell me. You gave depth to your face. You gave it dramatic depth."

Constantine Quiche didn't entirely understand this film director. He had not talked to this director before. He had not been told that he must do something about the shallowness of his face. And the voice was compounded a bit by the voice of that 'agent' Amelia Lilac resounding in his brain. "Dummy, the accident was supposed to happen to you and you botched it. You were the one supposed to be killed in that scene. You actually took the man's attention by your incompetence. You couldn't even gather your wits enough to read your lines off of the prompter's panel, and he thought that made you seem mysterious. Well, no harm done. We help him and he helps us, and he needed another utility actor. We'll get you killed some other way if we don't change our minds again. We'll find another place to stick you in within a few minutes. Meanwhile, be amenable. And remember that you are still slightly paralyzed in limbs and tongue and wits."

And the film director was talking as if Constantine had worked for him before, and he hadn't. And now that Director of that masterpiece-in-progress "The Thirteen-Sided Room" was saying something else that didn't quite fit in.

"We had a little flurry a bit ago," said this director who

looked as if *both* of his eyes were glass. "It was a police call that said that you had been found murdered in your lodging house room. This gave me a little start, especially since I had just selected you (I may as well be frank about this) for the role of the man who was to be killed by 'accident.' It was this call, and the sudden hunch I had that I had better be able to produce you live if there was already a wild report of your death, as well as the interesting silent performance that you gave as the Thirteen O'Clock Man, that made me decide that you should not be the one to die by 'accident.' In fact, if things got sticky, and they are a very little bit sticky even now, it seemed like a good idea to be able to produce you, not only live and well, but also with friendly inclinations towards myself. Cigar, Frenchman? Drink? It's very good stock. Ah, we'd better do something about that rope burn on your neck. Then we will go over to your room to see who it is that's dead in your place while wearing a face very similar to your own. I find it sometimes helpful to show a little patience when dealing with various sorts of police. They are an excitable breed."

Constantine was in a hole and he couldn't think of any way out of it. He smoked a cigar and drank a wine-and-tar drink, and suffered unguent to be put on the rope burn on his neck and on chafings where the various straps had held him to the wall in the thirteen-sided room. About this lodging-house room that was supposed to be his, he didn't know where that was. About the person with a face very like his own, well, his appearance wasn't really extraordinary. Lots of men looked a little bit like him. But he didn't know at all whom he had been taken for: someone the Director here had been talking to previously, apparently, since he was called about the death. Who would know this stuff? Possibly Amelia knew. Possibly it was all an accident or a coincidence. Whatever person had been found dead in the lodging-house room was probably the person who lived there. That was the opinion of the best detective in the world.

He had the feeling that it was a very chancy thing to get mixed up with another dead person (there was the person he had killed in Marseilles the night before; there was the person killed by "accident" in the scene just

filmed, and Constantine might still make an issue of that).
Constantine had a temptation to break and run for it: but
he seemed to stand high with the movie director who now
carried the police citation in his hand. And he was used
to working with police in whatever town or land. The
Director seemed to feel that it was all a routine matter,
and perhaps deaths were more routine on Sandaliotis.

They went in a quick carriage. They arrived rapidly at
a poor building in a poor street, by Sandaliotis standards
at least. They went in, and the police had it all under control. In an upstairs room, there was a good-looking man
sitting at a table alone (but there was a dinner setting opposite him, and someone had been dining with him). The
man had been shot to death, or anyhow he had been done
in by a contusing and blood-letting instrument of some
sort. Constantine guessed that it had been of an ungel or
melting bullet sort. Very possibly no shot would be found
in the man, and that was getting common in the new killings.

The man did look quite like Constantine Quiche. He
looked impossibly like him, in fact. Constantine knew that
people were waiting for him to say something, but what
could he say?

There was an odor almost too slight to deserve that
name. It clung about the place of the missing diner. One
could hardly be sure to which sense this clinging thing ap-
pealed. It may even have been the sense of sight. Possibly
it was a light fog or mist rather than an odor.

Constantine had the untenable feeling that Sandaliotis
was somehow a parallel world to Earth and that this dead
man was somehow a parallel person to himself, even that
this *was* himself. Constantine felt shrunken by the death
and by the feeling that a part of himself had gone now.
Well, but he had to preserve whatever was left of himself
here.

"We have identified him by his fingerprints as Constantine Quiche," one of the police told Constantine. "We
know him by reputation. His reputation is that of the best
detective in the world."

"You have identified him by his *fingerprints* as Constantine Quiche?" Constantine asked, hardly bothering to
throw anything over the nakedness of his wonder.

94

"Yes, Mr. Chataigneraie," the policeman said to Constantine, "by his fingerprints. World Interpol gave us the information quickly. You two are of absolutely identical appearance, yet you do not have the same surname? You are not full brothers then or twins?"

"No, not brothers," Constantine said. "He is my nephew, although we are the same age. I am not sure what name he has been going under. I did not even know that he was—that is to say that I did not know that he was in any trouble, and surely not that he was in any trouble that would lead to his being killed."

No, it was not true that the dead man looked exactly like Constantine. He had a face that was slightly, very slightly, shallower than that of Constantine. Constantine was sure of this now, but none of the others seemed to notice it. They all commented that the appearances were identical.

And yet the Director had noticed it *once*. He had, in fact, told this man that he would have to do something about his too-shallow face, that it didn't pick up light and shadow well enough.

But did the Director realize the relationship now and know that he had talked to them both? Who could say what that Director realized?

"Why are you so nervous?' one of the policemen asked Constantine. "I have not seen so nervous a man all this day. Are all Frenchmen as nervous as yourself?"

"Believe me, we are a people who can get awful nervous awful fast," Constantine said. "But, ah, really there is not much to tell." Then Constantine motioned that policeman to follow him, and they went off together a little space away and talked together. And then they came back.

"Has he been staying with you here?" that policeman asked when he and Constantine had returned.

"No. I have not been in touch with him, not for several weeks," Constantine said. "But we were always quite good friends. And, in fact, he always carried a key to the door of my rooms here."

Constantine felt that he had to throw that in, to explain the man's having been there and having been enough at home there to have a guest for dinner. But he wished now

95

that he had tried some other tack and had said, for instance, that these weren't his rooms at all and that he knew nothing about this dead man. But all of it was blown when the policeman asked:

"What *is* a key to the door of rooms?"

Then Constantine knew what had been a little bit different about all the doors of all the buildings that he had seen on Sandaliotis. They had no keyholes or locks and they could not have been locked in an ordinary way. Well, what does one say to explain that he hadn't noticed that this was a country without locks, and that he had just plain put his foot in it? But the policeman didn't pursue the question of what was a key to a door.

"We must ask you to leave for a while, Mr. Chataigneraie," the policeman said.

"They keep calling me that, I had better accept it," Constantine mused. "It is as good a name as any, and it is no doubt the name of the poor dead man there. What kind of cops are these anyhow? There are a dozen things that would point out that this is not my place, though I never claimed that it was. There are a dozen things that would point out that this is the dead man's place and that he was very much at home in it. Ah, and there is one thing, the fingerprints, that point out that he is me. I wonder whose fingerprints I am wearing now."

"We must ask you to leave for a while," the policeman repeated as Constantine did not seem to be paying attention to him. "We want to go over your rooms minutely and you would be in the way here while we do it. Step out please. Go have a few wines or something. Do not come back here within one hour, and two hours would be better."

Yes, it was a very slight odor where the missing diner had sat, and a very very slight remnant of fog or mist, lavender or lilac in color, and right on the threshold of visibility. And who do we know who is always wrapped in lilac fog?

"Yes, two hours would be better," Constantine said. He felt that he had gotten a reprieve from a sticky situation. This was all tricky, but Constantine would have to handle himself with foresight and creativity and dignity. "I will

96

be available, of course," he said, "and now I wish to be alone with my grief."

"What grief?" the policeman asked. "Oh, I understand, you mean for your nephew. But he is only second degree of kindred, and grief is felt only for those of the first degree. Or is this somehow Frenchy?"

Constantine went out from the rooms of the dead man who had a shallower face than Constantine's own but who otherwise looked quite like him. He went out, and he came to Joe Primavera's wine-fine. He felt himself to be followed, so he went in there. He thought that he would drink and shuffle out his thoughts there. But the movie director came in also (he had been the one following) so thoughts would be a little bit hooded. There would be more talk from the Director. He liked to talk in his sounding brass voice.

It was just eighteen minutes after two o'clock in the afternoon.

"There is a possibility that the 'Thirteen-Sided Room' will be in trouble for being too true," the Director said after they had ordered wine. "You see, I believe that there really is a thirteen-sided room in this city, in a dungeon that has a name very like 'The Dungeons of Tertullian.' I run into this everywhere on Sandaliotis, that the things I believe I am creating out of my head are things that have been lying in wait in the very ground, things that are at the very roots of Sandaliotis. The Dungeons of Tertullian which I have rented on a short-term lease were once a part of a complex known as Amusement Central, a little pleasure park with entertainments in the middle of the city. I projected back to consider whether these toy dungeons built there to amuse the kiddies might not have real origins. As I come to the close of my work on the picture, I am haunted by those real origins and I know that they are here.

"Now the fact is that the Sandaliotistics are the least cruel people in the world. That is what puts such a shivery touch into it when one examines their hidden tales of dungeons and torture chambers. It is as if the dungeons were natural things like caves and were not built at all, and as if the torture were also a natural response with not much more connection to the *people* involved in it than have the weeds of the Earth. On Sandaliotis, I cannot come up with any creative concept at all without something bursting up from the black earth of this country, and looking and seeing that my concept had been buried and waiting here all the time.

"Every people, even the best of people, has a riven soul, and a consciousness above and an unconsciousness below. It has a garden of bright creatures, and it has a garden of demons under them. It has the bright mansions above, and the dark caves below. This is common. However, as is the case with old Thalassocracies or ocean kingdoms such as Crete, Sandaliotis has its national unconscious under-ocean rather than underground. That unconscious lives in submarine rather than subterranean caves. So I believe that the original dungeons were submarine ones. In the Tertullian Dungeons of the old amusement park, you might see, when the lights are on as they seldom are, that the walls are ocean painted to represent sea plants and sea fish and depths.

"Then there is the Sandaliotis euphemism for drowning (with the Sandaliotistics is seems to require an euphemism), 'Hanged with a rope of water.' I believe that in the original dungeons that water-cocks were opened by the clocks and that the men impaled on the walls were drowned."

"You are not a citizen of Sandaliotis?" Constantine asked.

"No, of course not. Who ever heard of a Sandaliotistic movie director? I come here from Italy. And there are many things about Sandaliotis that I do not understand at all."

"There are very, very many things that I do not understand," Constantine said.

"Oh, but you're French. I'm different. I should be able to understand. So, when I do a picture like the 'Thirteen-Sided Room' I do not mean to dabble in the local politics or to make cryptic references to such. I don't even know where their politics lives at, or whether they even have that thing that I call politics.

"What I do is create and direct psychological thrillers with a heavy historic and folklore underlay. I am very good at this. I try to do these pictures as cheaply as pos-

98

sible: how cheap I can do them is one measure of how good I am in this business. That is one reason why I come to Sandaliotis. The scenes are already all here and set up, and the actors are already all here and ready to act. Nowhere is there such scenery on beautiful Sandaliotis; town or country, it has no equal. And the people here are all natural actors. They are not capable of any artificial or awkward movement or disposition. And they are vivid, that is the main thing. I could watch them doing nothing forever: walking, talking, lounging. And so, I have discovered, can most of the rest of the world. These people pull the eyes right out of your head looking at them. They project drama in everything that they do. I don't know why this is so, since most of their doings, when analyzed, prove to be pretty prosaic. But these are the people with the dramatic gestures, and they are beautiful people. You have noticed that? Oh, they are wonderful.

"And they are intelligent. They can learn their lines quickly, and they can improvise. And their language, it has become the language of psychological thrillers everywhere, with nobody noticing that it has taken over. People who deny that there is any such land as Sandaliotis will understand and talk the language of this country and believe that they are understanding and talking their own. It is positively pentecostal. The Italians, the Portuguese, the Spanish, the Ladinos all fall into this, and even the French. Even the non romance barbarians of the north seem to understand it easily, for they flock to the movies and find no difficulty at all to it. Can you imagine having to dub in anything for Sandaliotis? Even the Japanese say that they do not need dubs. They understand, and all the peoples seem to understand, the multicadences and multimeanings that these people give to the most simple lines that I write.

"But of course it is the medium as well as the tongue. I believe that all really good psychological thrillers, such as my own, can be comprehended (and I do mean the words of them) because of the movement and impact. This is an hypnotic and perhaps a telepathic thing. I have often recommended psychological thrillers as a means of teaching languages.

"Everything is scenic on Sandaliotis, and the people especially. The towns and countrysides here are almost too good to believe in. 'Who took the frames away?' I find myself asking, for every scene that I encounter here is like a hugely adequate theatre scene, or at least a painted masterpiece. And the plots and turns are rooted right in the black earth here and in the colored buildings. Did you know that many of them, even those of the most painted appearance, are of natural-colored rocks? The peninsula here is made out of a mad color box. It is fantastic. There is contrivance, there is device, there is construction in everything. But the place itself, the country and the cities, the people themselves, how shall we take them? This is a garden of prototypes in everything, a garden of creativity."

"Director, you are like that also. Above ground you are brass sunshine and brass chatter, and an arty appreciation of everything. And underground, or underwater, you are the grotesque and fishy cruelty. Why did you deliberately kill a man in that scene in the 'Thirteen-Sided Room'?" Constantine was hot about this.

"I did not do that," the Director said. "Am I such a beast? Or such a devil fish? I simply let the odds operate. In our thrillers, we play some very dangerous scenes, and we have not had as many deaths as we should have statistically."

"Who sets and appraises the statistics?" Constantine asked.

"I do," the Director said. "So, being ahead of the odds, we have a certain freedom to operate. We borrow an 'accident.' Well, accidents do happen, and there is no way out of that. We hate accidents, but we do not hate the dramatic value of them. It must be there when you want it though. If an accident is overlong in coming, it causes tension all around. So we have that accident now when it is convenient to us and to our thriller-in-progress. We do not wait for it to pounce on us at a possibly inconvenient time."

"You take the accidental out of the accident," Constantine said. "And you kill a man and justify it with a statistical manipulation. And possibly you will win the grand prize for the most effective scene this year. I was the one you would have killed, for an effective scene, you had not settled on another with a change of mind."

"But I did not settle on another," the Director said. "It was another creature, over which I have no control, that settled on that other rather than on yourself. Should I take the blame for a thing when I can put that blame on an ungainly bird? You were the one to whom the accident was apparently going to happen, yes. And then that ungainly bird named 'accident' (but can anything on Sandaliotis be called ungainly?), that bird hovered over you, but he did not alight on your neck. Instead, the bird veered off and alighted on another person. And that other person died of accident. But there was never any question of our 'killing' anyone. Do you not understand that, Frenchman? A Sandaliotistic would understand it."

Constantine made a sign with his hand to a person not clearly seen: and that person went to do his bidding, apparently. This was most strange, for Constantine knew very few persons on Sandaliotis.

"I don't believe that a person of Sandaliotis would understand such a reasoning or justification at all," Constantine said then. "They are beautifully direct."

"Not always," the Director said. "Sometimes they are beautifully devious people, when you look at their devious side. And they are a totally naïve people when you look at their naïve side. They are the bright surface people who just happen to have big cellars stocked with 'everything in reserve.' Pick what you want, and they have it. What I pick is deviousness. Oh, I have become a slanted one since I have been here! One draws whatever he wishes right out of this earth. It pulls out easily for the earth is always moist and subterraneously irrigated. And what are these people really like? I don't know. You find in them what you look for. They are mirrors. How can I see them without myself getting in the way of it all? I cannot decide whether these people are absolutely guileless or whether they are the most conniving people in the world."

"Need they be the one or the other?" Constantine asked. "It would seem that a devious man like yourself would not look for absolutes. Need they be the absolutely most guileless, or the absolutely most conniving?"

"Yes, I believe that they do need to be the one or the
101

other," the Director said. "For my own purpose, creative psychological thrillers, they have to have these absolutes in them, perhaps both of the absolutes at once, but not blended. I am a devious man who must work with absolutes. Both my mind and my thrillers are built out of them. In such things, I need an expert to tell me what is forgery or what is genuine. I will not necessarily select the one above the other, but I want to know which is which."

"I know that expert," Constantine said. "But I don't need an expert to tell me that you are a forgery."

"Wait, wait, wait!" the Director cried, holding up his hand. "I don't know what kind of French fish you have turned into, but suddenly you have the power to do me a harm. I feel such things. Wait and let me explain why you should not do this. Let me explain what will go out of the world if you prevent me in my creations."

"Quickly then, explain it," Constantine said, "for the feet of your jailers are even now at the door."

"Fine old melodrama is what I offer," the Director stated. "I provide better melodrama than anyone else in the world, fuller, juicier, more popular. I give stronger emotions than anyone else in the world; and people love to experience strong emotions. Some of them experience vicariously and some of them directly.

"People maintain the myth that they are hard working and much abused, and that their requirements and needs are very few. People, as a fact, are not very hard working, and they are not very much abused. Mostly they have a pretty easy time of it. But they are right that their requirements and needs are few. These few cannot be reduced, however. There is a hard minimum that cannot be broken. That is what I cater to. It is what someone always must cater to if things are to hold their course.

"People have the need to feel important, which need functions as the inverse square of their *being* important. They have the need for something to abuse, for something to be superior to, and for something to hate. And the most important of these is something to hate."

"You are not an Italian," Constantine said, as if to change the subject.

"For some years I have lived in Italy, yes," the Director insisted. "When I am not at work or at play in some

102

other places, then I am probably in Italy. Now, man, I provide in my melodramas, in my psychological thrillers, in my smashers, just this minimum of things that the people must have. If the people do not have them, they will turn sullen, and then they will explode.

"When, for instance, I show thirteen men in the agony of death on the walls of the thirteen-sided room, I give the people something to feel important about; for they play at being God, looking through the God's-eye of the panoramic camera in the ceiling of the room. There is the need of something to abuse, something to feel superior to, something to hate. All these things are satisfied by the writhing creatures stretched out on the dank walls where they babble out their brains in rambling words as they die. All my dramas are very therapeutic. If something should happen to interrupt this beautiful flow of thrillers, then I would not guarantee what would happen to the people of the world. The people are already getting tense and jerky. Some of the people would certainly explode. If enough of them explode, the world goes with them. What I really provide are adventuresome safety valves."

"You are a little world saver indeed," Constantine said, "but you are not genuine. You are a forgery. And here are the people now who will deal with you as a forger and murderer and breaker of every law."

"Oh, Frenchman, you close me down for a few 'accidents' that give the people what they want to see!" the Director wailed. "The laborer is deserving of his hire, and the creator of his tools of creation. It is a judicious thing that one man should die for a scene. He stands for a hundred, and we save lives by it. You will take all the joy out of my creations and out of the world. You will take all the verve and spontaneity out of the world."

The police came in then and took the Director away, but he was not dampened at all by it. He was always a cheerful man, that one.

How had Constantine engineered that little business? Oh, by being the best detective in the world. That's about all it takes. And by being part of World Interpol. That counts too, if you give the sign to another person who also is part of World Interpol. World Interpol has men on every police force everywhere nowadays.

103

"You know what the Thirteen-Sided Room really is, don't you?" Joe Primavera, the proprietor of the wine-fine, asked Constantine when the police had gone with the director. "I heard the Director speak of his picture of that name."

"No, I don't know these levels of meaning," Constantine confessed. "I have never heard of the Thirteen-Sided Room until today."

"It is the Sandaliotis national epic," the wine man said. "It contains all our drama and all our poetry and all our music, and all our stories and all our genealogy and all our history. And you are about to ask whether the version that the Director is filming is accurate?

"It is an accurate version to about the extent that one flinder of hardened mud is a version of the Earth. The Director's version is part of the depiction of one of the 6,227,020,800 permutations of the epic. There are that many scenes to the epic. These are all the simultaneous combinations of the thirteen persons in the thirteen places or roles."

"The thirteen persons, are they Christ and the Apostles?" Constantine asked.

"Very often they are. Though the Divine Person, taking also sometimes the role of the Father and sometimes that of the Holy Ghost, and of other of the 'Persons' who are adhered to in the more attenuated heresies, will play each of the thirteen positions or roles in turn, while each of the other twelve beings is in each combination to each of the others. In fact, each person plays each role about a half billion times while all the others are ringing all possible changes. There are multiple depths to all the persons, not merely to the Divine Person.

"As you know, the real zodiac, the Sandaliotis zodiac, has thirteen units or constellations, and thirteen positions. That is the true and holy zodiac. The other, the false zodiac, leaves out the Divine Person, so it is called the Infidel or the Devil's zodiac, and Christians may not employ it or calculate upon it. The false zodiac was cast out of Heaven at the same time that Lucifer was cast out, and for the same reason: that it was incomplete. As you know, Lucifer fell first into Sandaliotis, which is said to be in the shape of his sandal. Then he fell on through the bottom. The crater he fell through is still in our land, and one may look down into the pit there."

"Especially in the complete arrangement of the National Epic, there would seem to be a lot of death speeches and a lot of crucifixions," Constantine said.

"Oh no, they are only a small part of it," Joe Primavera told him. "All the scenes are not death scenes or even sad scenes. The majority of them are gala. There are only a few death scenes and only a few crucifixions. Trees serve for many other things besides crucifixions. The very earliest name of the epic, as you may not know, is 'The Room of the Thirteen Trees.'"

"What other things do trees serve for?" Constantine asked.

"Trees are for climbing, for fowling, for taking nuts or fruits or bee honey from them, or taking game animals. They are for reigning as from thrones, for watching as from watchtowers, for declaiming as from stages or forums. They are for cutting timber out of, for tapping turpentine or syrup, for trimming for ships' masts, for riving as for roof beams. They are for visiting with tree spirits. They are for ascending from on space flights. All these uses are in the epic. There are a number of reasons to be in a tree other than to be crucified there."

"What happened to the Lords of the False Zodiac when it was thrown down to Earth, down to Sandaliotis?"

"They're still here. That's all in the epic too. The giant crab, the giant bull, the giant ram, the giant water pourer, the giant twins, they are among the living prodigies of our land and are still found on our hills."

"The Director, he is not an Italian."

"Oh, he was born here on Sandaliotis, whatever he says. But now he is a citizen of the floating world, being now an Italian, now Greek, now Japanese, now Egyptian, now Spanish, now French. He is an opportunist and he will have a profitable time of it even in prison, where he will not be for longer than an hour."

"Do you suppose that he killed my 'nephew'?"

"No, but perhaps he believes that he had it done. It was really done by a dolphin. Your 'nephew' was as curious about things as you are yourself. As to the details, nobody knows them yet. Your 'nephew' was at first the best

105

detective in the world. Now he is dead and you become the best detective in the world, though you thought you were so before. As the best detective in the world, you will be able to figure this out."

Three other men came into the wine-fine then.

CHAPTER SEVEN

The three other men who came into the wine-fine of Joe Primavera were Angelo DiCyan, the Master Forger from Salerno in Italy, Troy Islander the ship owner and importer-exporter from Civita do Nord in Sandaliotis, and Hugh Najtingalo the mine operator whose headquarters were right there in the City of Ichnusa of Sandaliotis. These three arrivals found themselves at once in the congenial company of Joe Primavera, the proprietor, and of Constantine Quiche, the best detective in the world.

It was just five minutes after three o'clock in the afternoon when these five persons fell to at a table over boar and snails and barley bread and good red wine. Joe Primavera's wine-fine was the best such place in Sandaliotis or indeed in the world, and himself and his four guests shaped up to a superior tableful, even for those fine premises.

"Oh the air is full of crackling wits!" Joe said, but he often said that to encourage people.

"I want information," Constantine told them all bluntly. "I want information that only intelligent persons can give, and I find myself in intelligent company. The question I want to ask of each of you is 'What is the nose on your face like?' My whole day is ruined if I don't get some clear answers to this."

"Of plain noses on unplain faces," said Hugh Najtingalo, "there is always a problem. A person cannot easily see the nose on his own face. I have an idea that it was placed exactly where it is so that he will *not* see it. And feeling it with his hands will not give a clear idea of it either. The old phrase 'as plain as the nose on your face' means 'not plain at all.' Which nose are you talking about, Constantine Quiche?"

"I am talking about Sandaliotis, gentlemen," Constantine said. "I have an assignment that consists partly of finding out just what is going on here on Sandaliotis. Three of you, Primavera, Islander, and Najtingalo, are citizens of Sandaliotis, and you have to know something about this place where you have spent your lives, this place which is closer to you than nose itself. Where has it been? Why is it here now? In what way is it different from other lands? Is it real, or is it contrived?"

"I suppose that it does indicate something that Sandaliotis has been made manifest and visible to all the world today," Troy Islander said, "but I'm a little lost as to what it does indicate. It's as though a multitude of people should begin to shout 'We can see the color violet! We can see violet!' To those who could always see violet, the world doesn't shake much at this announcement. To us who could always see Sandaliotis, or almost always, nothing much has happened except that certain foreigners have recovered from a queer eye disease. And we may resent the undue attention to this. It's our own nose on our own face, and we might resent having it twisted."

"But haven't you been puzzled that large numbers of foreigners have not ordinarily been able to see your country?" Constantine asked.

"As to myself," Islander said, "large numbers of foreigners have puzzled me in steeper ways than this little failure to see the obvious. Large numbers of foreigners are clear mad."

"But all you Sandaliotistics can see Sandaliotis all the time, can you?" Constantine kept asking. "That is important. Recall it clearly, I ask you. Can all of you really see Sandaliotis all the time?"

"No, I can't," Najtingalo admitted. "Most of the time I can, but not all the time. It may have bothered me as a child, I'm not sure of that. It may be a fact that all of us had these gaps in seeing our country when we were children, before we learned to compensate for it. It's possible that seeing Sandaliotis all the time, or almost all the time, is a learned convention. I believe that it is. The missing land is noticed more out in the country at my mines than in the cities. I have discovered that there are very many of my workers who do not see the country even as well as I do. There will be days when hardly half of the miners will be able to find the mines that they have been working in every day. 'They aren't there today,' they will say. 'We can't find them. We could work them if we could find them. The land they are on isn't there.' And they are sincere when they report such difficulties.

"And when I hear some of the most susceptible of them mention on a certain day 'The land is *in* this morning', to me it is no more than if they should say 'It's foggy today' or 'There's snow.' I don't pay a lot of attention to what goes on outside my place. If a few of my mines can't be mined when 'The land is out,' well then that is allowed for. I will have a mine, for instance, that can be worked only a hundred and eighty days a year because, to the majority of my workers, that's all the days it is *there*."

"And I don't pay a lot of attention to what goes on outside of my place," said Joe Primavera, "except just for the loafers' bench out there and the two tables that I set up on the sidewalks. But there will be days when it is so 'foggy' that I can't see across the street. It won't seem to be foggy though. It will just seem that there isn't any other side of the street.

"And then there are the days when I step out and whoooo! It ends up right there, a meter from my door. Not even a guard rail! I'm going to put one up, I swear. I'll put one up tomorrow just to be safe the next time it happens. There will be space before me and below me, clouds drifting below me, and an open ocean far below me, eight hundred meters or so below me. And directly under my shop, no more than ten meters under, the land that my place is built on will end. I will be on a little slab floating in the sky, myself and my building, and three or four other buildings. But that very weird state may last no more than half an hour. It's disquieting though."

" 'I sometimes wonder what the vinters buy/One half as precious as the stuff they sell,' " said Constantine. "That's a quotation. Are there days, Joe, when you drink more of it than you sell?"

"Yes. A few of them. But I don't pay a lot of attention to any of this, Constantine. And I believe that you do not pay a lot of attention to the nose on your own face, even on the days when it feels a little bit foggy."

"I might as well give you my preliminary report on the work I have been doing for you and for World Interpol, Quiche," said Angelo DiCyan and the Master Forger. "Sandaliotis, as revealed in my quick survey, is not really a forgery. It is genuine, as far as it goes. And it goes a good ways sometimes, and then it stops abruptly. But it isn't any false production that is so frequently coming to a sudden end. It is a remarkably valid production. I still believe that you should give me a four year contract to unravel this mystery. It's difficult to complete such a massive undertaking in part of a day."

"Did you discover yourself listed in the Sandaliotis accounts of the subject as a Master Forger of art works?" Constantine asked.

"Oh yes, they have me there. They give me good notices. Quite a few of their facts about me are wrong, but that is to be expected. But there is one thing that I have noticed about Sandaliotis, Constantine, which you as a foreigner should also notice. I do not know whether I could make the wonder of it stand out for any of the natives of Sandaliotis here, but it is a wonder. It is that there is no repetition on Sandaliotis at all. Oh really, that's so! That's the opposite of not being able to see Sandaliotis because it is somehow so jaded that it falls too low for the notice. When Sandaliotis is here, it is here with a freshness in every detail.

"There is only one typical pebble on all of Sandaliotis. That pebble was taken from a north-flowing creek at the top of the sandal, and it is now in the Museum of Tensor Geology at Bastia. Out of the billions of pebbles on Sandaliotis, that is the only one that looks like the nondescript pebbles of other countries, and as such it was thought rare enough to go into the museum. There is only one conventional leaf on all Sandaliotis. That is from a Green Bay tree, and it is in the Institute of Arborology at San Vito. Oh, there are other small stones of sorts, each one of a different sort, but there is only one classic pebble. And there are other plant breathers, vaguely like the green or blue 'pages' or 'leaves' of a plant book. But there is only one classic leaf, that one that seemed so blank and dumb struck that it is shown in the institute. All the other leaves are, like leaves of a book, written over with entirely different messages, each one from each, in the shape or the color or the texture, or just in the living signature.

"There are other things that completely avoid sameness where it might be expected. The automobile which I have heard that you abandoned in North Town today, Constantine, that of which you were so proud, was the only one of that exact model. There cannot be two alike run off their lines, or the lines will rebel. There will be a breakdown, and then there will be handwork. And when the repair on the line is made, there will be changes incorporated in that repair. I tell you that there is no duplication here. Two jars of beer will not be the same. They may be of almost the same name, spelled almost the same on the jars, and they may be of nearly the same flavor. But no two will be exactly the same. I have asked several citizens about this and they have never noticed it. They will not know what I am talking about. I will point to two jars of beer taken out of the same case and ask why they differ. 'Oh, one of them is spelled wrong, isn't it?' they will finally notice. 'And the other one is spelled wrong also, but of a little different wrongness. I suppose that someone was careless when they went through.'

"Someone is careless when they pass these things off so lightly and so mysteriously. Possibly though, in my Italy, there are anomalies which I do not notice and which some hypothetical alien would howl at. And perhaps he would point them out to me and I would be mystified as to what he was talking about and why he was making such a stork's nest out of a straw stack.

"I believe though that Sandaliotis is so constituted that if it cannot come up with something new in every detail, it

111

will not come up with anything at all. And these are the gaps. Oh yes, that isn't a very good theory. Who knows a better one?"

"The fact that Sandaliotis has been made manifest and visible to all the world today," said Joe Primavera the proprietor, "and not merely to the people of Sandaliotis itself (this is a thing that does not happen so strongly as today more than two or three times a century), this might well indicate that either Sandaliotis or the world is coming to its end. That also happens no more than two or three times a century. I don't believe it is Sandaliotis that is ending though, and yet we must consider this too. This may be the Day of the Holocaust. Why then is only one of us ready and girt, with his pilgrim's staff in his hand and his zone about his waist?"

"Oh, if the world ended, could Sandaliotis survive?" Constantine asked.

"Yes, I believe so," Primavera said. "The answer to all the inconsistencies may well be that Sandaliotis isn't very tightly attached to the world. I believe that is one purpose of the world, to survive if the world slides over the edge of the abyss; to belay the rope that the world is on and to bring its slide and its ending to a halt. Or, failing that, to be the new world, as it has some instances of everything on the world already on it. It seems to me that the first case, stopping the slide of the world, happens pretty often, and the world gives no thanks for it."

"But which one of us is girt and ready?" Constantine asked.

"You are," Joe Primavera said. "You have a parachute packed around your waist. That is to be a pilgrim, ready and girt."

"I have been meaning to ask someone about that," Constantine said. "Why am I wearing it? Does anybody know?"

"You are the best detective in the world and you don't know why you are wearing a parachute all this day?" Troy Islander asked.

"No, I don't. I don't understand it at all. If I even think of taking it off, a fetish screams at me and warns me not to touch it. This is only one of the many loose ends that I can't connect up. It's as though someone should say 'Nay,

112

there aren't eleven ends to that rope. There's only two. It's just the way the knot's tied that makes it look like eleven loose ends.' Well, I will have to list out my own loose ends and try to find out why they seem to be loose."

"Give us one, Constantine," Troy Islander said. "Maybe it will identify the knot and give us a clue to the other loose ends. And it's always easier to tell the other fellow how to tie up his loose ends."

"A three-hundred-mile-long object in the sky," Constantine said. "It is either a physical object or it is a delirium. If it is that, it is such a delirium as will be recorded by sensitive and sophisticated instruments. A three-hundred-mile-long object right over our heads, about a thousand miles high. Why is it instrumented if it isn't there? And why in hound-dog heaven can't we see it if it *is* there? Damn the dog bomb of an island anyhow! Oh, there it is. You can see it right there!"

"Yes, so we can," Troy Islander said. "It echoes and corresponds very roughly to the shape of Sandaliotis here below. It subtends an angle of about fifteen degrees. Three hundred miles long, did you say that it was, Constantine? Oh, that would make it about a thousand miles high, wouldn't it? It's really rather clear and sharp today, is it not? But what was it that you were wondering about it?"

"Damnation, Islander! I was wondering why no one else is noticing it."

"But I *am* noticing it. I have been looking at it ever since you called my attention to it. It's clear and sharp, I said. What else am I to say about such an island in the sky? Oh, the clouds are moving to cover it up again. I wonder who is marshaling those clouds anyhow? It's likely that none of us would have been able to see it if you hadn't made a breakthrough in fury and exasperation to see it."

"What if it's a bomb?" Constantine asked.

"It would be a big one then, Constantine. It would do real damage to the earth if it went off," Islander said. "It would probably destroy the earth. For any lesser job, a bomb that big would hardly be needed. But I don't think it will go off. It doesn't often.

"There are parallels to it, you know. And this island it-

113

self has been noticed for many centuries as an irregular and irrational object in the skies."

"Now we are doing better, Troy Islander. Tell me about the parallels, and tell me about this thing itself," Constantine begged.

"As to why it hasn't been more noticed, Constantine, well, a three-hundred-mile-long object in the sky isn't very noticeable even when it's no more than a thousand miles high. Lose it for a minute against the bright sky, and you'll have to search for it again to bring it within focus. Let its outline be broken by clouds here and there, and it takes on the appearance of a long cloud itself. But these objects (the three-hundred-mile length is a frequent estimate) *are* very often sighted. They are sighted mostly by crackpots because crackpots see more out-of-the-way things than do other people. They are classified as crackpot phenomena because there is no noncrackpot category to put them in. But there isn't much doubt that they really are up there, quite a few of them. They are among the original tall stories, about a thousand miles tall. Some of them have a local habitation and a name. Others of them are drifters forever.

"There is 'Hogan's Bobsled' that is regularly observed and charted by a group of drinking gentlemen at a place called College Station Texas in America. Their meteorological observations are accurate and are verified. The rationale that they give for this 'Island in the Sky' is, ah, far out, much more than a thousand miles out, I would say. Well, there *is* something up there that remains in the immediate 'up there', that looks like a bobsled (a large, compounded or coupled sled once used in North America), and that was discovered by someone named Hogan.

"All of these phenomena are probably Fortean.

"There is Schnitger's Steamboat, *Dampfboot Schnitgers*, that hangs in the sky over Old Heidelberg in Germany and has been loved by whole generations of students there. Under very high magnification, people have been seen on the Steamboat, so it is said. A very high magnification seems to be endemic in the styles of some of the students in Old Heidelberg. It is hard to know where fact leaves off and whimsy begins with the Steamboat, but there is considerable fact to it.

"And, in the skies over Poland, is to be seen Pad-erewski's Porpoise. Copernicus himself sighted this many times and he could not account for it. Really, he didn't try to. It would not fit into any theory that he had. As it very often got in the way of his observations, he prayed that it would go away. But he couldn't pray it out of the way and he couldn't account for it. Polish students still make a cult of the porpoise. It is curious how all these manifesta-tions are somehow attached to groups of 'students', just as poltergeists are usually attached to persons just a little bit younger.

"And finally, out of a hundred of them, or at least half a hundred, we come to the one that we can see right now. This is the manifestation known as Thibeau's Torpedo. Ah, is it not beautiful in the afternoon air! Notice how the clouds are still trying to disguise it."

"It reassures me that the rest of you are able to see it," Constantine said.

"Why should we not be able to see it, once it is pointed out to us?" Troy Islander asked. "Are we blind men that we should not see it? The Torpedo, like the other mani-festations, is a cult of a group of students, students at the University of Ichnusa. Why are you especially con-cerned about it, Constantine?"

"It seems to me that the Torpedo overhead is somehow concerned with the appearance and disappearance of San-daliotis?" Constantine said uncertainly.

"Why?" Troy Islander asked. "Is Hogan's Bobsled somehow concerned with the appearance and disap-pearance of Brazo's County, Texas? Is Schnitger's Steam-boat (it is sometimes called Schnitger's Sausage also) concerned with the appearance and disappearance of Germany? Or Paderewski's Porpoise concerned with the appearance and disappearance of Poland? (Perhaps, in this one case, it is. Poland disappears and reappears quite a lot through the centuries.) Greatest detective in the world, are you not chewing on too many different things at one time?"

"I am advised that the local 'Island in the Sky,' the 'Thibeau's Torpedo,' may be antimatter," Constantine said.

"Oh certainly, certainly," Islander agreed. "That is a

115

frequent guess of all of them, that they are enclaves of antimatter and antithought."

"The latter must be extinguished," Constantine said firmly.

"Antithought can be extinguished only by cancelling it out with an equal amount of positive thought," Hugh Najtingalo the mine operator said. "And I am not sure that there is enough positive thought in the world to extinguish that beam in the sky. Even if there be, there are better uses for it."

"Would you, possibly, tell us a few of the 'loose ends' that are bothering you, best detective in the world?" Joe Primavera said. "The Torpedo might be a loose island, but I wouldn't call it a loose end. We are all anxious to help you. We doubt if you became the best detective in the world without the help of very acute persons such as ourselves. Name some of the loose ends and perhaps we will be able to belay them for you."

"There are two friends whom I have been counting as my very closest friends in the world," Constantine said. "These are named Salaadin and Regina Marqab, the beautiful couple from the floating world. I spent last night at and near their place between Nice and Monaco. These are my two best friends, I repeat, but in truth I cannot now recall ever seeing them before last evening, though I then saw them with a powerful recognition. They seem to be coming apart today, having a split and behaving irresponsibly, but I do not care one thing about this. It is almost as if they were intruded into my mind as decoys, and my previous memory or pleasant impression of them also intruded there. You must understand that I do have an affection for them almost too powerful to bear, but where is it from? It is a very pleasant and glowing memory, whatever its origin. The memory is certainly better than last night's or today's facts."

"When you were last in Ichnusa with the incandescent couple, you cut a pretty good swathe," Joe Primavera said. "You look blank at that. You might also refresh your memory by reviewing your appearances with them in the rotogravure journals of two months ago. You three also cut a grand swathe on the blue coast of France and

116

Spain. Well, they are loose ends one and two. What follows?"

"There are three 'agents' who are loose ends three and four and five," Constantine said. "There is the agent Julien Moravia who tried to have me arrested in Civita do Nord this morning, though it was a clownish attempt. There is the Agent Amelia Lilac who tried to paralyze my limbs and will with an infusion in this town this afternoon. She is the woman who carries her own shade around with her. There is the agent John Seferino who will attempt to obstruct me to my very death tonight, and perhaps he will attempt the same thing on the world."

"Loose ends three and four and five," Joe Primavera said. "How much slack do you have, Constantine, do you know?"

"Slack? For what, Primavera?"

"For tying the loose ends together, Constantine. Is there enough for a sailors' short splice? Or for a long splice? Or for an elaborate knot?"

"I don't know, Primavera. The slack is in time, of course: how much time I have left before I can dispose of them or they of me. The sixth loose end concerns the 'double' of one of our mentioned agents, which 'double' I killed earlier yesterday evening in Marseilles. I am not sure whether it was the basic agent, or the surrogate and decoy of that agent whom I killed. It was the double of the agent whom I knew the best and should have recognized for sure. It was with this murder or encounter that I passed through the door to unreality. Everything has seemed unreal since that time, including present company."

"The sixth loose end properly recorded," said Troy Islander. "It isn't at all difficult to be the best detective in the world, is it? One simply finds the most intelligent companions in the world and spills it all to them."

"I hope it will work," Constantine said. "The seventh loose end is myself as the best detective in the world. I am very foggy about how I came to be so. I remember being a hard-working and honest foot policeman in a medium-sized French city. After that is an empty interval. Then, sometime yesterday. I was Constantine Quiche the best detective in the world and I was assigned to a very

117

mysterious case. There's the gap of a long season between the two states, and the only memories I have of the interval are symbolic shreds and pieces. Well, it isn't too unusual for World Interpol to give a man a swept-slate mind for clearer work on a case, and then giving him his old clutter back after that case is finished. But there's quite a few inconsistencies about it all."

"You do seem a little bit different from the Constantine Quiche, best detective in the world, that I was talking with a month or so ago," Hugh Najtingalo the mine operator said. "Several times I have wondered whether you were the same man. And then I check you over in my mind, your voice, your gestures, your overall and detailed appearance, your way of flying an idea like a tail-heavy kite: and yes, you are the same man. But you are the same man slightly changed. Or you are as near to the same man as trickery can make you, in which case you yourself would seem to be unaware of the trickery and disguise."

"You talked with me a month or so ago, Najtingalo?" Constantine asked. "Where?"

"In this very room. With this very company in this very wine-fine. You do not remember it?"

"May I break in on this, Constantine?" Angelo the Master Forger asked. "I have been suspecting something all the while today since you were in my workshop at Salerno at noon. Do you remember searching my workshop and rooms there several times in the past during the World Interpol intervention in international art forgeries? You seemed a bit blank when I mentioned it."

"No, I don't. I don't remember searching your place," Constantine said.

"Do you remember me at all before today?"

"No. I don't think that I do."

"Then how did you happen to come to my place in Salerno? How did you remember the way? How did you know that I was Angelo the Master Forger? Why did you think that I could help you? How did you even recognize me when I arrived there?"

"I don't know. I don't know these things at all. Loose end number seven, myself, is a bad one.

"Loose end number eight consists of attacks on my car

118

and presumably on my life. But they were not strong enough attacks. It was as if they were more warnings than attempts, but I was never told what I was being warned away from. Loose end number nine is Sandaliotis as a mirage, coming down from the air into place and becoming solid. This does not agree with the accounts of citizens of Sandaliotis that Sandaliotis is always in place but is sometimes not seen by the outer barbarians. What I have seen with my eyes is a contradiction of this."

"Mirages are tricky," said Najtingalo. "You did not see what you thought that you saw. It would not be lawful to see our land coming down from elsewhere."

"Loose end number ten is my superior at World Interpol, Grishwell. There is an amnesia about him, but induced amnesia is common in World Interpol work. Nevertheless, I know him only by telephone and I do not remember knowing him before, and I have no idea of his appearance. And at this moment I remember him much less well than I did this morning when I talked to him on the phone for the first time today.

"Loose end number eleven (I have them in my mind in this original number order and I cannot change their numeration) is the bomb in the sky, which you say is Thibeau's Torpedo, a Fortean construct, and which I can see right now in spite of its camouflage of clouds. But it isn't in accord with Grishwell's description of it this morning, for he specifically said that it could not be had on visual. Am I being subjected to a visual decoy right now? And by whom?"

"I suppose that it would have to be one of us here present," Angelo the Master Forger said. "No one else has been close enough to you to get a good mind-grip on you for such a thing."

"Loose end twelve is my parachute. Why did Grishwell tell me to wear one? Why did I immediately buy one? And why was there a mod parachute shop so readily at hand? Is it still there? Or just how elaborate is this hoax?"

"I have heard of the mod parachute shops," Troy Islander said. "I thought it was all a euphemism for the purveying of something other than parachutes. Well, in fact, I know that it is. And they really had parachutes

119

there? How rum! This loose end may be looser than you believe."

"Loose end number thirteen is a devil named Haziel whose sandal Sandaliotis is said to be. But your land is also said to be the land of Lucifer himself. There *is* a world or planet named Haziel, however, one of the closest of them. And there is no world named Lucifer that I know of."

"As a matter of fact, there are several worlds named Lucifer," Troy Islander corrected. "None of them is near enough for likely involvement, however, and perhaps Haziel is."

"Loose end number fourteen is antimatter," Constantine said. "It keeps climbing back into this case when I think I have got it out. Is Haziel an antimatter world? Grishwell, if there is such a person, believes that it might be.

"Loose end number fifteen is the director of films. This man has a brass voice, not unpleasant to me, but very artificial sounding. I fancy (and I am as full of fancies as he is when I am in his company) that it isn't the voice of a man but of some masquerading thing. And his eyes appear like two *glass* eyes, even though they are moving enough and merry enough. Is he an 'agent'? He is something more than a director of films. I believe that he is the director of the apparition of Sandaliotis.

"Loose end number sixteen is the Inquisitor in the not-very-successful first scene that I played for the 'Thirteen-Sided Room.' I believe that he is a prisoner, dazed and doped. I believe that he has really been blinded and deafened and unbalanced. And I believe that he really is an Inquisitor from somewhere where the office is at least equal to a world ruler. He is needed here for the authority that adheres to him, but he is made into a deformed clown and stumbler.

"Loose end number seventeen is the Five O'Clock man who says that he is an agent. Therefore he must have been that, either in the scenario of the play or outside of it. But what sort of agent was he? There is much more to him than has showed.

"Loose end number eighteen is the man who was killed
120

by 'accident' in the thirteen-sided room. Who was he? Why was he killed? Why was I *not* killed then?

"Loose end number nineteen is my 'nephew,' the dead man with my ah, ah with several of my characteristics. The dead man whom the local police have somehow identified as Constantine Quiche the world's best detective, in place of myself.

"Loose end twenty is the continuing puzzle of Sandaliotis. It is a drifting ship, and the crewmen give contradictory and impossible accounts of its situation, and its origin and its destination. Ship-owner Islander, is that not odd conduct for crewmen on a ship? But Sandaliotis is here right now, and what happens to the other things that should be in the place that it occupies?

"Loose end number twenty-one is the man in this party who will betray me tonight. And that is the most of the loose ends that I have."

"Oh, I believe that we can splice up an even number of them," Troy Islander said. "We can surely splice up any twenty of the twenty-one. In fact, we must do it if we are to preserve your reputation of being the best detective in the world. Which one of us will betray you?"

"Whichever one of you dips his hand with me into the dish of snails, he will betray me," Constantine said. That sounded like an echo of an old quotation.

So they set about the business of splicing up the loose ends. They hadn't much slack for even short splices. And yet, being persons of very acute minds, they began to get it done. They got several of the splices executed. Then they got all of them effected. Twenty of the twenty-one loose ends were securely spliced in now into a rational explanation and perhaps accusation. This wasn't done completely to Constantine's satisfaction, but it was done to the satisfaction of the other four. They were well-executed splices and perhaps they would hold.

On the parts of the splicing that Constantine didn't understand, he was a little abashed about questioning that distinguished and highly intelligent company. Nor was he even certain how he knew that they were such a distinguished and highly intelligent company.

Then, as they wined and dined, Constantine reached his hand to take more snails, and another personage

121

dipped his hand in at the same time. Constantine, in spite of his prophesying it, didn't notice it at all. But the other personage looked long and hard at Constantine, and kept his hand in the snails for some time.

"This is the second very pleasant meeting that we five have held here," Joe Primavera the proprietor said. "The first meeting exactly one month ago. The second one to-day. Let us propose to meet here again exactly one month hence. Let it be here even if Ichnusa is then no more than broken pieces of rubble on the bottom of the ocean."

CHAPTER EIGHT

"Let it be here even if we ourselves are no more than fish-cleaned bones," Troy Islander said. "Stranger meetings than that have been effected where the heroic will was present."

But Constantine Quiche didn't at all remember having met with these same men in this same place one month previously.

It was five minutes before four in the afternoon when the small party broke up at Joe Primavera's wine-fine.

"Angelo, may I have another one of our own forgeries of Doctor Korkolon's controversial guardsman pills," Constantine asked as they broke up.

"Certainly," the Master Forger said, and he gave him one. Constantine put it under his tongue and forgot about it. But he was uncertain and flighty.

"You are jittery, Constantine," Angelo said. "That is the penalty for being the best detective in the world, I suppose. If you would switch and get on the wrong side of the law, you would not have these worries, and you could sleep at night. You would no longer have the weight of the world on your shoulders. Your peace of mind should be worth your trying the crooked way once."

"Ah, no, no, Angelo," Constantine said firmly. "I will have to do without that sense of peace and well being. I am committed."

In the street again, Constantine was perturbed to see his own name in an advertisement.

"Also in the cast, Constantine Quiche, the World's Greatest Detective, with sensational revelations about World Interpol, in thrilling scenes filmed only today."

What sort of thing was that? It was an advertisement for a drama to be shown that very evening, and the name of the drama was 'Interworld Duplicity, a Psychological Thriller!' This was part of a double-bill, the ad said, and the other half of it was 'The Trillion-Dollar World-Jack, the Holdup with a Message! The Last Psychological Thriller of Them All!' This latter one had an ominous feel about the very signboard of it.

"I will bet that it is the same Director doing all of these," Constantine told himself. "And I will bet that someone is 'accidentally' killed in each of them to point up a big scene. I had better be careful. The accidentally killed one might still be myself. With his fluid ways, the Director hasn't necessarily completed the filming of either of these."

On a kiosk phone there, Constantine called Grishwell, his superior at World Interpol.

"Constantine, I can get the 'news' from the news," Grishwell said quickly. "There is a lot of it and it is subject to every interpretation. But what is really happening there? What is the latest development on the big bomb and the big conspiracy? And how is it on the big rogue peninsula?"

"Nothing is happening," said Constantine, "but it maintains a brisk pace nevertheless. The island in the sky that you said was never on visual is on pretty clear visual here. And it may be an antimatter bomb in its nature. The peninsula in the sea has remained on visual all day, and I have been on it all day except for one short trip to Italy. But both the sky object and the peninsula are shimmering. Sandaliotis here seems to be made mostly out of green foam. Some of those bounding green meadows appear quite artificial. For a while I will be almost convinced of the existence of Sandaliotis. Then I will blink my eyes to clear them, and it will be all green sea-foam again. There are two different versions going on here, Grishwell. It's as though two narrations were going on at the same time. There are these two different trends or pushes going on, and someone has put a large price tag on each of them. In each case, it is one trillion dollars."

"What are you doing to set things straight?"

"Not much, Grishwell. I think I'll go to a show tonight. There's a double bill that will be on everywhere. One drama is 'Interworld Duplicity, a Psychological Thriller.' It's partly about World Interpol, I think, and I'm in it, though I don't know how I am or what I'm doing in it. And the other half of it is 'Trillion Dollar World-Jack, a Hold-Up with a Message.' "

"Does the double bill correspond to the two different versions of something that are working there, Constantine?"

"No. Not quite. The second of the dramas does correspond to one of the versions. But the first one seems to be a red snapper drawn across the trail. Instead of it, or in addition to it, there should be a melodrama entitled 'Interworld Duplicity, the Great Real Estate Heist.' "

"It is important, Constantine, that nothing be done to dim the great image of World Interpol," Grishwell said.

"Not very important, sir. I was taught in my training that the image was to be burnished only after everything else had been taken care of, after every other duty had been performed. Myself, I have been chopping that image up and using it for bait. And I've been getting quite a few strikes at it too." Constantine hung up the phone on Grishwell and left the kiosk.

And he ran right into a lilac fog. He was caught in the fragrant arms of Amelia Lilac, special agent and lady of the afternoon. He felt again the slight needle punctures that were more common than not with kisses nowadays. He was thankful that he had used another forged pill from Angelo to counteract the effect of strange invasions. He had no wish to be further paralyzed in various functions, and he had no desire to be made more amenable. Well, let the needle and the forged pill fight it out between them.

"Really, Constantine my minor passion, you are too

125

easy," the lavender-shadowed Amelia said. "Will I never find an opponent who is able to call out my full talents? If you are the best detective in the world, then tell me what the worst one is like."

"Oh, he's not bad at all, Amelia," Constantine said. "I work with him on cases sometimes. The general reaction of people who deal with him is 'he's pretty good. If he is the worst detective in the world, what must the best one be like?' It's sort of a tribute to me really."

"It's a shame that you can't live up to it, Constantine, my treasure and my patsy," Amelia said. "Really, we had quite a bit to do with your getting to be *known* as the best detective in the world. You're not the best, of course. But we have to look ahead on these things and select and arrange a little bit."

They went to the Imperial Hotel which was near, and to the 'Gardens of Delight Suite' that Amelia had taken, permanently, for all that Constantine knew. There seemed to be a continuous slow-paced party going on in the 'Gardens of Delight.' Other agents were there. One can always tell when a person is an agent, but one can never find out what a good agent is agent for. There were hustlers and representatives there.

"Which one are they on?" Constantine asked himself. "Which narration is this a part of? Is it a part of the 'Trillion Dollar World-Jack'? Or is it a part of Interworld Duplicity, the Great Real Estate Heist'? It would help me slightly if I knew which of these jags this group of people was on."

There were many of those real-estate agents there, but these seemed to be very far up in the hierarchy, top agents of agents' organizations. There were some of those tourist-strangers who clearly were not natives of Sandaliotis, and who just as clearly liked the place. They had those pleasant but odd appearances that indicated that they were either Scandinavians or Off-World people. It is very difficult to tell persons of these two groups apart.

"This is Constantine Quiche, who is the best detective in the world," Amelia introduced Constantine to her mixed mob. "He has only two things wrong with him. He is weak in the head, and he kills people. He killed my sister yesterday evening in Marseilles, but he may have had a reason. I would not be so crude as to ask him about a thing like that. I mention this to you all only because he is so colorless and I don't want him passed over too lightly. Really, he may be worth your attention, girls, and I do want him entertained. Maybe he will kill one of you, girls. Don't you find something very attractive in a man who kills girls?"

Amelia was an adept with more than one sort of needle.

There were half of a dozen girls there, girls much prettier than Amelia Lilac, girls not nearly as beautiful as she was. Surely she had selected these girls to show herself off. Were they needle-puncture girls also?

"Come to me, killer," one of those pretty girls said to Constantine. But these girls were not from Sandaliotis, except maybe one of them. Where were they all from then?

There was a sudden change, in light, or in shadow, or in ambient. What was it?

"Did a light go off?" Constantine asked one of the girls.

"No. It's more as if a dark went off," the girl said. "She turns it off sometimes when she relaxes." It was the mysterious lavender-colored, lilac-colored shadow-and-nimbus colored thing that had always attended Amelia Lilac. It had gone out. It wasn't there now, but Amelia was still there somewhere. Her disguised presence gave uncertain indications that she was still there, but Constantine realized that he wouldn't know Amelia without her cloud.

"And what case is the best detective in the world working on now?" a bouncy young lady of attractive chubbiness asked him.

"The case of Sandaliotis and all its mysteries," Constantine said. "And you are one of those mysteries. I will bet that you were not on Sandaliotis yesterday. Why are you here today?"

(The best detective in the world had always been proud of his powers of observation and recognition: he knew that there was a girl in this room whom he had paid very special attention to; and he would not recognize her now because an accidental aspect of her had been 'turned off.' Well, would any girl be Amelia Lilac if she were surrounded by that lilac-colored aura? Was there a fine disguise drifting around here waiting for some woman to put it on and turn it on?)

"Oh, there are so many reasons why I am here today," the bouncy girl said. "I am here because I knew that you would be here, I suppose. I really *did* know that you would be here, Constantine Quiche. And that really *is* part of the reason that I'm here. We do want you to be entertained."

Even this bouncy girl could be Amelia Lilac.

"We like you so much," the bouncy girl said. "We simply must be with you."

"We like you not at all," said an ill-mannered but pretty young man. "It is because of World Interpol, really, that we have you here at this time. We have put a leash on you." (Even this young man was prettier, but less beautiful, than the nimbused Amelia Lilac.)

"The deal is too big to have it messed up by you," the pretty young man was still saying. (Did the 'deal too big to have it messed up' sound more like the 'Trillion Dollar World-Jack' deal, or like the 'Interworld Duplicity, Great Real Estate Heist' deal?) "And World Interpol, in its bumbling way, messes up a lot of deals," the young man said. "But how could we keep World Interpol out of a deal as big as this one? Oh, we couldn't."

"But how could we keep World Interpol out of it *effectively?*" the bouncy girl cut in. "Oh, we could! We can! We do!"

"We keep World Interpol out by letting it in," said the pretty man. "So we arrange to let it in with a patsy representative, the 'world's greatest detective,' that's you. We have you assigned to it, we have you nailed to it, but we cannot allow you to accomplish anything on it. But we cannot simply extinguish you either, not while the deal is still on. Should we do that, should we make away with you too early, World Interpol would simply send out another agent to take charge, or they would send several of them. So you must move about, you must circulate and be seen to circulate, you must be seen in very many places, you must make phone calls, you must convey reports. And you must find out nothing, or at least you must tell nothing.

"And you must be amenable. Of course you're a prisoner, and of course we can extinguish you at any time. And we *will* extinguish you in all good time. You cannot mount any opposition to us even in your thoughts. You cannot find the world or the machinery to phrase or plan such opposition, for we have introduced scramblers into you, and your own thoughts will scramble themselves when they try to climb out of their prescribed ditches.

"But, for the present, see to it that you are amused, see to it that you are seen, see to it that you appear to be working on the case even if you don't know anything at all about the case in hand. It is sufficient that you are slightly paralyzed in your faculties, and that you do not get any idea of making or communicating any discovery.

"Be amenable and live a little while longer. Yes, a couple of hours longer."

(Amelia Lilac, without her lavender shadow and aura could be any of them here. *Could* she be the pretty young man as well? Oh no, not that. That would be going too far with it.)

"But we do want you to be happy," the bouncy girl said. Constantine, by this time, was taking liberties with the bouncy girl. As a detective, there was something that he wanted to find out about her substance and texture.

"Believe us, we always have our best interests at heart," the bouncy girl said. "How did you kill Amelia's sister in Marseilles?"

"I broke her neck."

"Try mine, darling," the bouncy girl said. "I have a superb neck, and I love men to do violence to it. You didn't use a snapdragon to break her neck, did you? That's cheating."

(The girl in Marseilles had had a superb neck also, and a lavender shadow ambient. Was there more than one of these shadow-ambient disguises?)

(What could be done with one of those disguises if it were three hundred miles long? Would such a long and powerful shadow ambient as that not change almost anything out of recognition?)

Constantine had killed the girl in Marseilles with his hands, but it had been close. She had almost killed him. She would have succeeded with most men.

Well, why had she tried to kill him? It hadn't been in the script for her to kill him yesterday evening if it wasn't in the script for them to kill him now. Why had she tried it then? Constantine looked into the eyes of this present girl. Oh, there was a quirk of insanity there. It couldn't be mistaken for anything else. But it was like something that she was under only part of the while, and out from under it often. It might be that the insanity adhered to the shadow ambient disguise and not to the person. Well, out with what he was thinking then! It is a good trick sometimes to blurt the questions out, and often it takes people by surprise.

"What could be done with one of those shadow ambient disguises if it were three hundred miles long?" he asked. "Would it not change anything almost out of recognition?"

And the girl paused a moment as though she would pretend that she didn't know what he was talking about.

"No wonder Amelia told us that you were weak in the head!" she cried. But she did know what he was talking about, so she came around to the other side of it then.

"Oh my darling," she said then. "You are charming, charming! *But this thing must not be interfered with!* You are like an enchanting child who comes to one with a rose-red mouth, and then fastens into one suddenly with poison fangs."

"Are the fangs anything like the puncturing needles that paralyze one slightly in the various faculties, that make one amenable?" Constantine asked.

"No, not like that at all," the girl said. "Oh my treasure, do you know what you are about to throw away? A short and happy life that still has about eight hours to run, that's what you are about to throw away. I'll never willingly throw any of my life away, no, not one minute. And you are also throwing away the chance for a much longer and happier life than that."

"What is the essence of the disguise?" Constantine asked. "What is the essence of either the small disguise or the large one? What is the name of it? Is it the veil? The *velo?* The *peplos?*"

"Oh, I suppose it is something like that," the girl said. "It's an illusion, and it can cover some crude work underneath, for a while, for a quick and profitable while. It covers other illusions, rougher and more material illusions. There are things done by it that just couldn't be

130

done without it. And it is enlivening and awakening as well as disguising. Do you not ever underestimate it!"

"You *are* Amelia Lilac, out from under that lavender-shadow disguise for a moment, aren't you?"

"Of course I'm Amelia. My voice isn't the same without the shadow cloak, and none of the appearance is the same. But I am Amelia. Who else cares for you? Who has been keeping you alive when you keep blundering closer to things? I have been. I mean it. Who else selected you out once, some months ago, to be a man on the rise until you had risen to be the best detective in the world? Who else would bounce you on her bouncy bosom? Texture and substance, you're testing, are you, Constantine? Test away. Do I remind you of a dolphin yet as I did in what you thought was a dream? Do I remind you of a human person? Test away, but you won't find the answers till I give them to you.

"But do not think lightly of the lavender-shadow disguise, Constantine. You have worn it yourself. You will wear a piece of it forever."

"I? How have I worn it, Amelia?"

"It is the illusion that can cover quite a few kinds of crude work underneath. It's the illusion that brought you the fame of being the best detective in the world, and you're really not even very good. We fling this veil, we fling this net out over the things that we want to manipulate, Constantine. And we flung it out over some islands and seas this morning. But we did an awful lot of crude work underneath first. And now we will have our quick and profitable harvest from it. *And you must not interfere!* I can, perhaps, save you completely if you trust me. And I will, perhaps, kill you with my own hands if you do not. I will kill you, Constantine, as I nearly killed you last night."

"Who was it that I killed last night, Amelia? Who was there?"

"I was there. And you killed no one at all. You will remember that I was in the illusion, that I was in the shadow cloak all that time, and there is a lot of room in it. I went out from me for a while and I left me there. And then, when you were gone, I went into me again.

131

And then I went along the Grande Corniche ahead of you and arrived ahead of you while you were still confused.

"I have just said, Constantine, that I might be able to save you completely if you trusted me."

"And I haven't given you an answer, have I?"

"No, you haven't given me an answer, Constantine, and you're lost if you don't."

"Are you a bit mad, Amelia?"

"Oh, it's the old madness and the old aspiration. *And it must not be interfered with.* The old madness is simply the old existence. An old man told you today (Oh, of course I can hear what people tell you, I've got you rigged on audio reception) 'The Old Things reigned in the cult circuits a long time ago. And then, after they were clear discredited, they came to our island to end it all. But they do not die.' That old man was mostly right about us, Constantine. We did reign on the cult circuits a long time. And we were clear discredited. And we did come to some hills that were at the same time in the Island of Sardinia and the Peninsula of Sandaliotis. But we did not like to be discredited and displaced, and we did not accept it. We fight back again and again. There have been some huge and direful things that happened to the people of this globe because they dropped our cults. We live both in the green hills and in the ocean that is replaced by those green hills sometimes. And we are people of several fleshes, for we refuse to be slain in just one of them.

"Oh yes, I am of dolphin flesh, and quite a few other fleshes. Are you not finding that out with your investigations? But look out for us when we come up out of the ocean and whistle for our sky dog. We can blow you out like candles then."

"You are as clear a forgery as was ever dredged out of this sea, Amelia," Constantine said. He went swiftly out of the 'Garden of Delights Suite' and out of the Imperial Hotel. He still hadn't given Amelia an answer. All he knew was that he hadn't better make any pledge to one of those persons who was made out of that older clay. It is stylized and it is stiff, that older plasticine, and you may be hardened into one of its forms too quickly to get away from it.

But Constantine still kept a bit of something that he now realized that he had received from this Amelia many months before, when he had first met her. It was pieces of the hypnotic fog, of the veil, of the lavender-shadow disguise. And, by the use of it, he had been able to influence people to do almost anything he wished. He had been able to do this ever since he had had it, even in the times when he didn't realize that he had it.

He was trying, by the employment of it where it was lodged in a corner of his personality, to influence somebody to do what he wished now. He was trying to compel the pretty young man from Amelia's 'Garden of Delights Suite' to come out after him.

He waited in an alley that could be seen from hardly anywhere. When one had a piece of the fog, such things as hard-to-see alleys are always right at hand wherever needed.

The pretty man came into the alley as though not knowing where he was going or why. Constantine knocked him down. He picked him up then, and he knocked him down again.

"The first time was to get my attention, as in the old joke about the mule," the pretty man said. "But what was the second time for?"

(There was more to this pretty man than there had seemed to be.)

"I have an intuition that if we go down this way, we can find a place to talk," Constantine said. He put a knife blade to the back of the pretty man's neck and they went down the secluded alley.

"Oh really, Constantine, this tactic is not worthy of the best detective in the world," the pretty man said. "There are quite elegant clubs where we can go and talk. We can talk over the table of any coffee shop or bar. Or there are privacy offices, quite well appointed, that can be taken for a day or an hour or a minute. I have funds whether you have or not. This alley here is plain slum melodrama. Whatever we enact, it deserves a better setting than this."

"Oh, I like slum melodrama," Constantine said, "and this door will go right to the heart of it." They went through a decrepit door into what had once been an old warehouse. They came into a tall and shoddy room there.

133

"I don't want it elegant, I don't want it well appointed, I want it like this," Constantine said. There was a rope there.

"I knew there would be," the pretty man said. "What corn!"

Constantine made a noose out of it and put it around the pretty man's neck. He reaved the end of the rope through a pulley that was lashed to an overhead rafter, and he pulled the rope tight.

"This is incredibly juvenile," the man said. "Your performance in the 'Thirteen-Sided Room' has given you a heritage of ham, Constantine. I am quite uncomfortable already. When will I be permitted to sit down again?"

"Never again," said Constantine. "Neither in this world nor in the next. Now you will answer questions. Which version is your group working on: 'The Billion Dollar World-Jack' or the 'Greatest Real Estate Heist'?"

"The latter," the man said. "I learned about the world-jack too late to get in on it."

"The real estate deal, yes? All right, how did you make Sandaliotis?"

"How did we *make* Sandaliotis? I don't understand your question, Quiche. What is it that you are trying to ask—aaaeewwhmmm—so it is understand your question or hang, is it? All right. I will attempt to understand and answer your question then. There was a great quantity of improbable technology used, and an hypnotic fog was thrown over that. That's the answer. No wait, Quiche, don't pull that rope again! That really is the answer. I am telling this straight. It is improbable technology that we used. It is impossible technology. It can't work. It can't hold together. It is like lines drawn on water that we then erect a land upon. This is the most temporary, one-day thing that anyone ever saw. We are to convey title to all the land and to collect all the money before midnight tonight. That is the great real-estate heist. I wish it were sooner. I just don't believe that Sandaliotis can hold together till midnight tonight.

"I will begin in the middle. A broker for an off-world group came to us with an inquiry, and so we picked up an idea from that. The off-world group was an investment and resettlement conglomerate, and it wanted an equity in

134

Earth. It had equities in fifty or so other worlds. Diversification is the name of the game now, the broker said, and equity and property on Earth would add a straw to the diversity strawstack.

" 'About a hundred million equivalent acres, to use round figures,' the broker had said, 'one-third of it, in one or two enclaves, could be lightly settled with Earth people, and two-thirds of it to be clear of them. Figure a way to do that and we will buy,' the broker said. There was also a commemorative element to the tentative offer. The people the broker dealt with held to the myth that they were originally of Earth origin. They had been driven from Earth in proto-historic times, they believed. Now they thought that token numbers of them (fifty million or so) might establish themselves back here.

"Myself and my associates tackle many theoretical problems. The accidental fallout from them almost pays for the effort. We decided to try this one on a theoretical basis. Ah, Quiche, can you give me just a little bit more slack in the rope?"

"I don't see how I can give you another inch," Constantine said. "Talk, man, talk."

"There were three ways to obtain the land for which we had a potential customer," the man said. He was a pretty man no longer. He was a young man no longer. His face was now like one of those tortured faces from the 'Thirteen-Sided Room' psychological thriller.

"We could, for the first case, find a place that would fulfill all the conditions. (But where on Earth could we find such a place?) Or, for the second case, we could find a place that would fulfill all the conditions except the main one, and for that main one we could clear the land, sixty or seventy million acres of it, of its human fauna. (But we paled at the thought of clearing people off so much land that they stubbornly believed to be their own. That would take warfare, or at least armies.) Or, for the third case, we could construct a new land that would fulfill the conditions. (But how does one construct a hundred-million acres of land?) 'We can always put an impossible price on it,' one of us said 'like ten thousand dollars an acre for rough farm land or for rougher hill land.' 'That would come to a trillion dollars,' another of

135

us said, 'a truly thirteen-sided figure.' We made the proposal to supply it for one trillion dollars. It was accepted. So we examined the possibilities of constructing the place.

"We finally settled approximately on the third solution, that of constructing a new land to fulfill the conditions. With one exception we settled on that solution. We decided to construct an *old* land to fulfill the conditions. Folklore was one of the thousand subjects that we ransacked, and very quickly we came onto the folklore of Sandaliotis. We studied Weingarten's fanciful map of the place that was based on all the legends and descriptions. Then we superimposed it on an actual map of the same region. We found that all the cities, except North Town, fell into the areas of either Corsica or Sardinia. So did all the prominent elements of the landscape, the higher mountains, the old volcano remnants, the taller sea cliffs. There was our country, one-third of it in two enclaves (Corsica and Sardinia) already lightly settled with Earth people; two-thirds of it blank. All we had to do was construct the blank two-thirds of it, the clear two-thirds of it. And we did that.

"This is the thing that you will find hard to believe, Quiche. One reason that it is hard to believe is that it didn't happen, and could not have. A proof that it didn't happen is that, though we made a new country appear at about dawn this morning, and though we have maintained it in apparent being all this day, yet we will not be able to maintain it in being much beyond midnight tonight, if that long. It has been full of holes since the minute we made it, and the holes are getting bigger. It is a para-material illusion, and we will soon see what is the outcome of this first massive para-material illusion.

"We did have a mass of mentality, or at least of mentation, at our disposal to construct with. Sandaliotis was already strongly in many minds. People had believed in the existence of Sandaliotis for ages. People still believed in it. People said that they had been there, and that they knew how to go back there. Several prominent, though also eccentric, persons of the world had claimed Sandaliotis as a birthplace. Sandaliotis was a going cult. It was a fantasy place with a fantasy literature.

"A study that we made revealed that seventy-two per-

136

cent of the people in neighboring Italy believed that there was the peninsula named Sandaliotis that was larger than Italy. There was one quirk to this belief. Very many of those who held it believed in the appearance and fact of Sandaliotis on only one night of the year, on All Saints' eve. Nevertheless, there was fiber and material of belief, and it could be built upon. The 'para' or para-material illusion is belief and mentality.

"There were countless Sandaliotis Clubs in the World. Some of them were poetry or literature circles, some of them were song and drama groups, some were ethical or spiritualistic or religious groups. Some were antiquarian, and the materials that they gathered were fantastic. Sandaliotis had even begun to have a language; well, it resembled an illegitimate daughter of Esperanto, but it was claimed to be a very old sister of Latin; and it had a new-old literature of its own. We used much of this club literature in the setting up of several 'show' libraries in the new construction. Some of the Sandaliotis clubs went in for such things as spirit manifestation, alternate worlds, the old Mediterranean god-and-hero cults, and levitation.

"Working with some of them, we made studies in inculcated, sustained levitation. We found that it could be accomplished, that in fact it was being done regularly. We were strictly in mind country on this, but that mind country will support a lot of weight for a while. Persons properly inculcated, and self- or hetero-hypnotized, may for a period (for about a day at most, we believe) move about on a supporting medium that would not ordinarily sustain their weight at all, that would not ordinarily sustain a tenth or even a twentieth of their weight. Well, you see, we cut costs where we could. It isn't cheap building a country at least as large as Italy, even if we build most of it out of air foam.

"We worked with nonmaterial molecular lattice patterns. With these, the shape is all important, and there wasn't any substance. Once the molecular lattice pattern was established, it would continue to impose itself on its ambient whether there was any material in that ambient or not, whether there were even any scattered molecules there. The noncollapsible shapes will sustain themselves with no expenditure of matter.

137

"We worked with the Multiplication Virus (it is deadly only when it spreads to living substance). The Multiplication Virus will reproduce itself like wildfire on a rampage, and it does not much care what if any material it uses. It will grow furiously to a certain point dictated by its particular mutation, and then it will stop growing. We believed that we had brought about the proper mutation in the virus so that it would grow to fit our designated area exactly. Such material as it would use to form its virus crystals would be air and water and salt, from the local atmosphere and the sea.

"We worked with various gas plasmas. We worked with sustained electrical-field areas that continued after the cessation of their primaries. We worked with fox fires and swamp fires as patterns for short-life constructions. Oh, wc did a lot of things with air foam also. As to bulk, most of our work was with air foam. We believed that we could cover our designated areas of ocean with oscillating oil slicks and then let down air foam or fog foam on that. The electrical charge had to be maintained on the oil slicks, of course, and on the air foam also. The air foam was really the hair of the ocean standing on end with the electricity in it. That is all that we did do this morning, and it worked much better than I at least had expected. The largest variations we have got so far from drifting coastlines is about twelve miles.

"We had come to the point where we could lay down area-covering 'meadows' of shimmering green goop. From a distance they would look like convincing meadows. And they could possibly be walked on like meadows, by persons in trances, by hypnotized persons, and simply by great numbers of persons caught up in the contagion and epidemic of walking on air, on colored air with a little solid foam to it.

"We had gone what flimsy distance we could go with material and paramaterial things, and it was all very flimsy. For the rest, we would have to do with hypnotic form, the cloak, the mind-casting veil. In short, we would have to employ magic for the rest of it.

"We had one special expert of the Cloak or Veil or Shadow or Disguise phenomenon with us. This was the person code named Amelia Lilac. She was the lady of the

138

lavender ambient which fractures both appearance and reality and can cause crowds as well as persons to see and to believe almost anything that is wished onto them. She is one of the very old people, of the cult people. The effect of the shadow fog is very powerful so that even fragments of it can perform wonders. Amelia herself demonstrates bi-location and diplo-somatism (bi-bodyism). She has several different valid bodies that she uses."

"No, she has not," Constantine contradicted. "That bouncy body that she was using this afternoon, her half-dolphin body, it wasn't valid and it wasn't real. Only a toy."

"It may be that you're mistaken," the man said. "But, yes, we had already done something this morning that you asked about this afternoon. We *did* project one of those shadow-ambient disguises that was about three hundred miles long. That was really what made Sandaliotis 'appear.' It just fit our new country and it transformed it. Everybody believes in the lavender fog when it is first in their eyes. Everybody believes in it for about a day, and it creates reality for those who believe in it.

"We had run many excursion boats here today, to get a crowd of devoted and believing people, people who should look like native inhabitants. They were filled up with a sense of pageantry, for they were recruited out of the various Sandaliotis Clubs. They were full of play-acting and they had all the burning desire to make the play-acting come true. They were bright and shining Sandaliotis people, and they were everywhere. But many of the old-line Corsicans and Sardinians played parts also.

"Everything here is either Corsica, or it is Sardinia, or it is North Town, or it is Monaco. Or else it is that shimmering green goop of tenuous substance, the transmuted air and coloring matter. Oh, the green meadows of Sandaliotis! They are here today, and tomorrow they will be melted and gone. Well, we have sold the new land to an off-world group. We will collect by midnight tonight. And then we skip. Oh how we will skip! That is all that there is to tell."

"That is not nearly all," said Constantine Quiche. "What is special about North Town?"

"Only that it is more material than the other additions," the man said. "It's the remnant of our earliest and most material attempts, those that would have been prohibitive cost-wise for the whole area. There is some very ingenious lightweight scaffolding there, covered over again with a very ingenious use of the lavender fog, the reality cloud."

"And the city that we are in now?"

"Ichnusa, the capital of Sandaliotis? Oh, this is only the city of Cagliari of Sardinia somewhat added to. A few of the signs have been changed by the excursioning members of the various Sandaliotis clubs who are having their conventions here, and then the lavender fog is cast over it to make it a big city out of a little city. But it is still Cagliari as it always was."

"And the Italian Steps, that magnificent sweep?" Constantine asked. "There was never such a monumental construction as that in Cagliari before. Do not tell me they are not real. I walked down them."

"The Italian Steps? You really walked down those things, Quiche? Man, you were walking on air then. I mean it. But there are other things that I am not so sure are mere air. They may be mere thoughts, but then who thought them? I am one of those people who believed in the reality of Sandaliotis, as a boy and as a young man. I haven't made any contact with that old reality in all our fancy doings here, but that doesn't preclude it at all. There *is* a Sandaliotis somewhere. And they can't take it away from us, because they can't find it.

"But another thing, Quiche. When we add these various tawdries, the Italian Steps and such, we observe the first rule of fakery."

"And what is that?"

"We make the new things complete with the marks of considerable age on them. It's as easy as making them with the marks of considerable newness. We make a new world complete with its fossils and with its carbon-14 dating that shows considerable age.

"Even God employed that trick when He made the world, and that was not at all a long time ago. He made the world complete with all its age marks and its strata and memories and fossils."

"Have you or the things that you have constructed here

140

any connection with that Island in the Sky that is known as Thibeau's Torpedo?"

"A few connections with it, yes, but they haven't amounted to much. The people fooling with the Torpedo are mostly nothing people. And the people intent on pulling the world jack don't really need the Torpedo in the air for their purpose. Almost anything else would serve. Thibeau's Torpedo is a Fortean construct anyhow, and we stay away from that stuff. We just don't feel comfortable with it."

"And you really believe that you can get away with all this, man?"

"We can, man, but you can't," the suffering and flustered man told Constantine. "You yourself are trapped, Constantine Quiche. There is an emitting locator in you. You can't hide, for it is hollering your location all the time. And you can be killed wherever you are; all they have to do is ride in on the emissions of your locator and blast you with almost anything. Your locater is quite small. It was inserted into you, with other things, on the point of one needle."

"The person code named Amelia Lilac has given a perhaps-promise to me, and I believe that she intends to fulfill it. She is the only one who can locate me. My locater is tuned to her only."

"That's true, man. But her 'perhaps-promise' to you is a vain one, though she may hope to fulfill it. She cannot. People who are on the 'Great Expectation' as we are cannot leave living witnesses behind them. This is bad practice in very many cases."

"How much of this that you have told me is true, man?" Constantine asked.

"From a quarter to a half of it anyhow. I will tell you whatever I have to tell you to save myself from hanging. I will change my story to anything you wish if that will save me."

"Isn't it true that many earth persons were sold plots of the new land?" Constantine asked. "Quite a few million Earth persons in fact? Isn't it the case that most of the people here on 'excursions' are agents buying the one-day land for thousands of clients? Isn't it true that they have

141

already paid for much of it, those who have come today and millions of others besides?"

"Well, you know how it is, Quiche. One gets carried away by one's own salesmanship."

"And there weren't any off-world contacts at all, were there? It is all sold to Earth people, all the false land out of the falseness of your hearts?"

"I think there may have been off-world contacts, yes. Oh, the ninety-nine percent is heisted from Earth people for land that won't be here tomorrow, but I think there were a few off-world contacts also. We were conned badly if there weren't any. Some of them seemed like off-world people, and some of them are cutting themselves in on our things."

"As an old bunko-squad man, I bleed for you there. But your complaint is received a little bit late. You know that there are fewer people who believe in the Inhabited Worlds than believed in Sandaliotis even?"

"It isn't a few. It's a lot. It's a wide enough belief that we might build something on it, and with them we might not even have to cut and run the same day. I believe that our next Promotional Enterprise might well have to do with those Inhabited Worlds."

"You may be doing pretty well on this world," Constantine said. "Seventy million acres or so will total up pretty steep even if you won't get ten thousand dollars an acre for it."

"We are getting more than that, Quiche. Do you think that we sell the land only once? What sort of pikers do you take us for? This is big. And, as Amelia Lilac told you, we can't allow you to spoil it. We have worldwide electronic selling going on now, and that can mean multiple selling on very quick, one-day deals. After all, if this country and its land aren't going to be here tomorrow, why *not* sell it a dozen times today? If it won't *be* here, it might as well not be here a dozen times as not be here once."

"Man of the 'Great Expectation', you have a weird look in your eye," Constantine Quiche said, "and I don't like it at all. I have to keep reminding myself that yours is the neck in the noose and mine is the hand on the rope."

"I'm a bit mad, Quiche," the man in the noose said.

142

"I've been one of the persons of the lavender fog for some months and that brings on a touch of madness. You must try to forgive me for what I will have to do to you tonight."

"I also, unbeknownst to myself, have been one of the persons of the lavender fog for some months, and that has brought on a touch of madness to myself also. You must try to forgive me for what I will have to do to you right now."

"There's really no way you can harm me," the man said. "As Amelia Lilac did, I will go out of myself for a while and leave myself here. And then, when you are gone away, I will go into myself again. And then I will take a faster road than the Grande Corniche, and I will be there before you, wherever you go. I am within the illusion and protection of the shadow cloak now, and you will hang no more than a shadow if you hang me here. I will go and come back."

"You had best go very quickly then," Constantine said. "In any case, you will come back into a strangled body and one that will have a broken neck, I will make sure of that. Happy homecoming to you. There is no animosity, man. I only take your advice to leave no live witnesses behind. As you say, that's bad practice to leave them."

"One last question before I 'die,' Quiche," the man said, but he was laughing with his eyes, "for there is a remote, a very remote, possibility that I really will die in your noose. Why are you wearing that silly and cumbersome parachute around your waist?"

"I don't know," Constantine said. "I really don't. I can only say that I am wearing it because I was told to wear it, and I was told it by someone who seems intolerably vague now."

Constantine pulled on the rope to hang the man then, and he got a good start for a moment. Then there was a short difficulty. The man was caught in quick panic, but he reacted in psychosomatic protest. There was no doubt that he was still in the body. The rope froze in the pulley. The man was using mind on it. The hands of Constantine cold froze on the rope. Then there was a struggle. The two men, both of whom had been slightly under the mind cloak for some months, battled for it there. Constantine

143

had the advantage. He also had, as he found in the mortal combat, the stronger mind. And, after all, his was the hand on the rope. He forced it, and then he got free motion on it, and saw fear and doubt come into the face of the throttled man. Constantine hanged the man there until he was dead, and he was pretty sure that he had not got out of it, not got away. Probably there wasn't any such thing as going out of the body like that, though the man apparently had believed that there was. Constantine broke the man's neck to be sure of it.

"That takes care of the small end of the fog for a while," Constantine said. "And now I must go for the big end of it. Where next will I find an encounter to lead me inside the other half of this riddle?"

He went out from the old building and out from the alley, and he ran into the Five O'Clock Man in the street.

CHAPTER NINE

It was exactly five o'clock in the afternoon, so the fate clock was keeping more strict time as time ran out to its end.

"I know you, man," the Five O'Clock Man said to Constantine Quiche, and he seized him by the throat. It wasn't an unfriendly grasp that he put upon him, however, though it was firm. The man only wanted to delay Constantine and to talk to him.

"You were in Gethsemane with me, in the garden with the thirteen death trees," the man said. "You had a part in that Drama."

"I was in the Thirteen-Sided Gethsemane with you, yes," Constantine said.

"You were one of those who fell asleep when you should have prayed," the Five O'Clock Man said. "And now the country, which is our body and soul, will be destroyed."

"Which country is that?" Constantine asked.

"Why, it is Holy Sandaliotis. What other country is so preyed upon and destroyed? What other country has so many prodigies to announce its death?"

145

"What prodigies are those, friend?" Constantine asked him. "I hadn't heard of them."

"Oh, calves talk and sing dirges. Eagles catch fire in the air. Kittens hatch out of owl eggs and such. All the usual. I am the Agent Deserted, yet I have been the faithful agent all the time of my service. Now my primary is being struck dead. It is my root. Without it I must wither and die."

"What is your primary and who strikes you dead?" Constantine asked.

"Sandaliotis, in whose clay I was formed, is my primary. It is the cheap-shotters who strike her dead. Whenever a country or a world is brought down, it is the cheap-shotters who do it."

But the Five O'Clock Man himself seemed pretty vague about it, and he would mumble to himself a while.

"Some of them in the Thirteen-Sided Room didn't know that it was real," he said. "Some of them, and I am not sure of yourself, thought that it was only scenes in a filmed drama. But it was real and vital, and the world was weighed there, and perhaps lost. I was the patriot for a while, you know, and I learned the patriot's lines. I am a good patriot. That was before you were brought into the room. Then they changed me and gave me the role of the Agent Deserted. But all roles are the same when we come down to the end of the world."

He was silent for a little while, and he was nervous and discouraged.

"Sandaliotis is the last country in the world that a man would die for," the Five O'Clock Man said suddenly after a while, and this startled Constantine. They walked.

They came to the great Tarshish Tower which Deutero Scripture says is the exact model of the Tower of Babel. About the one or the both towers there has been some misunderstanding—"and it may as well be put right on this the last day of the world," the Five O'Clock Man said.

"The Towers were *not* designed to reach Heaven. The tapering and the setback clearly begins too lowdown for the towers to reach such prodigious heights, even by primitive standards. The Towers were designed to call Heaven down to Earth, to reach Heaven in that way.

146

And, in that way, they were always successful.

"The Tarshish Tower, with its thirteen-faced clock, has held congress with every sort of lightning and thunder. And it has itself been the Burning Bush. Do you not notice, now that I point it out to you, the trimmed bush shape of it? It is scarred and mottled with the old and loving fire, and it is imprinted with the divine wisdom. There are fire messages graven fine all over it in every tongue. It was to the Towers that the tongues of fire first came down with messages to Earth. A Tower is only a sharpened and tuned mountain, and this fire on the mountain has been the beginning of communication. Notice the variety of the faces of the tower, man."

There was a Roman Face and a Greek Face to the clock in the Tarshish Tower. There was a Carthage Face and a Jerusalem Face and a Babylon Face. There was a Han Face with older Chinese characters than they have now. There was a Damascus Face and an Alexandria Face and a Tarshish Face from the tower-givers themselves. There was the Sandaliotis Face or Host Face. Hosts in Sandaliotis who were waiting to greet and welcome out-of-town guests would always wait for them under the Sandaliotis Face of the Tower.

There was the Nial Face of Hibernia. There was a Middle American Face in the contorted stone motif of the Maya. And there was the Constantinople Face that was quite the most recent of them all.

Now this tower was not a new thing, and it was not made out of air. And yet there had never been anything like it in the small city of Cagliari or Sardinia. This was an encrusted-with-age tower.

"One hundred generations ago, an ancestor of mine died under the Roman Face of the Tower," the Five O'Clock Man said. "That is why our coat of arms shows a dead man at the bottom of the Roman Face. It was only a small thing, a scuffle with daggers, I believe. The cause of the fight is now forgotten. But a family likes to have an old device on its coat of arms.

"Strabo, writing during or near the lifetime of Christ described this Tarshish Tower at Ichnusa on Sandaliotis," the Five O'clock Man continued. "He described it just as it was then, just as it is now. Except for the Constantino-

147

ple Face, that is; it hadn't yet been ornated or dedicated. He wrote instead of the Illium Face which then made up the old count of thirteen and which now is no more."

There was a patina of time in layer after layer on this tower. And there were waves of contemporaneity swirling about the base of it. It was here that one might stand and sooner or later see every person in the world go by.

Surrounding the Tarshish Tower was the Roman Circus with the thirteen major streets leading into it. Some of these stoned streets had names that were very old. One of them, the Strato Napoleon, was comparatively recent. But there were vast accumulations of time in the whole area.

"Nine generations back, one of my ancestors was a cobblestone foreman when they gave the newness to the new-named Strato Napoleon," the Five O'Clock Man said.

West of the Roman Circus were the Ninety-Nine Fountains of Nekros with their reflecting pools. They were shockingly beautiful. Yes, they were made out of mere air and mere water, and one might almost believe that they had been made this morning. And they were made out of mere stone, but it was a stone that had been hammered by many centuries of water. And some of the fountain fittings were bronze, not brass and not iron.

"The water in several of the fountains is very old," the Five O'Clock Man said, "and some of the fish in the pools are of very ancient species. There are carp there that were given for the pools by the Emperor Hadrian of Rome, and they were of the oldest variety known in the Roman world. Now they are of the oldest variety known in the world entire."

Spray came into their faces from the fountains. It was fresh with the freshness of centuries.

"The fish are of old species, perhaps," Constantine said, "but how would the water be old? And who would know it if the water in one place were somewhat older than the water in another?"

"Oh, the age may be calculated by the patterns of the halide crystals in the water," the Five O'Clock Man said. "It has to do with the original shape of the halide-salt crystals formed from the dissolved minerals. There is a small difference in the materials of the crystals, between

148

those from old water and those from new, a difference in shape and pattern. Crystals follow time fashions, and these are old-fashioned.

"You will notice the several Etruscan Fountains in the old part, in the central cluster there," the Five O'Clock Man said. "It is almost forgotten that the Etruscans were among the earliest colonists of Sandaliotis. And you will notice a group of Egyptian Fountains there. But Egyptian Fountains do not leap up as other fountains do. They roll up regularly and sedately. There is a difference of mind set that accounts for this. There are all very storied waters and rocks here."

North of the Ninety-Nine Fountains was the big Basilica of the Húndred Martyrs, the oldest still-standing basilica in Christendom. It was the see of the Patriarch of Ichnusa. It had one hundred bells, each known by its tone to all the people of Ichnusa.

West of the Ninety-Nine Fountains were the splendid Italian Steps going upward in a flighty sweep. There was a bird-flight contour to them. They were a hundred meters wide and three hundred steps up (but they were three hundred and one steps down. The difference was due to a symbolism and warning. The way to Hell, it was said, is made up of a series of steps, three hundred up and three hundred and one down. And, one who follows them and does not break out of their trap, will go down and down lower yet, and he will believe himself to be maintaining a level.

The steps were made out of colored stones that looked painted and sometimes were not. They were blocks of garnet of different colors, and of rose-colored shale, yellow slate, old redstone, and green turquoise.

"It was only eighty years ago, in the time of my grandfather, that the Italian Stairs received a major repair," the Five O'Clock Man said. "Two million new stones were set into them to replace stones that were broken or too badly worn. The old replaced stones and fragments were hauled to a place west of the City where they filled up a miasmal swamp and heaped themselves up over it. Today it is still called 'The Field of the Old Stones'."

There were ten thousand bench loungers and step loungers on the sweep of the Italian Steps, and they were all of the Beautiful People. People as scenery! And they were Sandaliotis people and Sandaliotis scenery.

Constantine Quiche and the Five O'Clock Man sat on a bench and became bench loungers for a while.

"I am the Deserted Agent," the Five O'Clock Man said. "I am an agent for the 'Society for the Preservation of the Antiquities of Sandaliotis', and I am deserted because people have ceased to care about these antiquities and their own deep past. Our once-thriving society has dwindled in membership. Quite lately there has been introduced a feeling of contempt for the old things of our country and the wish to replace them with cheap-shot products.

"I say that this feeling has been 'introduced,' for it has come to us as a contrived and alien thing which I do not understand at all. This feeling has been building up for critical weeks and I have tried to warn people of it. But how do you warn of a feeling that cannot be weighed or held? I have known for some weeks that the destructive attitude would culminate on a target date, and that it would be today. And this morning, I felt it like the blast from a furnace. There are people who want to destroy our country completely, physically destroy it. They intend to do it today, or to do it before the night is over with tonight. They will let all the juice leak out of it first. And then the day remnants of it will break up into pieces of no weight at all and will drift away on the sea. These people want to make it that we have never been. I don't understand this at all. Do you?"

"A little bit, Five O'Clock Man, a very little bit," Constantine said.

"I tried to convey this threat in an impassioned speech in the Thirteen-Sided Room, but my warnings all came out as nothing talk. They had decided, at the Room, to kill me for what I had tried to say (for what I really did say, I believe, but they changed my words and my sounds with some kind of garbling mechanism that they had there). Then somebody else was killed in place of me. They were playing Corsican Roulette with the death selections for a while there, but I do not know who was spinning the barillet of the revolver. I am half sorry that it

150

was not myself who was killed. If my country does not survive this day, why should I want to survive it?"

"Do you understand what it would be like if there were an Island of Corsica, and if there were an Island of Sardinia, and if there was nothing else of Greater Sandaliotis?" Constantine asked.

"Yes, I have seen the maps of the Sandaliotis-Must-Be-Destroyed incendiaries, those hate people," the Five O'Clock Man said. "Oh, that is the great nightmare, that is the horrible premonition. The Destruction and Disappearance of Sandaliotis is in our national Epic, but we can no more understand it than we can understand our own death before it comes. Three great nations have sunk into the sea in the past, and there is the prophecy that the fourth great nation will disappear into the sea in the future. Do you believe that this future might be today or tonight, man?"

"Yes, I believe that it might be," Constantine said. "It may already have happened, quite a while ago. It is hard to set accurate termination dates on things."

"Yes it is. We tend to exaggerate the length of our sojourn on the earth," the Five O'Clock Man said, "and we tend to exaggerate the length of years of our nation, however old it may be. To the angels, we must be like ants who built a fine hill or hive or nation only this morning. But they thrive in it in their generations, and they develop an intense feeling for its arts and its history and its religion and its hearths. They become very patriotic about it all, those ants do. Have you watched ants during the destruction of their hive or hill? They are in a panic. They are in a desolation. And their burning patriotism cries out in voices that are too small for us to hear. The ants believe that they are destroyed in their incredible ancientness, and yet their reality was built only this morning. How long ago do you think that Sandaliotis was built, man?"

"Only this morning," Constantine Quiche said sadly.

The Five O'Clock Man began to moan.

"Sandaliotis will fall to the enemy whom we cannot even see," he said. "It will fall into the enemy the ocean, but the ocean is not of itself our enemy. We are an ant hill invaded by an army of evil and alien fire ants, and

151

they will not leave us one grain of sand upon another. I have felt these people for weeks (these alien, attacking, army ants) and I have seen them everywhere today. I cry out about it, and I am laughed at and told to shut up. But this is my land. This is my mother whom they intend to exterminate. I will *not* shut up! Help! Help! Help! Police! Guards! Street Sweepers! Assemble! Repel the attack! Protect our country that they are destroying right now!"

The Five O'Clock Man had become very excited, and he continued to roar out that persons were stealing and destroying his Land, Sandaliotis. By and by, officials or public servants of some sort came and took him away.

Well, what about that Five O'Clock Man? How could he have been an old citizen and patriot of Sandaliotis if there hadn't been any old Sandaliotis? Had the Five O'Clock Man been created very recently, complete with all his memories and fossils? When had he been created? Yesterday? Today?

If the realm of Sandaliotis had been created only today, but created at a great age and with all the built-in vestiges of that great age, what would happen when it was uncreated again? Could the uncreation go smoothly?

Constantine Quiche did a number of things then, such things as only the best detective in the world will do between five-thirty and seven o'clock on an evening. He may have blown the whistle on the biggest real-estate deal around, but that couldn't be quite certain till the payoff later that night. He figured out quite a few things. He analyzed several very strong and rank animals with only a hair or two of each of them to go on, and he made reports on them.

Then, just at seven o'clock in the evening, he ran into that 'agent' named John Seferino. This was under the Constantinople Face of the Tarshish Tower which, as every guidebook tourist will know, was in the middle of the Roman Circus.

"What were you saying last night that thieves were trying to steal, little Constantine?" Seferino asked him with easy mockery.

"Monaco," Constantine said cheerfully. "But they didn't get away with it. I thwarted them."

152

"Be careful whom you attempt to thwart tonight, Constantine," Seferino said. "This gets too big for you."

"It's the big end of the log that I'm looking for now, John. Do you know where I can find it?"

"Yes. I'm standing on it. Leave it alone. I told you that it was too big for you."

"Ah, John, I'm eaten up with curiosity. I just have to find out what this is all about."

"Tune in at nine-thirty tonight then, and have your curiosity satisfied."

"Tune in where, John?"

"Any station in the world, Constantine. It will be on them all."

Seferino had the pace and spring of a wild animal. He had a grinning ferocity that Constantine hadn't known in him before. And he had his great size; now it couldn't be overlooked, but Constantine had used to overlook it. And Seferino had never seemed to have much depth or strength or vigor before. Maybe he had only been popping ferocity pills now.

"You are to have dinner with me tonight, Constantine," Seferino said. "And we will have it at once. How would mushroom quiche please you for the opener?"

"Neither such opener nor such host would please me. I'm choosy."

"You have the right to be choosy as to the food. That's ancient custom. But you may not be choosy as to the host. You have the right to be choosy as to the food because you will be a condemned man eating his last meal ever. But I will be your host and your guard also, and you cannot be choosy there. You will come with me pleasantly now, or you will come with me with an iron collar around your neck and with my hand in the grip on the back of that iron collar. Did you ever notice what large hands I have, Quiche? Did you ever notice how large a man I am all over?"

"No, I never noticed it, John, and I do not now. To me, you are small within and small outside."

But Constantine went along pleasantly with that agent named John Seferino who was said to be from Istanbul. They went to Messina's German Restaurant, one of the finest in Ichnusa. This was just off the Circus, on the first

153

block of the Barbarossa Road which was one of the great streets that led into the Roman Circus from the North.

They waited for a moment in the little anteroom and had small glasses of red wine from the wine spiggot, and crab meat and cheese from the sideboard.

"Treasury men and bankers of the world are in a great scurry and fever right now," Seferino said. "So are mareschals of various countries, along with their figure-heads. They have got the big word, though the peoples of the world won't get it till nine-thirty tonight. This is the biggest hijack ever. Heads of countries are agreeing to it now, or heads of countries are rolling. But the new heads of the countries will agree. There is no way out of it."

"Why not?" Constantine asked. "That gun isn't loaded." It seemed like a clever thing to say, but Constantine wasn't quite sure what he meant by it.

"That gun *is* loaded!" Seferino cried furiously.. "And the world had better behave as if that gun were loaded, or it's going to be too bad for the world."

A waiter with moustaches and a walk like a walrus led them to a table. This was all in the middle of a burnished elegance that couldn't have been burnished only since this morning. Seven maids with seven burnishing brushes could hardly have done it in seven years.

"You were guessing, little detective," Seferino said. "You don't even know the name of the gun I'm talking about."

"Thibeau's Torpedo."

"Oh well, I suppose you do know it then. It's had lots of names. But you do not at all understand the great mor-phic aspects of it or its topological dynamism. There are several of these morphic entities, all very old. One of them will be an island in the Aegean Sea, for instance. Then it will disappear from there, and the next time it is seen it will be a Star in the Pleiades. And the next time after that that it is seen, it may be a peninsula on Earth."

"It is not identical with Sandaliotis," Constantine said.

"No, of course not," Seferino agreed. "It is, as they say, a gun, or a torpedo. It is (how frequent is the length in this particular area of mythology) three hundred miles long. It is fused, and it is loaded.

"Four other guests momentarily, waiter. And we will

begin with mushroom quiche. This man may want an opener in addition to that. Let him have it then."

Oh, what an overly civilized, urbane elegance was there! Could such an elegance be attained in less than a hundred thousand nights of high dining? Van Venduhouder, the famous epicure, has given the opinion that no restaurant anywhere can remain at top elegance for more than a hundred thousand nights (why, that's scarcely three hundred years!) without losing its edge. That is why there are no restaurants at the same time really old and really elegant in the world. (Van Venduhouder gave the opinion that such restaurants that time had run out on, those that have lost their glow and lift, should be wrecked and their areas converted to pastures for asses.)

The other four guests arrived. They were Salaadin and Regina Marqab. And Julien Moravia and Amelia Lilac.

"This will be a delight," Salaadin said. "It is the same enjoyable company as we had last night. What fate has arranged this, I do not know. I would have said that it would have been impossible for such a constellation to happen twice."

"This will be a delight," Regina said, and she kissed Constantine.

"Really, I believe that the needle stabs detract from it somehow," Constantine objected. "It is an ill custom in my opinion to mix such things. Whatever happened to the plain and simple girls with their sweet and needleless kisses?"

"I think maybe they all got trapped into something, Constantine my unburied treasure," Regina said. "If it weren't for the needle money that they pick up on the side, they just wouldn't get along at all."

"At least this dinner combination cannot happen again *after* tonight," Amelia spoke out of her lavender cloud. "After this dinner we break the plate so it can't happen again. You're the plate, Constantine. Constantine, my love and my subsidiary life, you have a bad habit of killing people, and for that you will have to be put under restraint of a perpetual sort. No, you will not be able to dine with us again. My own bonfire, you cannot dine ever again, with anyone.

"But do you not all agree that he is a delightful dinner companion now? See the slow fear flush spread over his face (aided just a little bit by the trepidation element from the infusion), and by the defiance (which really doesn't belong there). He is so like a boy, and I love him. I believe that the best suppers of all must have one member who will be dead before he comes to his next meal. This is the special sauce that the restaurants do not list."

"You *do* know that you're communicating, don't you, Constantine?" Salaadin asked.

(They had already begun on the mushroom quiche. Constantine had not countermanded it, so all assumed that it was his favorite supper opener.)

"You are communicating, Constantine, under intense amplification, to your superiors and to others who are tied into them. Every reaction of yours is going to them: the fear sweat of the palms of your hands, the skip beat of your heart, the crawling fright that courses along the whole surface of your skin, the burning trepidation thirst for the whole length of your tract. We have let the people at World Interpol know that this is the only way they can receive a communication from you. It will be effective. It will tell them that you are afraid and that they should be afraid."

"It is really a triumph of my own," Julien Moravia said, "but we have had a bit of forces-joining in several groups. It was Amelia who introduced the monitor and transmitter into you. The pretty man told you that it was an emitting locater. It is that, and it is much more. And Regina has now introduced a back-up transmitter into you. We hate failure when it can be prevented by simple precaution. Are we not thoughtful to help you arrange your thoughts and inmost feelings and reactions and then to communicate them for you, selectively and with our own reinforcing, when you are not able to communicate them yourself?"

"How is the marrying business, Regina?" Constantine asked. Naturally he was not frightened. He was the best detective in the world on one of the most diffuse cases to be found, and he could not permit himself the luxury of fear. Yes, his palms were sweating, and his heart was into the skip beat. The crawling monster was crawling all over

156

his surface, and the thirsting monster was prowling all his tract. But he wasn't scared.

"Oh, that wasn't myself who was doing all that marrying this morning," Regina said. "That was an unfocused person you refer to, she who was marrying every hour. That was a simulacrum of myself. We use a lot of simulacra in our doings."

"She was no simulacrum," Constantine said. "She was yourself with the veneer cracked. There was something very natural about her, Regina (oh, that very limited nature of her!). She was so amoral, so brainless, so skittish. That was yourself, Regina. But now you are taken over by a simulacrum. And possibly all of you others are taken over by them."

"I agree with Amelia that the best suppers must contain one member who is eating his last meal," Julien Moravia said. "(By the way, Constantine, that was not myself who harassed you in North Town this morning. That was a simulacrum of me.) I am something of an expert on these last-meal suppers. I have attended several thousand of them in my very long years. I attended that of Gautama (What a picky eater he was! He was really a drag on an otherwise excellent meal!). There was that of Socrates, that of Christ, that of Julian the Apostate (he was formally executed by his own soldiers, whatever other account you may have heard of it), that of—"

"He was *not* executed by his own soldiers. He is here present," Constantine said. "And he was on the cult circuit a while before he came here." No one seemed to understand what Constantine was talking about, except possibly Julien.

"—that of Count Dracula," Julien Moravia continued. "Oh, would it not be a fine touch if we had a sharpened stake of holly here on the table as we had then! That blood pudding that the Count ordered as the central dish of his last meal was rather good, but we are not blessed tonight with a victim with imagination. Then there was the last meal of the Bristol Strangler. Oh, so many of them! All of them had to die, you know, because they were meddlesome in one way or another."

They were into the salmon in aspic now. Constantine

157

hadn't gainsaid them, so the salmon had followed the mushroom quiche.

"You will get to see the transmission tonight, Constantine," John Seferino said. "You will be confined and fettered. You won't be able to move, and you will hardly be able to breathe; but you will be able to see the transmission. It would be lost irony if you weren't allowed to.

"You made lucky guesses, or you put lucky names to several things. That is the main reason for your sad and premature death. You even had the name of Thibeau's Torpedo. It isn't the right name, of course, but it is a going nickname for it. Know you then that the thing is real and that it's up there indeed! Know you then that Sandaliotis is a little bit real also, for all that it will crumble into nothing tonight. The Torpedo is a gun pointed at the heart of the world. And it will force the payment of the biggest ransom ever paid."

"That gun is not loaded," Constantine said. With perhaps exaggerated calmness he took a drink of—ah, it was that damned, antiquated, Falernum wine! It was the same as they had served the night before. It was not the best of wines.

"That gun *is* loaded!" John Seferino cried furiously.

"Constantine, my passion, my pet, my secondary heart," Amelia soothed it over. "I will apologize for that touch of anger from Seferino. Let us have only pleasure at this table. We will entertain your last repast with anecdotes that are both strange and true, and in particular we will give you the anecdote of the Torpedo in the Sky. We know that it is true because we have lived upon it."

"It is no more than an illusion," Constantine said, fishing for what they would tell him, but without much of a hook or line. "It is a Fortean Construct only. It has solidity, perhaps, and visuality sometimes. But these are both empty qualities with it."

"Oh, it's real enough," Julien Moravia said. "With this, as with very many other things, the unreal elements are not in contradiction to the real; they are in addition to the real. The Torpedo (what an awkward name for it!—but we would rather not speak its own blessed name) is a frequent station for out-of-the-body travels, but that doesn't preclude its being visited and inhabited by persons very much in their bodies. It is an illusion, yes, inasmuch as its appearance in the sky (when it sometimes does go visual) is not at all its true appearance.

"It is a Fortean Construct, yes, but that isn't near all that it is. It is a three-hundred-mile-long shaft of anti-matter, yes, and it can completely annihilate Earth on contact; and there is no defense against it, except the payment of the largest ransom ever. But it is much more than that, Constantine. It has been on Earth as an Island, it has been in the Pleiades as a Star, it has been in deep space as a space ship."

"No. Do not try to sell me that stuff. I am not in the used-torpedo business," Constantine said. "It is a Fortean Construct only, and the world has lost interest in Fortean Constructs."

"You have been to the Torpedo yourself, Constantine," Salaadin Marqab said. "You have been there in out-of-body travel. That is where you knew us, Regina and myself especially, and Amelia Lilac. And the others also. That is the only place that you ever knew any of us before last night."

"No. I knew you on Earth," Constantine said.

"Can you say where or when you knew us on Earth?" Salaadin asked.

"No, I can't," Constantine admitted, "and it worries me to have that hole in my memory."

"Let us fill up that hole in your memory then, Constantine, my other soul," Amelia Lilac said.

"About this out-of-the-body travel, it is in defiance of the laws of momentum. It takes off at broad angles (somewhat broader than three hundred and sixty degrees) and it changes direction easily," one of them was saying that, or a simulacrum of one of them at table. "And it arrives wherever it is going at zero elapsed time."

Yes, it now seemed to Constantine very much as if all the people at table with him in Messina's German Restaurant in Ichnusa of Sandaliotis were simulacra, and that these people here on the Torpedo (for Constantine now, by special dispensation, was both places at once) were the primary people. They were on the dazzling and direct Sky-Island that Constantine knew only by the code name

159

of Thibeau's Torpedo, and it was joltingly fundamental and material there. These primary people, though they were the same people as those he was dining with in the restaurant at the same time, were incomparably fierce in their sky manifestations. They were Sky-Animals, and they would raid anything up to a million times their size.

They were destroyers. They were annihilators. And it was all a numbing fear even to be with them. There was Amelia Lilac as she was on the other side of her veil passage. There was Julien Moravia in all his sinister deviousness, and there was John Seferino who came from a more distant Istanbul than the one on Earth. But Constantine Quiche *remembered* things on the Torpedo. He met those things again now, and they were more real than most settings on Earth. And there was an appetitive violence here that had no equal. This place *could eat you alive*. And any of the five persons here could eat Constantine Quiche instantly. Three Hundred Miles Long, the shaft, and it dwarfed Earth completely. One fifteen-thousandth the mass of Earth, and it could annihilate Earth, antimatter against matter, and make hardly a dent in itself. Then the power of the place overflowed.

There were sequences (though perhaps they were not time sequences at all; perhaps they were pre-emptory status only) that could not be put into words, or into visual forms at all, that did not correspond to any of the senses in their usual ways; and yet those sequences or whatever they might be called were brimming with absolute horror. They were clear on the other side of insanity.

(—only not quite.) From the other world of Messina's German Restaurant came a repeat of a phrase of Salaadin Marqab: "You do know that you're communicating, don't you, Constantine?" Yes, even on an out-of-the-body visit to the Sky Torpedo, Constantine was communicating the infectious and overwhelming horror that he found there. He was communicating it to World Interpol and to world. It was distilled terror that he was communicating, and (if it went uncorrected) it might possibly lay a deciding fear on the world.

A technical point broke through Constantine's mind then. A difficulty about being the best detective in the world is that pointed things are constantly sticking themselves through and out of the mind, awkward and imperiling. If the communication instrument were implanted in him, it was implanted in his body and blood somewhere. And if he were really on the Torpedo-in-the-Sky now, then he was here in an out-of-the-body experience. Thus he was not transmitting from the Sky Torpedo. He was not on the Sky Torpedo. He was still back in the restaurant and he was being given a mind ride by a quintet of very treacherous minds. He was being played for a mind patsy.

And then, after an unreasonable period of time, he was in the restaurant again in his own clarity.

"Where is my boar?" he asked crankily. "This is my last supper and I am supposed to have the best of everything. All of you are eating boar. Where is mine?"

"You ate it," John Seferino said, "and we are about finished."

"Did I transmit well?" Constantine asked.

"Excellently," Julien Moravia told him. "The world will believe that it is a technical first. And it will help to put the fear of annihilation into the world. In conjunction with the nine-thirty broadcast drama, it should convince the world to pay up."

"Is everybody ready?" John Seferino asked. How could that man be that big, and a person would not be conscious of it all the time? But whatever else of the visit to the Torpedo was faked, the incomparable ferocity of Seferino was real. He was a wild animal under a thin human pelt.

"Wait, wait," Amelia wailed. "Let me finish."

"You are a glutton, Amelia," Seferino said. Amelia finished like a real glutton then. But, after that, she pulled her lavender cloud around her again, as it were, and again she became perfect in all ways.

They were gathering up their things and themselves to leave, and settling the bill and such. There seemed to be a moment long enough for Constantine to volley a couple of them in. They had planted a transmitter in him. Then let him transmit something of his own.

"That gun's not loaded! That gun won't shoot!" he communicated with a mighty effort of his mind. He

161

prayed that his message would get through to World Interpol and to the world in general, to counteract some of the fear that he had been transmitting in spite of himself.

"Constantine doesn't look amenable enough. Something is wrong," Amelia said.

"I have a thing here for persons who aren't amenable enough," John Seferino vaunted. And there was an unpleasantness in the air.

John Seferino snapped an iron collar around Constantine's neck. He set one of his tremendous hands into the grip at the back of the collar and jerked Constantine to his feet. Then they were out into the dusk streets and moving with loud and happy chatter to cover up any awkwardness. They followed a way that was familiar.

They came to the building that had been called "The Dungeons of Tertullian" earlier that day. Now there was a sign on it: "Dungeon closed. Out of Business." They opened and went in, there being no door locks on Sandaliotis.

They took Constantine to the Thirteen-Sided Room and strapped him into his old place as the Thirteen O'Clock Man. They put the same noose around his neck, and John Seferino set a mechanism that would hang Constantine at twelve o'clock.

"I am mouth oriented myself," Amelia said. She stuffed something the size of a baseball into Constantine's mouth. It interfered with his breathing and with his swallowing. It interfered with everything about him. Amelia taped his mouth so that there was no danger of the thing popping out.

"It is only a small bomb, Constantine my puppy," Amelia said. "Really, I do love you like a puppy. It's primed and timed and will blow your head off right at midnight."

Salaadin and Regina and Julien Moravia were variously oriented, and they put their separate "bugs" into Constantine: but they are too bloody brutal to describe. But Constantine would die five different ways at midnight.

"The set will come on at nine-thirty, Constantine," Seferino said, "and you will be able to watch the drama that is a masterpiece of exhortation and intimidation and world blackmail. Admire it for its artistry if you cannot admire

162

it for its purpose. When it's over, entertain yourself as you think best till death comes for you at midnight."

They all went away and left Constantine writhing on the wall of the Thirteen-Sided room there. It was about a quarter to nine in the evening.

CHAPTER TEN

This was the time for introspection and not for transmission. It was not a time for transmission because all that Constantine could transmit was fear and apprehension; and fear and apprehension were the very things that certain opportunists were trying to heap up for all the peoples of the Earth for their disadvantage.

But there was much reason for fear and apprehension in the position of Constantine Quiche. He was trussed and bound and gagged and strapped up on a wall in a newly emptied building in a new part of a contingent city which, he strongly suspected, would suffer a pumpkin syndrome and cease to exist in a very little while. Apparatus was in place and ticking that would hang him, bomb his head off, and do three other things too bloody-brutal to mention to him at the hour of midnight, should his surroundings last even that long.

And moreover he was hardly his own man any more, what with all the piercings of the sophisticated needles that had introduced strange juices and apparatuses into him. An examination of reality was needed, but would that set the situation any straighter? Never had there been such a bunch of crumbling reality and pseudoreality around any man who was trying to order his thoughts and stabilize his world.

One sort of reality was that Constantine was perched several thousand feet high on a fill-in of green goop that was mostly air and coloring matter. The truth was that this green goop-filler of the newer part of the city and the newer part of the nation would not even support the weight of a man, much less that of a nation, except for the sustaining and feverish mentality behind it. And that mentality was of a crumbling, clay-footed sort, spinning and spun out of the illusion of the Lavender Cloud.

Constantine had had brushes with some of the people of this sustaining mentality, and they just weren't as mental as all that. They were showy projectionists and controlled hysterics, but they weren't mental enough to sustain a new nation for very long.

Constantine was choking to death. He was smothering. His heart and lungs were failing. All his limbs and viscera were cramping. Several different deliriums were disputing the area of his brain and his body.

"Hold onto this," he shouted to himself. "This is something like the facts of the case."

He was still a transmitting person with the communicating apparatus stuck into him, so these thoughts of his that attempted assessment were going out as well as his panic thoughts were.

"There is an unsubstantial mountain of air-foam, irregular in form and more than three hundred miles long, riding on a temporarily quiescent sea (the whole thing really resting on drifting oil slicks), and this air-foam goop is being presented as a magic new country of illimitable extent, and it is being merchandized by rogues as real estate, "the last free, fertile land in the world"; and the same goop is being merchandized over and over again to different buyers as real estate.

"This mass of unsubstantial air-foam will break up and disintegrate very soon, and everything on it will perish. This is part of one reality of an unreal sort.

"On a higher plain (higher in altitude only) there is a sort of beam or travant or strambolus drifting in the sky, and at present it seems to be about a thousand miles above Earth. It isn't known how much substance this beam has, or whether it is only a sort of beam in the eye, an optical illusion. Sometimes it is there to one sort of instrument and not to another sort. Sometimes it is on visual and sometimes it isn't. There have been a number of these 'sky mirages' known for quite a while, and mostly they *have* been regarded as mirages. Now another band of rogues, and some of them are the same rogues who are in on the inflated air-foam real-estate deal, are trying to fictionize this beam in the sky as a shaft of antimatter, under intelligent command, that is capable of destroying Earth or destroying whatever percent or part of it is decided upon. This would all seem hard to believe or to present, but the Illusion of the Lavender Cloud (a sort of hypnotic cult device) is over its presentation also.

"These are the facts as well as there are any uneroded facts in the case: there is a Fortean manifestation on the Mediterranean Sea, and it is largely artificial (mind and attenuated matter), and it is possible that all Fortean manifestations are artificial also. And there is another Fortean manifestation in the sky, at the altitude of about a thousand miles. And possibly there is a Fortean connection between the two things. But there is no reality in these things, only the mockery of reality.

"World Interpol, pick my message up and record it! You have equipment at least as sophisticated as have the Lavender Cloud people who put the transmitters in me. Take my appraisals here, and do not take my fears. But if you have another agent in the area, send him to me here and get me out of this."

Constantine felt a little bit better when he had summarized the crumbling facts of the case into crumbling words in his own mind, and when he had, possibly, communicated a little of them to World Interpol. If they were transmitted, either to World Interpol or to the world at large, so much the better.

He wasn't transmitting nearly as much of the "world-is-time-bombed" fear now as he had been, not as much as the rogues who had put him there had intended that he should transmit. Even though he was gagging on the time bomb in his own mouth, he was downgrading that fear and trying to transmit explanations instead.

The thirteen-sided room had not changed greatly since

166

early afternoon. The rats were gone, that's about all. Probably they had been sold. The panoramic eye that had been in the ceiling of the room now seemed dead and blank, though probably the big camera was still there and could be flicked on in an instant. Or maybe it also had been sold or pawned.

As before, there was very little light in the room, and its origin was hard to determine. Of the writhing snakes that were the superscriptions above the torture niches on the wall, most of them were asleep or in slow writhe. 'Gone to supper' was scribbled on the wall in a place where one snake was absent, but that was more likely written by a joker than by a snake. The markers on the thirteen clock faces moved very slowly. It was still eight minutes till nine o'clock.

The best detective in the world fell asleep. He slept restfully for seven or eight minutes. And then he was awakened by a great booming brass voice with its own cymbal accompaniment.

"Oh, *why* do you insist on introducing farce into everything that you do, Mr. Chataigneraie!" it was the Director calling out. "The market for farce is gone, and in any case I am about bankrupt and out of business. I thought I could recoup my fortune today; and I have done a great amount of business, and shot a number of films of one sort or another. If I can collect, I am in the clear and running again. And if I cannot collect, then I am sunk. Let me tell you something, Chataigneraie," (Oh, why did the Director still call him Chataigneraie, which was not his name?) "The people who talk in the biggest money, the people who curl your hair with their ostentation of trillion-dollar deals, those people are likely to be very slow pay. Watch out for them!

"That's good though! That's perfect right there! You're good, Chataigneraie. That's as fine a farcical-escapist bit as I've ever seen. I wish I were filming a 'Great Escape' film today. I'd use your act. I'd make a place for it somewhere. I wish vaudeville were back and I was in the middle of it. I'd surely find a place for your skit then.

"I love that touch of the ticking bomb in your mouth, and the way that you bug out your eyes and writhe and strangle. You have a true gift for pathos-comedy. Oh, I

167

suffer with you, I die with you, I laugh with you! Oh, your antic of having me arrested earlier today was also rare humor, Frenchman. I never forget a really choice bit of humor like that.

"I had just come back to see if I had left any cigarettes and liquor here when I was riding high today. Ah, these dregs are good when you're down to the dregs! I'm out of business now and broke, but I'll be back into business later tonight if I can collect on a couple of bills. Can I see the act though? Can I see how you really do escape from that one? It looks impossible, with the straps already so tight that they cut into your flesh and send the blood running down from their cuts. So realistic! I've always been a buff for the great escape artists, especially the comic ones.

"Oh, those bugged-out eyes of yours! And the way you make the veins in your throat stick out! Oh that bomb in your mouth, what a touch! Wow! And the slow sizzle and smoke of it, that is the master's touch. You are Prometheus bound to the crag with an apple in your mouth like a pig! And the apple is the explosive one of the family of fire. Oh yes, I'm sure you intended all the many levels of meaning. Great comics always do.

"Oh, you won't show me the escape than? Really, I don't blame you for that. I wouldn't show it either without an advance, but I really can't book you. I have nothing at all going. If I run into another producer or director, I'll tell him that you're down here with a great farcical escape act. Tootle, Chataigneraie!"

Oh great palpitating horror! That brassy Director left the place and closed the door after him. He went away and left Constantine there to die. That Director had brass brains! Constantine almost wished that he hadn't had him sent to prison that afternoon, for an hour or however long they keep such men. Possibly he resented it, and possibly the brass head had put it clear out of his mind. It would have been better if the Director hadn't come by for that brief moment and raised Constantine's hopes of escape. The desolation of this new-hope-dashed drove him all the way down. What were the chances of anyone else happening to come along to this deserted building before midnight?

But then the Director came back in.

"Chataigneraie, your act bothered me!" he said in his brassy boom. "I said to myself 'That act's too good. What if it isn't an act?' It is an act, isn't it, Chat—? No, I see now that it isn't."

So the Director unbombed and unfused and unnoosed Constantine, and unstrapped him from the niche in the wall there. He took him down and out of the former Dungeons of Tertullian, and to some small rooms that he had rented for that day. He bathed his wounds and galls with honey and oil and made him feel better.

"You're emitting," the Director said to Constantine when he had made him comfortable and when Constantine had somewhat recovered from his ordeal. "I am like a finely tuned instrument and I can tell when people are emitting. There is a device which may have been plaecd in you without your consent, and yet you are doing well with it, bending it a little bit to your own purpose. You give warnings. And it may be that you are tipping some scales."

"Not enough, I'm afraid," Constantine said. "There is a double band of rogues about, and they fleece the people individual and corporate. The biggest real-estate fraud that has ever been is persuading many thousands of agents to pay over the life money of many millions of persons for land that is only temporary and that has only a tentative existence here anyhow. And another band of rogues (closely connected to the first band, I believe) is hijacking the whole world with the threat to destroy this whole world. And they are taking their intimidation direct to the people with a planetary blackmail-threat program at nine-thirty tonight on every station in the world. It would gag a buzzard."

(Constantine had been talking for the Director, for World Interpol, and for World Itself, for anyone who would listen.)

"What is little known is that buzzards gag rather easily," the Director said. "But they do not give up easily. They will tackle the same piece of carrion again and again and again until finally they will keep it down one more time than they will bring it up. I've always admired this quality of persistence in buzzards, and indeed I have a lot of buzzard qualities in my own person.

169

"As to the presentation tonight, the world hijack explication and threat, I'm rather proud of it. When we have it on, as we will in a very little while, please note the credit lines. I am listed as Director of the piece. Most of the material comes from the double-rogues as you call them, but I shaped it up. I turned it into a piece of extraordinary art.

"I'm having a guest in to watch it with me. Possibly you know him. He'll be here very soon. He is a man of shimmering genius whose talents complement my own to a great extent. Ah, he is a master, a master, a master!"

"What sort of master is he?" Constantine asked.

"Well, actually, he's a master forger," the Director said. "He had gone back to Italy after completing a job here, but for some reason he returned here again later in the day. Sandaliotis is a temptress who is hard to refuse. And you tell me that you are not Mr. Chataigneraie at all? You tell me that, instead, you are Constantine Quiche, the greatest detective in the world? Oh, what a loss! Anyone can be the greatest detective in the world, but who else has such a consummate gift for farce as Mr. Chataigneraie? Or as yourself when mistaken for Chataigneraie? Oh I can never forget your bugged-out eyes and the apple bomb in your mouth in your great final act in the Thirteen-Sided Room. A great comic was lost in you, Quiche."

"Thank you, Director. And now I want to ask you (but how can one ask it in the deteriorating circumstances), are you a citizen of Sandaliotis?"

"By my soul, yes!" cried the Director in brassy enthusiasm. "But by my body, um, no. For Sandaliotis is a total illusion, but I am at home only in total illusion. It is what I am a citizen of. Oh, the great scenery, the great props, the wonderful facades, the fine effects, the convincing airiness! This is probably the finest day ever for those of us who believe in the 'Sandaliotis Effect.' Oh the shouting colors of our new cities today! Oh the glittering green pastures of our new countrysides! I have had a hand and a brain in almost every effect here, and I am sorry that most of them will be gone tomorrow. That's theatre though. There will be other effects, of course, and other

170

gala days. But for convincing and thrilling visual spectacle, today would be hard to beat."

"Had you a hand and a brain in the Italian Stairs?" Constantine asked.

"It chokes me up even to speak of them," the Director said, "they are so beautiful. Yes, I *directed* them. Cotton candy would be a hundred times as substantial, but he who eats cotton candy will hunger again. Gushing water is a hundred times as rigid, but he who drinks gushing water will thirst again. One who has enjoyed the Italian Stairs will have food and drink to last forever, even though the Stairs themselves will be gone tomorrow. We will go out and look at them by moonlight tonight one last time, myself, and my coming guest who also had a great part in their execution, and yourself. We will go out and luxuriate in them after the all-stations blackmail has been heard. There are only two things that subtract from the perfection of the Stairs: they will be gone tomorrow, and I haven't been paid for my labor on them.

"But tomorrow they will have become, in the world of the Roman poet Horace, who summered on Sandaliotis several years (it's cooler here than in Italy in the summertime), *'Pulvis et Umbra,'* Dust and a Cloud. Ah, here is the guest now."

The guest who was the Master Forger Angelo DiCyan came into the modest rooms of the Director with a sweep of grandeur that had to be a forgery. People in life are never that grand.

"Mr. Quiche the Detective, you have met the Master Angelo?" the Director asked.

"I have met him and have given a commission to him," Constantine said. "And I suspect that he has betrayed me, or intends to. He dipped his hand with mine into the snails."

"There is something wrong with that?" the Director asked with a bit of incredulity. "Surely it is the nature of a Master Forger to betray. And surely it is the nature of the Best Detective in the World to be betrayed. And I know that you would not have people, and especially yourselves, violate their own nature. As to the snails, that is a custom on Sandaliotis and nowhere else on the World, that the betrayer and the betrayed should dip their

171

hands together into the snails, and that the action should be quick and unnoticed. It is a little boorish of you to take notice of it, Mr. Quiche."

"I think so too," the Master Forger Angelo said. "Ah, but I am glad that you are taking your betrayal with such bad grace, Constantine Quiche. It makes me feel that I have done my job as it should be done. Actually I didn't get as much as I intended to for selling you to the rogues. And I don't suppose that they got as much on you from me as they expected. But I gave a pleasantly false shape to it, and the betrayal action isn't yet completed. There may be still one more item in my betrayal of you, Constantine Quiche, if the circumstance shall arise. If it does arise, I will betray you in that detail also. I would make it up to you in some other way if I could, in some way that wouldn't cost me money."

"Make it up to me in information then, Angelo," Constantine said. "I am still dealing with an incomplete case, though now it will have to be judged in its incomplete form. But I don't want to *leave* it incomplete, and you are on voucher from World Interpol to help complete it. Is there any real substance, true or false, to the Greater Sandaliotis that has appeared here today? Is there any real substance to the Torpedo, for that matter?"

"I told you this afternoon, Constantine, that Sandalitois was genuine, as far as it goes: and that it goes for a very little ways, and then it stops completely. But, lad, we have put a frosting on that little come-and-go cake! We have really covered the genuine but contingent land with forgeries for this gala show day. Every kind of forgery."

"Every kind of forgery? You have forged people? How about the Five O'Clock Man?"

"People? Of course we have forged people. The Five O'Clock Man? Of course we forged him. He has been one of our more effective characters, and he is still catching on big around town. There is a 'Free the Five O'Clock Man' campaign going on at this instant. I signed my support to it myself. I just couldn't resist an appeal like that. And we mostly forged him out of nothing at all; only a little bit of the local base clay, that's all we had to use. But how human we forged him to be! What a patriot! What a lover of 'The Eternal Verities'! (Those eternal

172

verities were not there for him yesterday and they will not be there for him tomorrow.) What a devoted antiquarian he is! What a feeling he developed for the mellow old flavor of Sandaliotis! He is so well done that it is almost impossible to tell that he isn't genuine."

"Isn't there any human element in him then?"

"Certainly there is. Would we forge a human character by using a nonhuman base? I said that we had made him from a local base clay. He was a poor Sardinian workman, and we forged him into a poor Sandaliotine patriot and antiquarian. A little concoction, 'Angelo's directional determinant,' poured into his brain was about all we needed to use on him. And then we proceeded to sculpture him from the inside. And it worked. In all honesty, Constantine, is he not magnificent?"

"He was magnificent, Angelo. He may not be now when he is imprisoned and persecuted beyond his limit. How many such persons did you forge?"

"Oh, about a hundred. It doesn't take very many if they are vivid. They are constructed to be doubt dispellers. One encounters such an empassioned person and says 'There *has* to be a Sandaliotis! This person is the burning tribute that there is. He loves it so much that it has to be.' We gave to all the one hundred or so human forgeries a directional or magnetic orientation also. They would always be where they would be the most effective. They were drawn to such places by a sort of magnet, and then they drew attention to themselves with a similar magnetism.

"About the Torpedo. I have done work on that also. I haven't done as much work on it as on Sandaliotis because there just wasn't as much work to do there. But my own work and everything else about the Torpedo is still hanging until we see whether the big blackmail will take effect. We don't know whether it is successful until we know whether we are going to be able to sell it. And it would be a violation of my ethics to make any premature disclosure as to the reality of the Torpedo."

"It is time for the Big Hijack Blackmail Presentation Program to begin," the Director said. "And, if everything goes wrong, this might well be the last movie ever in the world."

173

"No, I don't think so," the Master Forger said. "But it will be good. Our own contributions to it will insure that."

The program came on.

Power, speed, impact, percussion, momentum, bestial ferocity, savage attack, slashing drive that would cut anything in half, that was the impression first made by the spokesmen of the Sky Torpedo. These creatures (the odds teetered between their being human or unhuman) came through as calculatingly insane destroyers. The whole thing showed the unfocused destructiveness and the mad irresponsibility, and the absolutely direct aim at a staked-out and self-immobilized target—Earth. The creature John Seferino (finally now, it came through just how big a creature he was) appeared as frightening in his menace. The Violet Dragoness (she may have been the dynamically chubby Amelia Lilac herself under all those dragon veils, Constantine thought) was ruthlessness itself. This was an animated horror announcing itself and preparing for instant action.

"The Japanese are still the best on the horror-movie circuit," Constantine said, to have something to say, and to show that he was educated in these things.

"The Japanese are *not* the best," the Director boomed with anger in his sounding voice. "*We* of the International Floating World are the best, and this that you will see now is the best horror movie ever made. Both Angelo and I have worked on Japanese horror movies, and both of us have worked on this one, and we know. What other horror movie would have a live chance of blackjacking the whole world in open combat?"

It was the parts that struck directly into the mind by bypassing the conventional senses that were the most devastating. It was the subliminals and the hyperliminals that were scoring in the most telling fashion. There were the voices going on all the time, delineating the threat in sharp and arrogant metallic words, and there were the harmonics and subliminals of those same voices hammering the points in.

Earth would be destroyed if it did not pay one trillion dollars ransom. It was so outrageous a proposition that it should have sounded funny to somebody somewhere. Ap-

174

parently it didn't. This was a clear and targeting proposition, and it did not sound amateurish the way it was put. There were checks and guarantees. Earth would be put into a sort of slavery, but it could be called a benevolent slavery if it would make people feel better. Earth in that constricted state would be kept under the gun for exactly one year, starting tonight. The transfers of funds would be made in various forms. It was all very professional in its phrasing and proposed implementation. There would be about a hundred-thousand different boodle-collections, all huge. Tailing or recording would be tantamount to resistance and would be sternly dealt with.

"It is too cumbersome," Constantine said. "It couldn't stand up for a week even if it were started. Certainly it could not stand up for a year. People would be onto it soon. Time would work against it."

"It is *not* too cumbersome," the Master Forger Angelo said, "and time will work for it and not against it. I am the author of the shape of that part of the proposition, and I know what I'm doing. If it is accepted tonight, even with the reservations that it won't stand up and that it can be punched full of holes, and with the 'let's get out from under it today and take a good look at it tomorrow' reservation, if it is accepted tonight on any terms, then it is accepted forever.

"It will be easier to keep it imposed every successive day. Do you not understand the 'Exponential Growth of Sustained Hypnosis Effect'? It was once in folk form as 'Nothing succeeds like success'. That is what we are working with here. The acceptance factor is strengthened every moment that it is accepted. It is out of such acceptance that reality is made. We will arrive to the reality that Earth will pay tribute to the Torpedo.

"Have you some idea of playing a hand in the challenging of these propositions, Constantine? Be careful. You do not know everything that came into you by the sophisticated needles. And you certainly do not know everything that came into you by those pills that I gave you to counteract the infusions of the needles. You are a very vulnerable man, Quiche."

Then, while the great overcurrent of impression flooded in with its naked savagery and threat, the scientific sup-

175

port for the successful attack was marshaled; the probability of success was laid out reasonably and convincingly. Science was one of the things that the peoples of the world understood. Some of these nonsensical (in the meaning of by-passing the conventional senses for intuitive encounter) assaults were understood only by the emotional. But the scientific assaults were instantly comprehended by almost everyone. And the mathematical implementation of that scientific assault, why that was like gobbling buttered nubbins right out of the field. The people went for it.

This seemed like the clincher. Even Constantine felt himself convinced by the unarguable, interlocked mathematical movements that the Torpedo was the clear and present threat to the world. He knew that it wasn't, but he was almost convinced of it.

"There is no way out of it," he said. "How do you disprove proof? The mathematical exposition is so clear to everyone, and so devastating to any other theory of explanation, that the premise must be accepted. Unless there should be a misdirection at so high a level as to be almost beyond belief, unless there should be an absolutely master forger involved in this mathematical presentation—" And Constantine stopped his words there. He felt rather than saw the sly grin of the absolute Master Forger Angelo. But what of the several billion viewers in the world who hadn't been close enough to sense the sharp edge of Angelo's grin?

Oh, the Torpedo-is-Unstoppable faction was leading on points by a large margin, but extraneous voices and comments began to cut through the unanimity. How had they got past the program filters?

"Actually, the Sky Beams are largish and rather stupid animals," a conversational voice came out of the program somewhere. "Oh yes, a fellow or a group could have one of them under rather loose control. In former years, the more dashing sportsmen used to have them fight as dogs are fought. There was a secret arena where they were fought. There would be very high bets on these 'dog fights' between different sky shafts. But the fights themselves weren't very much. They sky beams were too listless and lacking in fight. They couldn't do hurt to any-

176

thing except another 'dog,' another sky beam. They are on a different level from people or from material objects.

"No, no they are *not* made out of antimatter. Somebody is trying to take advantage of the gullible with such statements. They are made out of nonmatter. There's a difference. Nonmatter can't annihilate anything except itself."

This casual little bit that seemed almost like a snippet of a private conversation may have caused some slight confusion on the presentation.

"What voice was that cutting in with such nonsense about dog fights?" Angelo DiCyan there in the room wanted to know. "I should know that voice."

"What voice was that cutting in with such a silliness about dog fights?" John Seferino, a creature on the dramatic presentation itself, wanted to know. "I should know that voice, and I think I do. It's the voice of a man who will die quite soon."

That naked threat of reprisal may have got up as many backs as it knocked down heads. Actually, it had been the casual voice of the best detective in the world, but however had he managed to project it onto the program presentation?

Could there possibly have been a lessening in the momentum of the great hijack program then? The mathematics and the science of it were shown again to demonstrate that the Sky Torpedo *was* antimatter, and that it was not nonmatter; to demonstrate that it *could* annihilate the Earth in an instant, and that its harm was not restricted to other dogs or to other sky beams.

There was no lessening in the *intensity* of the presentation, but there may have been a little flaking off in the quality of the conviction carried.

Then a dog bomb hit the program. How were the unauthorized voices getting onto the presentation anyhow?

"Hogan's Bobsled challenges Tibeau's Torpedo to a dogfight!" rang a proclamation over every station in the world. In the background was the weird sound of little aggies laughing, a blood-freezing sound. But that was all.

But can even the mathematical equations that are so dear to the people suffer such an interruption without abrasion? And can there be an overkill in going over the pertinent mathematics of the case again and again? Look out! Here comes another dog bomb.

"Schnitger's Steamboat challenges Thibeau's Torpedo to a dogfight!" rang out the new confrontation, and there was a sound a little bit like German students giggling into beer steins.

But the presentation found new momentum then, though it sounded a little bit forced. Iron voices were telling it 'the way it is,' and they were only an inch from leaden voices telling it the way it is. And everyone was waiting for another jolt. There would be another, however frantically the jamming engineers tried to prevent it. Dog bombs always come in threes.

"Paderewski's Porpoise challenges Thibeau's Torpedo to a dogfight," came the tin gauntlet whanging in, and somewhere there was the eerie sound of Poles laughing.

The program continued for another forty-five minutes of intensity. It ended with truly terrifying threats. And even the ensuing silence was filled with direful echoes. Well, who had won?

The Director, the Master Forger Angelo, and the Greatest Detective in the World, Constantine Quiche, all walked out of the Director's modest rooms and into the moonlit streets.

"The decision will be booed," the Director said, "but I believe that it will have to be given to the Torpedo People, and the world will have to knuckle under. The Torpedo people won every round on points, and they scored all the knockdowns. And dog bombs don't even go into the official scoring."

"I don't doubt that the Torpedo advocates have won," the Master Forger Angelo said. "So we will be living under their dominion for a while. I would feel better about it if they paid their bills though. Just how will we force them to pay us when they have a strangle on the world?"

"Yes, I keep telling you, Grishwell, that the gun's not loaded, that the gun won't shoot," Constantine was saying into a kiosk telephone. "Get that over to everybody and stop the nonsense. Don't pay. Don't pay any attention to the panics. That gun won't shoot!"

178

Then he hung up on Grishwell.

The three men walked over to see the Italian Stairs for the last time, in the moonlight. In an hour or so, the Italian Stairs wouldn't be there any more.

It was just eleven o'clock at night.

CHAPTER ELEVEN

They lounged on three great benches on the Italian Stairs. They looked up at the moon and the moonlit air that was about as substantial as the glorious sweep that they were on. They could see Thibeau's Torpedo in the sky also, and the giant beacon lights that someone had lighted on the three-hundred-mile length of it.

"The beacons on the Torpedo were my idea," the Director said. "Whatever effect they have in the intimidation or the hijack, they are still good theatre. I like them."

A man came by. He said that the main group of real-estate agents, the hundred thousand of them who were buying for their four-hundred-million clients around the world, were junking the deal. Too many things were happening. Too many pot holes were developing in the land, and persons were going through them and falling screaming hundreds and even thousands of feet to the ocean that was below the false land. A number of such cases had given a bad flavor to the whole enterprise. The great real estate heist was on the queer.

"I never thought much of it anyhow," the Director said. "I did work for it, but I never had any faith in it at all. It was childish beyond belief. My only regret is that I wasn't able to collect for my work. How could anybody ever have taken the great real-estate heist on Sandaliotis seriously?"

"The whole deal was a forgery," said Master Forger Angelo. "I wouldn't have minded that, but it was never a viable forgery. The whole thing is too ridiculous even to talk about."

"Would it have been so ridiculous if the real estate dealers *hadn't* pulled out at the twenty-third hour?" Constantine asked. "After all, they were fooled on it all day long. Would it have been so ridiculous if the pot holes hadn't begun an hour or two too early and so queered the deal?"

"Oh no, if it worked it wouldn't have been ridiculous," Angelo said, "but now it is. If it had worked, I would point out that I was in on it from the very beginning, as I was. Even as a failure, it isn't nearly as ridiculous as it would have been if we hadn't worked on it. Without us, it would really have been ridiculous all the way."

One of the girls who had been in Amelia's 'Garden of Pleasures Suite' came by.

"Oh hi," she said to Constantine. "I thought they'd killed you. I see that they haven't. You were wrong on one of the things they were guying you about. You didn't stop them from stealing Monaco. They really have stolen Monaco, but that's all they've gotten away with. The Monaco owners traded their whole principality for a hundred times the area here on Sandaliotis. And the trade's been completed. It's the last real trade that went through before things started to fall apart. It was shot full of holes at the end, but those Monaco people didn't back out. 'At a hundred to one, you've got to expect a few holes in your land,' they said. So you didn't stop them, but you were right in your first idea. They did steal Monaco and they have it now. Your friend Regina Marqab is princess of Monaco now, but there is some doubt who the prince is going to be."

"Why are you not with those victors in Monaco?" Constantine asked.

"Oh no, I busted with them all," the girl said. "We just couldn't get along. They'll kill me yet if they find me."

"Hadn't we better get off of Sandaliotis, or at least

181

down to old Cagliari?" Constantine asked. "Old Cagliari is only about a dozen blocks west, and then down, down, down in a valley. It should be safe there. It will still be old Cagliari in Sardinia after Sandaliotis has disappeared."

"Don't trust to it too much," the girl said. "That's where I come from. The people in Cagliari have always been plagued by rocks falling on their heads and killing them. Outsider people said it was all imagination, but the rocks always killed a lot of the people in Old Town anyhow. There will be another bunch of them falling on the town in a little while. It's Sandaliotis they always fall from, every time there's one of these little changes."

"Hadn't we better get somewhere," Constantine said. "Everything here will crumble just any time now, and there isn't anything between us and the old ocean except a little bit of green-colored air-foam. And air-foam always melts away when the mentality behind it gets tired."

"We have a plane waiting," the Director said. "I believe there will be tremors to warn us first. I like to wait till the last possible moment. It's more theatrical that way."

"How high are we?" Constantine asked.

"Quite high. A thousand meters," Angelo said. "We're much higher than Old Town. This is the Show Place, the City Built on a Mountain (and what is this mountain built on?), the cynosure of the eyes of the real estate agents, the eye buster of the gillies. And here is the beautiful heart of it all. I am proud of my own part in this. This is the Great Forgery that has no original in the same medium, though its grand design is to be found both in epics and in certain underwater meadows and constructions and caves. This is art. If you don't understand that, then take out your eyes and set them aside, for you are not worthy to look on this."

"I understand it a little bit," Constantine said. "I will keep my eyes."

A young boy came to Constantine on his bench there.

"I have a message for you," he said. "Madam Lilac says that she will meet you again in a very little while, deep below, deep deep below."

"Thank you," Constantine said. "I hope that I will not be able to keep that appointment."

182

"I'm going home," said the girl who had once been in the 'Gardens of Delight Suite.' "I'm going down to the Old City if I have to fall down there. It isn't so great a distance down as all that except that all those winding scenic roads that go down there are falling away and getting gaps in them. But I will find a way down."

She left them there.

Portions of the Italian Stairs were collapsing now and dropping people to screaming death.

"Hadn't we better find safety somewhere?" Constantine asked. "Where is the plane?"

"A bit above here," the Director said. "The Ichnusa Special VIP Port is the highest place in the city. I always like to cut these things as close as possible myself—a sense of crisis is absolutely imperative for best artistic effect, and I wouldn't have it any other way—but we'll go on up now if you're nervous."

They started up other sweeping, outdoor stairways, much higher and steeper than the Italian Stairs but not nearly so wide. These were now full of gaps and quite dangerous. But the Director didn't seem to worry about that, and Angelo didn't.

"I don't believe that Angelo and myself will break through the air-foam," the Director was saying, and they were practically climbing up night clouds and moonlight now. "Walking on air is an art, and both of us are artists. But I could see how a detective might fall through the stuff. I doubt if the detective arts are sufficient to sustain one where it really gets thin."

"I doubt it too," Constantine said. "It's like walking in fog, and all the breaks in the fog are underfoot, and there's no ground there anywhere. How much further and higher is it?"

"Not much further, not much higher," the Director said. "Do you believe that we have somehow lost a battle here, Quiche, with our experiments in Sandaliotis-making and in illusion construction?"

"I don't know who has lost," Constantine said. "I have, with one more false step."

"No, we haven't lost," the Master Forger Angelo intervened, "for there has been no battle here, nor any program or purpose. Those things will be unsheathed the

183

next time, or the time after that. This has all been a little practice session, a manoeuvre. We have been seeing what we can really do. We have found that we can do with the world as we will. Some of the younger rogues want to have fun and torture out of it, and that is the privilege of the young, I suppose.

"But very soon we will decide what we really wish to do with the world, now that we have found that it is so easily dealt with. Have you any other loose ends, Constantine?"

A section that Constantine was about to step on fell away, and it showed emptiness all the way down to the Sea. He stepped on another section.

"My Sassari car," he said. "How could it have been made in Sassari of Sandaliotis?"

"Your Sassari car is a little bit like my Sassari airplane here," the Director said, and they had suddenly arrived at the beautiful plane, already fired up and breathing with power. "They aren't very substantial. They are a lot of mentality-sustaining illusion poured over a little bit of material. But you rode in your auto, and we can ride in the plane."

"Let's get in it quickly," Constantine said. "This business of walking on crumbling clouds is a killer."

"Have you ever wondered to which Sandaliotis clan or totem I belong, Constantine?" Angelo the Forger asked.

"No. No. I've never heard the names of any of the clans or totems except the dolphins and the sardines. Let's get in the plane and fly to safety."

"I belong to the totem of the Lilac Snails," Angelo said. "And we of the Snails are all traitors. The last part of my betrayal of you is that I hinder rather than help you to escape if I'm in that position. And I'm in that position now."

Angelo stamped on a section of the air-foam of which the Ichnusa Special VIP Port was constructed. That section broke away and sent Constantine Quiche tumbling through space, falling, falling.

He would have fallen screaming as the other people had been doing, but somehow his voice didn't seem to be operative. And he couldn't reason clearly about his situation.

"Why are my hands clawing at my belly?" he asked. "What is the matter with them anyhow? They should find something better to do than that while I am falling to my death."

But the hands knew what they were about. They loosened the parachute and sent it streaming up behind (which was above) him. And pretty soon it opened with a jolting force.

"Thanks, Grishwell," Constantine said. He was alive and descending through the illimitable night, and he could not yet tell what sort of land, or more probably water, was below him.

Several of the Ninety-Nine Fountains were still leaping from their bronze nozzles in the sky, but their pools were all fallen and gone, and so was all else of beautiful central Ichnusa City.

"Loose ends, loose ends," Constantine said. "Could I short splice any of them while I strain my eyes to see what is below me?

"How was the dead man, my look alike, identified as Constantine Quiche by his fingerprints? There is only one answer to that puzzler. He wasn't. He hadn't been so identified, but one of the policemen said that he had been. He said that because Amelia Lilac had put it into his mind to say it. She had just been there, because she was the one who had killed my lookalike. We were two lookalikes on the case because vast World Interpol sometimes puts two lookalikes on a case to confuse the enemy."

It was water below, churning, foaming shoal water, and there was a queer center area to it, not so clattering, but louder with a sullen roar.

"Two of us were put on the case and each of us was tagged as the Best Detective in the World. Well, which one of us *was* the Best Detective in the World?

"Myself. I'm still alive, and he's dead.

"But how many more seconds can I say that I'm still alive?"

Things were getting a little bit more plain below, more wildly plain, perhaps.

"And what was that business about my killing Amelia

185

at Marseilles, and her being alive down the road an hour later? How was that really—Oh, oh, no time for that."

It was a sort of vortex of water in the center of that extent of churning and foaming crash water. It was a vortex, a maelstrom, and a very huge flow of water was plunging down into it. It seemed to be colored water in the moonlight, and all-sized pieces of air-foam were riding on it.

Constantine could control the direction of his descent a little bit by tugging on the ropes of his chute. Sure he could send himself down the vortex to drowning death, or he could send himself to pounding death in the shoal water. Or he could aim for—

"Mighty slim chance there," he said. "Mighty steep odds against it. But the two main ones, which one?"

What had the boy said to him at his bench just before the bottom began (literally) to fall out of the world?

"Madam Lilac says that she will meet you again in a very little while, deep below, deep deep below."

"And I say that she won't!" Constantine cried against it. "She's fishy. I don't care if a dolphin isn't a fish. She's still fishy."

He tugged the lines to carry himself away from that central vortex. He refused to descend deep, deep below into the lilac depths of the ocean.

There was the churning, hammering shoal water that would break up a ship or a man. And what else? Mighty steep odds against it. Oh, there was a little bit of solidity out there, about big enough to stand on. But it was a way, a chancy break-neck way where one might stay alive and sometime get to clear water or to help. If only—

And the odds against it weren't as steep as they had seemed at first. None of that hundred-to-one stuff. The odds were no more than ten to one against it now.

"Just one chance," Constantine said. "Just one way. Oh, Director, you said that you liked to cut it close. Director, you should be down here. This is really going to be close. You said that you wouldn't have it any other way. I would, but I haven't."

He tugged the ropes till he broke his hands on them. And he would have to hit—

"The best detective in the world should be able to reduce those ten-to-one odds against," he said. "Sure, he should find a way in those last ten seconds to reduce the odds."

He was into those last seconds. It was, in fact, ten seconds till twelve o'clock midnight. This would be cutting it very close. What consummate artistic effect! What absolutely imperative sense of crisis!

"Maybe I've shortened the odds too much," he said as he swept in on it. "I'll lengthen them a bit now, I'll tempt fate by pretending to bungle it, for artistic effect, for the sake of crisis—and at the very very last second I'll try to—"

The Three Armageddons
of
Enniscorthy Sweeny

SECTION ONE

THE LIFE AND TIMES OF ENNISCORTHY SWEENY
(1894—1984)

I

This introductory sketch of the life and attributes of Enniscorthy Sweeny should really have been written by someone who knew him well. But who would that be? Did anyone know him well?

Only about half of the people in the country. People knew him spontaneously and they caught the essence of him. This is the most puzzling part. People understood him, and they didn't know any of the facts about him at all. All they knew was a wooly clutch of facts that weren't so.

But we who winnow the facts find that we know him hardly at all; we find that our facts are less than the popular facts. The more we delve into them, the less we know him. And the less we know him the more we like him. Strange.

The proverbial man in the street has said it rather ineptly: "Even the people who hate him, well, they kind of like him too. No, I think he's wrong to turn the world inside out the way he does, but I still like him. If the world's going to be wrecked, it's better to have it done by someone that everybody likes."

The fact that there is something world wrecking about

191

Enniscorthy Sweeny is a popular idea of unknown growth. There is nothing in the facts, or in the 'facts,' or in the *facts* either, to support it.

Was Ennis Sweeny the man who left the iron door of hell open to the changing and ruination of the world? Or was that door open all the time, and did he call attention to this by trying to close it? And where did the idea of these intruding things come from? And however were they linked with such a kind and mild man as Ennis Sweeny? Why have some people accepted the intruding things as if they might be true?

Now, at the death of Enniscorthy Sweeny, the people are divided between two equally irrational responses.

"These things were never even thought of until very lately," half of the people say. And the other half of the people insist, "No other things were *ever* thought of till just lately. This is the way that it has been for all those decades; and the conclusion of it is the way it's going to be. Like it or not, it's so."

And there is only a very small rational minority to question it from any side. And all that the rational people can ask is "What things? These are fictions and not things at all."

2

Perhaps this attempt to outline Enniscorthy Sweeny should have been done with the aid of some of the experimental writing. It should be noted at the beginning what sound track should be played during the reading, and at what pace. And then the account would have to be read at that pace, and with that accompanying clatter.

It also should be noted what smells should be played by which capsules of 'The Evocative Nose' or 'Keystone Effluxes' or whatever commercial line of smells seems best. But we don't know what noises or smells to recommend as accompaniment. What did Sweeny sound like anyhow? Oh, he had a pleasant clatter to him. What did he smell like? He didn't seem to smell at all, some people said.

His wife, Mary Margaret, says that he smelled like timothy hay. Pleasant, that's what. But had she ever smelled timothy hay? No, she didn't think so. Then why the comparison? She just had the impression, she said, that he smelled like timothy hay.

But this sketch is given without accompaniment. It will not even have the subliminal flashes of 'Forms Incorporated' flicking the shapes and appearances.

Belloc once wrote that a test of prose explication might be the describing of the tying of a bowline knot, without a sketch, and without using technical or cordage terms, so that one who was not familiar with the name of it could tie it without hesitation or misunderstanding. Try it.

A similar or even more stringent test of prose explication might be the describing of the face of Enniscorthy Sweeny to one who had never seen it or enjoyed it. The phiz isn't easy to put into words, and what other than words is there to use? Enniscorthy didn't like pictures of himself to be taken: he was an honest primitive in that. There aren't any good pictures of him at all, and there aren't any pictures that look like him.

The face was skinny and ruddy. The nose was powerful and beaked; not like that of a bird of prey but like that one of the Roman-nosed water birds. The nose was always peeling, as though it were growing out from the inside and flaking off in those strips. And the face was inseparable from the voice which was instant midwestern Irish, so different from Boston or New York or New Orleans Irish. Oh, the rapid and skinny words of it! It was as harsh and perpetually sun-burned as was his face, and as strong and rough and high-humored.

The face was larger than it seemed, for it a bit more than filled the front of the head that was as long as a horse's head. The eyes and lips and nares were quite light, and all the rest was burned dark ruddy. It was like a very fair man looking out through a smoked and beacon-red mask.

The hair on the head was black and tan and red, with coarser and longer white hairs (this was after he was thirty years of age) outgrowing from the pile of it like lank winter-coat hair. Shorthorn bulls will sometimes have hair of that roan mixture of colors, but seldom will people have it.

Well, it was an unfinished face. A darker priming coat or undercoat had been applied to it (it looked very much like the rust-inhibitor paint that is sometimes given to machinery for a first coat), but the finishing coat had not been given to that face.

Enniscorthy Sweeny has been called an unhandsome man, and yet he was good-looking enough. He had a lank symmetry and a balanced originality in the arrangement of his parts. There was no weak feature to him, but some were more outstanding than one is used to. The mouth was large and mobile. The teeth were good but biggish. He grinned a lot, and he smiled sometimes. His ears would have been much too large for most faces, but they went well with his face of record. The ears were hairy and tufted about the tragus.

Someone once asked his father how big his son Ennis was by now. "How big compared to what?" the father asked in turn. It wasn't a bull or jest. There was something unrelated about the size of this person Ennis, and no body could say whether he was large or not. But he was always swift, and he always seemed light of weight. If he had had any real weight, then he would have been breaking all the laws of momentum all the time, the way he changed directions. And usually there was a puzzling finality about his face. It was as if he had considered several other sorts of faces and decided that this one was the one he would keep.

This 'finality' face was that of an old man, you ask? No, not that, though I never knew him until he was an old man by the chronology. It is said that the 'finality' appearance was very early, as though he had selected his face (this weird impression has been reported by several persons) almost in infancy. If, that is, he had any infancy.

It was his mother who wrote that he had really been born as an adult, albeit a very small one for the first several years of his life. And he had the face of an adult of uncertain age for all his life. It was an unchanging face that he wore for the biggest part of a century. It was the only face that he ever had.

This baffling appearance that was so completely separated from any chronology was a puzzling thing about him. One might at any time have answered the question

194

'Is he old?' with an echo of his father's question 'Compared to what?' His age and his size were simply not to be compared with, were not in the same category with, those of the other persons around.

At his death, some people actually said that it was a shame that he had been carried off so young and with so much of his promise still unfulfilled. And yet he had been much older than most of those who said this, and some of them had been pretty old. But old or young, or large or small, he was a highly good-natured boy (yet a boy forever) with those rough and burnished and peeling features.

No, we have failed it. Our prose explication is not at all equal to describing the face and form of him.

And yet Enniscorthy Sweeny was popularly known. He was recognized everywhere by persons who could never have seen him before. How could they even have heard of him? A few hundred people in the musical world could have known about him, and a few dozens in the journalistic and literary world. But how did the millions know about him? How did they know his name that they had never heard and recognize his face that they had never seen before? At spectacles and concerts in towns not his own, he would be recognized by people, and they would interrupt to applaud him. He didn't need a spotlight to pick him out for the people. His peeled beacon face was a bright enough spotlight. How was he always as familiar as old shoes at first sight? And why did the people applaud such ungainly old shoes?

3

The suspicion that Enniscorthy Sweeny was a genius is one that has to be put down firmly, and still more firmly, again and again, by almost every one who ever knew him or his work. He had too many talents to be a genius: that is the shotgun view of it. Really, he was a spacious bungler. There isn't much doubt that he was a bungler, always an interesting and sometimes an exciting bungler, in everything he did. And there was a spacious element in everything of his work and life. He had all the room he

195

needed, always. He worked approximately in the same medium where other people worked. But where other people were most often straited and restricted, Ennis Sweeny always had plenty of room.

"Only Enniscorthy Sweeny, certain nations of monsters, some tribes of giants, and the archangels have always sufficient room to work in; and they have this because they bring part of their own space with them," an impresario once said as he watched Sweeny work (he was building a piece of stage scenery at the time). "Only Sweeny and the giants and archangels are given all the colors they need and all the sounds they need for any work at hand. Only Sweeny and the archangels can exactly occupy that unmeasured space that is given them to work in. And only Sweeny can bungle a job after being given such preternatural equipment and opportunity."

"Yes, that is what he looks like and what he is," said a money backer of the enterprise, a man who also was lounging around and watching things. "The archangels have the same big, loose features and the same eternally sunburned look."

"You have seen archangels?" the impresario asked the money backer.

"In the old country, in my youth, yes, several times," the money backer said. The money backer was named Gregor Naldis and the impresario was named Ercule Rigutini.

Well then, like the archangels, those master builders of baroque structures, Sweeny was allowed spacious talent but not genius.

The suspicion that Enniscorthy was a saint required, perhaps, even more putting down, but put down it must be. Against the suspicion of sanctity was his pursuit and persecution of the few people that he just plain did not like. Against it was his sometimes excessive grabbiness in money matters, though his grabbiness always depended on his immediate need for money. Against it was his gift of satire and ridicule that stripped away skin and flesh and shattered bones. Enniscorthy made sure that, of the people he just plain didn't like, nobody else would like them either. But there are a few people who ought to be persecuted and flayed, and Sweeny had the shrewd sense

196

of knowing which they were. There are times when money should be grabbed relentlessly. And a ridicule deferred is a ridicule lost forever.

Against the suspicion of Enniscorthy's sanctity were a ringing half-dozen bawdy ballads that he sometimes sang. No, no, these weren't the ordinary raunchy things. They were rotten, tree-top rotten. And he sometimes feuded more hotly than a saint would have done. And yet, while not quite an attested saint, he was surely one of the super good guys. Except that—

—except that there remain, and stand up like heraldic and rampant beasts, Enniscorthy's horrifying and hellish creations, the "Armageddon Operas" and other things. Most demons would draw back from them in repugnance. Those things were crammed with ravening superevils.

But the suspicions that Sweeny was a genius, and that he was a saint, are not dead yet. They have outlasted the man. There is still a lot of logic in their favor, and Enniscorthy was a logical man. He did things so giantly grotesque that he had to have a genius for something there.

Sometimes he excelled maladroitly and gigantically, and against his own intentions. Some of his doings had to be immediately classified out of fact and into legend if there was going to be any peace of mind anywhere. And he made the giant strokes for small reasons and for no reasons at all.

There was the time when he was a journalist or sports reporter and went to do a training-camp story on the reigning heavyweight boxing champion of the world who was training for a title fight.

"Is it true that your timing is off a little bit, champ?" Ennis asked with that good-natured joshing that was a part of him.

"Get in the ring with me and find out," the champ said with the happy bluffery that was always around his camps. And he clapped the wispy Ennis on the shoulder with a big hand that knocked him rattling.

"Is it true that your footwork is not quite what it should be at this period of your training?" Ennis needled the burly champion.

"Get in the ring with me and find out," the champ dared him with a pealing hoot.

"Are the reports true that, due to your long layoff, your punches have lost a bit of their steam?" Ennis followed it up.

"Get in the ring with me and find out," the champ guffawed. And then there was a tinny tone to the champ's guffaw as though he saw something now that he hadn't at first.

"Yes, yes, all right," Ennis said, and in saying that he seemed to grow a foot taller. Surely he became a bit larger than he had been before. So, Enniscorthy, in boxer shorts, was into the ring in just about a minute, and there was considerable of the rowdy laughter that was always around the training camps of that champ. Well, Sweeny did look funny in the near-buff. He was as funny a looking stripped-bare man as there was in the world.

But when Enniscorthy and the champ squared off with the big sixteen ounce gloves, there was something very much wrong about the juxtaposition of the two men, something wrong with the confrontation of the champ and the rambling and rattling sports reporter. There was something very, very wrong.

Sweeny had usually been thought of as an unsubstantial man, not little exactly, but wispy. He was a person set apart and of no particular size. He always had a lightness and quickness that didn't seem to go with great bulk or great size. His whole style and movement were those of less than a big man. The big things about him were always grotesquely big. They just had never indicated that he himself was big.

So there was something very very mistaken about Enniscorthy Sweeny towering above the world's heavyweight boxing champion. The champion wasn't a giant, but he was a good-sized six-two and two hundred and eighteen; and a man of ordinary size had no business towering above him. The juxtaposition was a joke. Ennis would have to be seven feet tall and three hundred and fifty pounds if they were really on the same scale as they stood there. They couldn't be on the same scale. They couldn't be in the same picture without tampering. If Ennis had been that big, someone would have noticed it before.

There were intensely subjective elements in the encounter. It didn't seem possible to take an objective view of it.

People who witnessed the sparring must have had something wrong with their eyes. Our own guess is that the two men were *not* on the same scale when they stood there and when they clashed.

But the disparity of size was nothing to the disparity of speed. The champion had always been accounted as a fast man of hand and foot, but Ennis Sweeny made him seem slow as a sloth. Ennis blocked all blows easily when he wished to. He was like a fly-catcher catching flies. He was rather embarrassed about the whole thing; and yet he seemed to be, almost without limits, secretly pleased.

Sometimes he let the champion strike him a few resounding blows. The blows had not, apparently, lost any of their sharpness, and the champion was the puncher of the century. The champion was getting mad, and his blows jarred the whole ring, but they didn't jar Sweeny. There was no effect at all on Enniscorthy, though he was already so ruddy that a punch that did not spill blood would hardly show. The noneffect wasn't just because of the muffling of the big sixteen ounce gloves. The champion had cooled many a sparring partner while using the big gloves.

The thing became more and more wrong. And then Sweeny knocked the champion out accidentally. "Accidentally, with malice," said another sportswriter who was there.

Sweeny hadn't, so he himself believed, meant to hit the champion at all. He had been blocking the blows when he wished, and he had been taking the blows when he wished; and he had been feinting the champion almost out of his skin with a few lightning hand movements in between. Then one of those lightning hand movements flashed out a little bit too far. And the champion was the most completely knocked-out man that anyone had ever seen. And Enniscorthy was, at the same time, both the most embarrassed and the most tickled fellow around.

Ennis had sudden fear that he had killed the champion, but that had lasted only a second. Then Ennis seemed to be taken by the feeling that if he had killed the champion he could just as easily unkill him again.

A working sportswriter and former fighter, Nat Baumgardner, who was there, said that, after the disaster was effected, he stood next to Sweeny and found that the two of them were just the same height (Nat was an even six feet), and that Sweeny was much the slighter man (Nat then weighed two hundred and ten pounds).

Yes, but it hadn't been like that just a few seconds before.

There were two other anomalous elements in the disaster or the caper. At first it was believed by almost all the persons present that the champion was dead. But then he was found to have a little life lingering in him after all. It was still believed that his skull was crushed, and anyone could see that his jaw was clearly caved in as if it were crumbled-up cardboard. There was even a length of white and jagged bone protruding from the face of the champion, part of the shattering of the jaw bone or temporal bone.

But then, just two or three seconds later, the skull did not appear to be quite so crushed as it had been, nor the jaw so horribly crumbled up. And there wasn't any bone sticking out. That had been no more than an optical illusion.

Pretty soon the champion looked all right. Then he opened his eyes and he *was* all right.

"This is a completely awkward situation," Enniscorthy apologized. "I regret it. I repent of it completely."

"No, Ennis, not completely you don't," the champion said, still rubbing his jaw. "It's a blend, you know, nine parts and one."

"Nine and one?" Ennis asked.

"Yeah. Nine parts of repentance and chagrin. That's the corn, the corn whisky. But the tenth part is your secret delight in it all, and that comes through pretty rich. The tenth part is the rye whisky that flavors it all. It makes a good blend, a good drink. You wanted to do it, Ennis. You wanted to knock out the champion. And you always get a thing when you want it bad enough. Always. I don't know how you do it though. Do you?"

"No I don't," said Ennis. "I don't know how I do it, and I don't know how you knew that I have always done it. Now how can we undo it?"

"We can't," the champion said. "I won't tell about it, and you won't. But there are others here, and they probably think that they saw the knockout happen. There's no way to shut them up. Maybe it can be garbled though."

"Yes, I believe it can be," Ennis said. "I think that if I want it that way, it will become the case that the accounts of it will not be literally believed. Those accounts, even that of Nat here (and he is an honest reporter), they just might end up with one foot at least in the soft mud of legend."

And that's the way that the stories of it have ended up, as half-legend and the other half a discounted improbability. But it's a curious legend and it has lasted for quite a few years, quite a few decades really. The story is one that won't bear careless swallowing. One is likely to strangle on it if he swallows such a legend lying down.

Sweeny had been granted one of his boyhood wishes, that he should knock out the heavyweight champion of the world and that he should do it cleanly and decisively and with a really prodigious blow such as would almost fell an elephant. This thing was granted. Whatever else happened to the account, it was true when it happened; and nobody could ever take that satisfaction away from Sweeny.

As a matter of record, Sweeny was granted, or won somehow, *all* of his boyhood wishes, a thing that is absolutely unique in the annals of people.

But he wasn't granted all his boyhood wishes without much violence being done to the course of the rest of the world. Sometimes the world was moved pretty far off course during the fulfilling. So that brings it abruptly to the question:

What was going on here anyhow?

This question, in varied forms, would echo down the resonant life of Enniscorthy Sweeny for all the years of it.

4

Too much talent to be a genius? Was that possible? Too much badly focused talent is what he had. Ennis Sweeny had stood slightly lower than a doubtful genius as a sports-writer. Oh, his accounts were colorful and exciting. The accounts were often much more interesting than the events that they described. But Sweeny committed howler after howler of the sort that a working genius of a sportswriter simply will not commit. More than once his accounts neglected to state who *won* the event in question. That was to miss the whole point of it, wasn't it?

Yes it was. But Ennis committed that particular howler only a dozen times out of the hundreds of events that he covered; and there were strong reasons for the omission in each case. The reason was always that Ennis had gotten himself in so deeply on it that there was no other way he could get out. If, in that small number of outrageous cases, Ennis had written who had won, then it would have been a tainted result, an unfairly influenced outcome.

Ennis had many quirks in his lively mind, and one of the quirkiest of them was the belief that he could influence results, that he could *make* one team or contestant win by wishing it to win. He knew that, considering the power that he had, any wishing on his part was unfair. So he tried to put all partisanship out of his mind and make it of no moment at all who should win. In several cases, he put this aspect of the sport so completely out of his mind that he really didn't remember, when the contest was finished, who *had* won. He didn't remember, and he was ashamed to ask anybody. So he shot off the cannons of his prose in the loud hope that the thunder and lightning of his exposition would make the little detail of 'who-won-anyhow?' unimportant.

And, in several other cases, Ennis felt that it really did depend on him. He was himself so entangled with the fates of the things as to be a decisive element. If he wrote that one side had won, that side *would* have won. If he wrote that the other side had won, then it would have been that way. So he left the results out, and he looked like a fool. And the fates, after looking over their shoulders and being certain that he would not interfere, would go ahead and settle the things with their own customary unfairness but without the Sweeny element.

Yes, yes, Ennis Sweeny was as quirky as seven devils. And there were even people who tried to lay big money on him to hire his quirkiness for their gain.

Ennis Sweeny did have real genius as a flute player, and yet the flute field is thought of as rather narrow and of little real importance. Don't people remember the *Zauberflöte*? Don't they know that every flute is a *Zauberflöte*? He was very good on all instruments. For fear of laughter, we hesitate to say that he was the best jews-harp player and the best musical-saw player in the world, we hesitate to say that he was a genius upon those instruments. And yet, is it not more noteworthy to be a genius where nobody was ever a genius before than to be a genius on well-trodden paths?

Ennis had near genius as that most creative of artists, a cartoonist. It is said that he missed real genius and greatness here because of his lack of the killer instinct. That is needed in cartooning more than in any field that you can give instance of.

There is direct cruelty in every cartoon strip, or there is sublimated cruelty in it. But Ennis Sweeny was not capable of either. There is gentleness and kindness and the easy slowness of almost perfect peace in the real world very often, but these things cannot be found in the cartoon or comic-strip reflection of the world. The cartoon world is one of ornery giants.

Ennis was a close friend of all the great comic-strip artists of seven decades, and he knew to what frightening extent the worlds they glommed into were real. But he contributed horror and harshness to these works through a sort of osmosis, for he had strong influence on comic-strip artists as on other people. They all of them borrowed a great lot from his dark visions.

But there are other worlds of ornery giants, that of the grand opera, and of drama and melodrama, of vaudeville and variety, of band and orchestra music. And the world of the circus and the carnival is so also, and that of competetive sports, and that of gallery art. So is the pantomime world of silent movies.

The world of talking movies, however, is a bit different.

That one is the world of ornery dwarfs. The popular novels make up a world of ornery lop-sided people, somewhat dwarfish, sometimes giantized.

But all of these arenas require the killer instinct for distinctive work, and Ennis Sweeny had it not at all. And still he was rated as a near genius in every one of these fields. And, in every one of them, he stood as a confounding and anomalous and undoubted genius at least once, arriving there by paths that nobody else had ever walked.

But the world was slow to certify Enniscorthy as a genius, and in fact it has not done so yet. It was very much as if he were a superb mimic, imitating and transcending genius in field after field. But how could he be given the accolade in seriousness when he was only kidding about it in everything that he did?

(Ah, was he kidding when he, the man without the killer instinct, the man too kind ever to inflict an injury on anything, opened the iron doors of hell and invited all of the really horrifying things there to come out and mingle with us?)

Ennis scripted one of the best and most enduring and most evocative of all Broadway plays, "The Great Depression." It was absolutely purgatorial in its power and its passion and in its multitudinous humor and characters. There had not been anything like it in its depictment of the coupled hilarity and hellishness of real poverty, the rampant fun of it all, and the depraved suffering. There are things about half as tall in Russian novels and even in Dickensian English, but they just aren't as big and they aren't of such excellent shoddiness. This was the real Beggars' Opera, the great switcharound spoof, the "what-if-we-*were*-poor" ploy carried out with overflowing vigor. And the question is how could Enniscorthy have known of such things, how could he have built them, and out of what? He had never been poor, he had never known anyone who had been poor, he had known only a few very old people from overseas who had ever known anyone who had been poor.

The thing remains (for it is still produced fifty-five years after) solidly evil and completely cruel. It is totally dishonest. It is consummately depraved. It is completely funny. But surely it has genius.

Enniscorthy composed the great opera cycle of the century, the Tyrrhene Triptych. It is possible that Grand Opera was invented, a century and a half before this, to give a mature medium to this great work. It is great, but it is horrible. It is said that there is so much brimstone in the laughter that it yellows the teeth of all the singers. The parts of this triptych are Armageddon I, Armageddon II, and the quite recently produced Armageddon III, which is depravity and cruelty incarnate.

"It is not certain that the world will be able to survive this," an opening-night critic wrote earlier this month. And it really is not certain. The world cannot go on its usual way with such a revening monster in its midst.

This Armageddon III is subtitled "What Rotten Blossom Bigger Than the World!" Ten percent of the first night audience went and destroyed themselves, and though the percent of self-destroyers from subsequent viewings and hearings is down around seven percent now, yet this is quite serious. The opera is a carnivorous flower that is eating up the world. And we have as yet no idea of the extent that the lethal fallout may assume.

As opera, even as horrifying comic opera, these three cresting masterpieces of murder and destruction simply have no equals. Only two persons in all the universes could have composed anything like the Tyrrhene Triptych: the Devil, and Enniscorthy Sweeny. And we are not so sure about the Devil; he just hasn't the musical or dramatical or cosmic sophistication to bring it to such a level. Is it possible that any human other than Ennis Sweeny ever erected such evil and horror as he did in these?

But Sweeny himself once said that both "The Great Depression" and "The Tyrrhene Triptych" were scapegoats.

"I did them," he said, "and then I drove them out into the wilderness like laden goats. May all the wrath fall upon them and their loads! But may these things not happen in the world itself! If these things may pass from us, oh Lord, let them pass!"

The scapegoat tricks had opposite effects though. No one had ever heard of such abominable happenings before. But, once Sweeny had made such things known, then perverted cults grew up about them. And the cults, the "Horror-for-the-sake-of-horror" cults, are now about the most frightening things in the world. Ah, and they are about the largest groups; they run into millions of persons now.

The scapegoat apparently is the "goat" of one quarter of the Sweeny special coat of arms, and also is one quadrant of the answer to a queer equation that numerologists and mathematicians have worked out. The four quadrants are the Man (identified in some of these works as Enniscorthy Sweeny), the Goat, the Cuttlefish, and the Mushroom Patch. Very esoteric stuff!

6

If not a genius, couldn't Enniscorthy Sweeny at least be that greater thing, a saint? Ennis himself believed that anybody who *wasn't* a saint had blown it all. Ennis never quite blew it. And he never came as close to blowing it as he seemed to. In spite of his being an usher for all the hellish things, in spite of (on the other hand) his being the kindest person in the world, he didn't blow it either way. There is surely a mistake somewhere, and maybe he should be given the benefit of the confusion.

But whoever saw a saint with ears like that? Whoever saw a saint with such a pidgeon-toed gait that ate up the miles and leagues and parsecs? Who ever saw a saint who was perpetually sunburned and peeling in the most sunless of winters? Whoever saw a saint who shed his skin like a snake?

He was a mighty good fellow even though he might be responsible for the most threatening and massive evils ever. So, he was the harbinger of the latter days that mean the destruction of the world. Was he not a fine fellow for all that?

"It is a pleasure to be in the same room with him," said a man who was about as famous a statesman as there is in the world. "It is a pleasure to be in the same world with him, to be in the same creation with him. He infuses everything with his clear liveliness, though he *is* a most

206

peculiar infusing instrument. He makes all things better. He makes the whole world better."

So once more—
   —*What was going on here anyhow!*

That question, as we say, will echo down the corridors of the man forever.

7

There were, however, long lists of activities and occupations at which Enniscorthy Sweeny was not outstanding. He wasn't really a very good reporter for the newspapers and journals though he followed the reporting profession for more years than any other, and for more years than anyone would have thought possible.

Oh, on a story, he just didn't know where to stop. And when the men on the desk chopped him off, they couldn't be certain that they had chopped him off for good. Ennis believed that it was essential that he should get *everything* down in the record, if it were not already recorded some where. He said that things had not really happened until they were inscribed in the records somewhere.

"I have to get it all, the whole world," he would say to an editor who had tried to cut some trifling story. "If no one else has it down, then I *have to* get it. Don't you understand what you are doing when you cut me?"

"Yeah," an editor said. "I'm weeding. Do you have to get the whole world down, weeds and all?"

"Yes I do. If I'm on duty, and I am working in that particular medium, yes, then I have to get it all down, weeds and all."

"What are you, a recording angel?"

"One of them, Sam, one of them. We are a whole department, you know. 'Recording Angel' has always been no more than an editorial singular." The editor had believed that he was speaking figuratively, and perhaps he was.

But passages scissored out of his stories kept appearing at other places in the newspapers and journals. Snatches of them might be found, without any "continued from" tag on them, back in the "most-everything-for-sale" classifieds or among the muscle-builder ads in the journals. And then Ennis would lie and say that he didn't know how they had got there. Sometimes he was pretty pathological about all this.

"But I have to get it all down," he would insist.

"Why???" an editor among many barked in a firecracker voice.

"If ever it's an imperative, and I don't get it all down, you'll find out *why*," Ennis had said mysteriously.

Well, he didn't understand it himself, but there were sometimes big masses of things that he had to get down or something would fall apart. He was an unrestrained reporter when the voluminous urge was on him, and a good reporter hardly ever. And the editors treated him shamefully and they didn't seem to know about his fame or greatness in other fields. It was a mystery why he would keep coming back to those thirty-dollar-a-week reporter jobs (forty dollars a week after 1960). He could always make half again that much directing at the Metropolitan Opera House.

And Ennis Sweeny was not a good business man, though for short periods he might have been called a great one. He went into independent business a dozen times in his life: as the owner and operator of a carnival, as a maker of silent motion pictures, as a newspaper publisher, as a manufacturer of automobiles, as a horse-race-track owner, as an art dealer, as a builder of interurban railway lines, as an hotel owner, as a theatrical producer, as a manufacturer of player pianos and grind-organs, as the operator of a baseball franchise in the Three I League, and as a manufacturer of farm machinery.

In each case, Ennis made a great deal of money quickly. And then, in each case, he went through a period of a year or so of grinding doubt and doldrums. After that, he always managed to sell each business brilliantly.

It was after he had unloaded a business that the new owners always discovered what a really bad business man Enniscorthy Sweeny was, for each business was a shambles when he got rid of it. Yet the businesses had never appeared to be shambles on paper, and the papers were never falsified. No one had ever accused Ennis of fraud, and he was not capable of such. But people who bought apparently thriving business from him sure did get their fingers burned.

It was simply that Ennis could breathe a spirit into a business for a while, and then it would thrive. And then his spirit would go out of it and it would be a hollow hulk. But a good businessman will run a business soundly regardless of how the spirit listeth.

However it was, Ennis was never out of ready money from the sixth year of his life, when he first began to sell magazines and newspapers, originally in Blackwater Street in Chicago where he lived; and then through the whole world as it seemed.

And Ennis Sweeny was not a good prophet. He was not even a good prophet after the facts, and almost everyone becomes a good prophet on a subject when it is finished. Not Ennis though.

There was something wrong with his sequence, with his flow of time, in prophecy and in many things. It really seemed as if it did not matter to him whether a thing had happened yet or not. But he couldn't explain this odd detachment to other people.

"An event is like a box or other geometrical object," Ennis would say, "and it should be pretty much the same no matter which side it is viewed from. Let us say that we look at it from the south side (that is the past), or from the east side (that is the present), or from the west side (that is an alternate present), or from the north side (that is the future). The event will look a little bit different from these various viewpoints, but not much. You must not reject one view of it when you come to another view. They are all equally parts of it."

Ennis could not disassociate what he thought would happen from what had already happened. And often the two things were quite opposite. He was a poor predictor, a poor prophet, that man. Sometimes he would say, "I have lived this year before: I know this year." And he would give any number of instances that showed that he had indeed had a pre-vision of that year. And then he would bust on a major happening: he would have it completely wrong. He was a wretched prophet, or some people thought that he was merely a slab-headed kidder.

It is no good trying to put the life and letters of Enniscorthy Sweeny into sequence, for he was a creature who simply did not fit into the sequential system. His mother had said that Ennis was really born as a very small adult, and that he continued as that only slightly changed adult for the bigger part of a century. Size was one of the things that pertained to him as little as date: it didn't seem as if he ever really got much bigger. And he may have lived through the consecutive years as did other men, but his own cavalier handling of the passing time has thrown all the records into a fruitful chaos from which many choice things can be pulled, but not in any particular order. They can be guessed at, but they cannot be accurately dated.

From his boyhood, Ennis Sweeny kept copies of all his letters. Well, there was certainly system in that. And he preserved them in an array of large wooden trunks, each trunk finally holding more than three hundred pounds of writing or typing on onionskin paper. These were mostly his letters, but they were also the journals that he sometimes kept. It is not known what happened to the journals, often quite intimate and apparently designed for no eyes except his own, but these were carbon copies of only disconnected fragments of them in the trunks, and the originals have not been found.

These seven laden trunks that he left behind him at his death (there had been a legend of *eight* crammed trunks, but where was the eighth?—"I think he took it with him," one of his granddaughters said wryly), these coffers, these trunks do not leave an ordered record.

Ennis hardly ever dated a letter or an entry, and most of the carbons do not even indicate to whom the letters were written. They will be addressed to such unknown persons as "Heart of Oak?" and "Super-sleuth" who are not easy to identify. All of that is peculiar, for Ennis often noted the time of day when he began a letter or an entry (and even gave the temperature at that hour), and sometimes he gave the day of the week. A few times he would give the date and the month, but not a hundred times in twenty thousand letters did he give the year.

And he did not fill up first one trunk and then another. He had the quirk of keeping all of them filled to about the same rising level all during his decades. And he died just in time (filled with the youth of his years as he was), for all the trunks were jammed so full at his death that not one more onionskin could have been put into them. If there was a mysterious eighth trunk, it was probably near full too. Oh, his happy and rattling laugh (how could a man with perfect pitch laugh like that?) can be heard yet whenever anyone turns through his letters to try to find the beginning and end of things.

9

Here is an old incident from the very early life of Ennis Sweeny. It is in the hand and over the name of his mother, and she *did* date her letters. It was dated November 6, 1901 when Ennis was seven years old.

The letter tells of the President of the United States coming to the Sweeny house on West Blackwater Street in Chicago. There is no explanation of the President's coming there. There is only the certainty that he did come there if Irene Sweeny wrote that he did.

She wrote that the President of the United States put his hand on the head of young Ennis and said, "This is the boy to whom I owe it all, my rise and my position, the highest in the world." She gives no explanation of that statement or the following one. For the President of the United States also said "This boy is destined for the rise and the fall of many persons in Spacious America."

Could the mother Irene have meant to write the name of her oldest son Cashel instead of her youngest son Enniscorthy? Cashel was thirteen years older than Enniscorthy and was already a devoted precinct worker. No, that would not be possible. The mother plainly wrote what she meant to write.

Well, it was surely a bit of joshing on the part of the President then. President Standpipe himself had come from West Blackwater Street in Chicago, just four blocks away from the Sweeny house, and he made a point of knowing every family in those blocks along there. His presence at the Sweenys' was not really too extraordinary.

That is true. But he wasn't joshing. He meant what he said; and he said what Irene Sweeny reported him as saying. Irene Sweeny did not note very many things down on that one memo book that lasted her all her life, but what she did write down was of importance. Enniscorthy Sweeny *was* the person to whom Harold Standpipe owed it all, all his rise to the Presidency. And Ennis Sweeny was only seven years old at the time of this visit. He had been but six years old when Standpipe was actually elected.

Just what was going on there?

There was something unnatural about this, and about many other things that had to do with the intersection of Ennis Sweeny with the world.

Just what was going on there?—That question still reverberates down all the life and death of Ennis.

10

Enniscorthy Sweeny married the most beautiful and most desired woman in the world. She was so in the opinion of Ennis himself and in the opinion of very many other persons. And what was a lout like Sweeny doing marrying the most beautiful and the most desired woman in the world?

"Oh, I thought it might be fun," he said in later years when somebody asked him about it. "And believe me, it *has* been fun, every minute and day and year and decade of it. It was a sort of contest you know. There was another magus who had come to Chicago about that time and he believed that he could make his prospective bride into the most beautiful woman in the world. Well, in a way, we both had sufficient to work with, ample blocks of marble, that is, to sculpt from. His was a bit the largest, and still is. But the one I worked with was large enough, for I don't make many mistakes. There were two stages to it, you know: setting it up; and then grabbing it off."

"What are the two stages?" the asker asked.

"Wanting her to be that way," Ennis said. "Making her to be the most beautiful and desired woman in the world, that was the first. And then to have her for wife when she was that way, that was the second. I don't believe that anyone ever wanted two things more than I wanted those two things. When a person wants things that much, the Lord is rather driven into a corner if He doesn't grant them."

Well, how *had* Mary Margaret McGronsky Sweeny happened to be, or to become, the most beautiful and most desired woman in the world? That is an interesting question and it would probably produce an interesting answer if one could only know it.

It had been a rather prodigious flowering that began about the time she entered her nineteenth year, and that flowering went on all her life. But she had it won within two years. She was the best. She was clearly the most beautiful and the most desired within two years of her flowering out.

Sensational flowerings are fairly common as coming to girls at about the beginning of the nineteenth year. Margaret was one of those late spring sunbursts. Girls who flower earlier, at fifteen or sixteen or seventeen or eighteen, simply do not flower so prodigiously. But there had always been a lot of both the ordinary and the extraordinary flowering along West Blackwater Street.

People grew roses there. They grew purple tumbling wisteria Macrobotrys, and blue bird bushes, and lilacs. They grew exploding smoke trees. And they grew daughters. Every day during spring and summer, someone along Blackwater Street would have a new and sensational bloom of one of these species to show, and people would come from several blocks around to admire.

No one had very large areas to grow and to show such blooms in those blocks on Blackwater Street, just a strip in front of the house from five to nine feet wide. But that gave room enough for the little Smoke Trees and Blue Bird Bushes and Lilacs. It was room enough for the wisteria and the show-boat tulips, and the roses. And again, for the roses and the roses and the roses, for those were rose blocks.

And there wasn't a very large area for the display of

blooming daughters at those little houses on Blackwater, just a small space between the white front gate and the mauve front steps, three to seven feet maybe. But there were some real presentations in those limited areas in the mornings and evenings of spring and early summer. It is nice when people have flowers to enjoy and to take pride in.

Mary Margaret McGronsky was a sudden and prodigious bloom among the flowers of those humble blocks. She was an opera rose, she was a circus rose, she was a purple tumbling Macrobotrys. She was a blue bird bush. She was a smoke tree. She was all those things and much more. But before that she had been just a freckled and pleasant and chunky (full-bodied, we will say) girl. Even among the expert and talented flower growers on Blackwater Street she was sudden. And she was superb.

But she wasn't really the most beautiful woman in the world, not then, not yet then. It took another couple of years. But, however long it was, how did the amazing thing come about? Such extraordinary things do not just happen.

It was understood, instantly and all over the neighborhood, that that grinning and gangling red-faced kid, Enniscorthy Sweeny, had brought it about and would continue to bring it about. (He continued to bring it about until the last days of her life.)

Well, how does a young man, however strangely talented and gifted he may be, bring about such a change in the appearance and essence and personality of a girl in the neighborhood? This is not known, and it can hardly be guessed.

Ennis once wrote a mystic piece, for that ambitious little magazine *Architecture and Prototype*, entitled "On the Construction of the World." It explained several things that were theretofor thought to be inexplicable, and it gave unfortunate impetus to an evil cult, the evil apparently being grafted onto Ennis' idea by someone else. But it *did* give some very sound advice as to constructing a world.

Ennis was then asked, partly in banter and partly in earnest, by a close friend of his, why he did not write a companion piece "On the Construction of the Most Beautiful Woman in the World."

"Oh, I intend to do that, to do exactly that," Ennis had said. "I've done parts of it already. There are notes of it scattered through dozens of my letters. But it takes a lot of explaining, a thing like that, a whole lot of explaining."

One thing that takes a lot of explaining is the fact that everyone around there knew and accepted from the first that Ennis Sweeny *had* changed a nice and unordinary girl into an extraordinary person, the most extraordinary woman in the world.

Once more: *Just what was going on there?*

Enniscorthy Sweeny was tampering with the flow of the world's events and circumstances, that was what was going on. But Ennis had said about it: "There are two stages to it, you know."

Ennis had won a majority part of the affections of Mary Margaret before her extraordinary blooming, and half a dozen other young fellows had also won parts of her affections. But this new change in her was so stunning that it had to change everything about her. "Will you love me as a butterfly as you loved me as a grub?" No, she wouldn't. There was no way. She wouldn't love quite as she had done when she was only a slightly superior grub.

Do not underrate what Mary Margaret was, or the unique thing that she became. There are several instances to show how widely and highly she was regarded all over the world.

There was a German artist, one of the greatest artists in the world though now he is half forgotten, who saw the *gegenschein* of Mary Margaret from a quarter of the way around the world; and he came like a homing Magi to the manifestation. He came directly to West Blackwater Street in Chicago. He stood in the street there, before the McGronsky front gate, and he looked at the young woman, Mary Margaret, in the evening. Then he began to cry with an overflowing noise and emotion. People gawked at him there in the twilight and they didn't understand it. Even Mary Margaret herself only half understood it.

But there were understanding people about, those who had also felt the full force of the manifestation. Mr. Meistrel came out from across the street and had the sense to speak to the artist in German. He saw the end of something sticking out from the artist's coat pocket, and he improvised from that. Both he and the artist seized on it as an excuse for the artist being there. The thing in the pocket, the solace that the artist always carried, was a fife.

Well, of course the artist would play in their Horners' Windjammer Blackwater Street Band that night. And the band was to begin to play and to march in just ten minutes. The artist was a good fifer. He made an adequate temporary addition to the Windjammer Band, and he played with the band for three evenings. It was with this same neighborhood Windjammer Band that Enniscorthy Sweeny was then playing first flute.

And the artist had, or he made a good case that he had, business in Chicago for the three days that he was there. He had pictures in several of the Chicago galleries. He knew some of the directors of the galleries and some of the art dealers. He received plaudits and commissions, and it was as successful a three days as he had ever spent anywhere. Then he went back to Germany.

But it wasn't for plaudits or commissions that the great artist had come to Chicago. He had followed the living rumor that the most beautiful woman in the world was in that place. He had come there, and he had found out that the rumor was true. And he had been struck speechless and blubbering by the encounter.

There were a dozen other like instances. The most flamboyant director of the old Biograph Studios came there (none of the people who came there on the weird quest had to ask where Blackwater Street was or where the McGronsky house was—they homed in on the place by rampant instinct); and he wanted to make her the queen of the movies. She said no. She wanted to be queen of the Grand Opera. Randolph Street gentlemen, and also Broadway gentlemen from New York, came and wanted to put her into plays.

Her head was turned. And how was Ennis Sweeny going to win the most beautiful woman in the world even if it hadn't been turned? She could have been almost anything in the world. She decided on the most unlikely thing for her, to be the first opera singer in the world. That's a little bit harder to be than some of the other things. With all those experts, it just cannot be faked.

"But you can't sing, Mary Margaret, you can't sing a lick," Ennis had told her. "Not the Big Sing. You have a nice voice, but not for singing Big Opera. It would take you nine years study, and then you would be only mediocre."

"No, do not put me off with talk and excuses, Ennis," Mary Margaret said. "I have caught glimpses behind your own scenes. I know that you do unnatural things, and I have felt plenty of them being done to me. Make an opera singer out of me. Make me the best one in the world. Yes, and do it almost instantly. Oh, there are tryouts for supporting roles in the Chicago Summer Opera, and they start Monday. And how long do you believe that they will be able to keep me in supporting roles when I am the greatest in the world? You did the other things for me, and I don't know how you did them. Do this for me now. It's all part of the same thing."

"Maybe there are only so many great things I can do," Ennis had said. "Maybe my doing this will diminish the sum of them."

"Yes, it will. But do this for me now. Then think about the other things. If you come up short on one of the great things at the end of it all, well then you will just come up short."

Enniscorthy Sweeny, in a manner not at all understood, did bring it about that Mary Margaret McGronsky became the best opera singer in the world ever, in the times that have been, and are, and will be.

Once more: *Just what was going on there?*

Tampering was what was going on, tampering with the flow and motivation of the world itself and with the nature of reality.

But it took Ennis five years to win her after he had brought about her surpassing and continuing excellence. And those five years were loaded with all the perils there are. Burning brands and flaming flesh, but those perils were real!

There are grievous dangers in becoming the most beautiful and the most desired woman in the world while still

217

so young. There are particular dangers when one has become a great opera singer of international renown and has entered the gilded world of the several continents. And Mary Margaret was not, at this time, the wisest woman in the world.

She set herself on fire in the several ways of it. She engineered a colossal ruin for herself. She went in so deep that she no longer even had the choice between death and damnation. It looked as if it would have to be both. She was in danger of turning into the trash that is even beyond damnation.

"If I need you, how will I call you?" she had asked Enniscorthy several years before she had come to the bottom of the kennel.

"Oh, call me with your mind. I will be there at once," Ennis had said. "But what if it is too late or too deep when you call?"

"It won't be," Mary Margaret said, "not for you. You can always help me if you want to bad enough. You might hurt yourself by it, and that is bad; and you might hurt the world, and this is equally bad on a larger scale; but you can help me if you want to rob the other things to do it. You can always obtain any outcome that you really want. But I won't need you. Oh, get out of here, Ennis. I said that I won't need you."

But, about five years after her startling flowering and adornment, Mary Margaret had come down to the reeking bottom of it all. She was a burning brand in a noxious fire. She cursed the world and its Lord, and she slipped fatal crystals under her tongue. Then all her flesh crawled with living fire.

"I need you, but don't come," she said in her mind then. "It will burn you too."

Well, there was an ocean between them, and that was before airplanes made scheduled flights across the ocean. Ennis could not have crossed it in less than five days in the swiftest ship. He could not have got to and from those docksides in less than another day and night. Could Ennis get there at once even if he wanted to do so absolutely?

Yes, he could still obtain anything or do anything that he wanted to enough. He did it by his always cavalier handling of time. That is to say that he looked at the problem from all sides at once and took action when the crisis was still to the future for him. So he started six days before the last possible minute.

He snatched her as a burning brand out of that final fire. It was close. Oh God, the smell of scorched flesh! Well, had any one said that it would be easy to have the world's most beautiful and most desired woman for one's own?

Ennis had her in her perfection for a whole month. There was something baroque or lop-sided about that perfection and that enjoyment. It was perfect, but it was in the wrong setting and the wrong scale. Enniscorthy decided that it was on too slight a scale.

So he brought it about that Mary Margaret gave up one part in nine of her bodily beauty and received the equivalent of it in wisdom. With what she already had before, with what she acquired in the ordeal of the fire, and with the considerable amount that she received in the trade, she was pretty well blessed with wisdom from then on.

And she was still, for a while, the most beautiful woman in the world. But now it was possible that a more beautiful woman might come along. For five years there, that hadn't been possible.

What was this Ennis though, and what were the things that he could bring about?

What was going on there?

After this, Enniscorthy and Mary Margaret Sweeny lived in almost perfect amity and pleasure for another sixty-five years.

The first and one of the few returns of the smoking, scorching, flesh motif was when Mary Margaret sang the damnation role in Armageddon I, that hellfire comic opera that was the first part of the Tyrrhene Triptych. The damnation smell of fire-crawling flesh came on pretty strong in some of the movements that she sang there.

II

When Enniscorthy Sweeny was twelve years old he had gone into the Temple to preach. And all who heard him

219

were amazed by his wisdom and understanding. The Temple was St. Malachy's Church on Chicago's north side, just a block off old Blackwater Street.

The occasion of it was a religious retreat given for the high school students at St. Malachy's. (Ennis Sweeny was precocious: most of the other children were not into high school till they were fourteen years old.)

The priest who was retreat master had asked, on the last day of it, whether any of the young people wished to come forward to speak. Ordinarily it is very difficult to get one to come up, and if he comes he will be an insufferable showboat.

But Ennis had come forward to speak, and he had spoken with a great razzle. His fellow students were amazed at him. All of them had hung back when the retreat master, a Passionist priest, had asked if any of them wanted to ascend to the pulpit and propound his own views of the world, and of the Body that is bigger than the world, and of the final things, first asking aid of the Holy Ghost, of course. And Ennis had done this with a suddenness that was like a tidy spate.

He spoke powerfully and mysteriously. The clergy who had known him all his life were amazed at him, and the Passionists were also amazed.

"I did not know that he was so gifted," a sister said as Ennis, that adult from the beginning, that twelve-year-old adult now, talked on and on, intelligently and trenchantly. "He has always spent all of his time looking out of the windows and he never hears when a question is asked him."

"He is like the young Christ in the Temple," said one of the Passionists.

"But would a young Christ be chomping on chewing gum while he poured out his wisdom?" someone asked.

"What is chewing gum?" another of them wanted to know.

Although the year was 1906 and chewing gum was not really new, there were many people who still had never heard of it and did not know what it was. It was still a cult thing of racy and disreputable people.

"He isn't so much like the young Christ now," said one of them, noticing a change in Ennis. His wisdom and un-

220

derstanding seemed to be replaced by a hectic sort of power and an ill-balanced rapture. Oh, he was the worst showboat they had ever had.

He was a gawk now, a hang-dog clown, an elemental. He had trappings of elsewhere on him. He was an errant spirit. Perhaps he was not one of the Para-Angeli of whom Rhaptes said that they "Stumbled, but perhaps they did not fall." A twelve-year-old boy, and he had begun to set the world to quaking.

The speech became harsher and more ragged than it had been, and threatening. And then Ennis did several feats that can only be called poltergeistic. These showed his command, or at least his trickery, over matter. He caused little birds to fly about in the air and then to explode like firecrackers. Things like that.

And then he pointed to the big clock in the back of St. Malachy's and he ordered it: *"Vade Rursum!"* in a loud voice. "Run backwards" he ordered it, and it did. It spun backwards through twenty-four hours.

"This is the day that the Angel has stolen," Ennis announced. "I have stolen a day from the world and hid it. Does any one know where I have hidden the day that I have just taken?"

The retreat master put a stop to the farce. He took Ennis by the collar and hauled him down from the pulpit. He reprimanded him, and the other students laughed at him a bit. He whacked Ennis thrice heavily on the rump. He did this as one having power and authority. He sent Ennis off to go to confession then. And Ennis humbled himself and went.

12

The long life of Enniscorthy Sweeny presents a twisted series of puzzles. He was a good man. This was the absolute opinion of everyone who ever came into contact with him, except a very few enemies. Being a good man is something that can be faked for a few years, but it can't be faked for a lifetime. Ennis was good.

And he originated, invented, and propounded a series of evil dreams that can only horrify and sicken everyone

221

who comes across them. And still left till the end of his life was the presentation of the nine times worst of them, that fabled "Rotten Blossom" that betokened the end. If that last phase of it should happen, than all the good of the world would be in vain.

Ennis propounded his stark and evil dreams in several mediums with a handling that was probably genius. These things are so powerful that more and more people mistake them for reality.

But those in the form of opera, or *horribly* comic opera, those in the form of fiction, even those in the form of Broadway plays, they were not known directly to any large number of people.

Well then, they were known indirectly but intensely to almost all the people everywhere. The "Armageddon Cults", based on these horrible fictional happenings, grew and grew. Now they have somewhat more than half of all the people in their grip. And the cultified multitudes believe that these inventions have really happened, that they are still happening, and that the colossal final and engulfing rotten fruit of them cannot now be avoided.

What terrible thing is going on here? And how did this good man with the twisted good humor happen to father it?

There had been a thirteen-year-old adult who used to deliver milk with horse and wagons, and who played the flute. There had been a sixteen-year-old adult who delivered ice, and a nineteen-year-old adult who bought and operated a traveling carnival. He had been a vagabond innocent in a raggedly innocent world.

What had happened to that innocent young adult? Oh, he was still innocent for all of his years, and his soul was still pure. He would even take that soul out in his hands and show it to people so they could see how unblemished it still was.

But what had really happened to him?

And what had happened to the golden world of peace and the parousia, that ugly stories were bruited about it now?

A trick, a trick! Enniscorthy had set up the condition that no one can give a sequential account of his life. It escapes every effort. It can hardly be touched on.

SECTION TWO

A SHORT DISCUSSION ON THE FORMULAE
OF DOCTOR HENRY DEVONIAN

I

In the November 1910 issue of *Mathematics and Cosmology* there appeared a piece by Doctor Henry Devonian with the tantalizing title "Effector Formulae Governing Time and Consensus-Time, with Emphasis on the Saecula Unit." And, of course, after the appearance of this, the intellectual world was never the same again.

"Hell, it was never the same before," Elton Quartermas said. That's true. And the statement that the intellectual world was never the same again has been made of various other events also. The intellectual world is like running water, and anything at all can ripple it. Even so, there was only one possible early response to such a definitive set of statements and formulae (jolters they were) as Doctor Devonian published.

"It isn't new," the interested gentry responded to it. "It has all been previously stated in one form or another by Plotonius and Lucretius, by Anselm and Aquinas, by Cajetan and Cunningham, by Kant and Klubertanz. Nevertheless, the suggestions of Doctor Devonian must be looked into."

But these gentrymen were faking it. The statements, equations, and formulae of Doctor Devonian were quite new, and many of those who called them old weren't even able to follow the mathematics of them. And the drawing there, it hadn't anything to do with Devonian's "Effector Formulae." They used a little bit of art in *Mathematics and Cosmology* sometimes, and this piece (which looked like an old wood-cut but was only a drawing) showed a cherublike young boy, but with a sun-burned nose, being simply cherubic. But there was also an optical illusion to the drawing. That angelic and peeling kid could also be the end of one of the tentacles of a hellish monster that writhed in the background. It was a novelty piece done by Matthew Woodbine Senior, who was well known in the pages of *Mathematics and Cosmology,* both as a master mathematician and a droll artist.

"Oh, the *idea* of the idea is old," Wimbish A. McDearmott said (of the mathematical piece, not of the picture, though he was looking both at the picture and at the first page of the Devonian piece as he held the journal open), "but the main idea itself couldn't even have been thought of much earlier. Something like this was *suspected* by *everyone* from Plotonius to Klubertanz, true, but the angle of parallax was too small to give any observation at all with the mathematical equipment of former days.

"It was a little bit like taking annual parallax on fixed stars. You remember that that was the point where Galileo was wrong and his opponents were right. If the Earth moved, they said, it must move across the heavenly background. From its positions, six months apart, on opposite sides of the sun, it should observe the stars from a little bit different angle and against a little bit different background, its opponents said: and it didn't.

"It does," Galileo said, "and here are my different observations to prove it." But he had hypnotized himself and faked his own observations, getting the results he wanted to get. There weren't any such results. There couldn't be any such differences of observation. For the differences of the angle of observation on the stars he was playing with were on the order of an angle subtended by the diameter of a bird shot (maybe four-hundredths of an inch) at the distance from Earth to Moon. Angles as small as that could not be read with the optical equipment then available. And cosmological-behavioral angles as fine as those used in calculating the "Effector Formulae" could not have been read with the intellectual equipment available as recently as last year; I will go further and say that they could not be read with the intellectual equipment available as recently as March of this year.

"But now, as you may have noticed, there has been a quantum jump. Much of the very recent mathematics, that of the last three months in particular, is so sophisticated that there has to have been a biological mutation in a small group of elite mathematicians to bring them to such new understandings."

"Yes, there has been such a mutation," Elton Quartermas said. "I can feel it in myself. But these new equations are a danger to the world and they must be curbed."

(There was a little blurb above Devonian's piece "Mathematical speculations so disturbing that they may well drive men to murder.")

"And how will you be able to do that?" Wimbish McDearmott wanted to know.

"Perhaps by attaching amnestic corollaries to the equations," Elton proposed.

Doctor Henry Devonian had written in part:

"The intellectual development of mankind has so far been mostly a learning to talk. Man had intelligent speech from the first, of course. This is a matter of definition. Man is a creature with intelligent speech, so there could not have been a man without intelligent speech. To be a man is to have speech. Not to be a man is not to have speech.

"But further developments of this gift of speech have been expected from the beginning, and we have regularly fulfilled these expectations. Writing is a developed form of speech, expected of us, and fulfilled. And the "General and Particular Time-Consensus Equations" that I contribute here are new, quantum-jump developments of mathematical symbolisms and formulae and equations.

"We are now one decade into this latest century of the Lord, which I believe is the Golden Century of Peace and Parousia. Every century or saecula-unit must have its own mathematics and formulae, its own physical and paraphysical context. And this golden, quantum-jump century must have my own quantum-jump statements. They are these. Read them, and be struck smart!"

(But over opposite this opening page of the Devonian article was the optical illusion picture of good and evil, the innocent boy being the end of a tentacle of cataclysmic evil. Why couldn't that picture have been set opposite the opening page of Shipman's "The New Mathematics and Rural Reform?")

But the "General" and the "Special Time-Consensus Equations" that Doctor Henry Devonian then gave are not easy reading. A single equation thirty-eight pages long and containing eight thousand units is never easy. A second equation that is fifty-one pages long and contains more than eleven thousand units is likewise difficult, even for the sophisticated elite. And the elite persons in the world who belong to the mathematical-cosmological field number no more than two hundred. They almost exactly coincide with the subscription list of *Mathematics and Cosmology*.

And even these elite persons and their intellectual scions are not able to comprehend everything about the "General" and "Special" formulae immediately.

"It will take about three-quarters of a century for us to draw the full implications from these," Doctor Devonian had written in his summing-up. "That will be too late. The full implications will destroy us in just about three-quarters of a century if they are not counteracted. But how does one counteract the full implications of mathematical equations that he does not yet understand in their depth?"

Doctor Devonian then gave a little prose outline of the "General" and the "Special" formulae for citizens who were not of the elect:

"The mathematical and organic formulae comprising the "General Equation" indicate that the Interaction Index of the Enclave (known as 'Time' or 'Consensus-Time') will be keyed onto a single individual. The 'One Individual Crux' proves to be a mathematical necessity.

"I have been able to identify the individuals of eight different 'consensus-times' of the past and show that the one individual was paramount to *all* happenings in that consensus-time. This one individual is a requirement of the

226

happenings. Without him, they would not have happened, or they would have happened otherwise, which is to say that they would have been different consensus-times with different key individuals. But, without the one crux individual in each case, there would have been *no* times and *no* happenings at all.

"If the single key individual is withdrawn from the master equation of a particular time, then that equation will collapse, and that time will collapse with it. There are several apparent vestiges of such lost times or eras that were somehow voided of happenings and so became nonexistent.

"The "General Equation" is the statement of the nature of Happening. And happening is what comprises being. The "General Equation" applies to every time-enclave-happening from the Creation itself to the Parousia or Second Coming 'Till He Shall Return.' It applies to everything, the Fall of Angels and of Men, the Redemption, and the Waiting Centuries. The indication is that the present Golden Century is that of the Parousia, or the Coming, that it is the Time of the Final Things, which however will be a continuing final. They will not signal an ending but a perpetual beginning. And when that Time-That-Is-Bigger-Than-Time comes, we will be given a new time equation. (It should be a dazzler!) But first we must get there.

"For, if this century is not that of the Parousia, then it will be that of the False Parousia; it will be that of the horrifying and hellish reverse-coming, of the Second Coming of the Powers of Hell. (I have been told several times that preaching does not belong in theoretical mathematics. Well, if it doesn't belong there, what the hell does belong there?)

"Some may accuse me of impiety and say that I have left God out of the equations. But that accusation can only come from their careless reading. God is the thirty-seventh element of the 'General Equation' (how could I make that plainer than I have made it?), and the forty-fourth element of the 'Particular Equation' or the 'Special Equation.'

"This explanation or commentary moves then into the statement of the 'Particular Equation.'

"Oh how deprived are those who cannot read!" exclaimed Wimbish McDearmott. "They miss it all, or they get weak and derivative versions of all the big things."

"What do you mean by 'those who cannot read'?" Alistar Grogg asked him.

"Those who cannot read the sophisticated formulae of the new mutated mathematics may be said not to be able to read," Wimbish explained. "How feeble is mere prose beside the language of mathematical notation! Devonian does his best with it, I suppose, but his presentation just will not shake the world to its foundations; and it's necessary that it should do just that. We do all agree that it *is* world shaking and likely that it is world destroying? But there may be no more to say about it than he says in his notations and his prose; there may be no *way* to say more about it. Let us, however, go over the formulae a bit and see if we may not translate out a little bit more of their strength for the multitudes that may be called the 'short-end-of-the-stick' mankind."

Wimbish A. McDearmott, Alistar Grogg, and Elton Quartermas were met together over beans and books at the Rotating Vector, an all-night restaurant and piano bar and pool hall. Foundry men, packinghouse workers, pattern makers, printers, sewing-machine girls, railroad men, dray men, police detectives, hotel porters, piano players, livery stable workers, scrub women, and mathematicians all came into the Rotating Vector in the after-midnight hours for beans and beer, and cigars and conspiracy, and piano playing and conversation. Like met with like there, so there were really a number of small clubs assembled in the place sitting at the bean tables or lounging around the pool tables or leaning on the two pianos. The place always smelled like beans and beer and horses. (There were always hot horses tied at the back door while the team masters were inside for their long half hours.)

"If we do not have three-quarters of a century in which to draw the full implications from the formulae of Doctor Devonian, then we will have to do it in less," Alistar

Grogg said. "There have always been a few equations capable of blowing up the world, and there are more than a few of them here in this work. We may ask why, if even the "General Formula" contains so many explosive equations, the world has not been blown up before. And the answer is that the world *has* been blown up before, again and again, in a limited way, and sometimes not so limited. There is no age so poor that it has not had its catastrophe. I had hoped that our own Golden Century would be spared these things; but according to Doctor Devonian, and according to the most reasonable conclusions to be drawn from the formulae, it won't be."

"It won't be spared these things unless certain resolute persons devise a way to spare it," Elton Quartermas said. "There are strong indications, in fact there is mathematical certainty, that the catastrophes of our Golden Century won't be ordinary. They may be the terminal catastrophes of the people of this world. But what will happen to the equations if we *do* find a way to interfere with their disastrous processes?"

"There seem to be 'Protect-Our-Own' corollaries imbedded all through both the 'Special' and the 'General Organa'," McDearmott said. "I sense an organization (probably unnatural or unhuman) to which we might as well give a code name 'Friends of the Catastrophes.' It will destroy one or all of us if we attempt to interfere. I am not a believer in the 'Conspiracy Theory of Mathematics,' but there *is* a secret organization implicit in all the mathematics of the first part."

"Maybe someone else will do it, interfere with the equations," Quartermas suggested without conviction.

"Who else?" Grogg asked. "How can there be a working group of less than three, and in how many places will there be as many as three persons who comprehend these things? In Berlin? But in Berlin, they will recess their decision for decade after decade until it is too late. In Paris? No, they are not to be trusted in Paris. The slinky mathematicians of Paris might even join forces with the 'Friends of the Catastrophes.' In London? Don't count on it. In New York? But New Yorkers are bunglers, as the very mathematics of the 'Particular Equation' indicate. No, it will have to be ourselves. After all, the key person is in our town.

"I suppose that we should simply go and kill the young boy who fulfills the 'Equation,' and then let come whatever may come upon us. I hate to kill a young and innocent boy though; and I'm equally reluctant to be killed in turn."

3

"This moves then into the statement of the 'Particular Equation,'" Doctor Devonian had written, "and we are able, by relentless predication, to solve for the location and the name of the 'Crux-Individual' who is the key to our era or *saeculum*. In this case, he seems to be a 'dreadful key,' a baleful influence. He is clearly named in the mathematical context, but I will not publicly name him in the alphabetical letters of his name. But I might do it privately.

"If really interested persons will write to me at the address given at the end of this essay, I will send them the name of that person who is an essential function on which our *saeculum* is predicated. What possessors of this knowledge will do with it will remain my total unconcern. His blood be not upon my hands!"

("This is clear inciting to murder," Quartermas said. "He can't wash his hands of it."

("True, he's incited me to murder by it," Grogg said. "At least I won't be able to wash my hands of it.)

"To us oldtimers," the Devonian article continued, "it seems strange that a mathematical formula should arrive at the identity of a particular person as its answer. It has always been so, but our vision has heretofore been too narrow to see it. It is really as though the answer to a column of figures should turn out to be a person and not a quantity. Well, such is the case. And, of course, every person *is* a codified quantity; and every quantity is a person of either major or minor attributes.

"And the unlying figures and signs of the 'Particular Formula' indicate that things might be bad, very bad, for our Golden Century. It will get hot beyond the melting

230

point of its gold, beyond the vaporizing point of gold. The total wager, the 'Here-we-go-with-all-we've-got' smasher, is implicit in all mathematics. One cannot add up the most simple column of figures without the possibility of the answer being that the ground will break open under out feet and we will end up in hell. Ordinarily, though, the odds are tilted a little bit against such an answer.

"Well, a certain sixteen-year-old boy does represent a chasm opening under our feet and plunging us into bottomless—well, oblivion, if we are so fortunate. He does represent a possible withdrawal of humanity from the life affair, if indeed he does not represent something much worse. The damned vision of his, which has presently arrived at the 'reality-in-potential' state, is clustered about three smoking and spewing mountains, each of them deeper and more sulphurous than the previous one.

"What is going on with him? He is tampering with the flow of the world's events and circumstances. That is what is going on with him.

"He is tampering with the nature of reality, that is what is going on. This boy can make anything whatsoever happen if he desires it strongly enough. But does he *want* these *'abominations of desolations'* to happen? He protests, over and over again, on his very soul, that he doesn't. But the relentless mathematics indicate that perhaps he does. These are not imaginary inferences that we are drawing from the data."

"Certainly coming events may cast their shadows before them," Alistar Grogg was saying. "All that is needed is a tolerably well-focused light source on the far side of those coming events. This far-side light source is item ninety-nine in both the 'General' and the 'Particular Equations,' according to Devonian. Nor would I say 'according to Devonian' for it is according to everyone. The equations belong to the world, and they cannot be altered in any least item of them. It does not matter who first worked them out. They could not be otherwise in any detail. We find here also that the shadow of the coming event is a requirement of that event, that in fact an event grows out of its own shadow if it grows at all. It will first be a shadow or ghost of an event. Then someone will say *'Fiat solidus,'* 'Let it be solid,' or 'Let it be real,' and it

231

will become a solid event for that one who ordered it. And, in the great mathematics of contingent worlds, it will soon be a solid event for everyone, or it will be nothing at all, a shadow that has passed without memory.

"Oh, there are a few exceptions to this. There are a few cases where eventuality does not make up its mind at once. Sophisticated students of history have known for a long time that there exist opposite and contradictory history tracks in certain countries and eras, double validities of which one does not seem to have given way to the other. There are cases of this in tribal Sumatra, in rocky Arabia, in central Ceylon, in Madascar, on the island of Malta, and again on the island of Majorca, and in the eponymous 'boondocks' of Asia Minor. And sometimes these contradictory history tracks hold to their contradictions for as long as three-quarters of a century. Then it is finally resolved that one version is reality and the other version is unreality. But several times the resolution has been obliterated (along with the civilization) so that we cannot know which version proved to be real and which one proved to be unreal.

"But it is generally the case that the blood-fanged cannibal version will eat up the other one. Indecision and delay usually works to the advantage of the blood fangs."

(They were three poor mathematicians talking together in a crowded and noisy place after midnight one night. But anyone who looked at them shrewdly would know what they were doing. They were plotting murder.)

"So, what do we do about it?" Elton Quartermas asked his fellow plotters.

"You know what we must do about it, Elton," Alistar Grogg said. "We must put a stop to the indecision before it starts. The boy is already working to incarnate and publish his hellish visions.

"When he goes out to load his ice wagon for the first run on some early morning soon, and he does this about two hours before dawn, that would be a good time for something mortal to happen to this future sower of destruction."

Several persons, persons a little bit weak on the new mutated mathematics for all of their being professionals in the field (none but high professionals would ever have

232

seen the essay) had had to write to Doctor Devonian to obtain the name and location of the crux-individual of the "Particular Equation."

But there were other persons and groups (among them the three-headed group of Wimbish McDearmott and Alistar Grogg and Elton Quartermas) who didn't have to write to Doctor Devonian. They were themselves able to solve the name and location from the data of the equation.

However the answer was got, it was always the same answer. It was a boy named Enniscorthy Sweeny on West Blackwater Street in Chicago. He was the only answer who would fit into the calculations properly, the only thing for which the calculations could be solved.

4

Conspiracy, conspiracy! Can good men join in a conspiracy to effect an evil on the chance that it might preclude a greater evil as part of its results?

Well, there was a gangly and unformly sixteen-year-old boy with a head full of smoky dreams and the reputation of being able to get or to bring to pass anything in the world if he wanted it strongly enough.

This boy rose very early in the mornings, several hours before dawn in the winter, and loaded up an ice wagon to begin to deliver ice to commercial establishments first. There were then one hundred and twenty-five companies in Chicago that were in the business of freezing ice and having it delivered to customers on a regular schedule. The ice house of one of them, the one that Enniscorthy Sweeny worked for, was only a block and a half from the back door of the Rotating Vector Restaurant and Piano Bar and Pool Room.

This thing could be done easily. There was always a lot of noise and not very much light in that little half alley, half street in the several hours before dawn. There were the noises of horses and of men, and the squeaking and growling of drays, and the clattering of the whiffle trees of baggage wagons. There was the jangle music of harness rings and even chains. Horses often fell down there, and men often did, and no one thought much about either. Often the men were overdrunk when they came to work before dawn, and many of the horses were overworked and double-shifted. Who would think very much about it if he saw that a man or a boy had fallen to the ground? Who would believe that it was anything except a sad accident if a boy or man should be found dead with his head bashed in by something very blunt and thick, as thick as a single-tree perhaps?

The three mathematicians rehearsed it three different predawns first. Wimbish McDearmott went one early morning. Alistar Grogg went once. Elton Quartermas went once. Each was able to come up behind young Enniscorthy Sweeny as he waited beside his ice wagon for other ice wagons to load up. Each of the sophisticated mathematicians was able to come up right behind the young man with a heavy single-tree in his hands, and to see several good opportunities to kill that young man pass by. But all mathematicians are careful, and they check and recheck their figures and propositions.

So, on the fourth after-midnight of it, the three of them were in the Rotating Vector again, eating beans and drinking beer and smoking cigars and talking mathematics as they always did for those several hours. This would be the time.

"There is a woman outside asking for Alistar Grogg," said a waiter there in the Rotating Vector. "I might even say that she is a distraught woman."

"Tell her that he is not here," said McDearmott. "Tell her to go away. No, no, none of us must have any doings with women at all till this thing is accomplished. Like Indian warriors going out on a raid, we must eschew women completely for a while before the action. Such will give us strength and courage. We must eschew distraught women particularly."

"What does she look like?" Alistar asked the waiter nervously.

"Oh, all angry women look alike," the waiter said.

"Tell her that he is not here," McDearmott repeated. "Tell her that he went over to Holsters' Haven just a few minutes ago."

It was just half an hour before their target time. They

sipped, and talked mathematics and conspiracy, and smoked their cigars. Then, as the time for it came quite near, they called for the dice. They rolled for low dice.

Alistar Grogg rolled the low dice, so he would be the one to kill Enniscorthy Sweeny.

They finished their beans and beer then. Wimbish McDearmott went to get their hats. Elton Quartermas went to get their overcoats. They came back to the table with them to put them on before they went out into the predawn.

"What was that funny noise back here, Alistar?" Elton Quartermas asked out of the armful of overcoats. "It sounded like a firecracker."

"Well, come along, Alistar," Wimbish McDearmott urged. "You are the hit man and it's time for the hit. What's the matter? You look bad."

"What was the funny noise was the pistol," Alistar spoke in a very fuzzy voice. "What is the matter with me is that the woman shot me with it. I used to go with her till a couple of days ago. And lately I've been going with someone else."

"Shot you!" Elton cracked in a panic voice. "Where?"

"In the head."

"But that can be serious. Did it hurt you?"

"Yes. It killed me," Alistar Grogg said. He gave a little jerk then, and he was dead, dead sitting there at the table.

It was predictable. It was implicit in the data of the "Particular Equation." The "Protect-Their-Own" corrolary had come into play. The Friends of the Catastrophes organization (probably unnatural or at least unhuman) had struck. It had moved to prevent the small group's preventing the implementing of the desolating visions of Enniscorthy Sweeny.

Alistar Grogg was dead. Wimbish McDearmott and Elton Quartermas was still alive, but they were frightened and confused for the while, perhaps for a year.

But they still knew what they had to do. They had to kill the dreamer named Enniscorthy before he dreamed the end of the World.

SECTION THREE

EXTRACTS FROM THE LETTERS, FIRST SELECTION

I

This letter was written after November, 1916 when Franz
Ferdinand became Emperor. It was while the opera Armageddon I, the first section of the Tyrrhene Triptych,
was being presented for that first session in Vienna. It
probably was not opening night. It may have been emperor night that usually came a week or so after opening
night, or it may have been a still later performance. The
Emperor, though backstage, does not seem interested in
watching the opera, although he is intensely interested in
the subject and fact of the opera. So it is probably in De-
cember, 1916 or January, 1917. Enniscorthy Sweeny begins a dozen or more letters with "My Dear Tarnished
Friend," but this tarnished friend has never been identified.

My Dear Tarnished Friend:
    I met the Emperor Franz Ferdinand last night.
They have here (who would believe such a thing?) a
Royal Room backstage at the Burgtheater. We are at
the Burg. We are not at the State Opera House itself.
The State is being remodeled, but there is a Royal
Room backstage at the State also. It is hard to be-

lieve that the large and luxurious Burgtheater is only the second best opera house in Vienna.

"I love it," the Emperor told me. "It seems that it is the second best of everything that I occupy, but I accept all these second-best things. I do not live at the Hofburg which is the Palace of the Emperors and which has been for the last several months the mausoleum of the late 'Old Emperor.' I live in the little Karlspalast which is the second best of the royal palaces in the City. It seems also that I am only the second-best Emperor who is now ruling from Vienna. The best—well, I suppose that he is an ideal Emperor, and that I do not measure up to that ideal.

"I am also referred to as the 'Contingent Emperor' or the 'Caretaker Emperor,' although I am the legal Emperor in the true line in every respect. Do you know why I should be thought of as the 'Caretaker Emperor' or the 'Emperor of the Second Version'?"

"I, Emperor Franz Ferdinand, no, I don't know," I told him. "How should I know why they think of you in these ways."

"Because you, American Opera Maker, were the first one to think of me in these ways, on your road to thinking of me in still another way. I believe that you *do* know about all this, Mr. Sweeny of the Dark Librettos," he said. "I believe that you do know why I am only the 'Emperor of the Second Version.' It is because you have created a 'First Version' of things, and your 'First Version' is on the attack. It is already occupying low-lying areas in many minds."

Every young man, my friend, should meet and talk intimately with an Emperor. It is an essential part of the education of a young man, and it is too often neglected. The Emperor is a man of friendly voice and manners, and of unfriendly appearance. He is thick of face and body, and he has wild-boar mustaches. He looks older than his years. He has aged, they say, twenty-five years in the last two and a half years. It is only because he still stands in the shadow of the recently dead 'Old Emperor' that he

237

can still, with a straight face, be called the 'Young Emperor.'

"You did not intend to come to Vienna with the opera," the Emperor told me. "You try to stand apart from presentations of this work, Mr. composer of operas-that-go-Beyond, but I summoned you to come. The least Emperor can still summon the greatest composer. That power still adheres to us. I summoned you here to ask you questions. And you came.

"About the opera then, and about the libretto to it that spells things out much more starkly than the actual presentation, how did you know that these things would happen? *They will not happen,* but how did you know that they would?"

"What things, Emperor?" I asked him.

"The things in the libretto," he said, "the things of the 'First Version.' You must know that Vienna is the psychoanalytical capital of the world. It swarms with prototypes and with the makers of prototypes; but you are the tallest of the current prototype makers, and you come from over the sea. These things that are in your libretto of the first part of the Tyrrhene Triptych, in that awful Armageddon I that they are singing so awfully right now, they were in the archetypical nightmares of many of the Austrian people (and in my own nightmares) before your little libretto was struck off on the presses. How can this be?"

"That I don't know, Emperor," I said.

"But you can guess," he answered me. "Who are you that you have put my own nightmares, including the nightmares of my death by assassination, into the form of a horribly comic opera?"

"I am only a poor man who composes poor operas," I said.

"I did not go to Bosnia in July of that year," the Emperor said. "I did not go, because those recurring nightmares that always resolved themselves into my death would not let me go there. They made a coward out of me. I hadn't been one before that. But you have presented all these private hysterias of

238

mine in the form and context of Operatic History. Do you read my mind? Have you a window in onto my hysterias? How have you done this?"

"I cannot tell you," I said. "At least, I will not tell you."

"The things *can not* happen," the Emperor said firmly, as though he were giving an order. "There are enough responsible people in the world that we will not permit them to happen. The people themselves can have no idea how near they have come to happening. But the time of the crux happening (according to your opera and my nightmares) is now two and a half years in the past, and I am still alive and well."

"No, you are alive and ill," I said. "Who are you, Emperor, to say that a road can run only one way?"

"You are saying that these things *can* happen, man?" he asked.

"They are happening, on the stage of the Burgtheater out front right now," I told him.

"The stage of the Burgtheater is not the world," he insisted, "and time cannot be made to run backwards. I am safe from it."

"That stage may be the world for you," I said, "and stage time may run backwards. Many a man has died during a flashback. And no Emperor is ever safe. 'Being Safe' is the opposite of 'Being Emperor.'"

This was all a bit cruel of me, and I cannot explain that part of it. I certainly did not feel any cruelty towards the worried man.

But the Emperor began to groan and to sway in his thick-bodied manner. He was in some agony of mind, but I believe that was necessary for him. He cannot live on two life-tracks so publicly without this agony.

Every middle-aged Emperor, my friend, should meet and talk intimately with a young composer of dark librettos. It is an essential part of the education of a middle-aged Emperor, and it is too often neglected.

Enniscorthy.

This letter was likely written about 1907. There is a fair probability that the Pumpkin Seed to whom it is written is the Mary Margaret McGronsky whom Enniscorthy Sweeny later married.

My Dear Pumpkin Seed:

I bet this is the first letter you ever got from Blue Island, Illinois. I will be back this evening and see you then, and you won't get this letter till tomorrow, but I still want to write it to you now. I am only sorry that you decided not to come down to see the game. It is the greatest game that I ever played. I will go so far as to say that it is the greatest game that anybody ever played.

I had written the game out in every detail about two years ago. I had decided then to make it be a seventh world series game between the White Sox and the Giants, but it would take so damned much tampering to make pennant winners out of them for sure that I have meanwhile decided that my energy could better be expended elsewhere.

So I had the script of this game left over. I decided to use it for the game of today, with myself as the pitcher-hitter-hero. And I knew that I had it in my pocket when Mr. Stocker, our coach (Oh sure you know him, he's your uncle, I forgot), told me, "You will pitch today, Sweeny. I don't know why you will, since you never did pitch and I don't even know whether you can or not; but you will pitch today. I have three good pitchers ready to go, and Blue Island is one of the best suburban high school teams around. I don't know why I am putting in an underaged, third-string outfielder to pitch. Do you know why I am?"

"Yep," I said. "I know why. But it wouldn't be ethical for me to tell you."

Listen, Pumpkin Seed, this isn't any little cut-and-dried game that I win with a grand slam home run in the last of the ninth inning with two outs and two strikes and three balls on me. Give me credit for more class than that. And it isn't a game that just anyone can put together on the spot even if they have good control over things. I have lived with that game for two years or I wouldn't be able to do it now. Besides, we are the visitors at Blue Island, so we would be up in the first half of the ninth inning and not in the last half. Listen how I got around that one.

I didn't allow any hits and I didn't walk anyone in the whole game. But I had to let them get three runs so I could win it with a grand slam—no, *not* a home run, it's better than that. So I pulled out all the stops for our fellows to make some of the damnedest errors you ever saw. Oh, it was murder!

And I had to hit those home run balls every time I was up, and yet keep myself from getting any home runs. Ah, one of my towering blows hit a kite after it had already gone over the fence, and got entangled with the kite and broke it loose from its string; and it drifted in over the field again with the baseball still tangled in it. The shortstop caught the kite and the second baseman caught the ball.

And another of my towering blasts hit a chicken hawk, and the hawk and the baseball both dropped back onto the field. And a whirlwind caught another of my shots and brought it down to the third baseman's glove after every player on the Blue Island team had had a stab at it as it whirled around.

We were one fine-looking baseball team with our new red baseball shirts. I didn't have one, of course, being only a third-string outfielder till today, but I was wearing a red sweater that looked almost as good.

So we came down to the end of it. We were in the *first* half of the ninth, and Blue Island was ahead of us three to nothing. I still hadn't given up a hit and I had twenty-four strike outs, and yet we were behind because of all those errors and flukes. Then we loaded the bases, with three more flukes, on Blue Island this time. I'm telling you that those flukes take

241

more out of me than the straightaway stuff does. Then we made two outs. And I was up to bat and the count went three to two against me. It was now or never for me, and Blue Island had a big eighteen-year-old boy for a pitcher who was throwing speed balls that I had trouble controlling.

It was now-or-never time, do-or-die time, sink-or-swim time. The only thing that could save us was a grand slam—no, not a home run, dammit. It would be a grand-slam "something else" that only I of all the people in the world would have thought of.

It would be a grand slam bunt.

And you think that a grand slam bunt doesn't require total control of a situation! Boy!

I bunted down the third base line. The pitcher had it and could make a play to any base and end the game. I fell down so I would look like the easiest out, and all the runners had gone with the pitch. He threw towards first. He was laughing at me or he'd have made a better throw.

Easy now. This takes real control of things here. A yellow jacket stung the first baseman right on the nose. People out of the know will never guess where that yellow jacket came from. The first baseman crossed his eyes when he was stung on the nose and, instead of him catching the ball, it hit him on the head, incidently knocking him cold and then bouncing high and towards second base.

I put on a big holler so they would keep the play after me so I could keep it under better control, and meanwhile our runs were pouring over the plate.

The pitcher took the ball when I was already past there (it had bounced pretty high off the first base-man's head) and threw it to second, but the second baseman and the shortstop ran into each other and knocked each other out and I kept going towards third. The centerfielder cut it off and threw to third, but he stepped into a gopher hole when he did it and broke a leg. That put such a twist on the ball that it ran right up the third baseman's arm and hit him in the face and cooled him. The leftfielder was in with a sensational back-up play then and had the ball and

242

shot it towards home, and then he ran into the bench and went over and out. The catcher and pitcher were both trying to cover the plate and they cracked into each other and the ball made a billiard and knocked them both out.

I scored standing up, and we won the game.

And the last half of the ninth? Pumpkin Seed, there wasn't any last half of the ninth. You *were* paying attention, weren't you? The first baseman and the second baseman and shortstop and center fielder and third baseman and left fielder and catcher and pitcher had all been injured on the play. That left only the right fielder to bat for them in the last half of the ninth.

"I won't do it," he said. "The way things are going, a guy could get hurt out there." And the substitutes all refused to bat too because the game had got so dangerous.

They were bad losers though. They said that there was something fishy going on and that ours was a tainted victory. And our own coach, your uncle, Mr. Stoker, seemed to feel that way too, though he didn't say it. What he did say was:

"You had good control out there today, Sweeny. You had very, very good control. I have never seen such total control in my life. I have never seen a person who had *everything* under such good control before."

He looked at me with those funny eyes of his. They're kind of like yours. I think they must be family eyes. When *you* look at me like that with your eyes it means that you're seeing through me. Is that what it means when *he* looks at me like that, do you suppose? And wouldn't it be better, don't you think, if he should squelch all his suspicions? I *was* pitching for *his* team. We *were* on the same side. We *did* win.

I am certain that my feat is unique in baseball. If they play baseball for another thousand years, I bet nobody ever does get a grand slam bunt again.

This letter is probably written about 1911. Once more, it cannot be ascertained to whom the letter is written.

Dear Sergeant and Friend:

I know that you have a lowly place on the police force as yet, but it may not remain lowly. I believe that there is a way that you can prevent a crime and cover yourself with glory.

Well, there is a man who intends to kill me. He is bold about it, and he has told me to my face that he will kill me. This man is a maniac, and he must be stopped for the safety of society and myself.

This man belongs to one of those numbers cults. These people believe that they can deduct the future out of complicated mathematical equations. I understand their figuring a little bit and I have to admit they they are onto something. I believe that I could understand it completely if I had enough desire for that. I am easing up on the business of wanting to do different things badly enough though, as I feel that I may run out of powers on the other end of it if I use them all on this end. And my understanding the way that they figure out the equations isn't going to stop them from killing me.

I hesitate going to the law, except in as much as *you* are the law. I am still a minor, and I am an unprepossessing person, and what would my word be against that of an accomplished and personable man who is also a college graduate when I charge him with things that seem insane?

Here are the facts. The man who intends to kill me is named Elton Quartermas. He is a poor mathematician. Rather he is a poor man who is likely a very good mathematician. He teaches at Chicago Industrial and Technical Institute, and I don't believe that he is paid very much there. He spends time, late at night, at the Rotating Vector, a restaurant and piano bar and pool hall that is on your beat.

He has been following me and skulking after me and spying on me for some time, and last night I decided to have it out with him. I went to the Rotating Vector an hour after midnight and I sat down with him at his table.

"You have been following me and spying on me," I said. "Now I wait for you. Now catch up with me and see what happens."

"I will catch you up in my own time and way," this *man* Quartermas said.

"What do you want with me?" I asked.

"Dead," he said. "That's what I want with you. I want you dead."

"Why is that?" I asked as cooly as I could, but I was shaking a little bit inside.

"It's your dreams," Quartermas said. "Your dreams are disrupting the world and they are a danger to humanity. I want them stopped, but I do not believe that you are able to stop them yourself, or you are not to be trusted to do so. You will not stop dreaming these things till you are dead."

"What if I don't stop them even then?" I asked.

"But you will," he said. "The equation says that you will. There are people who keep on after they're dead, but you're not one of them."

"That is the most ridiculous bunch of stuff I ever heard," I said.

"I know it," he answered. "The only thing I can say in defense of it is that it's true. You are dreaming and devising baleful futures for the world. I believe it is more right that one man, you, should be destroyed than that the whole world should be."

"But what am I *doing?*" I asked him.

"Dreaming," he said again. "You are dreaming with an evil twist. You are dreaming dreams of great catastrophes, and the world is too frail a thing to be trampled by your dreams."

"What sort of dreams are these supposed to be?" I asked. "How could dreams possibly hurt anything?"

"They are dreams of Armageddon," he said.

245

"They will destroy the world unless you are destroyed."

"Why haven't you killed me already?" I asked. "You've surely had your chances."

"I've been in fear of the 'whiplash' or 'kickback corollary' to your own equation," he said. "But now I believe I have found a way to counter that. Be patient. I'll kill you very soon now."

"I will hand you over to the police," I said.

"On what grounds?" he asked me in a mocking way. "You will report the ridiculous things that I have said, and I will answer 'What's with this crazy kid?' He has jumped his trolley. You should toss him into the clink until someone has time to examine him.' And, boy, if that does happen, well I know someone in the La Salle street klink who will do a total wipe-out on you if you turn up there."

"There must be some way I can reason with you," I said.

"You reasoned with my friend Alistar Grogg," he said. "You shot him to death with a gun in a woman's hand. That was enough of your reasoning."

"I have never heard of this Grogg," I said.

"He has heard of you and he has lost his life over you," Quartermas said. "Well, perhaps it will happen to me also, but there will be a difference. I have devised—well, no, not devised—I have discerned a lock-in device or element in the "Particular Equation" that I may be able to take advantage of. If I die from this, then the lock-in will operate to the extent that you will die also. But the converse doesn't necessarily hold. If *you* die from this, I may escape it. But even if I do die and I take you with me, it will be worth it. It will be done for the world and for its quality."

"Sir, you are mad," I told him.

"That's likely," he conceded. "There's a humorous little preface to Hackberry's 'Three Algebras for Post-Human People.' It says that a workable level of creative madness will be necessary for anyone to master his opus. I mastered it handily. He says that going mad may simply be the stepping over a fence

246

that shuts other people in. He says that the test of whether a madness is benevolent or malevolent is what you step into when you step over that fence."

"I know what *you* have stepped into," I said. "You are a barnyard strutter. You have stepped into the stuff itself and you have it on your shoes now."

"Little Sweeny," he said to me. "I wonder if you know that your dreams are attracting fans. Yes, fans, devotees. There are people, some of them young and some of them not so young, who can hardly wait for your next blood-and-fire dream. They are turned in on you and your contrived futures. Some of these unfortunates are my own students and some of them are people I have encountered elsewise. They are unsavory people all; they are gore-oriented people; they are hatred-and-murder people; they are bring-down-the-world people. They have been looking blindly for a nucleus to form a cult about, and now they have found it in you and your dark visions."

"Man, no one can tune in on my dreams," I said.

"I can, and others can," he told me. "I do it a little bit sometimes. And they make me sick, your dreams. Horribly sick. Only your death can make me well again, and only your death can preserve the health of the world."

This man, who seems to be unhinged, tells me plainly that he intends to kill me. This man knows things out of the first part of the Armageddon I Libretto, things that I have not put on paper yet, things that I have not put into words yet but only into music in my mind; he even knows some things of mine that I haven't thought of yet. But now he has recounted them to me, or recollected them to me with his horror and hatred. So, he has recounted them to me; I am not above such feedback in advance. I will use them. They're good, and they mesh in well with the rest of it. I believe that if computers were sufficiently well advanced, the whole sequence of the Three Armageddons could be constructed from the mathematics for this time, from the 'Particular Equations' of Doctor Devonian, without using me at all. But, now I understand it, computers *are* sufficiently well advanced. I am such a computer and I am being used for this.

I am not sure whether I could have thought of these particular sidelights without Quartermas. I suspect that I would have. They were already in my mind, but very deep.

Friend, this man is criminally insane. And he is criminally insane on your beat, and that is your concern. Please, please find some way to have him picked up and examined. And find some way to have him held, forever, I hope. Have him held till he is over his delusions, and I believe that will be forever.

Enniscorthy Sweeny

4

This letter seems to date from about 1913. The "Moneybags" isn't identified.

Dear Moneybags:

I have been working with a notion that may not be new at all. I made quite a bit of money with it for a little while, and now I have lost part of that money back to the notion again. I should be way ahead on the deals, but I'm only a little bit ahead. It seems that my profits from this just evaporate away.

I believe that you yourself may have been involved with such notions along the way. I am almost sure that your father has been. You came to me a while back and asked for the return of a short letter that you had written to me two days before.

"It was the letterhead that was wrong," you said. "I used it by accident. I had been admiring some of them but I sure didn't intend to use one of them in this track. They aren't from this version at all. They're from a different track that hasn't even got this far yet and won't pass quite by here when it does. Please, Ennis, there isn't any way to explain it to you. Just give me back that last letter that I wrote to you."

Well, I'd like to have done that, Moneybags. I

248

took out the bundle of letters from you and they were all there except that last one.

"It has to be here and it isn't," I said. "And there isn't any other place it could be."

"Oh, I think it's all taken care of now, Ennis," you said. "It must have taken care of itself, as I had hoped that it would. And there *is* another place that it could be, and I trust that it is there. Forget it, Ennis, it's all right."

That's what you said. You're an odd one, Money-bags.

And then your father, the last time he offered me a job, he said to me:

"You would be almost ideal for this job, Ennis. I need a smart boy like you at my bank. For a bank messenger, Ennis. What, you do not rise to the term? I said, *for a bank messenger,* Ennis. You do not understand what sort of bank messenger I mean?

"Well, Ennis, maybe I'm not as sure of you as I thought I was. You're smart, you're smart, but you're not exactly on-the-money smart, and that's what I want. In some ways you're not smart enough and in some ways you're way too smart. How can you know so much and guess so little, Ennis? How can you?

"Oh, you say 'No' to it, do you?" (I hadn't really said 'No,' Moneybags. It was more as if your father had reached into my mouth with his hand and hooked that 'no' out from under my tongue. And yet it sounded in the air, and in my voice.)

"Well, maybe it's just as well that you won't, Ennis," your father continued. Forget it, Ennis, it's all right."

Well, your father and you are onto something, and it may be the same thing that I'm on. I want to know whether you know anything about Contingent Banking or Probability Banking or Multi-Track Banking, since you work in your father's bank. As I said, I made quite a bit of money out of it at first, and I didn't really know anything about it, but I believe that you do.

Well, what if I withdraw money from one of my accounts, *when it happens to be on another track?* And then I carry that money with me and deposit it into my equivalent account on this track. And what if the withdrawal doesn't show up, and the deposit does? What if I take things into another track and sell them there, and come back with the money. And the things sold are still here and the money is here at the same time.

What if I work at four different jobs in four different tracks at the same time, and find a way to have all the money come into this track. Would I not do quite well with such a deal? What if I can find out stock-market prices in several tracks at once and make smart-money transactions on the differences in the prizes? Well, all of these things do work, but they don't work quite well enough. Something always goes wrong and drains most of the money away.

Tell me what you know about these things, Moneybags, if you do know anything about them, and if you want to tell me. And, if not,—

then forget it, Moneybags, it's all right.

Enniscorthy.

5

This letter belongs to about the same period as the second one back, about 1911, when Enniscorthy Sweeny was approximately seventeen years old. It is written to a Charles Crachett or Crochett who is not otherwise identified.

My Dear Charles:

I have the music finished for the first part of my Triptych, *Armageddon One!* It is wonderful! It is horrible! I wonder why it does not burst into flames at every movement of it. And sometimes it does.

As you know, I, having a completely detached mind, do it without instruments, in my perfectly

250

soundproof loft room. The only sound there is the scratching of my pen as it peals and choirs its way over the music paper. The music sounds in my mind only. The instruments, which I see and hear in my mind alone, are not the same as any instruments in the exterior world, though there are several of them that I might build someday.

And yet I believe that my clashing and soaring mind-music has been heard outside. It has been heard rather widely.

People are hearing it, and I myself have not heard it yet. People are whistling transpositions of it. And people are understanding it, and I will never understand it myself. I will not allow myself to do so. I have heard, from sources both clean and tainted, that my dreams, in both their music and their narration, have groups of fans who follow them avidly. But the only forms that, so far, I have poured my dreams into are these soundless lightning-sheets of written music that nobody else has seen.

But another person, a grubby genius, will see what I have written tomorrow. He is going to orchestrate it for me. He came to me for it. He is well known, and I am not known at all. He has been listening to it, night after night, he says, and he had to have a piece of the dark and twisted thing, the thing, the snake that twists clear around the world, as he calls it. He knows that snake intimately, and he knows my operas before even they are written. He knows the names of the different sections that I have named only in my mind, *The August 1914 Tonalities*, for instance.

"What we are doing," he said, "is pushing the pillars of the temple awry until they buckle and crash; and then all the roof will thunder down on us and on everything. But the roof that collapses in thunder is the world itself. Boy, we are collapsing the world and breaking its foundation, why aren't you shouting about it? Oh, wonderful, horrible, wonderful again! The destruction is all that matters." That's what he said.

251

Well, he is a fine orchestrator, and I'm lucky to have him.

I am doing the words immediately. I am doing the running words on the music strips and I am doing the libretto at the same time. I am plagued all day and night with small fires in my loft that I call a studio. I pretend that I am puzzled by the fires, but I am not. Individual sheets of paper do, now and then, burst into flame when I have finished writing on them. And then I must beat out the fires from them. (It is mostly around the edges that they burn, so I am starting to use wider margins now.) When I have beat out the fires, I paste the music sheets onto still blank sheets and spray them with formaldehyde from an atomizer to keep the charred parts from crumbling.

Some of the sheets are in a great hurry and they burst into flame even before I am finished writing on them. All of this is a tribute from someone to some power that is in my work.

Charles, a small child with fangs stopped me early this morning. She (I believe 'twas a she) grasped my hand, and I imagined that I felt claws.

"Will we kill them all, will we kill them all, do you suppose?" she asked me.

"Very many might be killed, yes, little person," I told her.

"The part just a little while ago, just before we woke up this morning, I liked that," she said. "I like the fires and the booming and the awful way it smells. And then the people, when their brains are all blown out like you blow out a candle, and they all become spitting grubs like me, I like that part too."

I have my following, Charles. She couldn't have known who I was, and yet she knew me.

And, Charles, I was visited by a monitor last midnight. I do not know what a monitor is. When I was a small school boy, the monitors were students selected for a week to take care of the coats and caps of all the students, and to help to keep order among them. Well, this was not that kind of monitor, and yet he was a monitor.

"This is a horror," the monitor said to me. "You are using your power on sick and trivial things, on small pictures of the larger thing. Now, when it all winds down to the end of it, you may be short just the measure of power that you have wasted today. It may all go awry at the resolution and end of things, just because you will then be short of power and will blink out.

"There are only a certain number of us, and we need us all. When one defaults, it puts an insufferable burden on the rest of us. What side are you on anyhow?"

I wanted to tell the monitor that I wished to be on his side, but he was gone.

Enniscorthy.

6

This letter, to a friend we know only as "Strongheart," seems to have been written shortly after the fiasco described.

Strongheart:

I have suffered my first real failure in the arts. This hurts me everywhere, in spirit and body and money. And it hurts you in spirit, I hope, since you are my friend. It hurts your uncles in the pocketbook since they were the producers.

January 29, 1919 was the opening night of this play. January 31, 1919 was the closing night. So it was a bust. I thought it was a very funny comedy and I still think so. I myself made a little bit on it, on the side, from a hunch I had by which I thought I could make a lot. I was the impresario of the 'Lobby Bar' that ran for those three nights in the north lobby of Stabler's Theatre.

Our equipment was rented and portable, and we did a fantastic business at the bar. If the comedy had run three years instead of three nights, this concession would have made me really rich.

The comedy made most of the people who watched it want to run out and get a drink right now. It made the audience very, very thirsty for alcoholic drink. Well that was one of the effects that I intended, but I didn't mean it to be the overwhelming effect. The fact remains that it *was* a very funny comedy. The other fact, that there was no one left in the audience and that everyone was crowding around the 'Lobby Bar' before the end of the first act, made it look as though the play were a failure. Your uncles thought that this included failure, and they closed the play. But the play was a sellout all the three nights of it, and it would have continued as a sellout.

The happy customers who went out and got pickled in the Lobby Bar were truly pleased about the whole thing, and they would give a good report of the play, even if with forked tongues. And, on their snowballing recommendations, they would have brought other people in to continue to throng the play. And from it they would go to the bar. And we could all have been rich. The closing of the play was a misunderstanding.

These are the appropriate facts of the matter.

Enniscorthy

(This play, which opened at Stabler's Theatre in New York on January 29, 1919 and closed two nights later, was named Prohibition, A Farce. *Now it is almost entirely forgotten.)*

SECTION FOUR

"ON THE CONSTRUCTION OF THE WORLD"

This was written by Enniscorthy Sweeny for the magazine Architecture and Prototype, *November 1916.*

I

A world does not build itself. It is built. It is built knowingly by intelligent persons. *In Principio Erat Intellectus.* It isn't begun on chasm'd chaos though. It begins on a globe; for all things, rain drops and fire drops, plasma globs and congregations of gasses, rock-worlds, and water-worlds, all assume the rough globe form. The surface of the globe is bare, rock earth, slippery shale-in-formation, mud-earth. And jagged diamond-scattered earth. There are ghosts, but no organisms yet.

It begins then on the many-layered surface of the globe. There is the muffled sound of footfalls. That is the ironic beginning of it all: "The world is empty and void of all life. There are muffled sounds of foot falls," like the beginning of a short story. The footfalls are those of Panther and his panthers. And who is Panther?

Panther is Pan-Therion or Pan-Therium, the All-Animal, the prototypical animal. He is the cool-fever-flesh from which all others diverge. He is the composite ('you should have seen some of the things and pieces of things that went into him') and the generating force. He is the red-clay which is clay-flesh. He is also the Dream-Master.

But many mythologies say that it was the *Bear* who made the world. Yet, there is no contradiction there. The Bear is one of the very strong elements in the Pan-Animal. This primordial dream-master beast is in fact the "Bearcat" who appears both in the Prophet Elias and in Mark Twain and who is found in the common expression of today "Boy, is that ever a Bearcat!" It is Pan-Therium, the Bearcat that is in the beginning. It's the flesh that is the red grass. It belches the dreams out of its stomach and they battle for supremacy, whether they shall survive as 'Worlds,' or not survive at all.

When, in Scripture, Joseph's sheaf rose up (that happened on this same flat rock earth that is the *situs* or *topos*) and remained standing, and his brothers' sheaves bowed down to it, that was a dream-becoming-flesh, and it triumphed over the rival dreams. When in Pharo's dream (it also was on that same flat, rock-and-mud earth again, though Pharo describes it as a half-developed place on the banks of the Nile among reed-grass) the ugly, thin cows ate up the seven sleek, fat ones, that was another selection-by-combat of what would be part of the emerging world and what would not be. I often wonder how we would be today if the fat cows had eaten up the skinny ones.

The flat, rock-mud area is the basic arena; it is the *topos* or location of the unconscious, and also of all of the *limbi* or border lands. At the present time there is a twelve year old boy in Figueras in Spain who paints this *topos,* this floor of the unformed and the unconscious every day. This is the uncluttered and primordial earth, and it looks like a mauve pavement. The twelve-year-old Catalan boy paints this landscape as inhabited by a few flat panthers and bears and bearcats, flattened as if melted down to the flatness of pancakes. The flat beasts are draped limply over the folded and stepped flatness of the land.

The paintings are of the early mornings, so

256

shadows are thrown in contradictory directions from dawn and false-dawn (there is a selection-by-combat between them also). It is in the early mornings that these proto-beasts are as flat and limp as melted paper, for it is then that they have belched themselves empty of dreams. These dreams or eructations are painted as flying in the low air with their vulture heads and bat-wings, or canvas-and-strut wings.

This *topos*, this unadorned and unconscious flatland, is subject to change; but the changes are very contingent for a long time. If hills are wanted, they are dragged in on skids by creatures pulling them with ropes. If mountains are required, they are rolled in on wheels or log rollers. This is analogous to the geological mountain-bringing process. The mountains always come in on easy-flowing extrusions that are really wheels or rollers of magma.

When a *topos* has acquired sufficient ornamentation, it is blessed, or it is cursed. If it is blessed, it becomes one of the Holy Lands. If it is cursed, we don't know what it becomes.

Even in their first form, the lands are not quite flat. There are the ledges from which the statuary stones are quarried. There are the clay-pits from which the red adam-clay is taken and from which Pan-Therium came. But the *topos* still maintains the appearance of flatness or of stepped flatness.

2

The Panther or Pan-Therium denies that he is a creature. "My belched dreams become creatures as soon as they acquire flesh," he says, "but I am a precreature."

There are blind persons working in the quarries and the clay-pits and the dream-bogs at first. But they are cooperative persons, and they will share and spread such gifts as they have. One of them was able to see a little bit through slits that appeared in his head. Then he took a chisel and hammer and made eyes in the travertine heads of some of his fellow workers, and they were able to see. Others, with crumbled earth and water, made paint pigments in a mortar with a pestle, and painted eyes on still others of the blind workers. With the painted eyes, these also could see. Either way is good.

I myself am a newly born or newly wakened worker in these quarries and clay-pits and dream-bogs and new-greening botanical gardens. I have been set to work by an impulse and by the command: "Make Facsimiles!" But the persons around me, demiurges and archangels and underground-born gnomes, are all making originals.

"A facsimile is always a lie," a Tyrrhene-faced fellow demiurge said.

"No, in some cases it is only a cock-shy," a troll worker from under-the-rocks said. "This person is supposed to make dreadful facsimiles to ward off dreadful realities. Let him do it! The dreadful reality will come and see the facsimile of itself and say 'But that is myself. I am already here. There is no purpose in my being here twice.' Then he will go away."

"No. That is a lie about the nature of a bigger lie," a Para-Angelos told it. "That is serpent-logic, and it's false. The dreadful facsimile that this person makes will not ward off a dreadful reality. It will be the origin of that reality. It will be the invention of it. It will turn into that dreadful reality that will gobble up the world. The facsimile escapes being killed during its vulnerable period by this deception about its nature, this statement that is is merely a scare-bird or a scare-devil. Then, when it is too big to be killed, it kills."

"Well, but what am I to do then?" I ask.

"You have your orders," one of them says. "Each of us has his orders."

"My orders are 'Make Fascimiles!' " I said.

"Make them then, and be blessed," said one of the bigger giant workers.

"Make them then and be damned," said one of the dwarf workers from under the hills.

I am told to make them so I will make them. How

do I know who tells me? Nobody else tells me any other thing to do.

3

Notions are the beginnings of trends, and these are the small capillary and the great capillary roots and root-veins of new worlds. Notions are formed by the deliberate and studied connivance of someone. The mystery is how a notion is communicated. Apparently it is sown on the air. There is a new term, out of the not quite born radio, about this sowing on the air.

A doughnut baker at a morning doughnut-and-coffee shop is able to communicate the notion to the buying neighborhood that Bear-Claws will be a drag this morning, but the Apple-Fritters will be excellent, just the thing for tang and taste. The doughnut-baker does this when he is short of Bear-Claws and doesn't want to bake another batch, and long on Apple-Fritters which moreover are a little bit doughy and underbaked today.

This creating of notions is paramount in every sort of merchandising. It is the basic inventory control. The control and allocation would not be nearly as good even as it is in practice if it were not for the notion-creating that is outside the lines and frameworks.

A notion has to be transmitted to the senses, or at least to the interior senses. Odors, I am convinced, can be flung great distances by the mind. But the origins of notions, whether by subliminal sight or sound or odor, are not easily tracked down. I myself, on pretty massive-evidence, am a master at broadcasting notions, but my theory lags behind my practice.

That hell-stroke named the boycott which, like the iceberg, usually has only the tip of its nose above the surface, is the crudest form of notion-creating. It is the notion-made-flesh, but it is always a cancerous flesh. There has never been a good boycott. But do I

259

use this device myself? Maybe I do, maybe I do. I work much of the way in the dark when I am constructing a world. But I would hate to think that I am a boycotter.

A boycotter! What a hellish coward is a boycotter!

Three devils in human skins may speak six words each, and a person can be ruined. This is boycott. The same three devils in human skins may speak twice as many words each, and an abomination is elevated to success and respect. This is the other side of a boycott.

Nay, the words in neither case need to be spoken at all. They can be merely thought. "Think thoughts in key places, where they will be picked up by the avidly venal, and you have put another ring in the nose of the world." But this raises an important question. Am I one of the Boycotters? Am I a devil in human skin?

4

There was a friend of mine who had the lower part of his face slightly broader than the upper part. Well, he *was* my friend at one time, and he did have the lower part of his face *slightly* broader than the upper part at one time. Now he is no longer my friend, and the lower part of his face is *very much* broader then the upper part.

Originally the thing was so slight that nobody noticed it, and I surely had not. But I was looking for some abnormality in him, however slight. I snapped a candid camera-shot of him, full-face-on, from the front. I enlarged it. I hatched it off in small squares. I made measurements of it, and I made notations of the ratios. Then I locked the camera-shot up in one desk, and the measurements and notations in another one.

I drew caricatures of my friend then, and these showed his face very much broader in the lower half than in the upper. I left a dozen of these drawings around in the newspaper offices where this friend and I each hung one of our hats. I dropped the drawings on the floor. I dropped them on desks, I tacked them up on various bulletin boards of which there are always dozens and sometimes millions around news rooms.

People who knew my friend (his name was Skantling) looked at the caricatures and said 'What the Hell?' But they *had* looked at them, and at the broader lower part of his face. Their looking at these pictures became an activating act. It was a crude deal, but they would look particularly at his face the next time they saw him, and they would measure with their eyes the width of that lower section.

The next day I made another set of drawings with the lower width still more exaggerated. I put captions on them such as 'Skow-Jaw Skantling wanted for Megagnathis.' This was an assault, and I kept it up for nine days. By that time, everyone was calling him 'Skow-Jaw', and he was fuming and spuming over the thing. The slurs on him and his appearance had gone beyond fun, he said, and now they touched his honor. He would shout angrily over what he would do when he found out who was responsible. He would thrust out his jaw with an angry gesture that he had developed, and this made his lower face appear still broader.

I began to hear remarks about Skantling 'Such a fine man, it's a shame that he has a misshapen face!' And he did have. It was horribly misshapen. It was ugly. It began to be repulsive.

I snapped another full-face candid camera-shot of him. He caught onto me then and he knocked me down. But I got away from him with the camera-shot and I hurried back to my loft to make comparisons.

Oh yes, the two pictures, there was quite a difference in them. There was very much difference between the two lower-faces of those two pictures, very much, but not as much as I had expected. The first picture showed that Skantling had already been extraordinarily wide-faced in the lower regions. Well,

well, it showed that he had been. And he hadn't been.

Then I got out the measurements and notations that I had made from the first picture. They didn't check with that first picture, no matter how I marked them off. The change seemed to go by quantums or jumps. There were the notations that I had remembered which showed hardly any abnormality at all; there were the present notations which were not quite as I remembered them (they had shifted slightly in the direction of wide-jawedness). There was the first picture that was not quite as I had remembered it, and it was much greater in the lower width than either the remembered notes or the present and perhaps modified notes. And there was the second picture that showed the frightful abnormality.

Who had worked this change in my former friend? Myself? I suppose so. Was it real? It was real enough that it ruined him. If he had been born with such a deformity, he might have learned to live with it; but to have it come over him in just nine days when he was a grown man, he just could not adjust to that.

I believe that I have also been deforming certain events in the world. I make them broader here and narrower there. I deform them out of recognition, and some of them I do this to in as little as nine days. And the old accounts of them that I dig out, they are deformed also from my memory of them. But they are not so deformed as the final result.

5

I do not call myself a creator in the things that I construct, facsimiles or realities, whichever they may be. The name of the sort of craftsman that I am, *skaber*, was given to me by the same cloudy voice that told me "Make Facsimiles". It is only by accident that I have discovered lately that *skaber* is the Scandinavian word for 'Creator,' and now I recall

262

that all of the orders that I have been given were given to me in a Scandinavian accent. A god or demiurge with a Scandinavian accent? Sure. A Norse god. Or a Norse God who is behind all the gods.

This makes me feel that perhaps the holocaustic events that I am encasing in protective and preventive fictions do not belong to the ultimate holocaust but only to the Norse-version holocaust. They may not treat of the end of the ultimate world, but only of the end of the Norse gods' world. And the Norse *ultima* may itself always have been a protective fiction designed to encase and shield the universal *ultima*. But I only work in these clay-pits and quarries and dream-swamps. I am not in on the planning. Such a thing may be so.

But there is something about this designate-creationism that I and several others indulge in that is genuinely flamey and genuinely bloody.

A note: Horny music is especially effective for waking the dead and for raising hell. All my Armageddon operas are loaded with horn music, wood horn, ram and hvalros horn, brass horn. It is my job to wake the dead, and the unborn also. And it is my job to raise hell literally. Well, I didn't ask for the job.

For this almost-immediate future of divergent world-building that we go into now, this voice tells me (And Helvede! It is *still* a Scandinavian voice!) that unsuspected media will be used massively to reinforce our efforts to construct these paltry and deceitful worlds. New and electronic media, the voice says.

To me, the phonograph seems to be the most likely new device and medium for this, and yet I cannot see how it will ever equal the influence of the newspapers and journals and books and operas, and such shouting dumb-show pantomimes as I myself use in firming opinions and enclaves and counter-worlds. Perhaps the phonograph will accomplish this by reiteration. There are electric models and possibly even electronic models of the phonograph now. And this, the first one of the electronic media, has an advantage: it doesn't get tired.

I am told by the editor of *Architecture and Prototype* that this world-construction explication of mine is to be handled gently with moleskin gloves, that it is to be degaussed and then insulated with thin sheets of irony, and that it is to be printed in that limbo section of the publication that is titled *Illuminations on The Lighter Side*.

Maybe so, but in this particular enclave which is only slightly larger than the world, there is a Surly Shaper behind us designate-shapers, and he isn't laughing.

6

On what authority are changes in the world-structure made? On the very slightest authority sometimes, or on faked authority, or on no authority at all if these changes are accompanied by sufficient assurance.

There is a case back in the low Middle Ages when fewer counterchecks were available than now. There came a year 683. The world lived through it and ended it. And then the world was ready to start another year. The scribes and annalists each made ready to head up new annual scrolls to start the new year. But one of the most honored of all the annalists headed his scroll 683 again, and the other annalists heard of it before the day was over. (This one most honored annalist always headed up his scroll on the last day of the old year, not on the first day of the new year.)

Less honored annalists remonstrated with him, and it did them no good.

"What I have written, I have written," the honored annalist said. "You others, if you want to make total fools of yourselves, may write something different in the way of the year. But the year now opening will be known as the 'Year of the Goose, 683.'"

Some have it. Some don't. The honored annalist

had charisma above all his fellows put together and they deferred to him. They repeated that year, and perhaps they repeated it several times. There was the "Year of the Goat 683," the "Year of the Cuttlefish 683," and the "Year of the Mushrooms 683."

The leading annalist had authority, and he had honor, and that is what the new versions of the world were built on. I am surprised to find that I myself am his counterpart in many esoteric things. I myself have authority in namings and designations. I am deferred to, and very often my versions are followed.

But I hide hammers. I have several hammers hidden. A hammer is an advantage that you can use when you are driven into the next-to-final corner. A hammer is a sort of insurance. I make fictions as I am assigned to do, and many others also are carrying out collateral and equally weird fictions. But the others do not seem to play as many tricks as I play, they do not seem to hide as many hammers in their hurdles. I try to insure that the fictions that I am assigned to shall remain fictions. I set tricks into them from the beginning.

It is now the case that the catastrophes cannot really happen unless certain other things set into the fabrics of the continuities should also be made to happen. And they cannot happen unless other things are made to *unhappen*. So long as Hiram Johnson was elected President of the United States in 1912, for instance, the catastrophes cannot happen. And how is he to be unelected now these four years later, or seventy-two years later?

SECTION FIVE

"IN THE DAYS OF SILENT RADIO"

(This was written by Enniscorthy Sweeny for the magazine Psychosis and Metampsychosis, The Magazine of the Troubled, *February, 1924.*

I

These are the Good Years, this is the Golden Century, these are the Diamond Decades. Why, then, are we not cheering all the time instead of only now and then? Have we a surfeit of goodness? It takes a certain detachment or distance to see and to appreciate most deeply any really excellent thing. We are too close to it, for we are in the middle of it. A lifetime away from it and we would still be too close for full appreciation. And a lifetime from now, I hope, the Diamond Decades will still be going on.

There is no heresy in believing in the Golden Centuries. There is nothing wrong with utopianism or millennialism. There is, in fact, something wrong with people being in the middle of a millennium and not recognizing it. It has come to us, and we hope and trust that it will remain with us almost forever.

Our times are too rich and loaded with grace to be tied absolutely to fact. The art form of these poignant and picturesque years is high fiction, the transcending of frameworks, the flexibility and multiplicity of many-tracked happenings. "We live more lives than one when we live in grace." And these are the

266

time when the world itself lives in grace. Let us recall, by fictional technique if by no other, these years of benediction while we are still in them. People, these are the high times!

The tens and twenties of our century are especially the times of the star-dusted and gold-dusted young intervals of glory. Why certainly that is an extravagant way of writing about it. But it is extravagant living and it cannot be understood in any other way. It is not so much that these are the years when we ourselves are young. These are the years and decades when *everyone* is young, regardless of the count of their years.

There are constellations of magic now, and one of the most evocative and typical of the magics is that of the magic lantern. What built-in nostalgia is in that name! Oh, other names were given to it, the Biograph, the Kinemascope, the Movies, the Silents (they were called the 'silents' from the first in early recognition of the fact that they would not always be silent, that the ruination of sound would come on them); but the most popular name that endured right down to today (1924) is The Magic Lantern.

We went to the Magic Lantern on Saturday nights all through my childhood, and if we were rich (and everybody was pretty rich then) we went several times a week.

There is an enchanting parallel to the Magic Lantern, to the Silent Movies, and it is the Silent Radio. We always knew that the Silent Movies would not always be silent: and, also, we knew that the Radio would talk some day.

Oh, the days of Silent Radio! They still go on for some of us. Their hectic pagentry sounds to the inner ear only. There is sunshine and smoke on their days. The Days of Silent Radio are *always* remembered, for they do not consciously happen in real time, only in the reflection of the Golden Time that we are going through.

This will always be the answer to the question "Was it really like that?" Yes, it was really like that, and with abundance left over. The Silent Radio, the multitudinous drama within, was always an accompaniment, always a part left over, a bonus. There is a place where we do not have to decide whether whole clusters of things really happened or whether we only imagined that they happened. They happened at least on the Silent Radio. It's the magic emanation and broadcasting of the perennial indwelling drama.

It is said that great art must always be the representation of evil and of agony, and that there will therefore not be any great art in our happy times. This may not be quite correct. Out of catastrophes *that do not come*, out of the sparkle and health, we are able to say "We Must Have Been Doing Something Right." Doing something right is great art. *We Must Have Been Doing Something Right* is the name of the comedy of our times, and it is full and fervent art. "Great Art" is just a term that some one thought up. It isn't definitive.

2

"Socials" is sometimes the name given to them. They are "Get-Togethers," and in the Country they are "Whing-Dings" and "Hoe-Downs." There are Ice Cream Socials, there are Street Dance Socials, there are Sing Time Socials, there are Band Night Socials, there are Opera House Socials and Pie Supper Socials. They must have begun as small town and country stuff, but they have come to the cities now. There are Automobile Club Socials and Literary Night Socials. They are a social people in the Golden Century. And (with only slight exaggeration) it might even be said that everybody likes everybody in this social time. Yes, even the Hunkies and the Krauts and the Square-Heads and the Hokey-Pokeys and the Kikes and the Mikes. They all get along. Ours are the days of the prophecies, although there is still some scandal as to just who lies down with whom.

I believe that I am one of the peculiar spokesmen

of this century because of my exceptional good fortune in even these good-fortuned times. In my home, there was never a really wrong word between us, father and mother and children. We were all personal friends, we were all on the same side. And there is a hot 'diamondness' to my own later decades due to my being married to the most beautiful woman and best hearted wife in the world. More than half the men in this country sort of guess that they have this good fortune (I am sure that the percent never ran so high before), but I am *sure* that I have it.

We have experienced an exuberance together, my wife and I, that is the property of angels or of giants. I say that we are so fulfilled and fulfilling and unsated in this that we are people of prophecy. We two are named in the scriptures and the epics, though I will not say in which ones. This is our own time that has come. But this 'exceptional felicity' thing is no longer the exception. It is common now, more than ever before, I believe. Conjugal bliss is the rule and not the exception. It is the pleasant and underlying drama of all out silent radio.

When corrupting beings come to steal the gold of these times (and they *will* attempt it) they will start with this.

"Hail, wedded love, mysterious law," the poet wrote, and he wrote it for our age. (Sneerers sneer about this abundance of bliss, but it hurts their mouths when they do so.) "Sober certainty of waking bliss," a prophet wrote. And again "Bliss was it in that dawn to be alive." And also "Joy runs high." They were all speaking, in advance, of our era. "Laugh and be well," they prophesied and exhorted, and also "Continuance is well doing." All, all, all of them were speaking of us and our times. There must be one Golden Age to show to all the other ages for example. And it is ours.

Seven fat years, and then seven more, and then seven more again. The world is healthy. It licks the wounds of old sicknesses and accidents and they heal. The world today is fortuned in its families, in its neighborhoods, in its baliwicks, in its cities, in its provinces, in its nations, in its continents, in its entire globulosity, in its neighborhoods of worlds, in its galaxies, in its universe, and in its Father of Universes.

There is more wealth and more happiness than there has ever been. There is a better balance of law and of light lollygagging outside of the law. Arms have been beaten into plow shares and pruning hooks (What are we going to do with all those pruning hooks?—there is almost one for every prune), and peace reigns all the way from the Golden Sands of Samarkand to Clancy's Blackwater Bar.

All the killers are either gone or going, diphtheria, typhoid, small pox, pneumonia, cancer, war.

Do I sound a little bit like one who got his euphoria out of a bottle? I got a little bit of it there, yes, (it's a brand I never heard of before, Missouri Valley Blended Whisky, given to me by the wife of my bosom—'You try it first,' she said, 'and if nothing happens to you, then I'll try it'), and some of my euphoria I get from the very air I breathe and the ground that I walk on. "It is good to be alive, as the saints say. And my own rapture, you may charge, comes from a good digestion.

No, it does not. As a fact, I have a red dragon who is denning in my entrails, and I have a thorn in my flesh. I have a whetted sword that hangs over my head by a single hair, and the hair ravels and thins. I have assassins around every corner (three of them around one corner), and there is black earth making sounds that it will drink my blood. I still say "It is good to be here." Ours is the fullness of time. Oh, may not take that fullness away! Rome rejoices with Moscow and Mecca, and also with Shantung and Constantinople and Westminster and Waco, Texas. These are the good times.

There aren't really any old people now. There are people who have lived an amazing length of years, but they aren't old. Not as they used to call 'old,' no. And there aren't any deep ditches between the ages. No one person much notices the age of another. We are all of one family. Oh, there is a youthfulness so burnished and brazen that everyone notices the extra dimension of it, and the extra fun of it. But that isn't paid for from the other end. The dimension and the fun are not lost.

But, should the fire-spewing alternatives have happened, then there would be—then there would have been—old people again. There would be the deep ditches between the people again. These things are the fire-tarnish, and the tarnish would come back then.

(But we will talk no more about the fire-spewing alternative now. Should the improbable bad times come, we might have to talk about the alternatives then. But not now.)

We have kept all that people had before, and we have added to it in everything. We keep all the grand old musics, and we add jazz and ragtime, and perhaps something else. We keep the old dramas, and we add new dramas and new kinds of dramas. There is a poetry movement going on now such as has never been seen before. Even if the fire-spew alternatives should come and bring desolation on everything, there would still have been some of the most astonishing versifiers ever. The novels, the novels, they are ragged and unkempt, but they are better than many of the kempt novels that we still keep, and we will yet go through them with curry combs and brushes.

The art looks as if disasters have passed through it, but it also looks as if it had survived those disasters and as if the strewn pieces of it could be assembled into something quite superior. And it is better to have disasters in art than in life.

All the politicians are statesmen now, and all the statesmen have greatness dripping off their shoulders and forearms and running off their heads. It is the chrism itself. Everything is better. Was baseball ever as good as it is now? Was boxing? Was football? Was opera? Was band music? No, really, have any of these things ever been equalled in the past?

In mythologies, gold stolen out of hoards used to

turn overnight into acorns or twigs or stones or nut-shells or klinkers or ordure or trash. In our time, the process is reversed. All the minor and common things in their collectivity are turning into gold. What? Have ten million items of crass materialism been transmuted into new and transcendent gold in our own time! Is this the elevation of commonness with the improvement of everything opening up new aspects? For everything *is* better, hoes and hoecakes, shoes and saddles, baggage wagons and baseball bats (did our fathers have anything as good as the Louisville Slugger of today?), brass bands and bicy-cles (the New Departure Brake is really a new de-parture from anything that went before), fads and fashions. The accumulation of all these better-than-ever-before common things has turned into gold. How it shines! How it enriches and pleases!

Flying machines and automobiles! Did the phar-aohs have such. Did the Caesars? Telephones and telegraphs, phonographs and radios, electric fans and electric ice-making machines, photographs and mov-ing photograph-pictures, linotype machines, electric streetcars and interurban railroads. These things are new or almost new, and they can now be afforded by all. New-money, that's the thing, there is more new money than ever before, and it buys more.

Roller Coasters and Ferris Wheels and Whips. Ice Cream Parlors and Confectioners. Railroad Stations that would hold the Great Pyramid in their main concourses. New kinds of candy, new kinds of card games, new kinds of applejack, and new kinds of to-bacco.

Faster race horses and harness horses, faster race cars, better food and better drinking. Better night life and better day life. And people are getting smarter too. There is a new intellectuality astir. People talk about Freud and Jung and the cosmologist Einstein. We have archy the cockroach that we never had be-fore, and the Old Soak, and Hermione and Her Little Group of Serious Thinkers, and Old Judge Priest. Yes, and Cappy Ricks. These are characters out of books and papers who walk down town and are known everywhere. That is a mark of a creative age, that its created characters step out of the frameworks and move in the world. Maybe they always did it, but it didn't used to be the case that they were recognized when they walked down town. When everything is right with the world, then even the trifles of the world add up to gold.

3

There are two mistakes made in constructing practical utopias. One is to arrive to the state by such a bloody climb that the stench or gore will be on everyone in a worrisome manner and will be disguised only with the greatest difficulty. People are not completely at ease in such an utopia. The very ground they walk on cries out to them. The rats gnaw at their vitals. And then the persons and things that have been overthrown and gore will come back to live and pull down that utopia with red hands. Such at least I suppose to be the case. I have not myself lived under these conditions, and my intuitions of them do not have the personal feel.

And the other mistake is in making the utopia so grand that the people feel strange in it, keep it for a showplace, and camp outside of it. This condition might not be at all uncommon. There have been a dozen cultures that came to surpassing and curiously short-lived opulence and then lost control of it all as if they had choked on it.

But the right way to do it is not exactly to find a medium between these two errors (was ever a right thing found in a nest of errors, it is to plant the thing in a third spot that seems favorable though far less than perfect. Then the sign is put up: "Utopia if we can keep it," and the proclamation of it brings it into actuality. Our proclamation of the "Almost Perfect State" was made about three decades ago, and it has come into being to fulfill the proclamation.

When people construct utopias they usually get all the details wrong. And often they get the direction

273

and goal wrong also. But when we actually arrive to utopia (and we *have* arrived to it, praise God, if we don't lose it) then we find that most of the details are roughly right, for us, and that the direction is right also. We have now come to the right place, even if sometimes by the right road and sometimes by the doubtful road. We have had unearned luck. There is fun and pleasure and satisfaction to be had out of living in the world right now. We are out of the slough and we are up on the good land. These are the green pastures, and in us is scripture fulfilled.

Oh no, they are not quiescent green pastures. They are buzzing and clacking with life. We must not lie down in them for more than the canonical eight hours at one time. There are plenty of moving parts in the pastures, ourselves. And an unbroken greenness cannot be allowed. That would be a rainbow of only one color. That would put the whole thing out of proportion. The emerald green is the decoration and garnish, but it is not the main thing.

We break the monotony with all the lovely strength and roughness that we can bring, and we heap it up with more of everything. We are Chinese for a while, and we pile up the seven sweets and seven sours. Over the rural acres we spread that cosmic delight that is miscalled "Urban sprawl". We go to the well, and we intend to fill the bucket.

No matter how beautiful is a vessel or how fine its workmanship, it is always better when it is full than when it is empty. The green pastures must be brimming with life, and that is something that not everyone understands. Even the most unkempt of things add to the holy totality.

And the waters and wines and sour-kraut juices that are in the fine-worked vessels, they sprawl and heave and lunge. But they stay in the vessels. This is ourselves in the flooding pattern of our towns and smithies and arsenals and farms and wood-lots. Remove any roughness of them and you geld utopia itself.

One has heard of the "Dark Satanic Mills," but even these are better than no dark mills at all. Well,

274

route Satan out of them then and call them the "Dark Angelic Mills." Do you object to their being dark? Or to their being mills? They are probably light enough. Too much light is like too much noise, and it is the same shriekers who love too much of both of them. There is a beloved urban shade in most of the mills. Oh, clean up the damned mills then! And undamn them by it. But remember that their throbbing has got to remain.

"Holy Smoke!" is an expression of our own times, and it is an exclamation of astonishment and awe. We had an old neighbor once who loved the black smoke. He said that a sky full of smoke was a sky full of nutrient.

"Oh the Holy Smoke of the Chimneys of Gary!" this old neighbor used to cry out. He would take the street cars down to South Chicago and over to Gary just to look and admire at the wonderful industrialization. Smoke is a chemical reaction considered as life experience. Let us never completely do away with it, but we'd better cut down on its cinder content a little. Such solid and large things as are now to be found in the smoke, klinkers, cinders, dead cats, bales of burned wool, how did they ever get up in the air anyhow? Too much solid stuff in it is an excess. But the mills of utopia will yet grind and puff. Sweeten their puffing breath a little bit, and do not throttle it completely.

In utopia is heard, loud and foggy, the music of the oblate spheres. One of their new musics, and incomparable joy in our own times, is that of the new automobile horns. Earlier ages had them not, and later ages may refine their raucousness into something else. The same old neighbor who loved the holy smoke of the chimneys of Gary used to say that when the Angel Gabriel, on the last and first morning of the world, should blow that final big trumpet, the sound of it would be "Ah-OOOO-ga!!!" That sound is exactly right for the last trump.

Consider the great, and amazingly cheap, automobile horns of our own times, the "Specials." There is the Jiffy, the Combination, the Four-Tone Chime

Whistle, the Locomotive Whistle, the Rock Island Hooter, the Harrisburgh Howler, the Claxon, the Coon Shouter, the Roller Siren, the Bell Tone, the Gang-Way, the Blow-Hard, the Whistle Britches. And then there is the "My-Dog-Has-Fleas" horn whose four notes seem to say that. And these are just a few of the special horns that people put on their automobiles. This does not even list the fine standard-equipment horns and hooters that come on the automobiles.

But we wouldn't want all of utopia to be of one piece. There have to be some strange notes in its homey tone. For us dudes, there must always be the other side of the tracks to be heard from sometimes. The songs of the silent radio have a lot of variation.

But there is also an underlay of horror that will not go away.

4

Why is the silent radio, on some bands of it, always playing horror drama after horror drama? These outwardly silent and sightless, though inwardly they are soundy and pictorial enough, radio dramas of the private and group unconscious have their daily horror hours, and now they become hours that are as much as three hundred minutes long.

Inasmuch as the dramas are of the private unconscious, each person composed the scenarios of his own silent radio. In as much as they are of the group unconscious, all the personal scenarios are very much alike. There is cribbing going on there. But it is disquieting to see one's own privately contrived scenarios take on a rampant and public life.

When I was a little boy, there was in our block another little boy who made snakes. He had more imagination than the rest of us around there, and more creativeness. (Curse the brittle bones of him, he's dead now!)

But, in his snake-making or in anything, he never

276

sinned in the direction of excessive accuracy. I did, and I still do. I had a *Big Snake Book* that had been given to me by one of my funny uncles for a birthday; it was a thing that made my mother shudder and that brought out the secret love in my heart. I would go with my *Big Snake Book* to my creative friend and try to get him to make more realistic snakes. He used the book, and he did incorporate real information as to snakes' musculature and reticulatory motion. But he mixed up different kinds of snakes, and he gave all of them the teeth of carnivorous animals.

That little boy became the cock of the walk in our neighborhood with the terrible snakes that he made and had under his control. He would send the biggest bullies on Blackwater Street to running. His snakes ate dogs and cats. There was a story that one of them ate a baby out of a baby buggy.

Then the boy made one snake too big and it ate him himself. The eating was a terrifying and grisly thing and it went on for more than an hour. That biggest of his snakes was cranky and savage-natured from the minute that the boy made it. It knocked the boy down, and it swallowed his feet and legs clear up to his rump. The boy put up a big howl, and the rest of us did too. We raised a high racket, and grown people came there too. They battered the snake with boards and scoop shovels and spades and pick-axes and hatchets and saws. They couldn't make it release the boy.

We knew that it was all over with when the snake took a bigger gulp and swallowed the boy's rump and his whole body up to the middle ribs. The snake exuded black, tar-like liquids from its stomach. These covered the boy's chest and arms and shoulders and neck and head and made him easier to swallow. Then the snake would contract in spasms, and we could hear the little boy's bones breaking like sticks.

Big men attacked the snake with axes, but the axes bounced off it as if it were a very tough hard-rubber tire. Ladies of the block were saying the rosary out loud for the deliverance of the boy, and some of them were crying. A blacksmith rushed over with hot tongs to distract the snake, and this had no effect at all except maybe to make it even madder. A police constable shot a number of bullets into the snake from a hand gun. This did no good.

Then the police constable was crying gushes of tears and giving orders to some other policemen. The snake swallowed the rest of the little boy, upper quarters and head. So it was all over with. Then the snake made a sudden getaway over Meistrel's fence, and they never did find it again, or any pieces of the boy.

This really happened.

I myself, starting that day, began to make three snakes, of a more authentic but also more figurative sort. The first and smallest of them was big. The second one would be nine times as big as the first one, and the third one would be eighty-one times as big as the first one.

At first I was told (by whom, I do not know) that this making of the snakes was a purgative psychological action and that it was beneficient. It was only after I had been caught by this argument that I realized that there was a catch to it.

I have made one nonsilent opera on the Armageddon theme, and I am constantly occupied with two other such operas. These are the three snakes of mine. The first opera is light-hearted and satirical, and it is booming with anachronistic cannons. But the silent radio dramas that carry on the same theme underground or undermind are horrible, horrible, horrible. They have at this date (the beginning of the year 1924) knocked the whole world down and swallowed its feet and legs clear up to the rump.

They exude black, tarlike liquids that cover the upper quarters and head of the world. This noisome tar is the arrogance-sin of Sion and the money-sin of Sidon. It is the Moloch-sin of Carthage and the murder-of-the-children sin of Tyre. It is the Babylonian fishiness-sin or unnatural-sin. It is the Greek-sin and

278

the Sodom-sin. It's the Gomorrah-sin. It's three-staged Armageddon.

The bloody first-harvest of these dramas spooks me and degrades me. And the thrice-bloody aftermaths threaten to unhinge things completely.

Tirlement, Lorraine, Charleroi, Namur, Longwy, Montmedy, Soissons, Oaon, Rheims, Maubeuge. Yes, I suppose that these are the names of battles on the battleground of the group unconscious. The cultists of the "leagues" say that they were battles that actually happened within the last ten years. They are really the names of actions and abominations that are clear off this world.

Mons, LeCateau, the first bloodiness at Marne River, Ourcq, Aisne, Picardy, Artois, Verdun, St. Mihiel, Yser River, first blood of Champagne, Noyon, Montdidier, Bapaume, Armentieres, Ypres, Dixmude. Many of these happened once, and then happened backwards at a later time as if being run by a camera in reverse. Yes, of course I was the one who first devised all the names of these fictional battles and actions, but where did I get them. Yes, there are real places in France and elsewhere with these names. But why is there pretense that the battles were real?

Zamosc-Komarou, Lemberg, Czernowitz, Przemysl, Drina River, Tser, Jadar, Zemlin, Gumbinnen, Tannenberg, Masurian Lakes, Warsaw, Ivangorod, Cracow, Lodz, Limanova, Kolubara.

And the mixed blood-and-brine battles of Heligoland Bight, Scapa Flow, Yarmouth, Scarborough, Hartlepool, Dogger Bank, Coronel, Falkland Islands, Jutland.

Far-flung battles of the mind-swamps, Duala in the Cameroons, Swakopmund, Riet, Treckkopje, Windhoek, Dar-es-Salaam, Tanga, Mahisa, Tsingtao. Kars, Sarikamish, Van, Dardanelles, Sare Bair.

La Bassee Canal, Neuve Chapelle.

The winter battle of Masuria. Augustovo Forest, Przasnysz, Gorlice-Tarnow, San Lublin, Cholm, Novo-Georgievsk, Brest-Litovsk, Grodno.

Durazzo, San Giovanni de Medua, Isonzo.

Uskub, Elbasan, Mt. Lovchen, Corfu.

Kut-El-Amarna, Ctisphon, Koprikoi, Trebizond, Qatia.

The Ninth Battle of Isonzo,

Hi jaz, El Arish, Kut-El-Amarna again.

The Tenth and Eleventh Battles of Isonzo. Capretto.

Verdun, Somme, Chateau-Thierry woods, Arras, Messines Ridge, Vesle River, Argonne, Sedan.

That was a haunting harvest. But the aftermath is three times as haunting. That's to look into the faces of people who pass by and realize that they aren't people anymore.

Where are all these fictions at when they aren't being fictions?

The silent radio has its bad hours. I cannot turn it off. It has no knobs, and I have no hands.

SECTION SIX

THE CHRONOLOGY OF THE LIFE AND TIMES
OF ENNISCORTHY SWEENY (1894—1984)

This is to attempt an arrangement of the creative influences of the time, the world-arranging or creative events and works. Nothing of the Armageddon Variant is given here except the works of Sweeny himself. This is because there is not to be found any such material. It was in the minds of Sweeny and in the minds of certain cultists, but it does not appear anywhere as facts or events. A social psychologist has said, "Remove the Armageddon motif and happenings and the decades become trivial." They are not removed. They simply are not available to be put in. Trivial or not, this is the "Times."

1894   *Enniscorthy Sweeny born on West Black-water Street in Chicago.*
1896   *The Bad Child's Book of Beasts*, verse, H. Belloc. This was Enniscorthy's first reading.
1896   William McKinley Elected President of the United States
1897   "The Katzenjammer Kids," Comic Strip, Rudolph Dirks.

1897 "The Children of the Night," Poems. E. A. Robinson

1898 *The War of the Worlds*, Prophetic Novel, H. G. Wells. This was Enniscorthy's second reading.

1899 "The Interpretation of Dreams," Psychological Essays, S. Freud.

1900 Harold Standpipe Elected President of the United States

1900 "Quantum Theory," Physics Papers, Max Planck.

1901 "East River," Watercolor, Maurice Prendergast.

1902 The Electric Theatre in Los Angeles opens as the first theatre for Motion Pictures exclusively

1902 *The Wings of the Dove*, Novel, H. James.

1903 Pius X Elected Pope of Rome.

1903 Wright Brothers Make First Airplane Flight at Kitty Hawk, North Carolina.

1904 "Mont-Saint-Michel and Chartres," Essays, H. Adams.

1904 Theodore Roosevelt Elected President of the United States

1905 "Special Theory of Relativity," Mathematical Cosmology, A. Einstein.

1906 "Hairbreadth Harry," Comic Strip, Charles W. Kahles.

1907 "Une Fois Encore," Encyclical, Pius X.

1907 "Mutt and Jeff," Comic Strip, Bud Fisher.

1907 Ziegfeld Follies, Stage Extravaganza Review, F. Ziegfeld.

1907 "On Hypercomplex Numbers," Mathematical Theory, Wedderburn.

1908 *The Man Who Was Thursday*, Fantasy Novel, G. K. Chesterton.

1908 William Howard Taft Elected President of the United States

1908 "Three Algebras for Post-Human People," Mathematical Papers, Horace Hackberry.

1908 "Toonerville Folks," Comic Strip, Fontaine Fox.

1909   Discovery of the North Pole, Admiral Peary.

1910   "Effector Formulae," Mathematical Papers, Henry Devonian.

1911   "The Topology of Simplicial Manifolds," Mathematical Papers, L. E. J. Brouwer.

1911   "Theory of Harmony," Musical Theory, T. A. Schonberg.

1912   Hiram Johnson Elected President of the United States.

1912   "The August 1914 Tonalities," Musical Sequence, Enniscorthy Sweeny.

1913   The Armory Show, America's Introduction to Modernism in Art, and also to the Vested Unrealities.

1913   "Die Idee der Riemannschen Flache," Commentary on Riemann Geometry, Hermann Weyl.

1914   Benedict XV Elected Pope of Rome

1915   "The Birth of a Nation," Motion Picture, D. W. Griffith.

1915   "General Theory of Relativity," Mathematical Theory, A. Einstein.

1915   *The Genius*, Novel, T. Dreiser.

1916   Woodrow Wilson Elected President of the United States.

1916   "On the Construction of the World," Essay-Article, Enniscorthy Sweeny.

1916   'Armageddon I', Opera, Enniscorthy Sweeny, opens in Vienna.

1916   New York Day by Day, Newspaper Column, O. O. McIntyre. This represents the creation of a world significantly different from the current world, though thousands of persons in the O.O.M. world bore identical names to those in the consensus world.

1916   Josh Batman Makes First Solo Airplane Flight Across the Atlantic Ocean.

1916   The Sun Dial, Newspaper Column, Don Marquis (with archie the cockroach, Mehitabel the Cat, the Old Soak, Hermione and Her Little Group of Serious Thinkers, etc.) This column represented, it is said, the creation of a new world for every day of the week, either six or seven worlds. Who remembers whether the column ran in the New York *Sun* on Sunday?

1917   "Humani Generis," Encyclical, Benedict XV.

1917   "Andy Gump," Comic Strip, Sidney Smith.

1918   The Decline of the West, Historical Theory, Oswald Spengler.

1918   *My Antonia*, Novel, W. Cather.

1918   "The Girl of the Golden West," Opera, Puccini.

1918   *The Magnificent Ambersons*, Novel, B. Tarkington. This Insertion of a Variant World only a few seconds removed from the real world was successful in a limited way and may be a first at this. This "Tarkington Sector," not of wide extent, did exclude its better-documented equivalent and it survives as a standard version to this day.

1918   *The Moon of the Caribbees*, Play, Eugene O'Neill

1918   "The Bungle Family," Comic Strip, Harry J. Tuthill.

1919   "Prejudices, First Series," Essays, H. L. Mencken.

1919   "The Retreat of the Galaxies," Astronomical Reporting, Shapley and others.

1919   *'Prohibition, A Farce, a Play, Enniscorthy Sweeny.*

1919   "The Book of the Damned," Meteorological Instances, Charles Fort. Although Poltergeistic or Fortean universe go back thousands of years, the creatures for whom they are named did not assume flesh until the late nineteenth century.

1919   "Barney Google," Comic Strip, Billy De Beck.

1920   Warren G. Harding Elected President of the United States.

1920   *The Emperor Jones*, a Play, Eugene O'Neill.

This is actually an excursion into "Alternate Realms."

1920 First Radio Station, WWJ, Owned by the Detroit News, Goes on the Air.

1920 "A Few Figs From Thistles," Poems, Millay.

1920 *This Side of Paradise*, Novel, F. S. K. Fitzgerald.

1921 "Gesture," Oil Painting, Max Weber.

1922 Kirol I Elected Pope of Rome.

1923 "The Hunchback of Notre Dame," Motion Picture, Lon Chaney.

1923 "Moon Mullins," Comic Strip, Willard.

1923 "Where the North Begins," Motion Picture, Rin-Tin-Tin.

1923 "The White Sisters," Motion Picture, Lillian Gish.

1924 *In Our Time,* Short Stories, E. Hemingway.

1924 "Rhapsody in Blue," Music Sequence, George Gershwin.

1924 Calvin Coolidge Elected President of the United States.

1925 "The Rainbow Trail," Motion Picture Western, Tom Mix.

1925 *Roan Stallion*, Poems, R. Jeffers.

1925 "The Brown Danube," Oil Painting, A. Hitler. Hung in Alte Pinakothek, Munich.

1925 "Don Q, Son of Zorro," Motion Picture, Douglas Fairbanks.

1925 "The Gold Rush," Motion Picture, Charles S. Chaplin.

1926 *In Abraham's Bosom*, Play, Paul Green.

1927 "Long Pants," Motion Picture, Harry Langdon.

1928 Herbert Hoover Elected President of the United States.

1928 "Rerum Orientalium," Encyclical, Kirol I.

1929 *Look Homeward, Angel*, Novel, T. Wolfe.

1929 *The Great Depression, Play, by Enniscorthy Sweeny, opened November at Stabler's Theatre in New York and Ran for Thirteen Years, a Record.*

1929 "Rio Rita," Motion Picture, Bebe Daniels.

1929   *Sartoris*, Novel, Faulkner.
1930   *Secret Agents Six, Mystery Novel, Enniscor-
        thy Sweeny.*
1930   "Flowering Judas," Short Stories, K. A.
        Porter.
1931   "Quadragesimo Anno," Encyclical, Kirol I.
1931   *Mourning Becomes Electra*, Play, Eugene
        O'Neill.
1932   Alfred Smith Elected President of the United
        States
1932   "Horse Feathers," Motion Picture, the Marx
        Brothers.
1932   *Brave New World*, Novel, Aldous Huxley.
1932   *Studs Lonigan*, Novel, Farrel.
1933   "The Lone Ranger" comes to Radio.
1933   "Our Most Beloved," Encyclical, Kirol I.
1933   "Aesthetic Measure," Mathematics-and-Art
        Paper, George Birkhoff.
1933   "King Kong," Motion Picture, King Kong,
        Fay Wray, and others.
1933   *A Draft of XXX Cantos*, Poems, Ezra
        Pound.
1934   "Lil Abner," Comic Strip, Al Capp.
1935   "Porgy and Bess," Opera, Gershwin.
1935   "Gangbusters" comes to Radio.
1936   Franklin Roosevelt Elected President of the
        United States.
1937   "Mit Brennender Sorge," Encyclical, Kirol I.
1937   "Divini Redemptoris," Encyclical, Kirol I.
1938   *Of Mice and Men*, Novel, Steinbeck.
1938   "Superman" comes to Radio.
1939   *The Time of Your Life,* Play, Saroyan.
1939   Pius XI Elected Pope of Rome.
1939   "On the Function of the State in the Modern
        World," Encyclical, Pius XI.
1939   *'Armageddon II', Opera, Enniscorthy
        Sweeny, Opens simultaneously in twelve
        capitals of the world, a great tribute to the
        imaginative power of Sweeny.*
1940   Bernard Baruch Elected President of the
        United States.

1940   Commonwealth Southern Power Company
        completes conversion to atomic power.
1941   *Darkness at Noon*, Novel, Arthur Koestler.
        A selection of the Friends of the Catas-
        trophes Book Club.
1941   "Little Known Birds of the Inner Eye,"
        Goache Painting, Morris Graves.
1941   "The Maltese Falcon," Motion Picture,
        Humphrey Bogart and Sydney Green-
        street.
1942   *The Skin of Our Teeth*, Play, Thornton
        Wilder.
1943   *A Tree Grows in Brooklyn*, Novel, Betty
        Smith.
1943   "July Hay," Oil Painting, Thomas Benton.
1943   "On the Mystical Body," Encyclical, Pius
        XI.
1944   Franklin Roosevelt Elected President of the
        United States (second term).
1945   "Isle of the Dead," Horror Movie, Boris Kar-
        loff.
1946   *A History of Philosophy* (publication of
        first volume), Frederick Copleston.
1948   Robert Taft Elected President of the United
        States
1948   *A History of the Church* (publication of the
        first volume), Henri Daniel-Rops.
1950   "Concerning Certain False Opinions," En-
        cyclical, Pius XI.
1950   *Joy Street*, Novel, Francis Parkinson Keyes.
1952   "Music and Imagination," Lecture-Essays,
        Aaron Copland.
1952   "Art and Technics," Interdisciplinary Pa-
        pers, Lewis Mumford.
1952   Douglas McArthur Elected President of the
        United States.
1953   "The Liberal Imagination," Commentary,
        Lionel Trilling.
1953   "Shining Crown," Encyclical, Pius XI.
1954   *History of Technology* (publication of first
        volume), Singer and others. (It's the age
        of definitive multivolume histories.)

1956   *A Hatful of Rain*, Play, Gazzo.
1956   Desalting of Sea Water is being done massively, at a profit, and with a *gain* in energy.
1956   Dwight Eisenhower Elected President of the United States.
1956   U.S. Armed Forces disbanded as no longer needed.
1956   "The Dynamics of World History," Historical Essays, C. Dawson.
1958   John XXIII Elected Pope of Rome.
1959   "The Curse of Conformity," Essay, Walter Gropius.
1960   Richard Nixon Elected President of the United States.
1960   Federal Regulation that New Cars must have 500,000 mile fuel packs.
1960   *Hogan's Goat*, a Play, Alfred.
1961   Moon Landing.
1963   Paul VI Elected Pope of Rome.
1964   Lyndon Johnson Elected President of the United States
1968   Robert Kennedy Elected President of the United States

For the eight years from 1964 to 1972, apparently no train-of-events ever held majority acceptance. Therefore *Nothing Happened*. These were the 'Empty Years,' or the 'Years for Rent'.

1972   Barry Goldwater Elected President of the United States
1973   Mars Landing.
1973   United States Out of Debt for the first time in the Century.
1975   Jupiter Landing.
1976   Eugene George McWhortle Elected President of the United States.
1976   United States Debt restored with the Resolution "Don't Let Them Take it Away Again" passed by both houses and signed by the President.

1977   Pluto Landing.

1980   Charles Fourhorses Elected President of the United States.

1983   United States Armed Forces Reinstituted.

1983   Some people say that this year was repeated several times. Others say "Let it alone. It's fun this way."

1984   Ms. Agnes Klingle Elected President of the United States.

1984   Enniscorthy Sweeny Dies.

1984   'Armageddon III' Opera, by Enniscorthy Sweeny, produced in Palestine, in the Megiddo Amphitheater.

1984   The Situation Worsens

There is no way to complete this chronology since it becomes confused by the waves of the present breaking over it.

SECTION SEVEN

"Short Discussion of the 'Ambiguities' of Matthew Woodbine Junior"
Printed by the Holystone Press, Hicksville, New York, Summer 1938,
With the addition of material from the Holystone lecture "On the Nature of Amnesia."

I

The "Ambiguities" have been turning up in optics, in phonologics, in metronomics, in chronologics, in psychomesmerics, in chromics, in radio-electrics, in all of the sensible sciences. And the most sensible statement of the ambiguities is that there is an extra set of lines around everything, and an extra answer to everything. The ambiguities are to be found in the illegible dog-latin jottings of doctors to apothecaries, and the ambiguities are in the apothecaries' weights themselves. It is in the prescriptions, it is in the sicknesses, and it is in the cures.

In a frightening number of fields, this new phenomenon, that there may be two different answers to almost everything and that either will fit the requirements and situations equally well, this phenomenon prevails. I am sure that almost everyone has noticed that there are two different lines around everything and two different answers to everything. Almost everyone has noticed these duplicate things just as almost everyone has noticed that he has two feet.

Why do people so seldom make any mention of this then? Probably because they feel that it is all wrong, and because they are not sure that others have noticed it.

Well, it is all wrong. But others *have* noticed it. And we have got to drag it out into the light and consider it. It's as though one's mother had grown a second head. Shall we be silent about it on the chance that she herself doesn't know it?

Either we are mostly pleasant people living in a mostly pleasant world, as we had supposed: or we are people so compromised and trashed that we dare not show our own faces, and we are living in a world that we are afraid to look in its own face.

Do we sometimes wake up in the morning with the feeling that our hands and arms are black-red caked with blood to the elbows and that we have been committing horrible homicides all night? And do we hear a cracked, crowing voice sounding "What rednesses you have done so far, they are only the measure-in-small of what you will yet do in-large"? I do hear such voices. I do wake up red-handed and red-brained nearly every morning. And it's plain that one of the double lines that goes around everything is a red line.

There are covens or cults that attempt to give a rationale (or an antirationale) to these apprehensions and pseudo-memories. People meet together and they hold congress with the red things that are becoming more than shadows. I have infiltrated and joined one such cult-group, and I have attended coven meetings.

2

I did not join the coven or group in my own town of Hicksville but in Mineola, a neighboring town where I am not so well known. It might, I thought, be bad for me and for my Holystone Press if it were known in Hicksville that I had joined an organization like the "Armageddors," or had even attended the meetings of such a group. But I found that the group was quite open. And it was not at all what I expected.

I had been told that the Armageddors were either part of a movement of mad men, or that they formed an organization of mordant and sick humorists. It was said that these people believed or affected to believe, that the first

291

phase of Armageddon, the ultimate war that is to destroy the world, *has already happened.* They believe that it has already happened, not in Biblical or even more remote times, but quite recently, less than twenty-five years ago. They believe that this towering conflict, which they name World-Wide War, or World-Wide War Number One, did indeed happen in all its red horror, and that the results of it, the atrocious aftermath, are irradicably manifest in the world. They believe that the world is now in desolation and ruin from the first of three parts of fearful Amageddon. It would seem easy to say "Look out your window and see that it is not so." But the Armageddors apparently look out of other windows than we do.

Plainly the world is *not* now in desolation and ruin, either physically or in spirit. So plainly the Armageddors are mad or twisted.

But the men and women whom I met at that first session of an Armageddor group did not seem at all mad. And they did not seem to be mordant critics or sick humorists. They appeared to be intelligent and sane and informed, and to be deeply concerned about the affairs of the world. They were remarkable well educated persons with impressive backgrounds and accomplishments in college and business and political affairs and the current arts. They were the cream of the community by almost any standard.

And what was it that they really believed? Well, it was just about what the popular opinion had them believing. Well—they believed that the first of the three phases of Horrible Armageddon had already happened, not anciently but quite recently, within the last quarter of a century. And they believed that the world was now in desolation and ruin as the aftermath of that Armageddon I.

Well, this was the puzzle. They really believed these things. (I put it out of mind that they were twisted humorists: they weren't.) They really believed these things, and they were not at all the sort of persons who might be supposed to believe in turgid nonsense.

"Let us learn this lesson thoroughly, that we may not have to repeat it," was one of the sayings that was constantly in their mouths, and also on the walls of their meeting hall on motto plaques. And others were "May

God spare us from the rest of the Hellish Cup!" and "War no More, War Never Again!" and "With all our Minds, with all our Bodily Strength, with all our Prayers and Supplications, with all our Study and planning, may we turn it back!" These were all spoken and written exhortations there.

Their own name for themselves, however, was not the Armageddors. It was the "World Peace League." How was it possible for these people to be so intelligent and so sincere, and so *good,* and at the same time to be quite mad on this one subject?

The version of the people of the World Peace League as to what had happened was pretty well in accord with the little-known libretto of the well-known opera, *Armageddon I,* by Enniscorthy Sweeny. The story, the libretto of this work, is pretty well lost in the magnificent comic (or horror-comic) music of that great blood-and-thunder ramble. But none of those present had ever read the libretto, and few of them had ever seen the opera. And one of them who had seen it didn't like it at all.

"It is wrong to make an absurd comedy out of the Horrible War," he said. "It is wrong to turn it into a joke, even to a brimstone joke. "Brimstone comedy" is what some people call the opera, but the events themselves were and remain "Brimstone tragedy and Horror." They are, if they are not countervailed, the end of the world. The world is already one-third gobbled up by this hellish madness. So the Sweeny work is wrong. It is such light-handed and mocking response as this opera shows as may bring the wrath of God upon us again, and yet again. And nobody, no flesh at all, comes through that fire thrice."

But the people of the World Peace League say that the actual waging of this war did not take place in America, even though they call it The World-Wide War. That it did not happen in America, they explain, is the reason that we do not see physical desolation and ruin when we look out our windows. But there *is* spiritual desolation and ruin here; and in Europe the ruin is both spiritual and physical.

"I was in Europe last summer," I said, "and I did not see or hear of any such ruin, or of any desolation either

293

physical or spiritual. I saw health everywhere in the corporate body and in the individual persons."

"I also was in Europe last summer," one of my mentors told me, "and *I did* see overwhelming desolation and ruin (cleaned up as much as possible, and yet it was impossible), everywhere, on every hand. And in every face and in every mind and heart. Ruin and desolation, yes, and filled with the behaviorial rats that run in and out of such ruin and desolation. Where were you in Europe, sir? Let us analyze what you saw and what you were deceived into believing that you saw."

And he spread out a large map that had the outline of Europe.

That had the *outline* of Europe, yes. It had land where the land belonged, and it had ocean where the ocean would be. But that was almost all of Europe that could be recognized as such at first look.

The political contexts, the realms and the borders, were unreal. There were eruptions of new and resurrected countries across the whole center belt of Europe. Germany was greatly abridged, with her Eastern Wing in particular clipped. Poland had been dug up from the grave, and yet she still had the dead look on her. The Austrian Empire was reduced to almost nothing, a very small and tattered remnant. And there were all the new countries with comic opera names. Just who had worked out such a detailed hoax as this, and why? It was professionally done, there is no doubt of that. It even bore in one corner the name of a well-known map-maker, so it seems that there was a real case of fraud and infringement.

I recognized the map a little bit then. Some of the names of the new countries were out of Enniscorthy Sweeny and other fictioneers. This was the fanciful map that had been appended to one copy of the Sweeny Libretto of *Armageddon I,* and I suppose that it was faithful to the text of that monstrosity. And finer detail as to frontiers and realms, and the renaming of cities and provinces, were according to those of the clique who write in such little plump magazines as "Famous War Stories," "Famous Spy Stories," "Famous Love-in-the-Ruins Stories," "Famous Stories of Destruction and Depravity," and "Famous New-Werewolves-of-Europe Stories." (I will confess

294

that I sometimes read new-werewolves-of-Europe stories myself, but not as *fact*.) But surely these people at the meeting here were not the kind of folks who would mistake such gaudy fictions for realities.

I remember that "Czechoslovakia" was the name of one of the new countries on the map, and I remember the area that it was supposed to embrace. But the people of that area, the Bohemians or Cechy, the Moravane, the people of Praha, the Slovaci, how would they ever accept such an ungainly and falsely latinized name without laughter, or tears.

And there was a province in one of the other countries that actually bore the name of "Transylvania." Shades of Count Dracula! Transylvania!

I asked how many people belonged to the World Peace League. I was told that there were about a million active members in the world. What! A million? Then this unaccountable mania, this organized and promulgated mania, had already touched one person out of every two thousand in the world! Had there ever been such an inexplicable contagion?

This was incredible, that what had apparently begun as a fictional spoof should have claimed the fervent allegiance of a million intelligent and devoted persons. I do not understand it.

New systems of government were even devised for the new countries. A grotesque and illegitimate form that can only be called "Bureaucratic Democracy" was the thing pushed as asking belief. If ever there was bad utopianism it was in this concept of "Bureaucratic Democracy," what a shoddy counterfeit!

3

"Two Universes *may* exist simultaneously in the same place, if one of them is a Fortean Universe," so Doctor Henry Devonian once wrote.

And I myself was once taken in by a mathematical spoof that was almost as brazen as the World Peace League spoof. This was the pertentuous corpus of this Doctor Henry Devonian. His things were the "General

Equation" and the "Special Equation." There was a contagion on them, and many persons of good mathematical minds caught this contagion. I did.

These equations were new even in the ever-new world of mathematics. They were convincing. And they had an inner coherence. I myself, and my father also, did a great deal of work for and with Doctor Devonian on this great corpus. So it might be said that if I was deceived it was partly self-deception. Well, I was partly deceived by myself then, and partly deceived by Doctor Devonian. And I was much more substantially deceived by other entities and intelligences, and by one of them in particular which I am not able to put my foot on so far.

The "General Equation" and the "Particular Equation" are both of them nonexclusive statements. Yet they are absolutely tight and their relentless conclusions are not to be doubted. They are water-tight, but one cannot say that because a jug is absolutely water-tight there may not be water outside of it elsewhere in the universe. Nonexclusive equations being true does not prevent other and opposite equations from being true also. Almost all of the stunning and trail-breaking equations of very modern mathematics are nonexclusive.

A nonexclusive equation can obtain relative preeminence over other nonexclusive equations by strong coherence, by spaciousness, and by the computation of miracles. A miracle is required for an equation for it to be enshrined in the high company of ultimate equipoises.

One of the computed miracles of the "Particular Equation" was the naming of a young boy on Blackwater Street in Chicago as the "One-Individual-Crux" for our particular "nexus" or "world-of-time-event." And the twenty-eight years that have passed since the publication of the "Particular Equation" have proved that this individual (his name, Enniscorthy Sweeny, almost *had* to be selected by the relentless automation of an equation, and he was selected by what the uninitiates would have to call blatant numerology), that this individual is indeed a *crux-individual*.

In the matter of alternate presents, it seems that all roads lead to this Sweeny. His visions are now a part of the writhing record, and it is absolutely true that he is a mathematical necessity to the "Particular Equation."

You can check it and cross-check it in a dozen ways, and the answer will still be Enniscorthy Sweeny.

The mathematically possible answers of the other three quadrants are not acceptable. One of them is a goat in Turkestan (now dead, that goat, but the visions continue). One of them is a cuttlefish in the mid-pacific Ocean. And one of them is a mushroom complex (or possibly a toadstool complex) of two acres in Arizona. These three others will check but they will not cross-check. They fail on the rationality cross-check.

And yet I have the feeling that I, and the whole initiate mathematical world, are victims of a slight-of-mind in all this. Well, if we are the victims, who is the victimizer?

The victimizer will have to be one of a very mysterious group of superb mathematicians, "pure mathematicians" we will have to say, even if there are queasy elements in that purity. These superb and untrammeled and super-speculative mathematicians have an almost limitless mind-range for the reason that they themselves are incorporal. Every mathematician has felt their superior minds in the edge land that is just beyond proper equations. They are able to reverse our own processes, examining categories from the outside, and concepts from the inside. And there are (taking the medium of estimates that I have seen for the population of them) about three hundred billions of them. This is about a billion times as many of them as there are human mathematicians of competence in the universe. They are the devils, and every devil is a master mathematician. That is just one of the facts that we must live with.

The devils are hardly to be found in the fine arts at all, however strong they are in the coarse arts. They are weak in ethics and philosophy, and their psychology simply is not of the human sort. They bust whenever they tackle the physical sciences. They haven't any eyes onto the physical world at all so they don't understand it. Their sense of drama is sick, and their music is wretched. The only thing they have ever contributed to the graphic arts is shock. They have no refinement, no civility, no enlivening affections. They do not even have the common honesty on which all solid polity is based. But they do have mathematics, theoretical mathematics (practical mathematics would be impossible to them except on the basis of a stolen praxis), and they do have numerology.

Well, which of these three hundred billion of them is behind this particular slight-of-mind that has crept into the "Particular Equation" without its author being aware that it was an intrusion? Would it be hard to find out which of the devils was the particular victimizer?

No, not hard at all. Coming up with the name of this particular devil would be as easy as was coming up with the name of Enniscorthy Sweeny as the crux-individual. I believe that it would be fairly easy to solve this identity, using the devils' own numerology on them. And I believe that this little problem has already been solved several times. I am sure that everyone who has gone on a serious look for the answer has found it. They have found it just as—

—well, just as they came to the bloody conclusion, they have found it. In this case, the bloody conclusion seems mathematically linked to finding the answer. And four mathematicians of my acquaintence have come to just such a bloody conclusion. These four are Langweiler, Prinzhofer, O'Rimski, and C.S. Tzu, princes all, and fine fellows. They have all left the scene, and I miss them.

Oh, in each case, just as they came to the solution, they also came to its bloody corollary. Their brains exploded so violently in every case that several other persons in the neighborhood were also killed by the explosions. What cheap tricks of infernal vaudeville! Such stuff passes for humor in hell, and this shows what sort of entities we have to deal with.

Oh certainly, the bloody conclusion was implicit in all the tracking-down or spoor-number equations all the way, but my friends rather got carried away on the chase. I will have to be very careful that I am not carried away by it. Besides, knowing the name of the particular devil isn't all that important.

So the Devonian Equations are a mathematical spoof almost as brazen as the fictional spoof that has entrapped so many sincere persons as are to be found in the World Peace League.

And the crux is still there. The plurality of choices still haunts us. How can multiple present-times produce simple futures? If they cannot do this, then how have the simple and consensus pasts come about? Present-times, being moving parts, will always be multiple-choice because of Zeno's paradoxes, but futures and pasts should be fixed. How is a past fixed then? Or how is it made to seem to be fixed?

By illusion probably. Everyone in a single-world enclave accepts a single past for his world. But entities in other enclaves will have accepted other pasts.

For the easiest and most obvious example, the Devils believe that they won that titanic and tripartate battle (the prototype of Armageddon), and that they threw God and all his Michael-machines out of the centrality and into a straited place. (Mathematically, a centrality and a straited place are simply inversions of each other, equally valid.)

And many shadow forms have followed the devils in their historical believing on this point. The Titans still believe that they whipped the Olympian gods; and the Norse giants still believe that they whipped the Norse gods. The moon still believes that it flung the smaller Earth out of it, to fall like lightning into a slave orbit to give light on dark nights. But mathematical theory does not indicate who won. It only indicates breaks and separations.

In mathematical theory, there can be as many contemporaneous universes as there are free wills. Each free will is a variable function of the *General Formula*. But in practical mathematics, it is simply the case that not one will in a million is really as free as all that.

Even so, there's a lot of them.

The main ambiguity of our times is that the world is in the throes of unparalleled peace and prosperity going on and on. And, at the same time, the world is experiencing three-headed hell, Armageddon itself, in assault after cresting assault. It does not matter how many persons live in each version of this present time. If only one person lives in a version, that will still be a living and authentic version with a live chance (however slim) of ultimately becoming the only version. There are several of these interlocking ambiguities in our present-time enigma.

Well, I believe that I have a practical solution to most of the Ambiguities. This is it:

(Here follow fifty pages of solid and imposing mathematical calculations. They cannot be given right here right now. *Perhaps they will be given in an appendix. We will see.*)

5

There are howling inconsistencies to the whole business of the "World-Wide War," which conflict was supposed to have begun in the year 1914. The pseudo-technology of it is the howlingest of the inconsistencies. The true technology of 1914 was hardly used at all in these promulgated fictions that are striving to become fact. It was more like the technology of 1904 and 1894. Still less than the true technology of the period, it was a sort of projective technology of a kind sometimes used in popular fiction. It is quite archaic in all of its implementations. When it has to be inventive, it is only fictionally inventive.

Many of the machines (the "Iron-Clads" and others) are right out of the early fiction of H.G. Wells, a man who was in love with the time of his own sordid youth and who did not ever move beyond that time technologically. This is the old turn-of-the-century fantasy machinery. There is no real thought in these things. And there *was* real technology in 1914, and was completely ignored in these fictions.

For the first year of the World-Wide War, on several different sectors of the action, old-fashioned horse-cavalry charges were still actually used. How does fiction lag so far behind fact? How hard the nineteenth century did die in its action fictions! This is anachronism. It is also inexcusible sloppiness of concept.

Close comparison with the actual equipment of the small peace-time armies of the various countries in 1914, of those of England, France, Austria, Germany, Russia,

Italy, Turkey, and the United States, sharpens still more the contrast between the real and the imaginary state of armament and equipment. It is as though the fictioneers, almost the most conservative of persons, had not yet got the feel of the machine age at all and had merely hung a false front of it over the old horse age. One does not move into the age of automotive vehicles merely by shooting the horse between the shafts of the buggy.

The mystery remains: why do the people of the World Peace League and others of the psycho-war believers think that the war of 1914 was fought with 1894 equipment? This represents the interval that popular fiction usually lags behind reality.

Probably the weirdest discrepancy is in the aircraft. At a time when the Martin, Curtis, and Wright Companies had already come up with rather good planes, and when every air barnstormer had come to understand the air medium, the Dore-like creations of the anachronists rather give one the boggles. What bat-winged crates were these that are adopted by the believers in World-Wide War One? What were they doing in the air anyhow? They were lumbering after each other in "dog-fights" that were straight-faced burlesque. It is clear that the inventors of these fictions had never flown in any aircraft, that they had not even flown a kite for that matter.

And the "trench warfare" that is medieval or earlier. It really belongs to the lower Middle Ages. Before the age of gunpowder, castles were sometimes trenched about in this manner for protection against the bothersome volleys of arrows and spears, but that tactic was in 1914 as outmoded as fighting from chariots.

The Battle of Constantinople in 1453, when effective gunpowder artillery was used for the first time, still contained remnants of trench investure; but that was only a laughable lapse on the part of the Turks. They must have known better even then.

To resurrect the same lapse four hundred and sixty years later is hardly laughable. One is embarrassed for all the Armageddon believers in this. One is even embarrassed under the eyes of Bonaparte and Gustavus Vasa, not to mention Grant and Lee.

And the diplomacy (if it might be called that) which

301

supposedly led up to the World-Wide War is that of very early E. Phillips Oppenheim novels; and it is even more like that of the Byzantine "Intrigue" novels of five hundred years earlier. Dumas, a hundred years earlier, provided good "fictional" diplomacy, but the 1914ers had not come so far. Worse even than the time lag (perhaps there *was* such a diplomacy once, in comic opera kingdoms) is the simplistic handling.

The whole complex of treatments is that of popular writers of a somewhat earlier time trying to construct a pseudo-biblical conflict, writers who knew very little about warfare, or technology, or diplomacy, or events, or people.

6

War is a property of a Fortean or a Poltergeistic Universe. It cannot happen in a rational universe.

Here is a vista, an insight:

A prominent man, of well advanced age, under analysis or hypnotism, comes up with pseudo-memories of being a general during Wide-World War One. These are very valid memories. And they help to explain certain colorful trash and mementos and records that he has kept around to his own puzzlement.

When this person is led into such memories or pseudo-memories, is he wakening from an amnesia or is he entering into a delusion? Mathematically, these two conditions are interchangeable, one not more valid or more likely than the other.

Two opposite points on the rim of a rolling wheel cannot both be on the top at once: this is taken as an almost reasonable postulate. But they could both be on top at once if one of them were suppressed by Amnesia.

Of course, in Gyroscopic Topology, both points could be on top at once if the wheel were turning fast enough, faster than the speed of light. And in Zeno-Paradox Geometry, they could both be on top at once, for they would both be at every point on the rim at once. But, as a workable thing, in a practical universe, they cannot be. The situation is saved by Amnesia. If one of the points

302

can be persuaded to forget its prime function, then the difficulty disappears.

If it weren't for this amnesiatic condition, wheels would rupture and explode. Very rapidly turning flywheels do sometimes fly apart, those on machinery as well as those in brains and psyches. They fly apart from failure of their amnesia to operate.

"These two things cannot both be true at once," one person can say.

"They *can* be true," another will contradict. "I'll make them both true for me or I'll go bust trying." And most of the times that person will go bust, or insane, on that point.

There is really nothing wrong with having contradictory things occupy the same place and time, except that this causes insanity, in the earth, in plants and minerals, in animals, in people, and in machinery. The cure for this insanity isn't to have two or more things cease to occupy the one place at one time (it is impossible to bring about such a reduction arbitrarily), but to have all the contradictory things except one forced out of the memory of everybody. But forcing things out of the memory doesn't force them out of being.

There are always several contradictory trains of events happening. There are always several contradictory histories of what has happened. And one of them is only more real than the others because more people, or animals, or plants, or rocks, or machines, believe that it is the real one. All sane things suppress the memory and recognition of all the trains-of-events except one.

But not all persons or things remember and recognize the same trains-of-events. That's the difficulty. Most of the persons and things accept the same events and conditions most of the time, but all do not accept them all the time.

7

Things forced out of the memory have to be forced somewhere. It is sometimes said that they descend into the subconscious, but that's an inaccurate way to put it. It

303

is also inaccurate to say that the forgotten things go into another dimension. The problem can't be solved until the whole problem of "being" is solved. And this hasn't been done. The same enclave or country or world when seen as the area or arena of different situations and event-trains, will show the effect of its different interactions with the different events. The weather of the same world in the same years will differ somewhat according to the train-of-events. In several rare cases, we have been able to obtain dual weather reports for a decade or more, and these are startling in their ramifications. These things carry over more with the instinct-bound animals and birds than they do with humans. There are migratory birds that will fly from old Arctic ice-free areas of late glaciation time and fly over formerly glaciated areas that are further south (there are many cases of this unevenness of the old ice), and will not put down to feed there even when there is good feed. They believe that the areas are still glaciated, because their instinctive mechanism tells them that they are, and from one viewpoint they are. And there are Arctic reindeer that will graze certain valleys, pawing down through the yearly snow to do it, and will not graze other neighboring valleys at all, believing them still to have impossibly deep ice under the snow.

And, in the cases of islands that have sunken or disappeared, some of the fish will not swim over the places, still holding the area as of a "pattern impossible." Some birds and animals and fishes are able to make changes more quickly than others however.

But these things are all taboos, and birds and animals and fishes, and plants and minerals also, have taboos much more deeply bedded than do humans.

But the thing is not confined to disappearances or remnants as against survivals; it always happens between reasonable coexistences. And the kindling of ideas may differ vastly from one context to another.

But why cannot several contexts or event-trains live in the same time and place in harmony? Why must the condition bring on insanity or war if amnesia fails to work for it? Well, there *are* cases where two or more such contexts do live in harmony, but the people of the less accepted context must know just what is going on.

For more than five hundred years, there have been small elites living in different trains-of-events and in different conditions from the majority of the people. But what will happen when the elites grow so large that there is no longer *any* majority of the people? This is like lashing all the ballast to the tops of the masts or to the funnels. It makes a top-heavy and unstable ship.

There is the case of the "Una Sancta" elite which still lives in the world where the Reformation, "That Shipwreck of the World," has not happened. This group, being an elite, is rich, happy, virtuous, creative, full of grace, flamingly into the arts, constructive, conserving, and incredibly generous. All elites are so. This elite identifies itself with the seamless cloak, the woven flesh of the world.

And there is the case—but, no, we are pledged to secrecy on that one. It is the almost perfect society which believes that it is really the consensus society of this world; and in its members it is that. The almost perfectly secret society is that group that includes every person in the world except one. Should *every* person in the world belong to it, it would lose its magic. Should more than one person in the world not belong to it, it would lose its secrecy; for those two nonmembers would get together and tear its veils to shreds.

It apparently is in perfect balance with its membership and the world, and it has at least a tenuous reality. But I suppose that I am presumptive even to write about it. I am not a member of it, you see: so it follows that all of you who read this *are* members. Nevertheless, I am pledged not to reveal such hard details as I know about it.

The real split is between the world where war is unknown and the world where war is known. Can both of them be possible at the same time? This question has special aspects, and the General Law of Dualities does not apply to it.

The very idea of war has very strong nostalgic elements in it. The ideas of war, the fictional constructions of war, are very large in the childhoods of every person. The adult recollection of war is an attempt to recover our early childhood and our happy early chaos. It is a question whether we can be happy without the mental enjoyment of war.

And the idea of hell has very strong nostalgic elements to it. The ideas of hells, the fictional constructions of hells, are very large in the childhoods of every person. The adult recollection of hell is an attempt to recover our early childhood and our happy early chaos. It is a question whether we can be happy without the mental enjoyment of hell. But this is heresy.

The psychosis or pseudo-belief in a World-Wide War is of worldwide extent and of quite recent origin. Though it has different local and national variations, yet it is truly worldwide. This makes it unique. There has never been a worldwide psychosis except for a very few of those from the deeply buried and primordial strata. Has a universality been born this late in the day? There has never before been such a sickness that is both new and world-wide.

Weather is always local, and psychoses are forms of mental weather. They are storms. Tornados, for example, are found nowhere except in a limited belt in the United States. Other lands do have other storms, typhoons and so on, but each land has its own. Weather and psychoses are local. But this new psychosis seems to be cosmic.

What are we to make of this guilty belief that we have already had a worldwide war, in the lifetime of most of us, and that we are going to have two more of them which will complete the destruction of the world?

SECTION EIGHT

EXTRACTS FROM THE LETTERS, SECOND SELECTION

I

Here is one incomplete 'letter' of the peculiar sort of which more than one thousand are to be found in the Archives of Enniscorthy Sweeny. These might be called the "confessions." They were rough drafts of avowals that Sweeny intended to make to himself, to his confessor, to his God. Ennis went to confession once or twice a month all his life: and his careful examinations of conscience and preparations are written down in these rough drafts. Whether the actual confessions were put more concisely and tightly than these rambles, or whether they are expanded to even greater length is not known. If the latter, then they evoke sudden visions and intuitions of people waiting in the confession lines of a Saturday night, shuffling and silently grumbling at a "slow one" (there's one every Saturday night) in the box, with the people testy about one who takes more than the noncanonical three minutes and keeps patient people waiting to the point of impatience. So this is one of those untitled, written down introspections that can only be a bunch of "notes for going to confession."

I have been guilty of the sin of unhappiness quite frequently. This is the only name I can give it, the only name for it that might be a sin; for willful unhappiness *is* a sin; and mine is willful to a strange and unremitting degree. Several times when I have told this awkwardly, confessors have been puzzled and have asked 'What? What? What do you mean by the sin of unhappiness?', as if they had forgotten their theology on that point, or as if they had thought that a layman had never learned it. Well, I mean that this is the only name I can find for it, and it's a thing that *is* a sin to me. This is a *malus,* an evil, and *radix malorum est cupiditas,* the root of evil is cupidity. But my cupidity in this has a peculiar shape.

I perform speculations that may be unlawful and harmful. I have a war of voices in me over this thing, and one voice says that the speculations may be meretricious catharses for untensing the immediate ambient and also the world at large. But a variant voice says that anything that is meretricious cannot be good, and it says also that neither the immediate ambient nor the world at large was so very tense until these cartharses came along. And a third voice says that the whole bunches of stuff are the germs and roots of evil and catastrophe.

No, I do not devise these things myself. It's as though they were planted in me and I must excrete them. Yes, sometimes I take pleasure in these speculations, but sometimes I take pain. I am being manipulated, and not by loving hands, though sometimes they are cajoling and flattering. Sometimes they are accompanied by an abdominal kneading that is of porno effect.

I do not know why I am being used in this when there are so many other persons who would surely be more useful.

What fire-ants are these anyhow, they who milk me as if I were an aphid? Who uses me to disseminate horrors, and who uses other persons also? (A couple of little radio magazines have broken out with "fictions" of monstrous and horrifying under-mind
308

dreams that are very like some of my own speculations.)

I am sometimes an instrument for doing things whose purpose I do not understand at all, on orders that are simply not comprehensible to me, transmitting sick-dream stuff into public opera and drama. And there are several complications to all this.

There are two or three or more persons who have declared their intentions of killing me if I continue to act as this transmitting instrument. And there are several other persons who have declared their intentions of killing me if I *refuse* to act as this instrument. This is a dilemma that I have failed to solve by prayer or fasting. And it is an unfair puzzle in that the very idea of this instrumentality is in my mind only, and these several sets of killers cannot rationally have any knowledge of it at all. This complex of things and frustrations is behind much of my unhappiness.

Oh, but it *is* my fault. It is willful unhappiness that I take refuge in, however I got into such a situation. And willful unhappiness is always sinful.

(If Enniscorthy really told this part, just as he scribbled it down, it will account for the frustrated and unhappy look on the face of at least one priest. A very lot of them do have that pursued and harried look.)

2

This is a letter written about 1927 or 1928, apparently to a very close friend connected with theatrical production and also with publishing.

Dear Strongheart:

I am up to my hairy ears in private detectives and operators. And what is an honest man doing with such operators? He has to do with them when his honesty and concommitantly his life are challenged. My honesty has been challenged, perhaps rightly, by
309

what seems to be a shift or a clouding over of the cosmic categories.

I have six small armies of private investigators now, or at least I have six generals of such armies (Sextus is the code name I have given to the group of them), and each of the six swears that he has swarms of assistants or soldiers that he is placing on my cases. These apparatuses batten on me unmercifully: that is why I must always be on the lookout for money now, and that I must be careful to collect everything that can possibly be owing to me. Some persons lately have come to believe that I care for money for its own sake, but that is not so.

I buy my life with money, or I rent my life by the year or the month or the week or the day, even by the hour. There are, and have been for many years, two contradictory groups sworn to kill me if I do not change my ways, or if I do.

I have told you a little bit about some of my pursuers and intended assassins before. There is Alistar Grogg who is dead, but who has not slacked off his pursuit and persecution of me because he is dead. It is Grogg who gives me the worst feelings of them all, literal haunting and hexing feelings. I know he is dead, and that fact is nowhere in dispute. And yet he still comes and makes his presence known. He threatens my life. He seriously threatens to kill me by fright. He is all the rampant ghost stories rolled into one. And he makes me feel that I am the aggressive and evil one.

Grogg's two friends and associates, Wimbish McDearmott and Elton Quartermas, are still alive. Yes, and still weird. I am scared of these three, my friend. I am scared of them three thousand dollars a month's worth. Protection comes high.

And, friend, these three are the good guys. They are the advocates of the Golden Century and of the Diamond Decades in which we live. They are in fear and horror of the "catastrophes" that I and a few other persons create as fictions.

They, and other mathematicians of the school of Doctor Henry Devonian, believe that these fictions

310

are turning into facts relentlessly, and that I am a key to their turning. I do not know how my name or my fictions became embodied in the formulae of this Doctor Devonian at a time when my fictions were still deep in my own mind and hadn't been spoken or written, and when my name was still that of a most undistinguished little boy living on West Blackwater Street in Chicago. But my name, and part of the contents of my mind, *had* entered the formulae of this group of numerologist-mathematicians. They do not believe that the fictions can be a catharsis against themselves becoming facts, by turning them into works of art.

Come to think of it, I don't much believe it either any more, not when I'm in a glum mood. I have never regarded Grogg and McDearmott and Quartermas as enemies. I regard them as friends who are trying to kill me for the health and sanity of the world.

And on the other side of it all is the "Friends-of-the-Catastrophes" Organization (its members are probably unnatural or at least unhuman) who are a corollary to the *Particular Equation* of Doctor Devonian. The Friends-of-the-Catastrophes are intent on "preventing the preventing," on blocking any interference with the implementation and transmitting of what Alistar Grogg called "the desolating visions of Enniscorthy Sweeny." These Friends-of-the-Catastrophes intend to insure that the desolating visions shall become actuality. They really protect me as long as I keep working on these visions according to the time table that someone has implanted in my brain. But they tell me that I am very easily replaced.

There are three of these uncanny and unnatural menaces, these friendly enemies from hell. Whether they are human or not, they certainly have unhuman touches to them. I do not know whether or not they have names. Myself and the private detectives and operators that I have set up to deal with them have given them the code names of Marshal Mosco, Marshal Tosco, and Marshal Rosco. (The three private

311

detectives that I have set up to deal with these fa~~~~
some friendly enemies are code named Captains
Nemo, Remo, and Hemo.)

So my life is perpetually threatened by three
friends, two of them living, and one of them dead
(but ah—this situation has changed slightly lately:
another of the three is now more or less dead, but he
is not less active). And my life is perpetually saved
by three horrifying enemies. The enemies, the unhuman factors, have told me "Those three patsies of
the numbers-junk, they can destroy only your body,
but we can destroy both your body and your soul.
Stay with us. Do what we tell you to do. There is an
invisible, iron slave-collar that we have fitted around
your neck, and that is what is saving your life now.
All the death blows that have been struck at you
have been struck on that invisible, iron collar, and
they have been turned away by it. The collar has a
mechanism that can be triggered, to thought-triggers,
to contract suddenly and ironly. We can squeeze off
this trigger instantly by thought, and it will garrote
you too swiftly even to allow your soul to escape out
of your throat. You notice what happens when you
get into a fever to terminate and do away with the
fictions. You notice what happens, you notice what
happens—"

Yeah, I notice what happens. Death face-to-face,
do I know what happens! Strongheart, my friend,
you yourself have noticed what happens. The last
time you saw me you were curious about the heavy
scarf I was wearing around my neck in a warm
room. With your customary brusqueness, you shipped
it off. And you saw the premonitory wounds of the instant iron spikes. I came up with something pretty
good to tell you in explanation, as I thought. It was
ingenious. And you said "Your fictions, Ennis, are
wonderful, but they will never be mistaken for facts.
You worry too much on that score. People will always be able to tell the difference. But I wonder
what the fact is that you are trying to cover up by
such a fiction as that one."

The fact, Strongheart, is just as I tell it. There is

312

an invisible iron collar a
times my enemies thoug...
action. Even a slight action ...
the ultimate pain.

Of these three un... enem... slight
three thousand dollar... nth's being
six thousand dollars ...ection... that I ...red
with for the pr...ection... ave me...eservation...kes
and body. I ...have... ...yes, for a ...oul of
months. I have ...pro...es, for a couple o...
months. And t...en I...w prospects.

I know and ...you ...hat *The Great Depression*
will be a hit play. I...erything. Well, it will be a
hit play whe... I ge...shed (quickly, quickly on
that!) and get it pro... It will be the funniest and
most poignant play, the most extravagant and
most multitudinous It will be Dickens and Aris-
tophanes rolled tog... It will be the real *Beggars'
Opera*, as the work really bears that name has
failed to be.

But we both kno...hat such things take a little
time. We know that...can hardly go into New York
production before /he autumn of 1929. It will make
huge fortunes for all of us. But I will need considerable advances in the intervening months. I have just
told you why.

Really, friend, did you ever hear a better story
cooked up by a playwright hooking for a heavy advance? But are you sure that you can always tell my
fictions from my facts? I can't do it myself. Believe
me, I suspect that you will not be able to tell in this
case. But what I have just told you is all facts.

Yes, I have engaged the services of six different
private detectives who are supposed to be unknown
to each other. Knowing something of how private
detectives work, I suspect that they will not remain
unknown to each other for very long. Each of the six
has for his assignment the protecting of my life
against one of the six threats, Grogg, McDearmott,
Quartermas, and the Marshals Mosco, Tosco, and
Rosco. The arrangements are simple. I pay each of
the detectives a thousand dollars a month for as long

...nd when I am dead then I no longer ...should be good er... incentive for me alive.

I seem to be living the old mystery ...t Agents Six. In the... well-done mys-... an hires six secret... just as I have protect him agai... assassins. And it ...t that each of th... agents that h... has (in incredibly j... disguise ...se) ...ery assassin he is... d against. And... would belie... ve it?—se... f the Secret Agents despite the fact that ne has only himself to keep an eye on) bung... ssignments comp... ly.

You ha... ve not heard... et Agents Six? Do you not keep current with th... ch as this? Oh, I have an extra typescript that... end to you to read. I wrote it, of course. If yo... have your connection with Oppenheim Publish... ou might get this pub-lished and promoted—for... heed the money.

The secret agents, both... he mystery story and in reality, are pretty rum ch... ters. The one who is to guard against the dead m... Grogg (or Bogg in the mystery story), and the ...es who are to guard against the three unnatural and probably unhuman marshals, they are occultists, and more. They have to be for such assignments.

Read the transcript when I send it around to you. Or read between the lines of my obituary, whichever comes first.

Enniscorthy

3

Well, at least it is known to whom the following letter was written. It is to Pope Kirol I. It therefore has to be written between the years 1922 and 1938, but it is proba-bly written about 1932. There are problems about it, of course. Was it ever sent? Probably it was, and it wouldn't have made much of a splash, even though Enniscorthy had something of a reputation as a composer of exuberant and "brimstone-comic" operas by that time.

More important is the question whether there was ever a letter, outside of Enniscorthy's imagination, to which this letter is supposed to be the answer. There is at least the possibility that there was such a letter. For one thing, there was the well-kept secret that the Pope was an avid reader of old Police Romances as was indicated in the Sweeny answer. There is also the fact that in the papal files there is a note of a letter sent to Sweeny, although the files of Kirol I show more than three million letters sent (by name of the recipients) and most of these were no more than acknowledgements of contributions. But here is the letter:

Your Holiness:

It pleases me to know that I have a reader, even a fan, who is so high in the regards of both God and men. I am not one to be intimidated by presidents or by kings or by emperors. I am not intimidated by the great people of the opera or the drama or the world itself. Nor am I intimidated by you, for that is not the word for it. But I am awed by you and by the position that you hold between this world and the other.

But you raise up before me the ghost of something else, the ghost of doubtful principalities and Chronologies. For you write these words:

"You are the boy to whom I owe it all, my rise and my position, the highest in the world. You are the boy who is destined to bring about the rise and fall of many in *Terra Extensa*."

I read that, and then I felt your hand on my head, your big, man's hand on my little, boy's head.

Blessed man, do you understand what it is that you have written? Do you comprehend at all the meaning of the words that you have set down? It is tall insanity, and yet it's an insanity that I have encountered several other times. Let me tell you about one of those other times:

When I was seven years old, a large and pleasant and famous black man came to our house. He put his big hand on my head and he said: "This is the boy to whom I owe it all, my rise and my position,

315

the highest position in the world. This boy is destined for the rise and fall of many in wide America."
"The rise and fall of many in wide America" is what he said, and "The rise and fall of many in the wide world" is what you said. I pray that I am destined for the rise of very many and for the fall of very few.

The big black man who came to our house and put his hand on my head was Harold Standpipe, the President of the United States. And I remember the startled thoughts that bounded like jumped rabbits through my mind when he said those words and put his hand on my head.

"How does he *know* that I'm the one who did it," I thought. "How could he even begin to guess?"

And they are the same jumped-rabbit thoughts that dodge through my mind when I read your letter that I have just received: "How does he know that I was the one who did it? How could he guess?" Well, how could you have guessed? But I am not sure at all that I was responsible for your attaining your highest position in the world. That you selected the name of "Kirol" instead of "Pius," yes, I was responsible for that. I had quite a mind wrestle with you to force you to that. But I am not sure that I did bring you, the man, to your high position. As to your selecting the name "Kirol" that was just to preserve you from a little numerological trap.

But I see that you, by your position and blessing, are preserved from other traps and pitfalls. And certain words of your letter come to me as jolts of power:

"I saw your Opera *Armageddon I.* I do not accept it. So I prayed. And then I was able to un-see it again. Now I know that it has not been, it cannot be, it must not be. The question is closed. It cannot happen in this world."

I hope, of course, that you *are* able to interdict the happenings of the opera from becoming real happenings in the world. But are you able to do this?

But I rejoice, on a much lower level, that you have read and enjoyed my mystery novel *Secret*

Agents Six. It is good to have a Pope who is a reader of mystery and detective novels. Benedict XV, I am told, cared very little about them.

Yes, I am somewhat familiar with the Byzantine Novels of the first half of the fifteenth century, and in particular I am familiar with the 'Police Romances' of that period which you love. Wherever or whenever it appears, there is nothing ever quite so Byzantine as a Police Romance. Yes, I acknowledge that I am somewhat indebted to them. Oh, that was a dazzling half century before the fall!

And now I must tender you an appreciation for your own latest work, the superb Encyclical *Contra Fictionis Diabolicos* or however it is spelled. 'Against the Fictions of the Devil.' Good. You damn and you disable these fictions. You disallow them completely. And you see right through one of their stratagems: that of the rat-killer, and his promises, and his pipe. He comes, this rat-killer, and he says that he can divert the threatening rats away, by his art, by his artful piping, if only someone will give him the keys to the city so that he can find out all the rats wherever they may be. He will sublimate the rats themselves into a tune about the rats, he says. By making them to be rats in a tune, he will prevent them from being rats in the world. And so they will be obliterated and their threat will be dispersed.

But there is something dangling down and out from under the edge of the long cloak of the rat-killer. It is the tip of a tail, of a very long and thick rat's tail. For the rat-killer is really the giant rat-king, and he has not come for the destruction of the rat-assault but for its enhancement and support. Give him the keys to the city indeed!

So you have blown up my pretense of artful sublimation of the organized destruction of the world by turning it all into an art form. Did you see my devil's tail, red and ending in a red dart, hanging down below my cloak? Well then, you are right and I am wrong. But by now I am locked into my wrongness and they will not let me out of it.

317

You say that the "Desolating Visions" are blue-prints ("diagramme" is the word that you use), or action-prints for the Diabolical Destruction. I do not want to believe this, but if I believe in you how can I not believe in what you teach?

But where does that leave you, your holiness? Do you not know that you have acknowledged, in a queer sentence in your letter to me, that *you* are one of my fictions? At least, you may prove to be so, if other things also prove to have been so.

Your loving son—

Enniscorthy.

4

At least we know the code name of the person to whom this letter was written. It was to "Captain Nemo," one of the private detectives who was in Enniscorthy Sweeny's employ for many years. This letter was probably written about 1929.

My Dear Nemo:

You amaze me, as who does not these days. What, have I hired a contaminated person to protect me from the contaminators? You state in your last report that you once believed in the happenings of the World-Wide War. And you state that, for some years, you had memories or pseudo-memories of being a soldier in that war. "Of being a doughboy" is what you write. But "doughboy" is a term that I invented in my opera, Armageddon I (I am the only one who knows what "Doughboy" really means and I won't tell), and you say that you have never seen my opera. Never mind that. Persons of several cults have borrowed my terms in their own Heraldic-Masque Cult versions of the so-called World-Wide War.

Several analytic doctors have told me that there is

a remarkable consistency to these pseudo-memories of the hellish conflict. He says that my own input, from my various "visions," was possibly larger than that of anyone else, but that it might be no more than five percent of this material that has found its way to the group unconscious. He says that this war motif is archetypical, that all of past history and para-history is full of it. Some of the best-attested wars in history, he says, did not happen. I am glad to hear that part of his thesis. Even so well documented a thing as Henry VIII's sea raid into the Mediterranean and his assault on Rome may not have happened, nor even the Spanish occupation of London in the next generation. There is the possibility that both of these and many others were pseudo-actions.

I asked him whether there was a possibility that this is a pseudo-world that we are living in and that none of us ever happened. He said that, yes, there was such a possibility but that it was a low grade possibility, a possibility of less than three percent.

This analytic doctor tells me that there are two sides to all our visions, both the prospective and retrospective ones. We look backwards to Paradise Lost, and we look forward to Utopia. But, at the same time, we look backwards on horrible wars that never happened, and we look forward to nine times more horrible wars that must not happen. And, at the same time, and secretly, and with a contrary part of our minds, we want them to happen.

The analytic doctor also warned me of you, though I had not told him of you. He does not want to meet you. He says that he knows too much about you now and that you are the worst of the six. He also said that you may be the "only one of the six" who is a little bit murky. He advised me that a man should never let his confessor, his private detective, or his analytic doctor meet each other or there might be a psychic explosion.

But you once literally believed in the "destructions," Nemo; and the entity that you are to protect me from also believes in the strength of those same destructions. He is, in fact, one of the "friends-of-the-destructions." But, if you have both accepted the destructions as fact, you should have peculiar insights into each other's minds.

You tell me that you feel yourself being investigated and followed, even as you are investigating and following your assignment person. I tell you that we do not know where we ourselves leave off and another person begins. Maybe yourself and the person whom you feel to be investigating you are two sides of the same psychic coin. Maybe he is your target Marshal Mosco himself.

I'll tell you something else, Nemo, that I would not tell either my confessor or my analytic doctor. I also have pseudo-memories of being a doughboy in the World-Wide War. These recollections are overpowering at times, almost impossible to resist. No, it could not come from my opera which I actually composed nearly five years before the vivid memories. They simply are not on the same track with the Opera or any of my other "visions." But everybody seems to have visions about these things.

Oh, there are even cases of strangers glad-handing each other at first introduction and having identical pseudo-memories of soldiering together in that great war. Two such persons on meeting will remember the names of outfits that they belonged to, and the names of villages where great actions occurred. They remember the names and appearances of fellow soldiers. Strange, very strange.

And yet, the analytic doctor says that it is all to the good.

"We had *better* all remember it, even if it didn't happen," he said. "If we don't manage to remember it, in some form or other, then we are doomed to repeat it nine times over. We must be clear in our minds that it didn't happen, and yet on a deeper level we must remember that it did. It is all a premonition sent to us by God for our correction and warning. It will happen, and it will have happened, if we do not take it as a warning"

Strange and still more strange. And he is supposed to be the best analytic doctor in town.

Here enclosed, Captain Nemo, is the latest death note that I have received from Marshal Mosco; and Mosco, I do hope that you remember this, is the one of my possibly unhuman enemies that you are supposed to guard me against. Your laboratory analysis of the content and the semantics of this note, as well as of its physical materials, might lead to something. Be ostentatiously busy about the affair in any case. I believe that your prowling and scurrying does have a detrimental effect on Mosco's harrassment of you.

I'll write you or call you or see you several more times today. We must keep in touch while the enemy has stepped up his action. Yes, I would like to have Marshal Mosco "dead," if that is possible for him. I don't know for sure whether he might be called alive. But bring him in if you can get him into a helpless state, and we will see that he is either dead or disabled or dissembled.

With all good care and judgment we shall yet prevail against these plots.

Enniscorthy.

5

This letter is written to Enniscorthy's wife apparently in 1936 when he was in Europe and she was in New York.

My Dear Pumpkin Seed:

You are a crimson-hearted joker, I know, but don't drop those shoes that hard! Your last letter to me shook me. Kick the crutches out from under blind cripples if you want to have fun, or set small children on fire, but don't pull such tricks on me again. They go beyond fun.

Several times a year for these last two dozen years, you have shocked me with your artless, throw-away remarks. You are not here so that I

321

might see whether you quake with internal laughter when you pull one of these things, or whether you give no sign at all of your colossal kidding. You know all about my own complexes and hang-ups. Why do you do these things?

"Oh, a letter from you from Epernay in France!" you wrote in your own last letter. "Do you know that it is just nineteen years since you wrote me another letter from Epernay? You had just been made corporal, and I was quite proud of you to do it without influence from your great friends. And you had just discovered that war was a slimy thing and not romantic at all. 'Oh, will it *ever* be over!' you wrote. You needed me at that moment. Yes, and I needed you. And we were four thousand miles apart and the most terrible war in the world was going on. But to your question, I couldn't answer it then and I can't answer it now. It isn't really over yet, is it, Enniscorthy? Now there are people who say that it will start up again very soon. As a matter of fact, I can already *taste* it starting up again, in no more than five years. Some people say that it has already started up again in Spain. Did you notice anything about a war going on in Spain when you were there last month?"

So wrote the most wonderful, and at the same time the most exasperating wife in the world. Pumpkin Seed, Mary Margaret, don't do things like that! If you have such pseudo-memories, resist them, bury them! You know that just nineteen years ago we were together in Chicago, all that year and all the year before and all the year afterwards. Why are you so perverse?

Yes, I needed you nineteen years ago. I need you now. And forever. But do you need to devil me forever? Have a care what you do, wife of my bosom.

On a psychological level we must remember that great war. Yes, we must remember it as a vivid vision sent to us as an admonition and correction. We must remember it, so that it will not happen again, and so that it will not have happened the first time either. But we must also remember that it

322

wasn't real. There is high trickery required here, but when was that ever impossible for high persons such as ourselves? Preserve us in our distinction this day! And I will see you again within the month.

Enniscorthy.

SECTION NINE

CASHIERS POLICIERS

I

BRANAGAN'S REPORT

I am the private detective who uses the Code name Branagan. My assignment, going on for many years now, is the protection of the impresario, Enniscorthy Sweeny from a dead man named Alistar Grogg. This is a dead man who is also a mad man, a monomaniac with only murder on his mind. He believes that Sweeny must be removed from the world for its health and very survival. And he has discovered in himself the great psychic power and malevolence that only the misplaced dead have.

My credentials for this peculiar assignment are that I was picked for it by the "Shamus Salina," a multilist, saltwater basic computer that matches detectives to assignments; that I have long experience both as a policeman and as a detective; that I am an occultist with a Los Angeles degree and many years of study; and that I am also an expert in divergent behavior (madness). I have, in fact, been male nurse and strong-arm man in several of the largest insane asylums in the country. And I have also been strong-arm man in some of the most prestigious mortuary manses in the land and I am a smooth and strict handler of the frequent obstreperousness of the new dead. Some of them want to make a fuss about it, you know.

It would seem that the only harm that a dead man could do to my client Sweeny would be of a psychological or neurological nature. This is mostly true, but Sweeny was always a bundle of psychoses, in spite of being a relaxed man (he is capable of blowing his own brains out without ceasing to be easy and relaxed), and he is peculiarly vulnerable to this dead-man approach.

The dead man Grogg infests Sweeny and drives him towards suicide or self-attracting fatal accident. For a long time, Grogg infested Sweeny's daytime dreams but not often his night sleep. And it was a very selective, though murderous, infestation. I know now that it was a classic type of infestation, with the infestor-on-a-tether working up a hot fury of frustration.

In those first years, when Sweeny was out of the Chicago area, Grogg did not infest him at all. This set me to thinking and experimenting. But my target, Grogg, was a very hard man to experiment on, so the process was carried on for years.

If I were to get a good hold on the problem, I had to see this person Grogg that I was guarding my client Sweeny against. And Grogg was long dead and deep buried, I had seen him a little bit in the form of a blue plasmic gas that was his projective spirit, so it might be said that we had a nodding acquaintance. But there were only two ways that I could really see him clearly.

I could dig up his bones and see and handle them, and have them handy for however they might serve. Or I could manage to get myself infested by dead Grogg in the same way that Sweeny was infested. In this case, I would be able to see Grogg all too clearly, with inner eyes and outer, and with my own wailing nerves also: spectrally clear, freezingly and burningly clear. Whatever spirit of Grogg it was that was making the trouble, it was almost blindingly visible at the state of full infestation.

Finally I did both of these things. I dug up dead Grogg's bones to have them by me, and I got infested by him to a total degree.

But first, with the aid of my client Sweeny, I mapped out the area of the infestation. The only time that

Sweeny's night dreams were infested was when he stayed overnight at his sound-proof studio on Loftus Street on the rural north side. And it was also when working at this studio-loft on his music that his daytime dreams were most often and most deeply infested. The only other times when Sweeny was bothered at all were when he visited or dined on the north side, or when he happened to pass through the area going somewhere else. But the infestations were hellish, he said. They were designed to drive him out of his mind and out of the world, and they had finally mounted to the point where they just might do it.

"And when I am in my studio, I catch only the 'fringe' of it," Sweeny said, "and even so, I nearly die from it. But there are places I go through that would surely kill me were I there for more than a minute or so. It is for that reason that I must take a circuitous route from my home to my studio. There are death traps along the regular way."

Well just what was it about these "insanity zones" and "murder zones" on the north side? Were they subject to topological investigation and mapping?

Alistar Grogg was buried in Poor Scholars' Yard, a little cemetery off of North Potter Street. Sweeny's loft-studio was just a little less than a mile from the grave, but the direct route from his home to the studio came much closer to the grave. The studio itself, fortunately, was not quite in the murder zone, but Sweeny did pass through that zone of horror when he went by the shortest route to the studio, and even on the fringe of the influence, in the studio, it was "hell, hell, blue hell," as Sweeny said.

Sweeny and I began to investigate the topology of the assassination attempt. We found that, for Sweeny, there was a real "insanity belt" from half to three-quarters of a mile from Grogg's grave. Crossing that belt made Sweeny violent so that he would have destroyed himself if he had been there more than a minute or so. Even at the near mile distance, as Sweeny was at his studio, he became a very violent person, and this may explain the violent elements in his music and librettos for he did almost all of his artistic work right on the fringe of that "insanity belt." There were door jambs and side-boards in that studio that had Sweeny's teeth marks in them, as evidence of the state to which he was driven. It was fury right up to the extreme point.

If dead Grogg was trying to block the effect of the baleful and destroying fictions of Sweeny on the world, he was doing it wrong. At any point short of Sweeny's death, the fictions became more and more destructive. Grogg was abetting them in their violence, for the fictions became more catastrophic the more that Sweeny was in pain. And Grogg was not quite able, at the range of the studio, to kill Sweeny.

But oh, the screaming, the screaming of Sweeny as he went through one of the "murder zones" or "insanity belts!" He drove as rapidly as he could while going through them, and his tortured screaming was the most soul-shaking thing that I have ever heard. And yet the authorities always took a kindly view of the racket, and so did the people who knew him, and everybody knew him. After all, he was a composer of operas, and was that screaming so much different from much opera singing? Maybe he was practicing effects.

It was Sweeny who suggested that we see if there was an eye-of-the-hurricane aspect to these awful phenomena. He would have to risk his life to find out, but his curiosity was like to kill him if he didn't. I laced Sweeny into a straitjacket to keep him from injuring himself, tossed him into the back seat of the car, and drove at high speed to the grave of Alistar Grogg. Yes, there was an eye-of-the-hurricane effect. I could feel the passion seize Sweeny as we came close to the grave, into the terrible twisting and shearing of the psychic storm. And then I could feel the passion leave him again as we came quite close to the grave. Within an eighth of a mile of Poor Scholars' Yard the effect was minimal. We were in the "psychic shadow" of it, we were entering the eye. And, at the grave itself, there was scarcely a trace of trouble. Oh the peaceful eye of the storm!

"Oh, the malevolent influence of dead men!" Sweeny cried. "Even good dead man are of bad influence till they have found their final place. This one refuses to go to his final place till he has dealt with me, and so he becomes more and more harmful. But I'll not risk my life with this mad Grogg again. The only safe place I can live is in the

327

eye-of-the-hurricane, too close to him for him to fracture my mind and body. But I do not intend to take up residence in this boneyard on that account. We will dig him up and take his bones with us to my house. We will make my own home the eye-of-the-hurricane. And I must also devise a portable eye-of-the-hurricane to take with me whenever I go anywhere at a distance. With that done, life may be worth living again, but it would not be worth living were I forced still longer to cross the "murder zone" every day and to work on the fringe of it."

We dug up the mortal bones of Alistar Grogg. It was nice digging there in Poor Scholars' Yard, loamy and rich. We took the bones to Sweeny's house. And Sweeny, with a touch of the grisly humor for which he is famous, wired the bones together into a well-articulated skeleton and set that assemblage in a chair at the board-meeting table that he had in his meeting room.

"We hereby make Alistar Grogg the first member of our new club," Enniscorthy Sweeny said. "This is the Royal Assassins-and-Detectives Club. I can see right now that the club will finally grow to twelve or thirteen members. I make myself a member of it also now. And I make you a member, Detective Branagan."

"Save my membership," I said, "for it is plain that my assigment is completed here, successfully completed, I am happy to say."

"No, man, no, absolutely not," Sweeny contradicted. "I can feel the plasmic spirit of dead Grogg running and coursing about on the invisible cord that ties him to his own bones. Oh, he cannot turn sharply enough to get me this near to him, and yet he still turns and twists. I can see the blue flame of his spirit sitting like a carrion crow on the head of his bones right now. I can feel the evil scheming of this mathematical man. He is working harder than ever before on his assigned problem (my death), and he is working with the utmost flexibility. Depend on it, he will launch further theorems and theories. He will assassinate me with rogue equations. He wants me, he wants me dead, and he'll get me yet if he isn't prevented. You will stay here, Branagan, and you will counteract every action of this string of bones that you are able to discern. Use every resource you can get hold of to thwart him. We'll bring your occult library here, and you can study and watch and guard. Lay that dead man, Branagan! 'Laying the dead' is a good trick, and I am sure that you know many varieties of it. But Grogg is a resilient dead man. Be prepared to 'lay' him anew every day."

Then we devised a portable "eye-of-the-hurricane" for Sweeny to take with him whenever he left his house and went into the world. The first one didn't work, and Sweeny nearly died. The second one didn't work either, and Sweeny nearly died again. And the third and the fourth and following ones didn't work. But the ninth one worked.

It consisted of shavings from every bone of dead Grogg, along with small quantities of Grogg's own plasmic, gassy essence, all of this put into a little transparent locket which Sweeny wore around his neck. (It gave off a green glow.) It also contained a series of written, occult charms on small pieces of paper that I put into the locket. These would keep Sweeny in the state of permanent, but close-range and safe, infestation by Grogg. This close-range effect (in Grogg's own shadow) precluded any real harm to Sweeny.

It worked and it still works. Not that Grogg has given up on his harassments and his intended murdering. He institutes new actions every day, and I institute new counter-actions. This has gone on for a very long time now (what year is this anyhow?), and it will continue, for this holding action is the best we can hope for. In many cases of murderous pressure, an end may be seen in the death of the assailant: but Grogg is already dead. I will never abandon my post while life remains in me.

Grogg, tethered as he is to his own bones, roars and paces and plots red murder. He is determined to kill Sweeny yet (nor does he always use the disclaimer "for the good of the world"), and I am determined that he shall not do it. And I myself am permanently infested by Grogg.

Now here's an odd thing. In Sweeny's mind there is the suspicion of the theory that each of the six detectives that he employs (myself Branagan, Flanagan, Hanagan, and the Captains Nemo, Remo, and Hemo) is actually (in incredibly ingenious disguise) the same person as the one he is assigned to guard against. I do not know where Sweeny came up with such an idea, but it is to be found now imbedded in one of his fictions. This is a stretched-out piece of superstition, but it may possibly be true of some of the other five. Ah, there's a couple of weird ones there, on each side of the battle!

But how could it be true in my own case? Grogg is both dead and mad. Here are his bones sitting in a chair right across the table from me. There is his blue plasmic tethered spirit perched like a carrion crow on top of his skull. How could I be he? "How indeed?" asks Grogg's blue plasmic brains, now hovering half a foot above his own bone head. The theory will not hold up. How could I be this dead man, in ingenious disguise, hiring myself out to guard against myself? I am not that good at disguises.

And there's the beginning of another theory in Sweeny's mind. This is that all six of the detectives that he has hired (again in incredibly ingenious disguises) are all of them the same person. Well, I will acknowledge that three of us, myself and Flanagan and Hanagan, do look quite a bit alike and that we have picked up many mannerisms from each other. This may be because (a thing that all three of us just happened to remember again very lately) all three of us were doughboys together in World-Wide War One. But those other three detectives, the coded captains, some of them aren't even humans, I don't believe. No, no, this theory is even weaker than the other.

The whole business is impossibly wrapped in nonsense and stuffed into an insanity, but it pays well. It lifted me out of the twenty-dollar-a-week ordinariness into thirty-dollar-a-week opulence.

Sweeny believes that he can prevent wars and disasters from happening, and from having happened, by turning them into fictions, including Grand Opera fictions. And dead Grogg believes that Sweeny's fictions will grow up to be facts unless Sweeny is killed before he engenders too much of that baleful stuff. These two represent the two sides of the same insanity. How could there be war again? How could there already have been war in our Golden Century? This is the twentieth century of the Diamond Decades. We could no more have real wars in the twentieth century than we could have massive assaults by cave men using stone fist-hatchets.

One philosopher has said that we *do* have wars, terrible wars, in this twentieth century, but that we have relegated them to our unconscious, and so they are hidden away. And another of the philosophs says that *all* wars were always fought on the unconscious level (intensely physical and material though they all were) and that it is only by accident that memory of them can ever break up into our consciousness. This war of words and concepts, in fact, threatens to start a war of blood.

Nevertheless, Grogg and I now get along well together. We turn necessity into accommodation. Grogg is pleased that his bones, since they have been brought to Sweeny's house, are near enough to that old restaurant and piano bar and pool hall, the Rotating Vector, to allow his spirit, on its tether of not much more than a mile, to visit there. And I often go there with him, I in the flesh. Two other declared assassins of Sweeny, Wimbish McDearmott and Elton Quartermas, are often there also. And so are Flanagan and Hanagan who are assigned to watch them.

So we play out our game of death-and-beyond in a form of accommodation. And we play other games, both at the Rotating Vector and at Sweeny's house, at the big table in the board-meeting room when in his house. The bones of Grogg are now so finely articulated and so well balanced that they will move at the slightest impetus. They will move at the impetus of Grogg's own plasmic spirit or whatever. So Grogg can do just about everything that he did in life, but he does look funnier doing them now.

We play checkers. He beats me. We play dominoes. He beats me. We play chess. He beats me. We play two-handed hearts. He beats me, but not every time. He will not Indian wrestle or arm wrestle with me. He knows that I could beat him there. We play the Death-of-Sweeny game. I beat him. Every day that Sweeny lives through to the end means that I have beat Grogg that day.

Mary Margaret Sweeny, Enniscorthy Sweeny's wife, came in the other day and she said "I can hardly tell you two apart any more. Which one of you is Grogg? Which one is Branagan? Oh, you two have come to look alike!"

Mary Margaret knew Grogg a little bit in the old days, when she was a little girl. Her mother used to make doughnuts and Mary Margaret would sell them in the Rotating Vector and other places. And she says she remembers me when I used to go around picking up old iron with horse and wagon and taking it to Fledermaus Foundry for a penny for three pounds for it. I used to make a lot of money hauling iron with that old horse and wagon.

"I am Branagan," I said. "I am the one with flesh on his bones."

"Have you looked at yourself in the looking glass in recent years?" Mary Margaret asked me. And she brought a looking glass for me to look into. I held it up to my face, but—Zing!—it broke into a thousand pieces. And all three of us laughed.

I wonder what I do look like now-a-years? Would I recognize myself if I passed me on the street?

For the several years after that, Mary Margaret often joined us in three-handed games of cards or dice or dominoes or checkers or chess. We had fun. We were three outstanding players at every game. But then we passed to four-handed and five-handed and twelve-handed and thirteen-handed games. For, in the last many years, we have never been without considerable company at table, at whichever place, as more and more of the detectives and their targets (those of both sides who are involved in the Death-of-Sweeny battle) have joined us on a permanent basis.

I was glad for the permanent company of Flanagan and Hanagan after they moved in on us. Those two had been doughboys with me in World-Wide War One, and then Hanagan had been a Warrant Officer in World-Wide War Two also. He would tell us about it all, and we would compare memories and impressions and experiences of the two conflicts.

This is the most interesting case that I have ever been on, and I am delighted that it lasts for so many years. Poor Grogg, so dead and so mad! And so harmless. Yes, harmless, except that he will find a way to kill Sweeny if, even for one day, his activities aren't counteracted.

Poor McDearmott and poor Quartermas too! All poor mathematicians, they have such *driven* and devoted minds. Poor Flanagan and Hanagan! Poor Captains Nemo and Remo and Hemo! Poor Marshals Mosco and Tosco and Rosco! Those three are devils out of hell, I accuse them, but they say that they are not. There are a hundred different nations of devils, they say, and hell is only one of the hundred.

All of us play out our lives here in the interplay of wars and fictions of wars.

2

CAPTAIN NEMO'S REPORT

This starts in the early years of the police romances, probably about 1920.

I am Captain Nemo, the Detective, and my assignment is to protect the composer of music and creator of operas, Enniscorthy Sweeny, from the murderous kindness of a creature named Marshal Mosco. That is all that I can tell you about myself, and the reason is that it is all that I know. I have the mind-scrub characteristic, as have most of us nonorganic web persons. Everytime I go on a case or am assigned to a new task, all previous cases are scrubbed from my mind to give me clarity and room to operate. This gives us web persons efficiency which we always need because of our general lack of substance. This gives me myself a lot of uneasiness and fear also. I suffer from the Who-am-I?- Who-am-I? syndrome.

I suspect that I am not a human person. I would like to be clear on this subject but I am not able to be so. Well, how then do I pass for a human person? Oh, badly, and with great difficulty. I have always been confused as to who I was and what I was supposed to be doing. It was only a few years ago that I was told that this wasn't the universal case, that many people *do* know who they are and what they're doing. I accepted that theory.

I accepted it too readily. For, quite lately, I have about

decided that I might have been wrong in accepting it. I may have been right the first time in believing that everyone, like myself, really is confused about this whole business and that each person has good grounds to doubt his own humanity.

But there is strong evidence that *I* am not a human person. I gaze at the genes of human persons, and I gaze at my own, and they just are not the same. I consider their nomenclatures, and then I discover that I myself do not have any to consider. I have, so far as I know, no name except my code name of Captain Nemo. If I am not a man, what am I then? I am a private detective, that is all that I can answer; and I do not know how I happened to be one.

There is a quip about that multilist computer, the Shamus Salina, that if it cannot come up with the correct detective for a job, it will invent one on the spot. So, perhaps I am an invention of the Salina computer. Or perhaps I am the quip.

(My employer, Sweeny, tells me that I am one of his fictions. And I brag that he is one of mine, not I one of his. But one of us has to be wrong.)

I do know, in a literal way, how I came to receive my present assignment, that of protecting the great Enniscorthy Sweeny against the force known as Marshal Mosco. I was chosen for that assignment by the Shamus Salina we were just talking about, that talented multilist computer that matches detectives to tasks. The Salina specializes in the match making, so I suppose that I am somehow the right person to trail and defuse the troublesome Mosco.

Mosco persecutes Sweeny with his constant burden of "Just keep on with what you're doing, Sweeny, just keep on with it. Good, good, good. But if you ever even think about stopping it, I'll kill you, I swear I'll kill you. Just keep on the way you're going." That would bug anybody to distraction.

Yes, I'm the right person for the assignment, except that I'm afraid of Mosco. Of him especially, but I'm afraid of almost everyone and everything. I have never seen a more fearful or more apprehensive person than myself. This is part of the evidence that I am not a human person. Organic things generally, and human persons in

334

particular simply do not know the emotion of fear. It is completely alien to them, and they cannot understand it even when it is explained to them. Their blood pressures will not even triple at the sound of the words "war" or "catastrophe."

But web persons, network persons, crystal-form persons, unbodied spooks, quasi-machines and mechanical and mineral things generally, they do feel fear as the major emotion. So also do a few of the lesser organic beings. It is fear that splits the mountains and makes fissures in the low lands. It is fear that draws the iron in to hide in particular hills. It is fear that makes machine metal scream and howl from mental-material stresses of temperature and momentum. It is fear that sends ghosts into whimpering terror at the approach of humans.

As a nonorganic web person (I suspect that's what I am) I am tortured by fear whenever I must deal with alien species, especially humans. Those things are capable of killing you and eating you. I suspect that my assignment, Marshal Mosco, is not completely human either; but he is surely loaded with rampant and intimidating genes of some sort. People, I'm scared of him.

(About six years go by here, but it isn't the business of this report to deal in exact dates.)

Marshal Mosco orders Enniscorthy Sweeny to continue to promulgate the catastrophic visions, or to suffer tortures of the iron collar that has been put around his neck. Other persons in this particular struggle have threatened Sweeny with death. Marshal Mosco (along with Tosco and Rosco) threatens him with life. The Marshals state that Sweeny will not be permitted to die; that he must remain alive now and provide scripts for the Armageddons: and only after the last persons on Earth have all died of the terrible wars and catastrophes will Sweeny finally be permitted to die.

(About eight years go by here.)

I have evidence that most people cannot see the iron collar by which Sweeny is tortured and threatened, and that Sweeny cannot see it himself. And, if I were human, I suppose that I wouldn't be able to see it either.

But, whatever I am, I seem to have very "seeing" eyes compared to the people around me. This talent for seeing

335

things that are invisible to many other persons may be some sort of advantage to me, and I need every advantage that I can get.

Enniscorthy Sweeny really cannot see the spiked collar that is set around his neck and is triggered to torture him when he tries to back out of a deal that he never really agreed to.

And Marshal Mosco really cannot see the krypto genes in his own "body." Well, there are a lot of things I don't know about, but I do know something about manipulating key krypto genes. (Whence does this para-biological expertise come to me? Never mind, I have it, and perhaps the Shamus Salina discerned that I had it when it chose me for the Marshal Mosco assignment. Mosco has a weakness, a genetic weakness, and not everyone would be able to take advantage of it.)

Sweeny's spiked, iron collar is grotesquely misplaced. It's whole meaning is misunderstood because it is around his neck. It is really the "Crown of Thorns" that so many of the holy bearers of the invisible stigma suffer from. But Sweeny's holiness has always been misplaced by about eight inches, and so is his crown.

Marshal Mosco's krypto genes have gone amok and burst their lattice. Any expert could have deduced that from his bug-eyed look. Mosco is really a Metamorphic Demon, and as such he might be supposed to have almost total power over a human victim. But a burst-lattice matamorphic is always vulnerable to a good mutational engineer who happens to be on the spot. Even a nonorganic web person such as myself, assuming his expertise, can shoot the arrow into the Achilles-lattice of such a Metamorphic Demon and change him out of all recognition. All that is required is the ability to see genes and lattices, and a true genius for design and form. I have that genius, and I have the eyes that can see just about anything that is.

And I can mutate Marshal Mosco into almost anything that I wish to. But what can I find to mutate him into that I won't be afraid of?

(About ten years go by here.)

I couldn't find anything to mutate Marshal Mosco into that I wouldn't be afraid of. There isn't, as a fact, anything that I'm not afraid of. So I mutated him into the form where he can torture Sweeny the least, and where he can yowl his mouth off the most. That mouth yowling will divert him. He has always been in love with the sound of himself. Turning murder into cater-yowling will divert and nullify that murder, for a while at least; as Sweeny's turning war into opera and fiction may not divert and nullify that war at all. There has been discussion on this latter point recently.

I turned Mosco into a *kalo pisicho,* as we called it back home. A sudden sinking thought! I no longer remember where "back home is." Another sinking thought. I am more scared of the *kalo pisicho* (of the big ones especially, and Mosco has turned into a big one) than of almost anything else on Earth. Well, it's for the greater good, the Sweeny good.

Well, we are in a nightmare, that's what we are in. And, as is common in nightmares, we scream, and we make no sound. Being a web person, I have had much more experience with nightmares than has even the most hag-ridden human person. We have to warn the world that it will be eaten up. And we can't make the world hear us at all.

We can't make the world hear, Captain Remo says, because we are all fictions of Enniscorthy Sweeny and he is rigging things to conform to his own private conflict.

Yes, but now things are going badly, and we cannot trust them to follow proper courses.

The world has now suffered a second sledgehammer blow right over its planetary heart, nine times as severe as the first blow was. It doesn't matter whether we consider these blows real or not. A third blow there will kill the world, and even the after-effect of this second blow may do that yet. (It isn't so much the horrible things that have happened; it is the degraded attitudes of the people after the happenings that destroy all hope. They blink, and they go on. But it isn't the same selves that go on. They become immeasurably deformed.)

And the third blow is being manufactured of the same materials that the first and second ones were made from. And it's being manufactured by the same group of weird

337

giants who have been destroying the world for so long. Among these weird giants, is our employer Enniscorthy Sweeny. He seems out of place in that company, but he is in it. (Of course we don't understand this part of it: we're not supposed to.)

Wars! Wars! Or at least the vivid pictures of wars. (And the blood is overflowing the pictures and running out of their frames and down the walls.)

Wars! Wars! Or at least the operatic sounds of wars.

"What if it should turn out to be true?" a person worries out loud, and he has just had a shoulder and arm blown off. Have people no longer any sense of physical or mental or moral pain. They certainly are tough, but don't they overdo it?

"It's all so real that it might as well be a real war," a child says, and the child's flesh is on fire. "I think that they use thermite in the fire to make it look more real. It makes it feel more real too."

"If the world were really on fire," a philosopher reasons with us, "then people would try to put the fire out. But they don't really pay much attention to it. They gawk at it a little bit, but then they walk away and forget all about it. This proves either that the people have very slight attention spans or that it isn't real fire that seems to be burning the world. None of it is real, perhaps, or it would be more noticed. That stench of burning flesh is a fair facsimile of the real thing though."

Yes, and that was one of the better philosophers.

It's as though one, half breaking the shackles of the nightmare, should finally be able to shout to people: "You are all going to be destroyed if this goes on this way."

And they should replay: "Tomorrow, maybe, but probably not today. It's too late today for us to be destroyed. Too many of the destroyers have already gone home."

It's as though a husband, coming home in the evening, should ask his wife: "Anything interesting happen around here today?" And she should say: "Nothing much. A big dog did kill and eat two of the children, but nothing much else happened," And then the husband should say: "Nothing much happened down town today either. Did you happen to notice which two children the big dog killed and ate. There's one of our children that I always kind of liked."

Is the world insane? Yes, probably. Is that sufficient excuse for it to allow itself to be destroyed? No, but it is being used for an excuse. Should a private detective code named Captain Nemo be asking such cosmic questions as these? Yes, if nobody else takes the trouble to ask them.

(About four years go by here.)

We are not completely loved at the Rotating Vector even though most of us go there, in the body or out of the body, every after-midnight. (I tremble, I tremble, will they throw us out for misbehavior tonight. I believe that I have corundum bearings in me which make me tremble and suffer all fears.)

At the Rotating Vector, they grouse at Alistar Grogg because he will not wear flesh. And he has been a pretty regular customer in that place for near a half century. It looks bad for him to come in looking like that, they say.

They grouse at Marshal Mosco because he looks like a big, black tom cat now. And he talks like a man. It is indecent not to be clearly one or the other, they say. (What if they should see him as he really is?)

They grouse at me because I don't weigh enough. (Can I help it if I weigh only three pounds, and still look like a human? That's a characteristic of us web people. We're unsubstantial.) And they grouse at me because my feet don't always reach the floor because I'm so light. All this grousing scares me.

They grouse at Marshal Rosco, and they should. And at Captain Flanagan, and they shouldn't. But we tell them that we are important by an accident. Wherever we are, there it is that the "war of the world" is being fought. We must be shown a little consideration, we tell them, because we are the people of the arena where it is all taking place.

Sweeny is now very rich, and some of it trickles down to us. His great opera, *Armageddon II,* is surely the opera of the century. Never has there been a work so seminal, so creative. The influence of it grows and grows, year by year.

"That 'creative' stuff has *got* to stop!" Wimbish McDearmott shouts hoarsely. "It's the end of the world if

339

it isn't stopped. Oh, why does Sweeny make it so difficult to kill him!"

"That creative stuff has *got* to keep on," Marshall Rosco shouts still more hoarsely. "We will see that it does keep on."

3

FLANAGAN'S REPORT

The pieces begin to fall into place. And the ghost of Sextus begins to form.

Oh yes, I am the private detective named Flanagan, and I almost began my story at the wrong end. No occultist I, like some I could name. I am as hard-headed as they come. And I have the assignment to guard the great composer Enniscorthy Sweeny against a very hard-headed assassin—Wimbish McDearmott. This is a continuing assignment that has gone on for so many years that all the people and anecdotes surrounding it have merged together. A situation and syndrome has grown around us which represents police work at it worst and successful accommodation at its best.

There have been six of us detectives on the assignment of protecting Sweeny, for more than six decades, and now we merge into one person, Sextus, the Six-Pack.

We have no way right now of telling whether we have won the game or not. If the world survives in working condition for another two years (to 1985) then we might be supposed to have won it. Really, though, we have never even known the rules of the game. But Sweeny is still alive, and we were hired to keep him alive, against three cold-minded mathematicians who have been in a hot fury to have him dead, and against three underworldly types who have wanted to keep him alive on perhaps unacceptable terms.

Well, it's been a rich, rum business, full of the juices and anecdotes. There have been thirteen persons (eleven men and two women (those two, however, were a bit mannish in appearance) killed by mistake in place of Enniscorthy Sweeny. Sweeny, with that gift for the "extra"

340

that all fine dramatists have, is able to make random people play emergency roles, to imitate him by unconscious mimesis, to look like him in the accidental moment when it is critical, and to die in place of him.

There was Ellis Swinton, who traveled in hogs, all through Iowa and Illinois, and brought them into Chicago by the hundred-car train loads. Well, Swinton had a long, red, peeled face like Sweeny's, and he had a strong and high-ranging voice that was quite a bit like Sweeny's. But what prompted him to come into the Rotating Vector that night when he had never even heard of the place before? And what prompted him to rise to leave just at the time of night when Sweeny usually rose and left? What possessed him to put on Sweeny's overcoat instead of his own?

This was the very night when Elton Quartermas (Hanagan's assignment, and not mine) had decided to kill Sweeny finally, after having had rehearsals for it three nights in a row, unnoticed (presumably) by Sweeny.

But how was this diversion worked? Sweeny had been sitting quietly in the Vector with two friends when a tipster had come and told him that tonight was hit night. The two friends had been there every night when Sweeny arrived and they had remained every night after Sweeny had left, and they really had nothing at all to do with this. After Sweeny had been tipped, he looked around the room, and his eyes stopped on Ellis Swinton, the hog factor. Sure, Swinton looked a little bit like Sweeny, more than anyone who was in the Vector right then. And he looked a little bit more like him after he had risen, almost as if he were forced to do so by something he didn't understand, and had put on Sweeny's overcoat instead of his own. And Elton Quartermas later said that Swinton had the sound and smell of Sweeny when he went by Quartermas' table and out into Drayman's Alley.

But Quartermas had carefully trained himself for this murder, and he shouldn't have been deceived. After all, he could see Sweeny still sitting at his table there if he had happened to look.

But Sweeny was an expert at creating illusions and at flavoring an environment. So he created a Sweeny-flavored illusion out of Ellis Swinton, and Quartermas fol-

341

lowed Swinton out and killed him in the alley. And by that deed there began that Long Police Classic, "The Drayman's Alley Murders." The series ran for forty years and totaled thirteen murders that followed very similiar patterns.

This account of the death of Ellis Swinton was the true one. I was present and saw everything. In fact, I was the tipster who tipped Sweeny, even though Quartermas wasn't my assignment.

The other twelve persons who were killed in subsequent "Drayman's Alley Murders" over the next forty years were:

Charles Gamaliel, a pauper. He had his skull crushed by the traditional heavy blunt object.

Peter Kopsky, a plumber. He had his skull crushed by a half-brick swung in a scarf.

Hamilcar Grigsby, a rug salesman. He was throttled by a piano wire with two wooden grips.

Carter Bonance, a stave maker for a barrel manufacturer. He was throttled by a 100-pound test fish line with two wooden grips.

Columkil O'Mara, a foundry-worker. He had his skull crushed by an unknown instrument.

Holiday Lockwood, a lady barber. She was throttled by a heavy yellow silk cord with two wooden grips.

Jim Portugal, a commercial artist. He apparently died of fright. Witnesses said that he was attacked by a skeleton. The witnesses were sober.

Vincent Blunder, a brewery employee. He had his skull crushed by a heavy instrument.

Arthur Whiteindian, an automobile chauffeur. Died of fright and the blow of a light stick. Witnesses said that he was attacked by a skeleton. Witnesses were not sober.

Walter Violin, a stone mason. He had his skull crushed by a heavy instrument.

Estelle Gopherson, a lady butcher. She apparently died of fright and by wounds made by a small bodkin. Witnesses say that she seemed to be attacked by an invisible person using a visible bodkin.

Joplin Wagstaff, a hotel porter. His skull was crushed by a blunt instrument.

All these murders happened very late at night or very

early in the morning in Drayman's Alley, and all of the victims had just left the Rotating Vector, a restaurant and piano bar and pool hall for working people and promotors. No two of the murders happened in the same year, and the average interval between them was about three years.

People in the neighborhood, and indeed in the entire city, were indignant over every one of them. But indignation always cools a little bit within three years. And they were so widely separated in time that the pattern of them was not always apparent: that only stood out from the retrospect of the years.

None of the dead persons seemed to have been robbed. A few of them had little money on them; but with what they ordinarily carried and what they had spent in the Vector, they might be supposed to have but little money on them. And several of them had wads of money on them. And none of them seemed to have been molested, unless being murdered is a molestation. And the persons seemed to have nothing at all common in their past lives, and only one weird thing in common in their present deaths.

The police never did solve any of the murders, but they had some good leads and they tracked them right back to the perpetuators. They had straight talk with the murderers (three) and they knew that they could never make any cases. With one of the cases they would certainly be howled out of court and greatly discredited. So it was not faulty police work here. It was just a faulty "the way things are." A case against a person in the matter of murder requires not only proof, but also probability or at least possibility as well.

Wimbish McDearmott had been the blunt-instrument man of all the crushed skull murders. He had the heavy forearms found on most mathematicians and blacksmiths, and he could have crushed a bull's skull with any weighty instrument in his hand.

Elton Quartermas was the strangler. With a couple of wooden-gripped blocks on the ends of the murder line, wire or rope or cord or whatever, he could not only choke a person to death but almost decapitate a person with his violent and spasmic lunge. He may have been even a more powerful man than McDearmott, and his murders were the most livid and bursting.

Alistar Grogg was the principal of the skeleton murders and also of the invisible attacker murders. He scared people to death, perhaps, but he also inflicted death blows, slight, but possibly mortal. It was the combination that did it, the startled heart leap when seeing Grogg in such an unnatural state, and a blow of some kind on the then vulnerable person. Alistar usually when he went out, to the Rotating Vector or other place, wore gloves on his hands and a hood or cowl over his head. But it is known that he took off the gloves and threw back the hood when he confronted a victim.

Thirteen murders. All of them were murders by accident, and yet it seems a little irresponsible to write them off so easily as that. And a common element *was* found in all thirteen of the murder victims, an element so weird that it makes the flesh crawl.

All thirteen of the dead persons looked like that great opera composer, Enniscorthy Sweeny. It was as if his live face were stamped over their own dead faces in every case. This resemblance was immediately noticed in every one of the murders (for some reason, people always knew the face of Enniscorthy Sweeny, all people, always); but in not one of the thirteen victims had this resemblance been noticed in life. There was considerable investigation on this point, and the point stood. These people resembled Sweeny at the moments of their deaths, and they had never resembled him before.

And now in thirteen graves (ten of them in the Chicago area, and three others in places where the victims had come from) people lie buried with the Sweeny look on their dust.

And Alistar Grogg and Wimbish McDearmott and Elton Quartermas have for years now regarded Enniscorthy Sweeny with horror, since (from their view) they kill him and they kill him and they kill him again, and still he is not dead.

I myself was within a hundred or so feet of each of the killings, and I don't understand them. Even the killings done by my assignment, Wimbish McDearmott, rather slipped up on me. But I do not really consider their happening as failures on my part. My assignment is to protect Enniscorthy Sweeny from McDearmott. I have no assignment to protect everybody in the world from him. Sextus fumes and says that "we" have the assignment of protecting everybody from everybody, but I am only one sliver of that "we."

I am not even sure that it is Sweeny who stamps his features on those unfortunate people—so that they may be killed in his place. Sweeny is a master of illusions, and he could cause people to see a similarity for a fleeting moment. But he couldn't stamp that similarity on the flesh and dust. This formation of features outlasting death is more than an illusion.

Captain Remo says "Someone up there is looking out for Sweeny, and I rather suspect that it is Sweeny himself. Sweeny does maintain a small apartment 'up there', you know."

But I myself suspect that it is someone who is here, and who belongs "down there." I believe that it is one or all of the "hellish fiends," Marshals Mosco or Tosco or Rosco. They are pulling these unearthly tricks. They insist that Sweeny be kept alive and be kept busy at his abominable creations.

During our decades, there have been about fifty other murders in our area by persons of our group, but these others do not have the coherence and neatness of the Drayman's Alley Murders, nor the same face-in-death weirdness. The other fifty or so murdered people were folks who tumbled to the role that Enniscorthy Sweeny has been playing in the world catastrophes, just as the mathematicians had tumbled to it, and who with fine logic came to Chicago to kill him and terminate that role. And they had been preventively murdered by the three hellish marshals, the "Friends-of-the-Catastrophes."

These last several years I do not have very much to do, and neither do the other five detectives of the Sweeny retinue. Sextus seems to have taken over our duties for us. But isn't Sextus just a sort of caricature-representative of the six of us?

Yes, I suppose so. But he has become a visible (and very audible) caricature, and he is doing most of our actual work. One of my fellow detectives in these cases says that Sextus is a real person and not merely a contrivance. He says that Sextus is none other than the celebrated Cyrus Manhunt.

"But Cyrus Manhunt is dead and buried," I told my friend. "You and I and most of the other three-thousand private detectives in the Chicago area were at his funeral."

"Yes, but it must have been a pseudo-funeral and a pseudo-burial," my associate said. "Cyrus Manhunt was full of tricks, and what better trick than to fool three thousand of the sharpest eyes in town all at once. Look closely at Sextus during his next period of visibility. He's Cyrus."

"As well say that he's Sherlock Holmes back from a pseudo-burial," I growled. "But, yes, damn, he does look like Cyrus."

I believe that Sextus is not Cyrus Manhunt, but that Sweeny or the marshal-devils or someone has put the stamp of the celebrated Cyrus Manhunt features on air, for Sextus is still mostly air. Sextus is a wraith. He is the wraith of the number six.

About Sweeny's work, those endless and topless mountains of music, and the rivers of words that run like waterfalls out of those mountains, is it really influencing and creating events in the world? Yes it is. And the music is much more powerful than the words in these creations. The librettos don't really matter. The words of the operas and fictions do not. The details of the "wars" are of no consequence. They would have to be monstrous distortions of real details anyhow, considering their form.

What matters is those mountains of sound and fury that contain and posit and institute horrible wars and horrible interbellums, and which probably also contain the end of the world.

Well, is it inevitable that it should bring about such destructions?

When it is all that loud, it is probably inevitable, yes. Heaven and Earth shall pass away, according to Scripture, but the effect of "noises-too-loud" can never pass away.

It is remarkable that the Sweeny thread-of-life should remain uncut. It has writhed on the chopping block for more than seventy years now, and mad butchers with heavy choppers have been taking swipes at it daily. How can that be?

Sweeny is no longer wearing or being tortured by the invisible iron collar. This is something that only his private detective could know. The collar was taken off for invisible repair, and then (by high trickery and diversion) it was mistakenly put on a different person. And Sweeny has been faking it for the last year or so. And he will fake it for the rest of his life if they do not catch on to him.

He moans and groans with real art, and he has a little bodkin (I think that he took it away from Alistar Grogg) with which he makes slight cuts and piercings on his neck. And he wears that scarf to hide the horrible marks that are there (only now he wears it to hide the horrible marks that are not there).

Somewhere, though, there is an obscure person who does suffer the collar. This person suffers and suffers and suffers untold agony every time that the powers decide that Sweeny should be punished for his truculence. And this person doesn't understand the garrotting horror at all.

As we go into what may be called (according to one of the flitting theories) the last two years of the world, we have been having a set of terminal conversations and banterings. These are about old police cases that have been solved or botched, and the pointing up that the solutions were often wrong and that the botchings were often right. These are discussions of where the bodies are really buried and who the manipulators really are. And we have heady discussions about the disintegrating world also. We have now become a *ménage à treize,* or a thirteen-sided triangle.

But Mary Margaret Sweeny, Enniscorthy's handsome wife, calls us the "Old Mens' Menagerie."

The thirteen of us are the six detectives, myself Flanagan, and Branagan, Hanagan, Captain Nemo, Captain Remo, Captain Hemo; and the three assassins, McDearmott and Quartermas and dead Grogg; and the three Friends-of-the-Catastrophes, the marshals-from-hell, Mosco and Tosco and Rosco.

We all live together at Sweeny's house now. Well, the reason for it is that we are all old men (except Sweeny

347

who is only old in years), and that we do not get around as well as we used to. It is easier for us to watch and to be watched when we are all under one roof. It is easier to plan murder and to plot defenses against it when we are all in one house.

Well, there are thirteen of us, and Sextus. That still adds up to thirteen. Yes, Sextus counts. He counts for six of us, or for twelve of us. But, with ourselves and Sweeny, we still come to thirteen.

We talk about the wars which are the sort of passionless killings that police and detectives hate. When there is no reason for a killing, the police will still ask "Who did it? Who did it?" even after the doer is executed for it. Now a war is a passionless murder of millions of people. And the asking "Who did it? Who did it?" will not ever be answered.

Several of us now believe ("There is not any several of us," Sextus sometimes says, "I believe") that two of the three cresting final wars have already happened and that the repressed memory of them is what is festering and poisoning the world. And we believe that the third and most terrible of them is about to arrive, and that if it does arrive, it will spell "thirteen" for the world. (In one of the old slangs, "thirteen" means "That's the end.")

Our nights'-long conversations sometimes become a little bit foggy just before dawn.

"We are all subsumed into each other," Sextus said last night (several last nights, in fact) "and I am the subsumption. There are no longer six detectives as free agents. There are only six detectives subsumed into me. There are no longer three free assassins and three free devils. All are subsumed into me to save on moving parts."

"You guys get together on it," Sweeny said. "Say, that's pretty good; Get together on it. I don't care how you resolve yourselves. I promise that I won't even count your marbles when the game is over with."

"All that is left now is the World and the Sweeny and the Devil," Sextus said. "And, as everybody except Enniscorthy Sweeny has guessed, I, Sextus, have subsumed the world, and perhaps I am the world. And likewise I have subsumed the Devil. And now I start on the Sweeny."

348

"As everybody except Sextus has guessed," Sweeny said "I am—" But I either slept or was subsumed then, for Sweeny's incomplete sentence still dangles at dawn, after dawn.

SECTION TEN

WHAT ROTTEN BLOSSOM BIGGER
THAN THE WORLD!

I

*This is a review by music critic Drugger Eastgrave, in
the Chicago Tribune of February 6, 1940, of the Enniscorthy Sweeny opera* Armageddon II, *following its first
home-town presentation in Chicago on February 3.*

This is a most difficult thing to do. I pick at the
edges of it and I seem to find that the sinking of
the world is implied even in those edges. Perhaps
the most appalling result (or concomitant effect)
of the mountainous Armageddon operas has been the
hellish wealth that, deriving from them, has infested
the world. It sounds of madness, of course, to say
that the world's new wealth of the last quarter century
and its projected wealth for the next four and a half
decades derives from an incomplete series of operas.
Ah well, I wish that it were no worse than madness.

The fact is that there has been massive money
bribery of the while human race, that it has issued
somehow from the catastrophic things of which these
operas are a cutting edge, and that something will be
expected in return for this expenditure.

Perhaps this is strange stuff for a music critic to

put in a music review, but it is intrinsic to the explanation of the most effective music ever promulgated. Some of the worst music ever is what it is, but also perhaps the most effective.

For us, the most direct and most immoral result of this music that has infested and rotted the world is that it has already degraded our national society to the point that people can pay thirty dollars a ticket to see itself, *Armageddon II*. The most corrupting influence of the two operas that have appeared so far has been turning America into the cartoon hog with the cartoon dollar sign printed on its ham-fat side. (The first such cartoon appeared just two days after the New York opening of the opera, *Armageddon I*, in January, 1916.)

Is wealth then, for certain, an evil? That is a secret of which God and the Devil each know only half of the answer. But the wealth created by these seminal operas is evil, yes. This is almost the same as if one asked "Is music, for certain, bad?" And I would have to answer that the music of *Armageddon II* is certainly bad, yes. The music of *Armageddon II* is the worst music that has ever been on Earth.

And where does that leave Enniscorthy Sweeny, the composer of this very powerful work? It leaves him as the cheerful and red-faced maker of the worst music on earth, no more, and much less.

But it doesn't matter to this music critic whether the music of this opera is good, or passable, or very bad (which it is). The main thing about it is that it is overwhelming, that it is world-overwhelming. In the stones and strata of the earth, there is good magma and bad magma. There is good lava and bad lava. The good lava is made from the melting of fine and uniform rock crystals; the bad is made from the melting of trash rocks. But either one can be overwhelming and destroying when there is sufficient volcanic heat and heaving mass behind it.

And there is sufficient volcanic heat and heaving mass behind the operas *Armageddon I* and *Armageddon II*. The heaving mass buries the old world and leaves a smoking stratum for the new. Persons

351

not even born yet when the opera *Armageddon I* was produced have not realized that they have lived all their lives in the variant world created by it. Some of them might have thought that they were living in an authentic and un-hellified world.

Many of those youngish people were in the crowds that poured out from *Armageddon II* the other night. Did they, or the older people there, realize that they had now been shifted into a nine-times more corrupt world which had just been created by *Armageddon II*?

Oh, as to details, the music of the opera, though rotten, is superbly rotten. The costuming and staging is splendid. And all the singing is powerful. The plot has all the unhinged unity of any shipwreck. And there is movement and force and power. Power above all! This is Destruction as pageant and presentation. One has the feeling that something very large will come out of all of this. Yes, like the destruction of the world.

But it simply doesn't do to review the Sweeny-*Armageddon* events by one of their minor attributes, their music. This would be a little bit like presenting as a monumental study "Attila The Hun and His Contribution to the Development of the Tea-Drinking Ceremony in the Fifth Century", even though Attila's armies may have been the first of the rabidly tea-drinking armies. And yet the music of the operas is much more important than the story line. The story lines, although the world is conforming itself to them, are silly.

People coming out from seeing and hearing the opera *Armageddon II* have the Sweeny look on their faces. There are disturbing photographs of such emerging crowds, in Europe for a year now, and at this Chicago opening the other night, to prove this. Sweeny is a pleasant-looking, cheerfully ugly man. Sweeny, millions of times duplicated, is not. He is not the face that the whole world should wear.

Others may not find the new hellish wealth (it can absolutely be traced to the *Armageddon* operas or

352

the Armageddon Wars, whichever you believe in) to be the worst thing that could come onto the people. But this hellishness is not only the debasement of all that is good. It is also the destruction of all the good elements in what had been mostly bad. He has debased war itself while multiplying the size of it first nine and now eighty-one times. If there is no joy in war any longer, why have war? But war has become the main thing, the tail that wags the dragon.

Of *Armageddon I,* it was said that it provided the pleasure of murder and of war at a price that everyone could afford. I thought at the time that this observation was wrong, and *Armageddon II* proves its wrongness. These operas do not offer the pleasures of murder and of war at all. They offer these abominations with even their hard pleasures completely removed. The look on the faces of the people who have survived the operas say "No clean pleasures. No unclean pleasures either. Only the uncleanliness without the pleasure, now and forever. This we subscribe to now." For the people *have* subscribed to it, dully and wretchedly, with bribes in their pockets.

I have been a music critic for forty years. I had not intended to quit for another five years. But the other night I saw *Armageddon II* and I felt it was all over with us. And just now I have gone to the mirror to see what manner of man I was. I saw Sweeny's face stamped over my own. So I quit. I will be a music critic no longer since they will not allow me to be a man any longer.

Some have said that the Sweeny-*Armageddon* operas are without precedent and without category. This is wrong. They do belong to an ancient category.

They are "songs of Nines." Each one of them is nine times as powerful as the previous one. But the world cannot survive *Armageddon III* if it is nine times as powerful as *Armageddon II.*

"A Square-Headed Answer" by Brig. General George
Dredgefellow, *in the* Deactivated Army Review, *June,
1970.*

It is time to have a square-headed answer to some
square-headed questions: have we had two world
wars in this century, or haven't we? And are we
about to have a third world war that, by general estimate, will end the world?

The first point of evidence is negative, and this is
a massive point. It is the testimony of the more than
four billion inhabitants of the world. These more
than four billion, with less than one percent dissent-
ing, simply do not believe that we have had these
wars. More important, from the absolute depth of
their convictions, they simply do not *act* as if we had
had these wars. They act as if they had never heard
of such things at all. And there is really no other
body of numerical and substantial witnesses to coun-
terweigh their testimony. This is all of the first-class
evidence there is, and it answers "no."

Let us go to the second-class evidence then, what
we may call the minority reports. It is evident even
from the road that it is pretty light-weight. We come
up with the following categories of second-class evidence.

1. The evidence of the psychologists as to the
status of this problem and the accumulated evidence on it in the group unconscious.
2. Newspaper and magazine and book reports of
the "wars," and transcripts of broadcasts that seem
to give evidence that the wars did happen. And
also the army records, some of them very detailed
and minute, that name massive battle actions and
records of armaments and movements and engage-
ments and issues.
3. Fiscal vestiges, disability allotments and sur-

vivor pensions being still paid at present that indicate that there were great numbers of wounded
and dead in the "wars." The cases of the dead and
the wounded run into the millions and the payments of allotments and pensions into many billions of dollars.
4. Attested "memories" of the wars, including the
gathering by the League of Peace of more than
nine million affidavits of persons saying that they
remember being soldiers and sailors and airmen
in the "wars."
5. My own memories of the "wars", analyzed as
introspectively as possible.

As to the first point, the analysis by the psychologists of the present content of the group unconscious,
they do speak in "war" symbols. They speak of the
mammoth, the behemoth, and the leviathan, all of
them bathed in hot war blood, the first of them now
dead and unburied, the second of them still ravening,
though in a diminished tone, and the third of them
to be heard approaching with a tread so heavy as to
roil both the land and the sea. Of these, the first of
them is very large, the second of them is nine times
as large as the first one, and the third of them is nine
times as large as the second one. These are recognized at every level of the unconscious as the Armageddon beasts.
The people burn incense and flesh to propitiate
these beasts, and they also perform perversions on
themselves and others in the sight of the beasts. But
when these offerings do not appease the beasts, they
laugh with a certain jarring tonality (Enniscorthy
Sweeny has used this repellent sound in the "August
1914 Tonalities" in *Armageddon I,* and in the "Pork
Chop Hill Afterblast" in *Armageddon II* with jolting
effect), and they accept the reign of the beasts.
To the first of the beasts, the people offered the
flesh of Ukranians and Armenians. To the second of
the beasts they offered the flesh of Gypsies and Jews.
To the third of the beasts the people now offer the
flesh of unborn children and of undead old people.

355

The offerings are required by the beasts, but the people don't really expect them to appease. But the destructions of these fleshes brings to the people what still passes for pleasure and joy in the group unconscious.

"The Group Unconscious has become a thoroughly contaminated and polluted pool," writes the psychologist Widdershins, "but the more that it is contaminated the more time and interest the people give to it. It is very large and swollen now, and the upper life is very thin. The conscious surface life has now become only oil-slick thin on top of the waters, and the unconscious depth below is abysmal. But the huge and prophesying corpses of the three great wars are the most prominent things in those depths, and the names that the corpses prophesy are names that flick in and out of the thin consciousness with surrogate meanings attached to them."

As to all this, I can only write that there have always been monstrous things in the group unconscious. It is the business of this unconscious to contain monstrous things. And the people on their conscious level (which has always been oil-slick thin and oil-slick colorful and scrappy and dirty), the people *still do not act as if the wars had been or as if they would be.*

On the second point, some of the evidence is very convincing, and there is no way at all to contradict it verbally or to argue against it. But there are ways to bury it. And the very lack of popular interest in these wars and degradations indicates that they are not valid even though we are not able to say just how they are invalid.

There begin to emerge several ways of down-playing the attested happenings though. The names of the five hundred battles of Armageddon II are sometimes given as evidence that there was an Armageddon II. But those were only the names of army games and maneuvers. I named some of them myself.

As to point three, the answer is probably fraud, unconscious and accidental fraud. Yes, millions of

356

persons are being paid billions of dollars in reparations of various sorts for Armageddon II. The fact is that persons get into government records somehow as entitled to receive certain sums of money. And there is no way to stop money payments once they are started. As the popular ballad says "The Worker is Entitled to the Works, and the Pig to his Place at the Trough."

As to point four, the League for Peace and several hundred other such nostalgic groups, whether they are "pop," "op," "camp," or "army camp," fulfill a need that people have to band together and to pretend to have had tall experiences. The Society for Creative Anachronisms and other allied groups give a certain note of historical authenticity to all this, and FIAWOL has a heavy hand in it; but it is all play-acting.

Yes, nine million persons did make affidavits that they really remember these things, and some of them really believe that they do. People are easily fooled. But there are tests for reality. If a thing is burned up, then there will be a residue of ashes and gasses. But if there is not such a residue, and the things appears to be unchanged, then it is not acting as if it were burned up. And the people of the world do not act as if there had been wars and aftermaths of wars. That is the test.

Point five strikes a personal note, a personal carillon really. I will confess it; for many years I believed in the reality of Armageddon II, and also of Armageddon I, though I hadn't taken a personal part in the first Armageddon, as being too young. I remembered vividly the months of combat and the months of connivance in Armageddon II. These were things that had happened to me and the world. I was there. I knew them.

We *lived* those war games, as we had been taught to, and they seemed to be more than games to us. They were real to me. My wounds were real to me, and they still are, however much I am told that they are purely psychosomatic. But now I have it all straightened out. I could not have become a general in the paper army if I hadn't gotten myself straightened out on those old things.

So, on all counts, we come down to the straight hard-headed answer: the wars did not happen. They could not have happened. And the third and greatest war of the series will not happen either. The clincher of their not happening is the fact that the people do not behave as they would if they had happened.

("Well, how would the people behave if two parts of Armageddon had happened?"

"They would reform their ways, and they would do penance even as the people of Nineveh did penance."

"Nah, they wouldn't. They would behave as depraved louts, just as they have always done, and just as they are still doing."

"In that case, maybe the wars and aftermaths did happen.")

We plan far ahead in the "paper army." We plan for the ultimate in war games, fourteen years from now. Oh, they have got to retire me before then! I could not stand war games nine times as violent as the last ones.

("Aw, what are you talking about? Nine times nothing is still nothing.")

3

This is a sermon given by Jeremiah Bradford, preacher and prophet, probably in the year 1983. (In the year 1983, the first time around, that is.)

And I saw, as it were, a sea of glass mingled with fire.

And in those days men shall seek death and shall not find it; and shall desire to die, and death shall flee from them.

Raging waves of the sea, foaming out their own

shame; wandering stars to whom is received the blackness of darkness forever.

This wisdom comes not from above, but it is earthly, sensual, devilish.

The tongue can no man tame; it is an unruly evil.

They were as fed horses in the morning: every one neighed after his neighbor's wife.

Let him go for a scapegoat into the wilderness.

In the morning you will say, Would God it were evening! And at evening you shall say, Would God it were morning!

Behold also a gallows fifty cubits high.

What, is there no rosin in Gilead?

And then you will see the Abomination of Desolation that was spoken of by the Prophet Daniel.

And if that time had not been lengthened, no one would have survived.

The valley (Mageddo) which was full of bones.

Which things are an allegory.

But now, friends, I will speak clear and without any parabola or allegory. The greatest war ever, Armageddon III or Final Armageddon, is coming if you do not mend your ways. The world was destroyed once by water. This will be the second destruction, by the fires and volcanoes of war. These are the booming fires that signal the end of it all. These are the steep-down gulfs of liquid fire of which the poet spoke. These are the red blossoms of our sin, war. This is the rotten blossom that is bigger than the globe.

"But it is not sin that begets war," an old general said once. "That is the old business of having apples beget oranges, for they are of different categories." And this general swiveled around towards his shelves with their hundreds of tomes on 'The Causes of War'. "What begets war is the momentum of faulty diplomacy; it is the interlinking of accident with event; it is the general irrationality of mankind; it is the law that "What can go wrong will go wrong"; it is the kinkiness of fate itself.

"And now we have eliminated war by eliminating
359

all the begettors of war. We have done away with faulty momentum and faulty diplomacy. We have done away with accident and fetish and false numerology. We have done away with kinkiness. And most of all we have done away with the irrationality of mankind itself.

"But we have not done away with sin, the great relaxer and friend of men, nor do we intend to. It has been a false linkage. Sin and solace will we now turn to, and we will not have to turn to war ever again."

But that old general was wrong, he was false, he was kinky, he was irrational. And he had on his face the new swiney look. (Sometimes this is called the Sweeny look.) He had the look of the mad animal the hyena, and of the devil animal the wolverine.

And yet he is quite personable. And he has a rational manner even though he himself is irrational. He and his are the sweet and pleasant manure around the roots of the great, rotten, red blossoms.

Historians, especially reasonable historians, have rejected old battlefield accounts of blood, swirling and swift flowing on those fields, up to the hocks of horses, up to the haunches of horses, up to their crines, great rivers of blood that can sweep down both men and horses and drown them. And they reject such accounts because they are irrational, and they point out that not all the blood out of all the persons who could possibly have taken part in the battles would have made such rivers of blood as that, nor one thousandth a part of them. But they are wrong.

There is natural and unnatural blood swirling together in those rivers of blood that feed the giant rotten blossom. All the fountains of blood will be broken open, and all the skies full of blood will pour down.

I cannot say repent by any other word except "repent." The war, if we do not repent, will take place next year, in 1984. The latter-day prophets, Wells and Orwells, both give that year. It is in Holy Scripture and in Devonian mathematics.

Repent, and again repent. But when the world is finally destroyed will it *act* as though it is destroyed? Or will it be the most casual and nonbelieving cinder ever?

SECTION ELEVEN

AFTERWORD ON THE LIFE AND ANTI-TIMES
OF ENNISCORTHY SWEENY

I

The tombstone of Enniscorthy Sweeny had been carved, many years before this wind-down, by Sweeny himself. He was an excellent stone carver, as he was excellent in the mechanical execution of all the arts. And what he had cut on his own stone was:

> "Enniscorthy Sweeny, 1894–1984. *Si iniquitates observaveris, Domine: Domine, quis sustinebit?*"

This would be un-Latined as: "If thou, O Lord, wilt mark iniquities, who shall stand it?"

Enniscorthy Sweeny would be full of iniquities and years when the days of this stone should be fulfilled; but the point is that Sweeny hadn't any hesitation, when he did this stone many years before this, about carving 1984 as the year of his death. But he took a lot of kidding about it as the year 1983 approached its midpoint.

"When are you going to die, Sweeny?" ill-meaning friends would ask him. "You'd better be getting pretty sick pretty soon now if you're going to make it on time. You don't want to leave things like that to the last minute."

"I will die when Zeno's Paradox is fulfilled," Sweeny

said. "I will die when Achilles catches the rabbit. Achilles is 'Death' and I am 'The Rabbit.' And the event is to happen in the first multi-second of the year 1984. There will be some pretty dodgy times before it happens though."

"It was a tortoise and not a rabbit," someone tried to set Enniscorthy straight.

"You are looking at him and talking to him," Enniscorthy said. "Do I look like a tortoise or a rabbit? I'm a rabbit."

Sweeny was correct in that it was a rabbit and not a tortoise in the Zeno Paradox. This is a correction that is very long overdue in being made. And Zeno's "Achilles and the Rabbit" paradox ran like this:

Achilles, trying to catch the rabbit, can run twice as fast as the rabbit can, but the rabbit has a head start of one hundred kondulos on Achilles. Achilles runs the one hundred kondulos to where the rabbit started from, but in the meanwhile the rabbit has run another fifty kondulos. And when Achilles runs those fifty kondulos, the rabbit will have run another twenty-five. And when Achilles has run that twenty-five, the rabbit will have run another twelve-and-a-half. So Achilles can never catch the rabbit, for whenever he comes up to where the rabbit last was, the rabbit will be half that far ahead again, however small a distance that one-half will be.

In Devonian mathematics, of course, Achilles does catch the rabbit, and he eats it while it is still living too. But Devonian mathematics has room for the dodging corollaries of the rabbit, and it will seem that Achilles does not catch the prey while time is going on, but somehow after a particular time is over with.

There is another statement of this paradox which, at first sight, seems to be too otherwise to be the same paradox. This is the Arrow-in-Flight which denies motion, or position, or time, or all three of them. For, if the arrow in flight is in any one place at any one time, then it cannot be in motion, for to be moving is to be in more than one place, which is impossible. But if the arrow is ever absolutely in one place, then it is not moving, or time is not moving. Sweeny is the arrow in flight, just as he is the rabbit.

And both of these are death-paradoxes. The arrow has
363

gotten word, while it is still in flight, that when it falls to earth it will be broken in two and cast into a fire. So it stays in paradoxical flight, since that is the only hope that it has for survival. And the rabbit knows that when it is caught, however much it complicates the paradox by dodging around, it will be eaten immediately. Some people, however, believe that it was the world itself that is represented by the rabbit, and not Sweeny.

The world's the rabbit, yes. And the more it is almost caught, the more it is a dodging, darting, cotton-tail kind of rabbit. It will whip back under the old briars and back into its old hole. The pursuer almost has to plug up all its old holes before he can hunt that rabbit down.

The unplugged hole that the darting and dodging cotton-tail rabbit of a world was getting back to was the year 1983. When a world is cornered and trapped as our late world was by its circumstances, there are only two places that it can go for safety: into a rabbit hole, and into a Zeno paradox.

It can go into only two places. But it can come out again into a third place. It can come out into a Chinese Puzzle or a Chinese Box.

(The Hollow Tree, the last haven of Sweeny or Prince of Prophets, is the topographic equivalent of the rabbit hole.)

(The Devonian-mathematical Stutter is the topographic equivalent of the Zeno Paradox.")

(The "Totality of Unchosen Alternatives" is the topographic equivalent of the Chinese Box.)

"If I am the scapegoat," Enniscorthy Sweeny said, "and I den in and dig in and refuse to be forced out to my destruction, then the world cannot be forced out of its haven to its destruction either. But I'll miss my wife."

The points of critical mass and critical momentum and critical heat had all been passed, and these were irreversibles when they were brought together. So the End-of-the-World War could not be avoided.

And it could not be delayed. And the courses of things rushing towards it could not be delayed either. But such diminished course as was still left to be run could be divided and subdivided and subdivided again and again.

This subdividing couldn't possibly slow it down even a little bit, but it might do something else.

The Zeno Paradoxes consist of halving and halving and halving again and again: and, if one never quits halving, then one never reaches the end. But, according to Devonian mathematics, the halving at every point represents a choice. One of the two halves at every point remains unused, since halving is always free choice as well as progression.

And where do the unused halves from every point go? They go into Chinese Boxes and into Chinese Box Puzzles. There will always be this unused accumulation of fractions in the Chinese Box. The unused total will always come to one less the smallest division.

So, when a year is used up, except for that very smallest fraction, there will be another year unused in the box, a year that is complete except for the subtraction of that same smallest division. There is almost as much year left over when it is finished with as when it began.

Enniscorthy Sweeny produced, a bit before mind-year of 1983, a farce-comedy called *My Name is Sweeny and I'm in Trouble*. In this farce, Sweeny (the role was written for him but played by a younger and more active man, since it was quite a strenuous part), Sweeny was persecuted by the world and its circumstances with relentless over-kill. The Sweeny character was thoroughly rotten in this farce and he deserved what he got; but there was a question whether Sweeny or the World was the more rotten. The Sweeny character did show a full rottenness with which the whole world could empathize.

There were farcical exchanges and action anecdotes between the Sweeny and the fates and fetishes that prevail. As part of this dialogue, Sweeny was struck by whanging lightning, and he lit up with torchy zig-zag words: "My name is Sweeny, and I am Everyman. My shirt-tail is on fire from the lightning and I'm in trouble."

This farce-comedy established once and for all who Enniscorthy Sweeny really was. He was "Everyman" and he had such variant names as Lemuel Gulliver and Richard Roe and Sean O'Shaughnessy. He was the uncommon man who is in everyone.

But it may have been the World that really had its

shirt-tail on fire, and it may have been the World that was the rottener.

At that time, just at the wind-down of the years, the World and its peoples had gotten mighty mean. They were the meanest and rottenest people that anyone *ever* saw.

2

There was a mystery about the year 1983, and that mystery came to fruit on the longest day of the year which was in late June, just when it was supposed to be. And that was the last thing in 1983 that happened when it was supposed to happen. After that longest day of the year (what should have been the longest day of the year), the days didn't get any shorter. There was something so massively wrong with all this that there was no precedent for it at all.

On that same longest day in the year (in the Northern Hemisphere, that is), the massive Enniscorthy Sweeny opera *Armageddon III* had its first presentation, secret and private. And yet there were more than four thousand persons (all of them secret and some of them private) viewing it.

It is the lopsided measure of Sweeny that he could be out with this mountainous opera and the farce-comedy *My Name is Sweeny* (the road-show of it used the title *My Shirt-Tail's on Fire*) at the same time. Had the opera anything to do with the days going awry and not getting any shorter? Had the farce-comedy?

As to the days not getting any shorter after that longest day of the year, it was first said that this was a subjective phenomenon, a hallucination, and of course the days really *were* getting shorter. But things had become blurred, and there were no real standards to go by. Pop philosophers had recently erased the divisions between the subjective and the objective, so there was no longer any use of appealing to the one or the other of them.

So it was faked for a while, for a week or so. People would hardly notice it within that time unless it were pointed out to them. The government weather service gave times of sunrise and sunset as they were supposed to be for those days, not as they really were. Or else that is not quite what happened either. Pop philosophy had really erased the boundaries of reality.

And then the comet theory prevailed for a while. A comet was approaching the sun. There is always a comet approaching the sun if one needs it for some sort of excuse. It was presumed that the comet was affecting the movements of the Earth and not allowing the days in the northern hemisphere to get shorter or the nights to get longer. But it really wasn't a very big comet, and no one had ever heard of any comet (even a big one) having such an effect. But—well, what do *you* think was causing it? We might as well go back to the theory that it was all subjective.

What did happen (by one of the possibly subjective theories) was that there were nearly one thousand consecutive days of maximum length. That's almost three years! Who ever heard of such a thing as that?

Well, quite a few people had heard of it. The people who had read the fictional story "The Three-Year-Long Year" by Enniscorthy Sweeny had certainly heard of it there. The world had acquired a reputation in these late years of pretty well following the fictions of Enniscorthy Sweeny. But, to complete the involution, it was this same Enniscorthy Sweeny with his skylarking fictions who had helped to fasten that reputation on the world. The coincidences in fact weren't as striking as were the coincidences in Sweeny's advocacy and seminal fictions.

Even so, something was a little bit wrong with things. Some people said that the days were off by maybe a millionth of a second from what they should be. Other people said that the days were off by several hours. They were off, that's certain.

There was an easy solution, of course, for a mechanically sophisticated people—Ptolemaic Clocks with Epicyclic Compensation. These clocks and watches, which were quickly manufactured in the millions and as quickly adopted, showed the hours as they should be for the particular days. All that it took was a great number of epicyclic gears inside. So, with the new Ptolemaic clocks accepted as the objective standard, the popular feeling that

367

the days were remaining at maximum length became a new subjective impression that was contradicted by the clocks. And, as such, it weakened and weakened still more until the people who were able to say with half-honest conviction "Aren't the days getting shorter now though!" And, again after a few months "Say, aren't the days getting longer lately though!"

3

Enniscorthy Sweeny, who had been called "Everyman's Everyman" by *Time Stutter* magazine, probably didn't have much more to do with the "wars" than anyone else did. He was able to present them in art form, and in pretty minute detail, a little while before they happened; but everybody has some little gift such as this. His operas, as well as his farces and fictions, were mostly concerned with the "wars," but such covert concern was only one of many hidden responses and rejections. Nobody had ever really accepted the wars; and there were as many ways to avoid their acceptance as there were people.

But it is unlikely that Sweeny really caused the wars by inventing them into opera or other forms. Well, to be accurate about it, forty-four percent of the people believed that it was unlikely that Sweeny was causing the wars; this was against the forty-one percent of the people who knew for a fact that Sweeny *was* causing them. And yet, only two percent of the people believed that the wars that Sweeny was either causing or not causing were in the realm of fact at all. There was something irrational about that response.

Sweeny then, in those stretched-out, latter days of 1983 (wouldn't that triple-counting year ever end!), did what the only rational man left in the world could do.

He climbed into a hole in a hollow tree and announced that he would never come out of it alive.

And several billion people in the world (all the people of the world had instant knowledge of Sweeny moves) all bawled out "Why didn't I think of that!" A few million of them did climb into hollow trees then, but this was not very many percentage-wise. Those with man-sized hollows in them are not to be found very often.

The world was actually in a jam in those extended days. It was (such was the prevailing vision of things) standing in the center of a huge cavern which was named "Mouth-Center," and it was looking right down into a big, black-red throat that burned with lurid and garish flame light. The world was the world of current presentation; and the mouth and throat were those of Armageddon III, that rotten blossom that was bigger than the world and was determined to swallow up the world.

There was even some threat of "up-tightness" in those final, scatter-brain days of the noncalendar. When as many as a thousand persons a day in a medium-sized city had to be executed for up-tightness then it could no longer be denied that there were up-tight elements.

And there was the constant wealth that was clogging everything. Streets and roads were almost impassible from the glossy cars that people bought, drove only once, and then abandoned; to go and buy later models that afternoon. Some people even acknowledged that they *liked* being rich and that they were impatient when the wealth didn't double every week. In the "public room" of every corporation, there were men flayed alive every week, and their hides nailed on the wall because they had not doubled the corporation's "well-doing" in the previous week. The recently passed "Non-Restrictive Act," that every person could lay claim to the salary of his choice from the corporation of his choice, had rocked the boat a bit. Persons had to be impressed and dragged (sobbing and screaming, some of them) to be invested as new corporation officers. Never mind, most of them would have their release within a week, and their varnished hides would be nailed up on display.

There were some persons who said that the year was really 1985 now, and there were quite a few persons who said that it was 1984. But, officially and popularly at least, it was still 1983, now and forever. And, as long as taxes had already been levied for the year 1983, they could not be levied for any of the further doubtful days or months that might attach themselves to that year.

("I suppose that I had better take up my den in the

tree," Enniscorthy Sweeny had said. "They won't know how to drive a goat out of a den in a tree, not a scapegoat. And the bigger things can't very well be resolved until they do drive me out. I'm an impediment. I'll have everything that I need here. But I will miss my wife.")

A very great war (in everything except name) had come to America. And a few people even called it by the name of war," but most of them still gave it other names. It was quite incendiary and bloody, but there were advantages to it. People did not have to *go to war* this time. The war came to them. It's homey to have the action near at hand with no need to add travel to the other burdens.

But there was adaptibility and even a little bit of verve for the world living in the shadow of the "giant red blossom." And there was an overwhelming lot of braggadocio and strutting arrogance. Private murder doubled every week. And the blood in the streets, while not yet even as deep as horses' hocks, was much deeper than mices' hocks. It drowned mice, and all but the strongest swimming rats with its swirling force.

"Will God be patient forever?" one of those street-corner prophets asked.

"He'd better be!" the people hooted. "He's about had it, and we've about had it with him."

The invasion forces from the Peoples Republic of San Simeon and such places didn't amount to much yet. It was the spontaneous wars between the local private armies, "The Reds," "The Blues," "The Greens," "The Volunteer Industrial Bombing Group," that were raising the levels of the rivulets of blood. Bombing by private groups had become legal. Almost everything was legal in those days of full freedom.

"May the Right of the People to Bomb always be respected" was a famous resolution of that day supported by almost every group of an activist slant, COPE, CORE, GORE, the Catholic Bishops, and KICKS (Kaleidoscopic Institution for Creating a Kinetic Society).

Assassinations and Group Exterminations were always on TV. One could be had up for "Secret Connivance" for engineering such acts without first alerting the media.

But there was no question of anyone wanting to do

things in the dark. People wanted light, and more light, and still more light. On even the most dim streets at night, the light level was kept at two thousand foot-candles, three thousand, even four thousand foot-candles. And noise too. The decibel rate was kept up over two hundred. And still it seemed to be too dark and too quiet. It was dark town and dull town everywhere, but new ways to enliven it were constantly sought.

But it was strut-and-swagger everywhere. The whole country, and the world perhaps, was one giant Dark Town Strutters Ball. There had to be action! Accelerated action always.

But a prophet whom the people had rather liked, who had always been a little bit in advance on everything new, who had given them accelerated action, had now taken up abode in a hollow tree. This was ridiculous. It almost amounted to up-tightness in him. He could be executed as an up-tight person any time for a trick like that. But, of course, Sweeny could always be executed by simply lifting his permit.

Sweeny did have a permit to allow him to live to beyond age fifty, and he was far beyond that. Only special and priviledged persons had permits to live beyond fifty: labor leaders; comedians; top people in pornography, rock, and media generally; and other consensus leaders. Sweeny had a top permit, an "All-Category" permit. But those top ones can be terminated easily.

(Who said that there couldn't be the Ultimate War before the start of the year 1984? The people and the prophets had all said that.)

There were furnaces on every corner now, for the disposition of bodies, so as to keep ahead of the stench. Some persons, after they had flung a few dead and dying persons into the furnaces, would laugh and wrestle with each other in front of those glowing ovens; and the stronger of them would throw the weaker in to their deaths. It had become a good way to settle arguments. "Let's decide this at the Furnace's Mouth," people would say, and they would decide things that way. It was a sort of virility kick to see who could toss whom into the furnaces. And it also helped to keep the streets clean.

But the bloodiness of the war or pseudo-war was increasing exponentially; and so was the number of persons who were willing to believe that this was the year 1984 indeed, and that the tricks with the sun and the calendar need no longer be played.

Enniscorthy had a pretty large chamber or cave in his tree, and he made himself comfortable there. Well then, he was Odin himself, hung up in his tree for nine days, as a sacrifice from himself to himself. (Remember that the original preternatural voices heard by Sweeny had had a Scandinavian accent.) He was the Christus crucified there (Sweeny spent part of his time in arm-extended, yoga-like contemplation, and to the people who looked in the hole at him it appeared as if he were stretched out and then nailed to the wall of his grotto.) And he was also a sort of Saint Enniscorthy the Stylite. A tree is a form of pillar, and Enniscorthy was like one of the old desert saints who spent their whole lives in prayer on the tops of high pillars. Enniscorthy did spend a lot of time in prayer now, as he had always done.

Enniscorthy Sweeny didn't invent all his notions right then. He had intended many of them several years earlier, in a popular pastiche called *Illuminations from a Hollow Tree.*

Sometimes Sweeny would preach to the people from the mouth of his tree hole.

"Aw, c'mon, Sweeny, come out of that tree," Mary Margaret would beg.

"I shall light a candle in this tree and it shall not be put out!" Sweeny would orate. "Is this not all written in the Book of Jasher?"

"Aw, c'mon down, Sweeny," Mary Margaret would coax.

"What more can I do for the people?" Sweeny would call out. "I have made the Earth to stand still in its orbit, and the Dreadful year to delay its arrival. I have given the people the choice between fun and murder, and they have chosen murder. I have given them the alternative between Bloody Opera and Bloody Armageddon, and they have chosen Bloody Armageddon. Hey, we could have had some bright fun in the world, but you'd rather have a dark fun. So now I have immured myself here for as long

372

as I shall live. It's a grand gesture, but I do miss my wife."

"Aw, c'mon down, Sweeny," Mary Margaret said.

" 'And the weaned child shall put his hand on the cockatrice' den,' as Isais said," Sweeny orated. "I am that weaned child, and I not only put my hand on that den, but I enter it and live in it. This is written on the fleshy tablets of the heart."

"Aw, c'mon down," Mary Margaret still crooned.

4

A fire can be lit with a kitchen match, or with a lady's small cigar lighter, or from any sort of pilot light or torch, or from a barbecue lighter. And then sometimes that fire will blast out of control. It will crest and crown and explode!

Ultimate Armageddon arrived, and the final rotten-red blossom did explode till it was bigger than the world. And that war began to swallow the whole world with its giant, gobbling fire. It did not matter who had lit that fire. There was no way in the world to put it out.

The blood was flowing haunch deep on the horses, and with a super-strong current.

They let the year 1984 officially begin then. There was no reason to block it any longer. One left-over thing to be destroyed though.

People set Sweeny's tree on fire to roast him to death. And the tree (it was very old and dry) crested and crowned in horrid flame.

Seven dark and smoky spirits of Sweeny jumped out of the tree and fell to the ground. Then they sank down through the ground as if it were water, and disappeared there. And one golden spirit of Sweeny flew out of the tree, and up and away, whistling (this is the absolute truth of it) the "Sly Pig Sequence" from *Prohibition, A Farce,* an old and almost forgotten comedy.

That, so far as we have record of it here, was the earthly end of the old and almost forgotten prestidigitator Enniscorthy Sweeny.

So Final Armageddon was burning and raging out of control, and the World was ending.

That's funny. The people didn't *act* as if the world were ending. But they didn't act quite as if it were going to continue either.

They behaved as though they didn't very much care whether it ended or not.

THE MANITOU

"Like some mind-gripping drug, it has the uncanny ability to seize you and hold you firmly in its clutches from the moment you begin until you drop the book from your trembling fingers after you have finally finished the last page."
—**Bernhardt J. Hurwood**

Misquamacus—An American Indian sorcerer. In the seventeenth century he had sworn to wreak a violent vengeance upon the callous, conquering White Man. This was just before he died, over four hundred years ago. Now he has found an abominable way to return, the perfect birth for his revenge.

Karen Tandy—A slim, delicate, auburn-haired girl with an impish face. She has a troublesome tumor on the back of her neck, a tumor that no doctor in New York City can explain. It seems to be moving, growing, developing—almost as if it were alive! She is the victim of

THE MANITOU
GRAHAM MASTERTON

A Pinnacle Book
P982 $1.75

If you can't find this book at your local bookstore, simply send the cover price, plus 25¢ for postage and handling to:

PINNACLE BOOKS
275 Madison Avenue
New York, New York 10016